a novel

CRUDE

AMBITION

PATRICIA HUNT HOLMES

RIVER GROVE
BOOKS

This book is a work of fiction. Names, characters, businesses, organizations, places, events, and incidents are either a product of the author's imagination or are used fictitiously. Any resemblance to actual persons, living or dead, events, or locales is entirely coincidental.

Published by River Grove Books
Austin, TX
www.rivergrovebooks.com

Distributed by River Grove Books

Design and composition by Greenleaf Book Group
Cover design by Greenleaf Book Group
Cover images used under license from
©Shutterstock.com/andras_csontos;
©Shutterstock.com/All Stock Photos

Publisher's Cataloging-in-Publication data is available.

Print ISBN: 978-1-63299-381-6

eBook ISBN: 978-1-63299-382-3

First Edition

ADVANCE PRAISE

"In *Crude Ambition*, Patricia Hunt Holmes shows she knows Texas in the way Grisham knows Mississippi—politics, environment, strong men and strong women, egos, oil, arrogance, influence and hunger for power. I don't think anyone could have nailed it better."

—Bill Sarpalius, former US Congressman
and author of *The Grand Duke of Boys' Ranch*

"I just finished *Crude Ambition*, and it's a winner. Well researched and compellingly written by a true raconteur. A Texas story at its best."

—former Texas Senator Don Adams

"A lively feminist thriller—set in the Texas oil and gas world."

—Elizabeth Gregory, PhD, director of Women's Studies
and professor of English, University of Houston

"*Crude Ambition* is the story of ambitious people in Texas, some of whom are crude, and some are good people who are ambitious for the right reasons. The plot takes us into a high-end law firm in Houston, a ranch in the Texas Hill Country, a fancy beach house in Galveston, and a company where the new wealth in fracking is an incentive to do almost anything. These interlocking places are the stage where stories of violence, betrayal, revenge, and loss play out—as well as generosity, love, and ultimately justice. The legal issues raised are eye-opening."

—Lois Zamora, professor of English and
Comparative Literature, University of Houston

This book is dedicated to my two daughters,
who prove that by working hard at what they love,
young women can be happy and successful in
both their professional and family lives.

"I've come to believe that each of us has a personal calling that's as unique as a fingerprint—and that the best way to succeed is to discover what you love and then find a way to offer it as a service to others, working hard and also allowing the energy of the universe to lead you."

—Oprah Winfrey

"You may encounter many defeats, but you must not be defeated. In fact, it may be necessary to encounter the defeats, so you can know who you are, what you can rise from, how you can still come out of it."

—Maya Angelou

"Ambition is a dream with a V8 engine."

—Elvis Presley

1

———

"Where is Laura?" Carolyn asked again, this time shouting. Despite the tremble in her voice, instincts told her she needed to be firm to get through to the men standing in front of her. It was two a.m., and Paul and Trey were barefoot and had fresh sand on their legs and feet. They were also her bosses. Under normal circumstances, she would never use such a peremptory tone with men in their position. They had the power to cut her career short right then and there. But it was clear that they were drunk and seemed confused and upset. And Laura was missing.

Like the beach house itself, the living area was enormous. The house belonged to Paul Robinson's father, who was a successful, independent oil man. He used it primarily to entertain clients and friends while Paul's mother, who disliked the salt and sand, stayed in their River Oaks home or spent summer months in Aspen. The architecture of the house was contemporary, with lots of windows and decks, but the interior décor was over-the-top "Go Texas," complete with cowhide rugs and a stuffed deer trophy over the mantle. The east wall of the living room had a giant window looking out on the Gulf of Mexico. During the day it provided a spectacular view of the beach and water. Now, clouds covered the moon and only the small white lights on the oil tankers patiently waiting out at sea to enter the Houston Ship Channel pierced the darkness. Carolyn couldn't see Laura anywhere.

She recognized Peter Kaufman, who she knew to be a managing

partner at one of the good midsize public accounting firms. She didn't think he had been at the party the day before. She was surprised to see him now, sunk in a big leather club chair, looking down at his glasses, which he was wiping with a white handkerchief. He didn't look at her. Beyond Peter, another man was standing with his back to Carolyn, looking out the window. He was very tall, dressed in jeans and a long-sleeved, white cotton shirt. He had a lit cigar in his hand, and the smoke from it gave off a distasteful smell. She didn't recognize him, so she ignored him for now.

"Laura couldn't have come downstairs without going through this room," Carolyn said. "Where is she?" She was looking directly at Paul this time. It was clear that he and Trey had recently been outside. "Did she go out on the beach with you?"

"No!" Paul and Trey both protested.

Carolyn gritted her teeth. Until ten minutes ago, she had been sleeping upstairs in the guest bedroom nearest the stairs. The sound of loud agitated male voices woke her. She looked at the bed next to her own to see if the noise had awakened Laura, the summer intern she had brought to the party at the beach house the previous day. But Laura's bed was empty, so Carolyn went downstairs to look for her.

She was wide-awake now, alarmed at the vehement tone of Paul and Trey's responses. With reluctance, Paul pointed to the dining room, which was around the corner. Carolyn walked over to it. In the middle was the big oak table, which had been filled with food and drinks during the day. It was almost bare now, the white tablecloth half on and half off. Two Corona bottles were turned on their side, the beer and lime slices spilling out into a sticky mess. More beer bottles were broken on the terracotta tile floor, and a tray of tortilla chips lay upside down among them, chips scattered everywhere. The room smelled like beer.

Carolyn slowly walked around the table to the opposite side, where the tablecloth was draped toward the floor. Laura lay there facedown, blood matted in her blonde hair, her left arm in a twisted position. She was wearing just her blouse. Her panties and capris were crumpled in a ball a few feet away. She was not moving.

"Oh my God!" Carolyn gasped, sinking to her knees beside Laura.

"What happened?" she yelled back to the men in the other room. *Something very wrong has happened here,* she thought. *And these guys are useless. Keep your wits about you, Carolyn.*

Still no answer. "Have you called 911 yet?" Carolyn asked, turning to where Paul now stood. His posture slumped.

"No!" he replied. "We can't do that!"

"Why not?"

"They would call the police." Paul stumbled and grabbed onto the table. As he did, the rest of the tablecloth fell to the floor, causing the remaining bottles to crash to the Saltillo tile.

"*That's* what you're worried about?" Carolyn choked out. "How about this girl? She's bleeding. Maybe she's dead."

Trey groaned.

Carolyn stooped down to get a closer look. She put her fingers on a vein in Laura's neck to see if she could find a pulse. *Thank God,* she thought. *She's alive.*

"My father will kill me if he finds out about this. Not to mention the firm. All of us could get in trouble, maybe fired. You too, Carolyn. Think of that," Paul said in a rush. He had a reputation for being cool and in control. But clearly he was panicking.

"All I know is that Laura needs medical attention right now. If you aren't going to get it for her, I'll take her to a hospital myself," Carolyn said, regaining her confidence. "Assuming she is still breathing when we get there."

Paul went back into the living room and sank down on a couch, unable to steady himself on his feet any longer.

"And what if the police stop you and give you a blood alcohol test, Carolyn? You might get arrested," Paul argued.

"I don't *believe* you all," Carolyn said. "What were you going to do? Drop her body in the bay?"

"Well, that's one idea," Paul murmured.

Carolyn looked at him in disgust.

"I was just joking," he said quickly, looking away. "I know. It's not a joking matter. This is terrible, terrible . . ."

Trey walked unsteadily into the kitchen and grabbed a bottle of Ozarka off of the counter, knocking over an open Bayer aspirin bottle, which fell on the floor and scattered pills everywhere.

Carolyn gently rolled Laura over, being careful with her bent left arm, and touched the young woman's face. Having grown up on a ranch, she was accustomed to seeing injured animals and people. She had treated sprains, cuts, and bone breaks on ranch hands before. But this was different. This was a young woman for whom she was responsible. Whatever had happened, it didn't look accidental. She guessed that Laura's arm was broken, and there was a bruise forming on her cheek. She was relieved to see that Laura was breathing, even though she was unconscious.

"Who's going to help carry her to my car?" Carolyn asked Trey and Paul. She scanned the room. When she got to the tall man in the jeans, she asked, "Who is that?"

"Just a friend of ours from UT," Paul said. "He and Peter were in the neighborhood and dropped by."

"In this neighborhood? On the west end of the island? At two in the morning?" Carolyn's voice was cold.

"It doesn't matter," Paul mumbled. Then he followed Trey into the kitchen.

"Maybe Carolyn is right, Paul. Maybe we should call 911," Trey said, shifting from one foot to another.

"No, this is my house and we can't do that," Paul said with finality in his voice.

"I'll help get her to the car, Carolyn," Trey said as he walked toward the dining room. "I am so sorry, so very sorry. I'm sure nobody meant to hurt her."

"Shut up, Trey," Paul barked.

"Really?" Carolyn said sarcastically, as she struggled to put Laura's panties and capris on her unresponsive body. She wanted to ask how they had come off, but then again she didn't really want to know the answer. *I can't believe this is happening,* she thought, automatically snatching her purse and Laura's from where they had left them earlier in the day.

Trey lifted Laura under her shoulders with her head resting against his chest occasionally lolling forward. Carolyn carried her legs. Laura wasn't heavy, but they were trying not to move her arm more than necessary. Trey backed out of the door, which had been left open when he and Paul came in from the beach. There weren't any lights on in the neighboring houses and no moonlight. It was dark, and the sand between the house and driveway was soft underfoot, so they moved slowly so as not to trip. A party was apparently still going on in a house at the other end of the development because they could hear faint rock music.

After Carolyn and Trey carefully placed the unconscious girl into the back seat of Carolyn's BMW 3, Paul followed them outside and roughly grabbed Carolyn's arm. "Take her to the ER at UTMB. My brother, Brian, is a resident. I'll call him and let him know you're coming."

Paul started to stumble back to the house, then stopped. He turned around. "And Carolyn, tell them that she was really drunk and just fell."

• • •

There were no other cars on the two-lane beach road at 2:30 a.m. on a Sunday morning in early August. There weren't any streetlights, and it was pitch black until Carolyn drove up onto the seawall. At that point, she began to hear the incoming tide roaring and crashing against the rocks. To her left were condos and stores, which were all dark now.

She could feel the tightness in her neck as she grasped the steering wheel of her car. Her feet hurt, and she realized she hadn't put on shoes before she left the house. As she drove, she talked to the unconscious girl, telling Laura that they were on their way to get help. She didn't know what she would say to the doctors. *Why were Laura's clothes half off? Why did Peter and that other man show up after midnight? Who was he, anyway?*

Less than twenty-four hours ago, Carolyn and Laura had made the forty-five-mile drive from downtown Houston to Galveston Island. Carolyn was a second-year associate at Edwards and Harrison, one of the oldest and largest law firms in Houston. Laura was a rising third-year law student at the University of Pennsylvania, one week into a 2001 summer internship at the firm. The recruiting office had assigned Carolyn to be Laura's associate sponsor.

They were on their way to a party at the beach house on Galveston in the exclusive enclave of homes known as Pirate's Beach. But this was no recruiting event scheduled by the firm; it was a private party. Carolyn was surprised and flattered when Paul's secretary called her with the invitation for Laura and her. She knew Paul was a firm superstar, but she had never worked with him, or even had a conversation with him of any substantial length.

Laura had been excited about going to the event. On the drive south, past the University of Houston with its distinctive, architecturally Greek-looking school buildings, she asked Carolyn lots of questions about the host, who else would be there, and how she should act. She was enthusiastic about the clerkship in general and carried on a lively conversation, asking all the right questions about how the associate program operated, whether women were mentored, and the chances of making partner. Carolyn liked Laura immediately. *She's done her homework and is ambitious. That's good.*

For the next several minutes of their drive, Laura quietly stared out the window at the many strip centers, shabby older apartment complexes, and billboards between the Loop 610 Intersection and Beltway 8, the two main highways looping around the city, many of which had signs in Spanish. It was a heavily Hispanic and poorer area of town.

"Why did you decide to take a clerkship in Houston?" Carolyn asked her, after they passed the intersection with Beltway 8 that separated the dense urban area of the city from the more residential and predominantly white suburbs to the south. "You're a long way from Philadelphia. Do you have family or friends here?"

"No," Laura replied. "I just decided to choose a city in another part of the country that feels like it has . . . possibilities. I'm really interested in your oil and gas practice. The business journals I read say that energy is only going to grow as an industry and there will be a great need for lawyers."

"You're brave to come so far from home," Carolyn said. "With your grades you could have had an internship with any of the Wall Street firms. Of course, they don't do energy work."

Laura laughed. "I worked at a Wall Street firm in a corporate practice the first half of the summer. I liked the work, but very few people ever make partner. Besides, this is the first opportunity I've had in my life to get away from the Northeast and try something new and exciting. I'm from a really small town in New Jersey. It's the kind of place where nobody leaves, and everyone knows everybody else's business. Life is predictable—women are expected to get married and have babies. I wanted something more, to be in a place where every day you learn something new or meet someone new. When the firm interviewed me on campus, I liked the people and saw it as a chance to spread my wings. Does that sound crazy?"

"It sounds familiar," Carolyn smiled. "I grew up on a ranch in South Texas where the only excitement is the annual county fair. Our land was outside a small town, and I dreamed of moving to Houston or Dallas, places where important things were happening. Now I look at the downtown Houston skyline as I drive in to work every morning and I feel like Dorothy looking at the Emerald City. It's beautiful and exciting. My ambition is to have a successful legal career and play a significant role in the city someday."

"That's exactly how I feel!" Laura exclaimed.

"Look to your left," Carolyn said. "NASA is just down that road. Beyond that is the Kemah Boardwalk and Clear Lake, which leads into Galveston Bay and the Gulf of Mexico. One day I'll take you down there and you can watch a continuous stream of cargo ships and tankers from all over the world in the Houston Ship Channel, carrying oil, cars, and everything you can imagine to the Port of Houston. It's the second-busiest port in the country. Hundreds of refineries and chemical plants line the channel. It's not just the oil wells in Texas that makes it the energy capital of the country—it's also the international commerce." As she spoke, Carolyn thought that Laura looked happy.

She's come to the right place, Carolyn thought. "It sounds like we're a lot alike," she said. "I love the firm. I think you will too."

After passing through miles of wetlands as they approached the coast, Carolyn drove up onto the wide causeway that connected Galveston Island to the mainland. There was a beautiful view of the island and the boats in the bay. They turned off the freeway at 61st Street and eventually onto the two-lane beach road that was the only artery running the length of West Beach. To the left was the Gulf of Mexico, and to the right they saw mostly pasture until they arrived at Pirate's Beach. The Robinsons' house was one of the largest on the front row just beyond the dunes. The party was already underway when they arrived. Carolyn could hear laughter and smell mesquite smoke as they walked up the driveway.

Laura was petite and pretty, with a quick and engaging smile. She mixed well at the party—attended mostly by young partners, senior associates and their spouses, and a sprinkling of summer interns—and seemed excited to learn more about Texas, Houston, and the firm. Carolyn tried to introduce Laura to their host, but Paul was in charge and busy and she never got the chance. She did point him out to Laura at one point, when the two women were relaxing, standing on the deck, looking in through the large panes of glass at the activity inside the house.

"He's handsome," Laura said. At the time, Carolyn thought nothing of it. Everyone said that Paul was handsome, as well as being an outstanding lawyer and business developer. Trey Jorgenson, another young partner in the oil and gas group, approached them and asked if he could bring them another drink. Trey was tall and blonde with blue eyes, betraying his Scandinavian ancestry. Carolyn introduced Laura to him.

"How are you liking the firm so far?" he asked.

"Everyone's been so kind, and it feels like an exciting place to work," Laura answered.

"Great! Where'd you go to law school?"

Trey was running through the usual litany of questions firm lawyers asked any recruit, so Carolyn took the opportunity to excuse herself and go to the powder room, leaving them to chat. When she returned, Trey and Laura were sitting together on a bench and seemed engaged in a lively conversation, which only ended when one of the caterers approached Trey and asked him a question. Trey excused himself, and Laura made the comment that Trey was "incredibly charming."

Everyone was having a good time drinking beer, listening to a small band, and eating boiled shrimp and barbecue. Two young men cooked the meat on a grill outside on one corner of the deck, as a caterer steamed the shrimp and served drinks. Carolyn lost track of the time.

At about nine p.m., Paul suggested to the few remaining guests that they had probably had too much to drink for them to drive back to Houston. He encouraged them to find one of the many guest rooms in the house and leave in the morning.

Carolyn realized she had indeed had more to drink than usual and was feeling a bit tipsy. She told Laura that it would be best if they stayed the night—I-45 was always a busy road, and there were a lot of drunk drivers making the return trip to Houston on a Saturday night. Carolyn could tell from the way Laura took a few steps backward and looked at the floor that she was hesitant about staying. But Carolyn assured her that all the men there were gentlemen, and they would be perfectly safe.

"Don't worry," she had said. "I promise to take care of you."

Now, driving an unconscious and battered Laura to the hospital in the dark, Carolyn remembered that conversation and grimaced.

2

———

Approaching the looming campus of the University of Texas Medical Branch at Galveston, on the populous east end of the island, Carolyn searched franticly for the emergency room. Spotting it, she parked her car in a fire zone and ran into the building. The emergency department was as bright as day, bustling with activity. Friends and relatives of patients, some crying, some praying, others looking tired and worried, filled three rows of folding chairs on the right side of the large noisy waiting room. A voice from a loudspeaker broke in, paging a doctor to report to a patient's room. Both a medical school and a teaching hospital, UTMB was also the Level One Trauma Center for a large area of East and Southeast Texas. It was always busy, but Saturday night was rush hour.

Responding to her frantic cry for help, nurses followed Carolyn back outside. They carefully lifted Laura out of the car and laid her on a gurney for the trip to an exam room. A businesslike Black woman in a nurse's uniform led Carolyn to a small windowless office marked "Triage," where she asked her a series of questions.

"What is your name? Are you related to the patient?"

"Carolyn Page. No, we're colleagues. I mean we work together. And she's a friend."

"Okay, friends," the nurse spoke calmly, trying to put Carolyn at ease. "And what is the patient's name?"

"Laura Petrillo."

"Where was the young lady when she suffered her injuries?" the woman asked.

"We were staying at a friend's house on Pirate's Beach," Carolyn replied.

"At what time did the injuries occur?"

"We turned out the lights in our room around ten. When I woke up at two a.m. I saw that she wasn't in her bed. I went downstairs to look for her and found her lying on the floor, unconscious and bleeding."

Something finally exploded within Carolyn, and tears rolled down her cheeks. It took a lot to unnerve her—hardened as she'd been by life on a cattle ranch—but the events of the past two hours suddenly took their toll. She sobbed for several minutes from sheer emotional exhaustion. The nurse silently handed her tissues from a box on her desk.

When Carolyn got herself under control, the woman continued. "Do you know what caused her head injury or how long she had been lying there?"

"No. I know she went to sleep right after we went to bed because she was breathing heavily. But I don't know why or when she got up. I saw a bottle of aspirin on the counter in the kitchen. Maybe she got up to get some."

"Had she been drinking alcohol or using drugs before she went to bed?"

"We had all been drinking during the day," Carolyn admitted. "But no drugs."

"Was anyone else in the room where you found her?" the nurse asked.

"The homeowner's son and another lawyer were there. And a couple of other people," she said.

"Did they say whether she was awake at any point?"

"No, they didn't. And I guess I didn't ask," Carolyn replied.

The nurse got up from her chair and walked to the door to see if Laura was still waiting for an examination room. Not seeing her gurney in the hall, she told Carolyn, "I think someone is looking at her now. Just a couple more questions.

"Do you know if she has any chronic health issues like epilepsy or seizures?"

"Not that I know of, but I've only known her for one week. She's from New Jersey and goes to law school at the University of Pennsylvania. She's interning at our law firm. She seemed healthy and happy yesterday. Will she be all right?"

The nurse closed her notebook and stood up. "That's all I need for now. You can wait in the lobby. Our staff will take good care of your friend and someone will page you when they are ready to talk to you."

As Carolyn walked back into the lobby, she was feeling unsteady. She saw a coffee machine and moved automatically toward it. She needed something to help her stay awake. *Poor Laura,* she worried. *Please God, let her be okay.* Then she wondered, *What in the hell did happen to her? Damn those guys!*

Carolyn looked toward the entrance. Two Galveston Police officers were standing inside, talking.

She shuddered. *I should report to them what happened,* she told herself. *It's the right thing to do.*

• • •

Carolyn was about to head toward the policemen when she heard her name over the loudspeaker. Hesitating, she turned around and hurried to the large double doors that led back into the examination rooms. A dark-haired young man in a white jacket stepped in front of her, blocking her progress.

"Are you Carolyn Page?" he asked.

"Yes, I am," Carolyn said anxiously, looking up at him. She assumed this was the doctor who had examined Laura. "Will Laura be all right?"

"I haven't seen her yet," he replied. "I'm Brian Robinson, Paul's younger brother. Paul called me as soon as you left the house and asked me to take care of you. I'm an orthopedic surgery resident. I'm sorry I wasn't here when you arrived. I was with a patient upstairs and just received his message."

She'd forgotten that Paul told her that he would call his brother and alert him that they were coming. Brian strongly resembled Paul and he appeared calm and serious. She began to breathe more slowly.

"I'll stay with you if you don't mind," Brian said. "My shift's over. And Paul is very concerned about Laura."

Carolyn grimaced, remembering Paul's lack of concern back at the beach house. "I'm sure he is," she mumbled.

On the other side of the big doors, patients lying on gurneys filled the hallway, looking especially ill under the harsh fluorescent lighting. They were lined up against the olive-green walls of the hall. There was an antiseptic smell. Doctors, nurses, and aides moved around quickly as if in an unspoken and well-choreographed dance. The apparent efficiency of the operation, even with so many patients to attend to, impressed Carolyn.

Brian led Carolyn to a curtained area near the end of the hall where Laura was lying in a hospital bed, a wide bandage circling her head and her left arm in a sling. A blue bruise had formed on her right cheek. A nurse was inserting an IV into her arm. There was another patient in a bed in the same area, but she was also unconscious. A young Hispanic man Carolyn assumed was her husband was standing beside her holding her hand and quietly praying. They both wore wedding rings.

Carolyn sucked in her breath. She felt queasy and lightheaded all of a sudden. She whispered to Brian, "How serious do you think this is?"

But all Brian said was "Hmm," as he crossed his arms in front of him.

"Did she tell either of you what happened to her?" Brian asked, looking at Carolyn and the nurse.

"The patient has been unconscious since she arrived," the nurse replied. "You can stay here. The doctor who examined her will be in shortly."

"She was unconscious when I found her," Carolyn said.

Brian pulled out the only chair in the room for Carolyn to sit down. "My brother told me that she was pretty drunk and was dancing by herself on the dining table before she fell off and hit the floor." He looked directly at Carolyn for a response.

Carolyn was wondering what her next move should be. *I should call Laura's parents,* she thought. *But all I know is that she grew up in New Jersey and is a student at Penn. The office would have her school address. But it's early Sunday morning. No one will be there.*

Carolyn turned to Brian. "I'm sorry. What did you ask me?"

"She must have been really drunk to get in this condition?" Brian said.

Carolyn felt he was prompting her. She didn't like that. "No. She wasn't. We talked for a while when we were getting ready for bed. I was the one who thought I shouldn't be driving back to Houston and decided to spend the night in one of the guest rooms, going back in the morning. We shared a room with two twin beds. I promised her it was a safe situation. I can't believe this is happening."

"Hmm," Brian said again.

"Seriously, Brian," Carolyn said, "it isn't helping me to understand Laura's situation if you just keep mumbling. Is that a medical diagnosis or a brother's obfuscation?"

Brian's eyebrows shot up and he looked amused, which had not been Carolyn's intent. Then he regained his serious face. "Sorry," he said. "It's a bad habit doctors have of reserving judgment until they examine all the evidence."

Carolyn was about to apologize herself for her sharpness, but just then Laura let out a moan and her eyelashes flickered. She shook her head and slowly opened her eyes.

Carolyn moved quickly to her side. "Laura, it's me, Carolyn. I brought you to the hospital."

The girl didn't respond. She looked around the room, obviously disoriented. When her eyes fell on Brian, her whole body jerked and she let out a strange, animal sound before she turned away from him.

"Laura," Carolyn said, "what happened to you?"

Laura moaned, but Carolyn couldn't understand her. A tear seemed to form and run down her cheek, and then she lost consciousness again.

Brian put his hand on Carolyn's shoulder and gently pulled her away. "It's not a good idea to push patients who are in shock to answer questions about an accident when they are still traumatized. Confusion is one of the symptoms of trauma. It's better to allow the initial shock to wear off before questioning them. Otherwise, they can become wedded to a story they dreamed or imagined, and which may not be true."

Carolyn felt annoyed. *He's patronizing me,* she thought. And now she wasn't sure she trusted him. Reaching over to hold Laura's hand, she leaned in to whisper, "Sleep now. You and I will sort things out tomorrow." Then she turned to Brian and frowned.

The attending physician entered the room. Dr. Art Jennings was sixty-five, had worked the emergency room at UTMB for thirty years, and, in that time, he had seen every gunshot wound, stabbing victim, burn victim, overdosed teenager, and other trauma imaginable. So a young woman with a broken arm, bruised face, and a head injury was not at the top of his list of worst cases. He looked at Carolyn and asked her if she was the patient's relative.

"I work with her and brought her here," Carolyn answered.

Dr. Jennings's tone was clinical. "We'll admit her and keep her under observation for twenty-four hours to make sure the head injury isn't worse than it looks. She has a fractured arm, probably from falling on it. But the rest of her injuries are nothing that time won't heal. We'll put her arm in a soft cast and sling for now."

Turning to Brian, Dr. Jennings asked suddenly, "What are you doing here, Dr. Robinson?"

"Miss Page is a colleague of my brother," Brian said. "They're both lawyers with Edwards and Harrison in Houston. Paul called and alerted me that they would be arriving and asked me to help them in any way I could."

"Edwards and Harrison," Dr. Jennings said, his tone softening. "I'm not a big fan of lawyers in general, but that's a fine firm." Turning to Carolyn and smiling now, he asked, "Do you know Tommy Lawler? We grew up together out in Abilene."

"Yes, I do," Carolyn said. Edwards and Harrison was one of the most prestigious firms in Texas. After working at the firm for two years, she was used to strangers asking her if she knew a friend who worked there. She appreciated that instant prestige was one of the unspoken benefits of her job.

"We'll keep the patient overnight, and you can call tomorrow and see when she will be discharged. Go get some sleep, yourself, young lady. And drive carefully. You look very tired."

Dr. Jennings checked the sling on Laura's arm before saying good night and leaving the room. Carolyn got up and absently placed Laura's purse under the sheet.

"Why don't I drive you back to Dad's house?" Brian offered. "You shouldn't be driving after all that's happened. Besides, you don't have any shoes."

Carolyn didn't want to go anywhere near the beach house. "No, that's all right," she said. *I've had enough of these Robinson boys for one night, shoes or no shoes,* she thought.

"You really shouldn't be alone. You could be in shock yourself. Why don't you stay at my apartment tonight. It's close to the hospital and I have two bedrooms." Brian lightly put his hand on her arm and seemed to be sincerely concerned for her, but he was still Paul's brother and Carolyn felt unsure of his motives.

"Thanks, but I need to be alone. I have some processing to do."

Carolyn sat down again. "Look, I know you're trying to be helpful. But there's something that's bothering me." She asked herself if she could trust him, and then took a breath and said, "It's the condition in which I found Laura that I haven't told anyone—at least not yet."

"Don't complicate this, Carolyn. You did the right thing. You brought this poor girl to where professionals could address her injuries. But whatever you think you saw—telling people about this whole thing might have repercussions that could adversely affect Laura, everyone who was at the house . . . even *you*."

"Such as?" Carolyn asked. Now she was on high alert.

Brian sighed. "Do you really want to draw attention to the fact that you and Laura were spending the night at Paul's when his wife wasn't there? You know . . . I'd think twice about spreading the details of this night around. Laura will recover and everyone will forget about it in a week."

"But we didn't do anything wrong," Carolyn protested.

"I'm sure you didn't," Brian said, sounding sincere, "but the old men running the firm sometimes make assumptions. I grew up around those old goats. Consider your reputations. One thing I've learned in my residency is not to do anything rash or fueled by emotion. Just think about it overnight and then decide what to do in the morning."

Carolyn tried to stand and walk away, but Brian put his hand on her elbow. "Please let me take you home, or wherever you want to go," he said. "After all, I feel kind of responsible since Laura's injuries happened at my family's house."

Brian looked sincerely concerned, and Carolyn was more tired than she had ever been. She thought for a minute that it would be nice to let someone else—someone with experience in all of this—take control. But she felt confused by the events of the night and didn't know whether to trust him. She gently removed his hand and said, "Good night, Brian. Thank you."

"I wish you would let me take care of you," Brian said.

Carolyn managed a slight smile before turning toward the door. *I wonder*, she thought, *what that would be like?*

3

―――

I
t was a short drive along Harborside Drive to Carolyn's destination. On her right, brightly lit jack-up rigs waiting to move offshore to drill for oil were docked across the channel in the Port of Galveston. On her left, some of the nineteenth-century warehouses that once held cotton, rice, and other agricultural products in the city's heyday sat abandoned. When she approached the old downtown area known as the Strand, all of the tourist shops and restaurants were dark. The only places showing signs of life at that hour were some seedy all-night sailors' bars. Tinny music from an old jukebox was the only sound breaking the silence.

The night desk clerk at the historic Tremont Hotel seemed unfazed that a barefoot, tired-looking young woman in rumpled clothes would lay an American Express credit card on the counter, and at six a.m. Carolyn went straight to her room, tore off her clothes, and crawled into the antique bed without even turning on any lights. She reached for the alarm clock to set a wake-up time but was too tired to figure out how it worked. She picked up her mobile phone, but the battery was dead. She decided she would wake up on her own in a few hours, hung the Do Not Disturb sign on the door, and took the telephone off the hook.

It was one in the afternoon when bright sunlight around the edges of the window shades and the noise of groups of tourists on the street woke her. "Damn it!" she said out loud. She had intended to return to the hospital in the morning, and now half the day was gone.

She pulled herself out of bed and went to the small bathroom, where she took a hot shower. She felt grimy inside and out. She didn't want to put on her clothes from yesterday, but she had no choice. She considered going to one of the tourist shops nearby and buying something clean to wear, but she didn't know if they would let her in without shoes and, more importantly, she wanted to get to the hospital as soon as possible. She remembered she had a pair of old flip-flops in the trunk of her car. They would have to do for now.

Back at UTMB, the hospital was quiet, a completely different atmosphere than the chaos of Saturday night. A young Black woman at the reception desk smiled when she approached. "Can I help you?" she asked.

"Yes," Carolyn replied. "I'm here to see Laura Petrillo. Can you tell me where she is?"

"Are you family?" the woman asked.

"I'm Carolyn Page. I brought her in here last night. She doesn't have any family in Texas."

The woman hesitated. "You know, under HIPPA, we can only release that information to family members."

"Please," Carolyn pleaded. "There is no one else in the entire state who can take care of her."

The woman looked around to see if anyone else was in the vicinity. Then she scrolled through a list of patient names and rooms. She looked at Carolyn and whispered, "She's in Room 322."

"Thanks," Carolyn replied, hurrying toward the elevator. When she reached Room 322, the door was open. A Mexican woman was changing the sheets on the bed, and a dustpan and broom indicated that she was preparing the room for the next patient.

"I am looking for Laura Petrillo," Carolyn said to her. "Have they moved her?"

"I think she's gone, senora," the woman replied.

"Gone! Gone where?" That's impossible," Carolyn cried. "She had a head trauma just this morning. She couldn't have been discharged yet!"

"I don't know anything. You check with the nurses down the hall," the woman said, returning to her task.

For the second time in twenty-four hours, Carolyn felt totally unnerved. *How could Laura be gone? And if that is true, where is she?*

An older white woman sat at the nurse station. She was flipping through some papers.

"Excuse me," Carolyn said. "I came to see Laura Petrillo, but she's not in her room. Can you tell me where she is?"

"Are you a relative?" the nurse asked.

"Yes, her sister," Carolyn lied.

The woman took off her glasses and put the papers down. "When the nurse went to her room after lunch to take her vitals, the patient was not in her room. The nurse checked the bathroom and then the rest of the floor. She couldn't find her, so she called Security and they did a search of the hospital. There was no trace of her. Her purse and her clothes are gone, indicating she meant to leave. If you ask me, she's gone for good."

"But I was told she was in Room 322 downstairs," Carolyn protested.

"Sometimes it takes a while for occupancy information to reach all areas of the hospital," the nurse said. "We think she's only been gone for an hour or so, and Security just completed their search."

"But doesn't she have to be discharged?" Carolyn asked.

"Yes. But sometimes we get people who partied too hard and either can't or don't want to pay their bill. Some skip out so their parents or husband or whoever doesn't know they were here. It happens. Galveston is a resort town, you know."

"Is Dr. Robinson on duty?" Carolyn asked the nurse. She hoped Brian might know what happened to Laura.

The nurse consulted her records. "No, this is his day off."

"How about Dr. Jennings? Is he here?" Carolyn asked.

"He's gone too."

"Can I have their phone numbers?" Carolyn asked.

"I can't give out doctors' personal information," she replied in a cool voice.

Not knowing what else to do and completely frustrated, Carolyn left. It was ninety-eight degrees outside and her car was like an oven. She turned on the motor and turned the air conditioner on max, but she didn't go anywhere for a while, instead trying to make sense of the past day. *Laura had her purse, so she could have taken a cab*, Carolyn thought. *But if she was confused and didn't know where she was, she might be wandering around on foot.*

Carolyn pulled out of the parking lot and began to drive slowly up and down the streets surrounding the hospital complex. The area on the northwest part of the island was known as the Victorian District. Before the catastrophic hurricane of 1900, which devastated the island with a fifteen-foot storm surge and claimed almost 8,000 lives, Galveston was the busiest port city on the Gulf Coast, more prosperous than New Orleans. Wealthy merchants, shipping magnates, the ecclesiastical hierarchy, and others built grand Victorian-style homes with turrets and gingerbread trim. Some had survived and even been restored. Carolyn drove up and down the narrow streets for an hour, but there was no sign of Laura.

What now? She asked herself. Laura had been badly injured. *Could she really have walked out of the hospital on her own? Could someone have abducted her? Surely not. No one knew where she was—except Brian.* Not for the first time, Carolyn asked herself how she could have allowed this to happen. In any case, she didn't know what else to do except to go home.

• • •

Once on Interstate 45, Carolyn's mind returned to the scene at the beach house. After she crossed the Causeway, the land on either side of the mainland was low-lying marshland for much of the way. She felt exhausted, but there wasn't much to distract her. One by one, she considered what she knew or had heard about the men who were there

Sunday morning. Most of what she knew about Paul and Trey had come from listening to gossip from her friend Cynthia Connor, who also worked at the firm. Cynthia and Carolyn had been in the same class of summer interns and first-year lawyers. Although they came from different backgrounds, they quickly bonded. Cynthia had gone to Harvard and stayed for law school, graduating with distinction. She was a tax whiz and worked in the employee benefits group. She also seemed to have her pulse on firm gossip and loved to share it with Carolyn, off the record, of course.

Although she was Brian's age, Cynthia knew Paul from having grown up near the Robinsons in River Oaks. Since the subdivision was developed in the 1920s for the elite families of the day, River Oaks, consisting of over a thousand acres just west of downtown along Buffalo Bayou, had been the center of Houston high society. Many of the houses were designed by famous architects and sat on broad, wooded lots. Southern-style white or brick-columned mansions mixed with large Tudor-style homes, many of which surrounded the meandering green edges of the River Oaks Country Club Golf Course. Azalea bushes were everywhere and bloomed spectacularly in March, drawing crowds of people who waited in line for hours to tour the featured homes and gardens of the wealthy.

Oak tree-shaded River Oaks Boulevard was known as the only street in the world with a country club at both ends. Lamar High School, a remarkable art deco campus where all the early residents sent their children, sat on the south end. The gothic stone structures of St. John's Preparatory School, erected in the late 1940s and one of the two best college preparatory schools in Houston, was located just across the street.

Exclusive, stately River Oaks Country Club presided on a rise at the north end of the boulevard, surrounded by ancient oaks and well-tended beds of flowers that bloomed year-round. The original club opened in 1926, but the current clubhouse was built in the 1950s in the style of a white antebellum mansion, complete with columns and a distinguished, ageless black-uniformed doorman to open the door and greet members and guests. Generations of residents passed down their membership, and the waiting list for new members stretched into the years. The club's ballrooms had seen fabulous weddings, galas, and charity extravaganzas. Many important business deals were made in the bar, grill, or on the golf course, where caddies carried the bags of the privileged.

Both the Connor family and the Robinson family were longtime members of River Oaks. Paul, Brian, their older brother William, and Cynthia all grew up at the club and had attended the same social and holiday events. As children, all of them were members of the swim team, which competed with other private clubs. Paul was the Junior Club tennis champion several years running, and Men's Club champion until shortly before he was up for partner and gave up tennis for work.

Cynthia's father insisted that his only child should learn to play golf, and she fell in love with the game. It suited her competitive nature. She was Women's Junior Club champion and captain of the golf team at St. John's School until she left Houston to go to Harvard. Later she made her debut at the club, despite her protestations that feminists didn't make debuts. Her parents insisted that was what young ladies did and she complied because she loved them.

Cynthia and the Robinson boys all went to Teddy Bear House for preschool and St. John's School for elementary and high school. William, Brian, and Cynthia were honor students. Paul earned Bs not because he wasn't as bright; he just had athletic interests and knew that, with his social acumen, he did well enough. All of the Robinson boys went to summer camp at Teton Valley Ranch Camp in Wyoming, where they rode horses in the national forest and mixed with the sons of the upper class from across the country. Their father told them the national contacts they made there would serve them later in life. Cynthia attended summer camp at Waldemar in the Texas Hill Country, the most exclusive camp for young Texas girls.

Paul was tall, with dark brown hair and brown eyes. He was unde-
niably handsome. Years of competition-level tennis had given him an
athlete's body, and his many medals contributed to his abundant self-
confidence. The partners at Edwards and Harrison saw their younger
selves in him and loved him. The male associates wanted to be like him.

Paul and his brothers came from old money, which in Houston
mostly meant the oil patch. Their grandfather, Jacob Robinson, had
been a wildcatter who came to Texas from Tennessee in the early years
of the twentieth century with only a few dollars in his pocket and
a sheriff trailing him. With a combination of raw intelligence, blus-
ter, and a little chicanery, he had managed to find one of the earliest
oil fields in East Texas and amassed a fortune before he died. R. A.
Edwards, one of the named partners in the firm, had met Paul's grandfather early on in his time in Texas and invested in one of his first
wells, which turned out to be a gusher. As the Robinson Oil Company
prospered and grew, Edwards and Harrison did all of its legal work and
grew with it.

The family company was still a client of the firm. Paul couldn't work
on any of the family's business because of the firm's conflict-of-interest
rules. But Paul's daddy made sure that his friends who were also in
the oil and gas business directed legal work to his son. As a midlevel
associate, he was already considered a rainmaker. So his tendency to
take off periods of time in order to entertain clients on the golf course,
a deep-sea fishing expedition in the Gulf, or a duck hunting trip at the
St. James Bay Hunt Club in Rockport were encouraged as business-
development time. He made partner early and everyone expected he
would be elected to the management committee one day, maybe even
become managing partner. He was married to Ashley Hunt, a popular
young woman he had grown up with in River Oaks. Cynthia had made
it clear to Carolyn that she was very fond of Ashley, saying that in marrying her, Paul had married up.

At Texas A&M, his father's alma mater, Paul majored in petroleum engineering and drinking at the Dixie Chicken. William, the Robinsons' oldest son, was being groomed to take over the family oil company, so Paul decided to go to law school. Like any smart son of River Oaks royalty, he attended the University of Texas law school, where an ambitious young Texan went before seeking a job in one of the elite law firms in Houston or Dallas. Paul could have had his pick of firms when he graduated, but the family wanted him to work for the family law firm. He agreed, correctly calculating that his chances for rising to managing partner status was probably best at Edwards and Harrison. In Paul's mind, managing partner of a major law firm was roughly equal to the positions of power that his grandfather and father had occupied, and that his older brother soon would.

Carolyn thought about all that Cynthia had told her about the Robinsons as she drove. It was a typical Sunday afternoon and many weekend visitors to Galveston Island were on the road. Traffic was heavy and moving slowly. Carolyn felt herself getting sleepy. She pulled into the parking lot for the McDonalds in Dickinson and went in to use the bathroom and get a cup of coffee and a homestyle burger.

Fifteen minutes later, she was back in her car on the highway, and continuing her mental inventory of the night's participants. Cynthia had told her that Trey came from a middle-class family. His father was a high school teacher and coach at Lamar High School, the public high school where Trey was a student in the International Baccalaureate Program. His mother was an elementary school teacher and active in the Methodist church. They lived in a modest, original two-story brick home in West University, a separate municipality developed in the 1930s for middle-class families, soon surrounded by the city of Houston. During the past several decades, most of the original houses had been replaced with new construction and the neighborhood residents had changed from middle-class to upwardly mobile high-earning professionals. It was a status symbol to live in West University now.

Trey and Paul had met at Texas A&M, where they were in the same company in the Corps of Cadets. They both studied hard, but also partied hard, and loved dominoes, playing forty-two late into the night at times. They went on to law school at UT together, and Trey lived in the nice four-bedroom house close to campus that Paul's father bought in Austin for his son. Cynthia told Carolyn that Trey was a good guy. "He's pretty much Paul's easygoing wing man," she said, laughing. He was tall, fair, smart, and attractive. Growing up, he participated in the Methodist Youth Organization and became an Eagle Scout.

When Carolyn approached the intersection of Loop 610 South and I-45, traffic slowed to a crawl. It was hot and progress frustratingly slow. Nevertheless, Carolyn continued her thoughts, turning to Peter Kaufman. He'd been the late arrival to the house. She knew that he was a managing director at the midsize accounting firm, Kaufman Stone. Cynthia said that word on the street was that his father was a tyrant who Peter could never satisfy. Carolyn had worked with Peter's associates on a couple of real estate transactions where his firm was also involved. She had the impression Peter worked on a lot of Paul's deals and that they were old friends, although they seemed very different from each other. Peter struck Carolyn as reserved, almost dorky. He was not unattractive, but he was one of the only men she knew who wore tortoise rim glasses and a bow tie.

Paul and Trey had always been cordial to Carolyn, but she was not part of their working group. No women attorneys worked on their deals. Reflecting now, she wasn't sure why she had been invited to the beach party. At the time, she'd felt honored. Now, she had the uncomfortable feeling that perhaps it had something to do with her being Laura's mentor. Laura was very attractive after all.

Then Carolyn remembered the other man who had been in the room when she'd come downstairs. *Paul said that he was a friend from UT. It's strange that he and Peter arrived in the middle of the night.*

Carolyn realized that she was drifting mentally and that she needed to pay attention to the road, particularly as she neared downtown. She put her thoughts behind her and concentrated on getting to Allen Parkway.

Her apartment was in a new midrise development, the Riata, where a lot of young professionals lived. It was close to downtown, and River Oaks Shopping Center was nearby. Everything she needed to live, her entire world, was within three miles of her apartment, maximizing the time she could be at work. As she entered, she noticed that the red light on her answering machine was blinking on and off.

"You have five messages," the mechanical voice said.

"Five?" Carolyn wondered. That was unusual. She pushed play.

The first two messages were from Paul, asking her to call him. The next message was from Brian, wanting her to call him to make sure she'd arrived home safely.

The fourth message was from Paul again, asking her to "give him a call so we can get our stories straight." He sounded desperate.

The last message was from Cynthia, telling her that Paul had called her asking if she knew where Carolyn was. "Are you okay?" she asked. "Why is Paul Robinson looking for you?"

The machine shut off and Carolyn pulled the plug out of the electric socket so that no more calls could be recorded. She took the phone receiver off the hook. Then she walked into the kitchen and took three Tylenols and turned out the lights before sinking down on the couch. "Damn! Damn! Damn! I can't deal with any more of this," she said out loud.

She stretched out on the couch, pulled a faux fur throw over herself, and closed her eyes. The last thing she thought before her exhausted body slipped into sleep was, *What in the hell is going to happen at the firm tomorrow when the shit hits the fan?*

4

———

arolyn's alarm went off at seven a.m. the next morning. She reached over and quickly shut it off. The cheery sound of "It's a Beautiful Morning" didn't seem appropriate. Unwelcome thoughts ran through her mind. *What will happen if Laura doesn't show up at the office? But what if she does? What if she comes in with a broken arm and a bruise on her face?* She felt sick to her stomach.

Her office was on the thirty-seventh floor of the Trans-State Energy Tower. Under construction in 1985, when the Houston economy collapsed along with practically all of the Texas oil companies and banks, it had finally been completed in the early 1990s. The *Houston Business Journal* likened it to a Phoenix rising from the ashes. The finished building was beautiful. Carolyn felt a tinge of pride every morning when she entered the marble lobby. *You're not in Kansas anymore, Dorothy,* she'd told herself the first day.

She had barely put down her briefcase when Cynthia Connor entered her office and sat down on one of the two associate guest chairs. She was carrying two cups of nonfat latte and set one down in front of Carolyn.

"Where have you been all weekend?" she demanded. "I was surprised when Paul Robinson called me looking for you. You don't work with him. Did he snag you for an urgent project he's been putting off until the last minute and you were the unfortunate associate who happened to wander by at an inopportune moment?"

Cynthia was tall and slim, with shoulder-length, naturally ash-blonde hair and brilliant green eyes. Her grace of movement reflected five years of classes at the Houston Ballet Academy. Men found her attractive but intimidating, and that was how she liked it. Her father owned a successful oil field equipment manufacturing facility on the ship channel that was founded by his father. He had no sons and had always hoped that Cynthia would come to work for him and take over the business one day. But Cynthia's ambition was to be successful on her own. She'd told Carolyn she valued her independence and didn't want to be seen as just another River Oaks trust-fund kid.

Carolyn liked and admired Cynthia. When she had first started at the firm, she didn't know how to dress professionally, or the right way to mix and network at social or business events. Cynthia, on the other hand, was sophisticated and worldly. She had spent spring breaks in Switzerland or Aspen skiing, and knew the streets of Paris and London well. She shopped at Neiman Marcus and Saks Fifth Avenue and delighted in mentoring Carolyn, fondly regarding her as her personal Eliza Doolittle project. Carolyn didn't mind at all; she was grateful.

Carolyn was about to confide in Cynthia all that had happened over the weekend and ask her advice as to how to answer the inevitable questions about her summer intern. Since she was Laura's sponsor, she assumed that the recruiting office would surely interrogate her. But she was interrupted by Cynthia's secretary, who called to say that she was late for a client meeting in her office.

Cynthia got up quickly. "Catch you later," she said to Carolyn.

After she was gone Carolyn sat, doodling on a pad to keep her hands busy. She was too anxious to do any work, so she spent some time just staring out the window at the Galleria in the distance. Three hours later, it was noon, and nothing had happened. No one came by her office. No one called.

She waited until she thought people had left the floor for lunch. Then she walked to the office assigned to Laura. The door was closed.

Carolyn knocked, but when there was no answer, she slowly opened it. There was work on the desk, but the computer was off and no one was inside. Carolyn closed the door again and quickly walked away.

The afternoon passed in the same way as the morning. Nothing happened. At four p.m., Carolyn realized she had skipped lunch and was hungry and decided to go to the snack bar on the next floor. As she got off the elevator, Trey and Paul were standing in the hall, drinking coffee.

"Carolyn," they both said, nonchalantly acknowledging her and continuing with their conversation about the Astros game over the past weekend. Carolyn was taken aback by their disinterest after the frantic attempts to talk to her the previous evening. She realized she was standing still watching them walk away and felt stupid. *Am I in an alternate universe?* she wondered. Laura was gone, no one in the firm seemed concerned, and Paul and Trey were acting as if nothing unusual had occurred. *They have nothing to say to me now?*

Tuesday morning, Carolyn went to Laura's office before she even went to her own. She found it completely empty except for the standard desk, chair, and bookcase. Carolyn walked in to look around. Feeling confused, she sat down in the desk chair surveying the empty space. She realized she was holding tight to the arms of the chair and there was tension in her neck. "Where's Laura?" she whispered.

She remained there for five minutes, thinking, but not coming up with any good answers. Finally, she decided, *I've got to get my work done, but I also need to find out what happened.*

She went back to her office and worked on a contract that was due the day before, but her mind kept wandering. Occasionally she would stand and stretch before sitting down to work again, but she couldn't get the tension out of her body.

Around eleven, Pilar, her assistant, buzzed her to say that a Dr. Brian Robinson was on the line inquiring as to how she was. She remembered the patronizing doctor, Paul's brother, with distaste. "Tell him I'm fine, but can't be disturbed right now," she told Pilar. "And thank him for his inquiry."

She had a lunch scheduled with a junior banker with whom she was friends and kept the appointment. When the woman kept chatting idly, however, about the poor male/female ratio for promotions at the bank, Carolyn couldn't feign interest and excused herself, saying she had to take a phone call with a client soon.

After lunch, she turned again to the contract she had been working on in the hopes that it would at least temporarily shut down the questions in her mind about what had happened to Laura Petrillo.

That entire day, no one contacted Carolyn about the party, about Laura, or about anything out of the ordinary. Other associates stopped by from time to time to gossip about the deals they were working on or to ask her routine questions. Late in the afternoon, she decided to call Cynthia and see if she could join her for a drink after work. Cynthia always had a good perspective on complicated people issues and firm politics. She was disappointed when Cynthia's secretary told her that she'd gone to New York for a tax conference and would be away for the rest of the week. Carolyn had forgotten about that. *It would help if I had someone to help me think this issue through,* she thought. But since she didn't have her best friend to confide in, Carolyn went home alone.

• • •

During the summer, the Houston office branch of the firm recruiting committee held a meeting every Wednesday morning. As an associate member, Carolyn always attended. Partners and associates sat around a rectangular table in a conference room. The room faced south, giving a good view of the towers of the Texas Medical Center in the distance. Paul was the partner in charge of the summer intern program. On this Wednesday, after a few introductory remarks, he reported that they would have one less summer intern going forward. Carolyn sat up straight, on alert.

"Who's that?" someone asked.

Paul ruffled some papers before answering. "Laura Petrillo, the University of Pennsylvania clerk. She came to see me at the end of the day last Friday. She was upset and said she was resigning from the firm immediately. It seems she has a boyfriend back on the East Coast. She told me she couldn't stand being without him and decided to move to New York City, where he's working. I informed the attorney recruiting office Monday."

The oldest partner on the committee spoke up. Because of his seniority and accompanying power, everyone had to listen. "The firm is better off without her if a boyfriend is more important than her legal career. I've always said we're wasting resources on girls who are just looking to find a husband and spit out babies," he said, slyly glancing at the few women in the room to see if he could get a reaction. But the women were used to his comments and ignored him. The young woman next to Carolyn whispered *dinosaur* under her breath.

Carolyn looked at Paul, who was not looking at her—deliberately avoiding her, she thought. It was all she could do to sit through the rest of the meeting, not hearing what was said after that. *Laura didn't mention a boyfriend to me,* she thought, *and I don't believe she told him that on Friday.*

After the meeting, Laura was the first to leave and stationed herself outside the door to the conference room. She had decided to confront Paul about what he had said. She would force him to tell her why he had made that statement. *What does he know about what happened to Laura at the beach house before I found her, and what does he know about where she is now?*

Several people stopped to talk to her while she waited, nervous but determined to find out the truth. She brushed them off, more or less politely. Finally, Paul came through the door, but to her dismay he was deep in conversation with the older partner who had made the disparaging remarks about female attorneys. She followed them as far as the elevator, but they ignored her. Before she could interrupt, they were gone.

Anger turned into frustration for a few minutes. But then the anger returned and Carolyn decided to go to Paul's office and confront him there. For one thing, after what Paul and his friends had put her through, she deserved an explanation. For another, she was sincerely worried about Laura's well-being. She rationalized that confronting Paul in his office was a better plan, since she could do it with the door closed and not cause a scene like she would have done outside the conference room.

Carolyn rode the elevator up to the fortieth floor to where Paul and the energy group had their offices. She found Paul's near the end of the hall, which was full of people, some of whom greeted her as she walked by. She wished they weren't so pleasant, but it didn't dampen her resolve. Boxes of documents were piled against the wall in one spot, evidence of an ongoing big transaction. When she arrived at Paul's office, his assistant was on the telephone and Carolyn decided to wait. The door to Paul's office was closed. When the assistant finished her call and hung up, she smiled.

"What can I help you with?" she asked.

"I'm Carolyn Page," she said. "I have an important matter that I need to discuss with Paul. Would you please tell him I'm here?"

"I'm so sorry, Ms. Page. That was Paul on the phone. He's getting a haircut now, and then he has a meeting with a client. He's gone for the day. But I'll pass your message on to him, if you like." The woman smiled again.

Carolyn felt deflated. She had summoned up all her indignation and courage for nothing. She believed that Paul had seen her waiting for him outside the conference room and now was avoiding her. *What a coward*, she thought.

"Never mind," Carolyn heard herself say. She felt defeated and realized the enormity of what she had intended to do. It was unthinkable that a junior associate would angrily confront a partner about anything. It would have been career suicide.

Walking back to the elevator, Carolyn ignored the people she passed. She kept her head low on the way back to her office. When she got there, she closed the door and sat at her desk, took some Tylenol, and tried, without a lot of success, to get on with her work.

Five minutes later, her assistant buzzed her. "Paul Robinson's assistant is on the line. She says you left without telling her whether you wanted Mr. Robinson to call you when he gets back in the office tomorrow."

Carolyn weighed the possible cost of what she had planned to do one last time. Finally, she said, "No, tell her the issue has been resolved." *Now I'm the coward,* she thought.

5

———

aura opened her eyes just after eleven in the morning. From the
sunlight shining through the window, she knew it was daytime.
But she felt panic when she realized that she had no idea where
she was. She tried to grasp the sides of the bed and realized with horror
that her left arm was in a sling. A woman dressed in scrubs entered her
room, and she quickly closed her eyes again, pretending to be asleep.
I'm in a hospital! Laura realized.

After the woman checked some machines above the bed, she left
the room. Laura tried to move her left arm. She felt intense pain in her
arm and her head. *What happened to me? How did I get here?*

She lay quiet for several minutes, trying hard to remember what had
occurred the previous day. Slowly, some pieces began to come together.

*I was at the house on the beach, at the party. But then it was night and
most of the people left. Carolyn was with me. She said that she'd had too
much to drink and wanted to stay over and drive back to Houston in the
morning. We went to bed upstairs.*

Laura's thoughts were interrupted by the loud siren of an ambulance outside of her window. There was shouting and then another
siren signaling the approach of a second ambulance. A nurse came into
her room and looked out the window, trying to see what was happening. She stood there for a while, before turning to leave the room.

"Can you see what's going on?" someone outside the room asked
the nurse.

"Probably a multi-car accident," she replied.

"Has Ms. Petrillo become conscious yet?"

The nurse looked at Laura and shook her head as she left the room.

I remember having trouble sleeping. I thought that if I took some Tylenol that might help. I went downstairs to the kitchen. A tall man was there. I don't think he'd been at the party because he was wearing jeans and a belt with a big silver belt buckle, and everyone else had been wearing shorts or sundresses or swimsuits.

When another nurse entered Laura's room, she closed her eyes and pretended to be asleep. She wanted to figure out what she was doing there before she talked to anyone—even a nurse. When the woman left after writing something on a pad, she tried to remember more.

I asked the tall man if he knew where there was some Tylenol. He said he had aspirin. I remember him shaking two tablets out of an aspirin bottle and handing them to me with a bottle of water. He wore a huge turquoise ring on the hand he used to open the bottle.

There had been a steady beeping in the background from one of the monitors beside Laura's bed. It turned into a long beep that was louder, startling her. The same nurse entered her room to replace the saline drip that was connected to the IV in Laura's arm. She continued to keep her eyes closed and breathed slowly and evenly so the nurse wouldn't notice that she was conscious. It was getting harder to do as she remembered the emotions she had felt the previous night.

Then he asked me if I was a local girl and where Paul had found me. He asked if I had any girlfriends with me. Those questions stuck in her mind, but other things weren't quite as clear. *Was I dizzy after that? There was a table and I might have grabbed the tablecloth because everything on it came crashing down around me and onto the floor—*

Laura's train of thought was interrupted by another loud siren from an ambulance coming closer to the hospital. She started, causing her broken arm to hurt even more. When the siren stopped, she shut her eyes and tried to calm herself.

What happened, what happened? Now Laura was panicking. Had she hit her head or blacked out? She felt the bruise on her cheek. *I heard a second man's voice—someone had their hands on me—they were laughing. Laughing at me!*

Tears welled up in Laura's eyes as the humiliating experience came back to her in bits and pieces. She felt violated, shamed, and embarrassed—emotions she had never felt before. She was a good girl, a strong, careful girl. But somehow, she had let herself be taken advantage of. She felt foolish. *I can never see those people again—any of them.*

Then another emotion kicked in: anger. She made a decision. Although it hurt to move, she got herself out of the bed. She quietly closed the door to the hall. She looked around for her shoes and clothes. She was moving slowly, her mind not totally clear, but she finally found her clothes from the night before in the closet. It was hard putting them on with her left arm in a sling. It hurt and she almost gave up at one point. She had to sit down on the one chair in the room and rest for a minute before continuing. As her mind cleared, however, her determination to get out of the hospital became more focused. She forced herself to keep going until she was more or less dressed.

She became dismayed when she realized that she would need money to get anywhere. But she saw her purse on the floor of the closet, in the corner. That energized her. She picked it up, looked in the mirror, finger-combed her tangled hair, and slowly opened the door wide enough to look down the hall.

She waited until she didn't hear anyone. Then she slipped out of her room and followed the EXIT signs to a back stairwell. Not hearing anyone on the stairs, she stepped carefully down two flights to the street level. There was a door, and, when she pushed it open, she found herself in an alley squeezed between the hospital and another building. Outside, she looked both ways and decided to follow the back of the hospital, past a set of dumpsters, until she came to a street.

When she crossed the street, she entered a neighborhood. Rows of mostly Victorian-style houses lined the street. Some had been freshly painted white or in pastel colors. Others were gray and weathered by time. A few cars were parked along the street. The air was hot and very humid, but she was near the harbor and a salty breeze made it bearable. The first person she encountered was an elderly man in shorts, a T-shirt, and Panama hat who was watering the flowers in the front yard of a pretty house.

"Can you please tell me where I am?" she asked him.

He stopped watering and looked her over, considering her rumpled clothes, her arm in a sling, and the ugly bruise on her face. Then he said, "The East end of Galveston, of course."

"Do you know where I can get a cab to an airport?" she asked.

"There's cabs at the Cruise Terminal," he said. "Straight ahead."

"Thank you," she mumbled and started walking again. But she could hear him mutter, "Damn druggies. Don't even know where they are." She felt even more humiliated and teared up again.

It was a long walk to the Cruise Terminal in the Port of Galveston, and Laura's arm and head still hurt. She had to stop and rest every few blocks. There weren't any benches along the way, so she had to sit down on a curb or a grassy spot in someone's front yard. Each time she felt like she could go on again, it was a struggle to stand up because of her injured arm, the pain in her head, and general exhaustion. A twenty-something young woman who was out for a run stopped and took out her earphones.

"Do you need help?" she asked Laura in a kind voice.

"I'm trying to find a cab to get to the airport," Laura mumbled.

"I passed one in front of the Peanut Warehouse on the Strand. It's not very far from here."

"Thank you," Laura said, not stopping.

The other people she passed pretended to ignore her. That was just as well, she concluded. She didn't want to answer any questions about how she had gotten in such a sorry state.

When she finally made it to the Strand, downtown Galveston's tourist center, she spotted a cab parked, waiting for one more fare.

It was now late Sunday afternoon and most of the tourists had left the island. Only the ever-present seagulls were everywhere, screeching loudly and scrounging for scraps left by people who had dined in the restaurants along the dock.

Laura approached the driver, an elderly Black man who was listening to R&B music on his radio, looking bored. There were no other cars around and only one couple across the street, strolling and eating ice cream cones.

Laura said, "I need to get to the nearest airport."

The driver looked at her skeptically, and again Laura felt conscious of her clothes, her face, and what she imagined must be a frightened look on her face. "Do you have any money?"

"I have a credit card," Laura said, struggling with her right arm to pull her Visa card out of her purse and show it to him. When his expression didn't change and he didn't say anything, she said, "And I have cash."

"Let me see," he said, looking skeptical.

Exhausted from her walk and mortified, Laura reached in her purse and pulled out sufficient bills for him to trust that she could pay.

"Please," Laura said. "I really need to get home and I don't think I can walk any farther."

The driver looked at her arm in the sling and then looked at the empty street. He had been sitting there for an hour. "Okay," he said, his voice softening. "The nearest airport is Hobby. I'll take you there. I live on the mainland in South Houston anyway. You got any luggage?" he asked.

"I don't need it anymore," Laura said, climbing into the back seat and closing her eyes, her head leaning off to the side.

"Hey, you all right?" the man asked, looking around at her and sounding concerned.

Laura didn't answer. Within minutes, she was asleep and didn't wake up until they arrived at the airport.

6

———

By the end of the week, Carolyn felt emotionally exhausted. On Thursday she had gone to talk to her mentor, Will Hopson, to tell him what had happened the previous weekend at the Robinsons' beach house and seek his advice about what to do about it. She was still worried about Laura and felt the need to make sure she was all right.

"I'm sorry, Carolyn," Will's assistant said when she went to his office. "Will is in Austin at the State Bar Real Estate Conference. He's on a panel later today. I don't expect him back in the office until Monday."

Carolyn was disappointed. She loved the firm and her law practice. Until now, she had absolute faith that her colleagues were people of the highest quality and ethics. She wanted desperately to continue to believe that. But the events of the previous weekend had shaken her confidence.

Friday morning, she woke up and made the decision to go home and discuss her moral predicament with her father. She had always trusted his judgment about what was right and wrong. She left work in the middle of the afternoon, not even changing out of her work clothes. Her assistant expressed surprise to see her leaving early.

Carolyn headed west in her car on Interstate 10. She was hoping to get ahead of the usual Friday afternoon traffic of Houstonians heading to the Hill Country for a weekend of rest and outdoor activities. She had grown up on a ranch in rural Kargon County, southeast of San Antonio. The nearest town was Greenville, with only a couple thousand people, and the entire county was mostly other small towns like it. Her father raised cattle and grew a few crops, just like his father and grandfather had done. There had only been one brief owner of the land between Mexican ownership and Carolyn's ancestors.

One of the oldest counties in Texas, Kargon had played a prominent role in the Texas revolution from Mexico in 1838. Carolyn had always been proud of her family's deep Texas roots.

Her mother, Elizabeth, had been a Dallas girl from Highland Park and met Carolyn's father at Texas Christian University in Fort Worth when they were both juniors. She studied art and literature but fell in love with the tall, good-looking ranch management major.

After graduation, they married and moved to his family's ranch. Her mother came from a highly social urban background, and it wasn't easy for her to adjust to the isolation and hard routine of country life. Sometimes she was full of energy and fun. She would arrange picnics alongside the Agua Pura Creek and take Carolyn and her brother, Cody, who was three years older, to the local Czech festival in Flatonia, the Octoberfest celebration in Schulenburg and other local events. But sometimes she became moody and depressed, staying in her bed with the curtains drawn most of the day. When that happened, Carolyn's father would make the children play outside so they didn't disturb her. Few people knew much about depression or bipolar disease in those days. People just left her alone. When Carolyn was only ten, the unimaginable happened: Elizabeth committed suicide.

Carolyn's father struggled to overcome his grief on losing the love of his life. Cody was thirteen when she died and was angry that his mother had left them. He felt cheated. As a teenager, he would sometimes take his anger out on defenseless animals that he killed for no reason. He had a temper that would occasionally flare up over small matters that he considered personal insults, resulting in physical altercations that grew more serious as he became an adult. Young Carolyn, who was the picture of her mother with auburn hair and blue eyes, sorrowfully watched how her mother's death affected the rest of her family. She wondered if it were in any way her fault that her mother didn't consider life worth living. Her father tried to assure her that her mother loved her, loved all of them; she was just sick and no one knew how to make her well.

Their father raised Carolyn and Cody after their mother died. Maria, who had worked for her grandparents as a teenager, cooked and kept the house. She was a nurturing soul who loved both children and tried to keep them well. Their nearest neighbor, Mrs. Prichard, who had been Elizabeth's best friend in the country, looked in on the family regularly, teaching Carolyn things her father didn't know how to teach a young girl. Mr. Prichard and Carolyn's father were close friends and lent a hand to one another when needed. The Prichards' only son, Kenny, was the same age as Carolyn and became her playmate and, eventually, her best friend.

There were plenty of hard chores to do on the ranch, irrespective of gender. Carolyn shoveled hay in the barn in 100-degree weather in August alongside her brother and moved the cattle on horseback with her father, brother, and the ranch hands. As a result, she developed a strong work ethic and self-confidence about her ability to tackle hard tasks.

She rode horses and fished and hunted with her father and brother too. She competed in local rodeos as a barrel racer and often took first place, much to the annoyance of Cody, who didn't have her patience and skill with horses. Nevertheless, Carolyn decided at a young age that she would not live the life that caused her mother to take her own. When she grew up, she'd move to either Dallas or Houston. She would escape from the country and become a successful career woman. She was determined to do something important, something meaningful. She did not think that ranch life and the repetition it entailed fit that bill for her.

Cody was average in intelligence, but lazy. Tall like his father, with his mother's auburn hair and blue eyes, he usually got along on his good looks without having to work too hard. He attended a couple of small colleges in Central Texas, but never graduated. As a child and through his teenage years, his only aspiration was to take over the ranch one day from their father. That was fine with Carolyn, who assumed he would take care of their father and the family ranch while she built her own life in the city.

Growing up, Carolyn read virtually every book in the county library. She was an excellent student and valedictorian of their high school. She felt proud when she smiled at her father and brother from the podium in the school auditorium. She majored in English and biology at Southwestern University, a Methodist liberal arts college north of Austin. During her final year, she took both the MCAT and LSAT exams. When she earned a perfect score on the law school entrance exam, her guidance counselor told her that law was her destiny. That was enough for her.

And she did well at the prestigious University of Texas Law School too. She finished at the top of her class and was inducted into the Order of the Coif. She was articles editor of the Texas Law Review and well liked by her fellow students. When recruiting season came, most of the top Texas law firms recruited her. She was excited when she shopped in the stores in Austin for an interview suit. Looking at herself in the mirror in a black skirt and jacket and white open-necked blouse and pearls, she knew that she was finally on her way to real life and a professional career.

It was natural that Edwards and Harrison LLP considered Carolyn a prize recruit. They had very few female lawyers and were beginning to feel the political pressure at the turn of the millennium to add some. So when this top UT law graduate came along who was not only highly intelligent and ambitious, but a native Texan to boot, they didn't waste any time in making her an offer. Carolyn was flattered by the attention and liked the lawyers. She accepted their offer and joined the real estate finance practice group in September 1999.

At first, she was happy with her choice of practice group. Real estate work was challenging, but she was accustomed to hard work and it made the transactions seem more exciting and important. Her analytical mind was suited to solving clients' problems. Those she served were the companies that were making headlines in the *Houston Business Journal* and *Houston Chronicle*. When she drove past an office tower that her group had helped finance or build, she felt proud.

By Christmas of her first year, however, she began to be unsure. The senior woman associate who was eligible for partnership that year, and widely considered a shoo-in by the women in the firm, was passed over without explanation. The next most senior woman associate said she saw the writing on the wall and resigned to become a partner at a midsize firm in town. A month later, the remaining senior woman associate was outplaced to be general counsel for a client.

Carolyn sensed the low morale among the few remaining female attorneys in the real estate group. She realized that a male associate who had started work the same day she did was getting much better work assignments with more client contact. One day, a secretary told her she would have to wait to have a document typed because the secretary was working on a partner's wife's Christmas card list. For Carolyn, that was the final straw. She knew she was every bit as capable as the young men in the section. For the first time in her life, she felt like she was being discriminated against because she was a woman. She decided to confront the issue head-on.

Will Hopson was in his late fifties when Carolyn joined the firm. He was in the prime of his career as head of the real estate practice group. His stable of significant, longstanding clients provided challenging work for him and the young lawyers who worked under him. He was tall and dignified looking, wore his gray hair longer than most men his age, and had a deep voice that could be intimidating when he wanted it to be. His manner was Texas old-school genteel. He opened doors for women and stood when they entered the room. Some of the young women lawyers who considered themselves feminists thought that was offensive. But Carolyn, raised by an old-school father, thought this was the way men were supposed to act until the disillusioning events of her first four months at the firm made her question what came with that gentility.

She remembered trembling inwardly but presenting herself as composed. She waited until after six one evening when the staff had gone home. She hoped that Will would be in his office alone.

Will smiled when Carolyn peeked in his office.

"Do you have a minute?" Carolyn asked.

"Why of course," Will answered. "I was just getting ready to leave, but I have a minute. What's on your mind, young lady?"

Suddenly, a term she had always considered respectful struck her as patronizing.

Carolyn sat down across from Will. For once, she wasn't smiling.

"Will, it has come to my attention that there is a problem here in the way work is distributed among the associates," she said.

Will was taken aback by his new associate's frankness. "I'm surprised to hear you say that, Carolyn," he said. "I thought we treated all our associates the same. Can you explain what you mean?"

"Yes," she said, trying to not let her voice betray how nervous she felt. If he took what she had to say the wrong way, it could end her career. "I've observed that David Berg, who started work at the same time as I did, gets the transactions with more challenge and client exposure; for example, the Trident Properties deal, the Martin Partners work, and the Four Acres Investment Group. At the same time, since we started, you've asked me to prepare form contracts for the Section, document the sale of partners' second homes, and close a few minor land sales. This means I'm not getting the same opportunity to learn on significant transactions as my male colleague. Is there a reason for that?"

Will reached for his pipe and looked as if he was giving deep thought to Carolyn's complaint. He shifted in his chair.

"I certainly didn't intend to unfairly delegate projects, although it is true that some of our clients prefer working with men. That's just what they are accustomed to doing and we want them to be happy with us. But if you're concerned, we should look at the matter."

Carolyn didn't respond or get up from her chair. She wanted to indicate that she was waiting for him to think and respond now, not later.

Will cleared his throat. "I'll tell you what. The next deal that comes in the door, no matter how big or small it is, I will assign you to work on it. How's that?"

She wondered if she should bring up the matter of female associates being outplaced when they get to the partnership level, but a voice inside her said, *Take what you can get. Small steps, Carolyn.*

The next deal that came in the door of Will's office turned out to be a huge land sale by the city's largest oil company to a major real estate development company. Good to his word, Will named Carolyn as the associate working with him on the deal.

Carolyn heard from one of the male associates with whom she had become close that David Berg wasn't hiding his indignation at not being given the assignment. He saw himself as the rising star and told a group of male associates that Will should have given him the plum assignment since Carolyn didn't have the same experience as him. But Carolyn worked hard and distinguished herself to the client and to Will. At the closing dinner for the transaction, the client singled Carolyn out for praise. After that, Carolyn and Will developed an excellent working relationship. He became her mentor.

Now, as she left the city, Carolyn mulled over her experiences at the firm while she drove. She'd worked hard to overcome obstacles that her male colleagues didn't have to face and she was making progress with her career. But the events of the previous weekend were a setback. She'd been put in the position of doing things she wouldn't choose to do and not even given an explanation. She had seen another young woman treated in a horribly crude manner. None of it made sense, and she felt helpless to do what she knew was right. There was no one she could talk to in Houston to help her sort through the predicament in which she found herself. She thought that her father would listen and give her the advice she so sorely needed.

7

———

Once she crossed the Brazos River and finally left Houston's urban sprawl behind her, the Texas coastal plain became flat, green, and open until she reached Columbus. Then it began to roll into green hills and valleys that were dotted with the occasional barn or farmhouse. Billboards advertising the local festivals and natural cavern tours, as well as the occasional oil pumper, broke up the landscape. The big sky was filled with white cumulus clouds. Bluebonnets and Indian paintbrush, courtesy of Lady Bird Johnson's native Texas plant initiative and the Texas Highway Department, covered the medians between the westbound and eastbound lanes of the freeway. Carolyn was approaching Schulenburg when she realized she was hungry.

Frank's Restaurant was just off the south side of Interstate 10, and most folks thought that the long, low restaurant was the best place between Houston and San Antonio to get a good homestyle meal. Carolyn pulled into the asphalt parking lot, which was full of pickup trucks and American-made cars.

The locals ate dinner early, and most of the tables were full. Carolyn heard noisy conversation and children's voices as soon as she stepped into the restaurant. A bakery with fresh-baked bread, pies, and cookies gave off a delicious, welcoming aroma. Nothing had changed at Frank's since she was a child.

Surveying the large dining room full of tables covered in red check tablecloths, Carolyn spotted a group of young people wearing jeans and trucker caps at a table toward the back. They were waving and try-ing to get her attention. It was some of her high school friends. Due to her workload, Carolyn's trips home had been short and infrequent, so she was happy to see them.

"Hey, girl!" redheaded, brown-eyed, slightly chubby Lou Ann Schultz cried, getting up to hug Carolyn as she approached the table. "I haven't seen you in so long I almost forgot what you look like. Still skinny, I see," she said, laughing. "Sit down a spell, have some pie, and tell us about your exciting life in Houston."

Carolyn smiled at her old friends. She had known Lou Ann and the others all of her life. Most of her friends returned home after college or the military or a short work experience in Austin, Dallas, or Houston, but Carolyn was one of the few who had stayed away. Her friends got together around backyard barbeques, festivals, and high school football games, married one another, and started having babies. A few made the commute into San Antonio or smaller cities for work. They were satisfied and content living the slow-paced life cycle they had grown up with and from which Carolyn had fled.

Lindel Hart got up from his chair and walked over to a table where there were vacant chairs. He brought one back, hugged Carolyn, and ordered her to "Set a spell!"

"Still not much of a social life," Carolyn said, anticipating their questions. "But I love it. It's exciting when you help a client close a big deal after a lot of hard work. You never know what the day is going to bring when you walk in the door in the morning."

"Mm, that's not exactly the case back home," Lou Ann said.

"Well, now wait a minute, Lou Ann," Lindel, the perennial optimist and comic, interrupted. "We got lots of excitement and variety in the country. Some years, it rains. Some years, we have drought. It's always a surprise which way the weather will go."

Everyone laughed, causing Brenda Sue Pinkney, who had been vis-iting with other friends at a table across the room, to turn around. She excused herself and walked over to the table where Carolyn and her friends were sitting. She was followed by a tall, good-looking man with slicked-back black hair, dressed in a preppy button-down white cotton shirt, khakis, and leather loafers. He had a sport coat slung over one shoulder, which made him the best-dressed man in the room.

"Are you on your way home, Carolyn?" Lindel asked. "If so, you're slightly overdressed," he said, appraising her navy-blue tailored suit, white silk blouse, pearls, and matching navy pumps.

"Honestly, you look like a man, Carolyn!" Brenda Sue shrugged in distaste. She said this in her slow drawl, intended to get everyone's attention. Brenda Sue had been the prom, county fair, and beauty pageant queen back in high school. She was of average height, had luxurious streaked light-brown hair and blue eyes, and a peaches-and-cream complexion. She was a natural beauty, and she knew it. Her father owned the local bank, and she had always dressed better and drove a newer car than anyone else. She had attended Stephens College in Missouri to get "finished" and returned to the University of Texas for her last two years to study childhood education and find a husband. Everyone knew this as the "Texas Plan," and at this Brenda Sue excelled. She married a law student from the East Coast she'd met in Austin and brought him back to where she was most comfortable and appreciated. He became the third lawyer in the county. Brenda Sue's daddy convinced him that since he was the only lawyer under the age of sixty-five, his future was guaranteed. Carolyn had never been a big fan of Brenda Sue, and the feeling was mutual.

"I would die before I'd dress like a man," Brenda Sue drawled, as she dug through her purse for her lipstick. "You haven't met my husband, have you, Carolyn?" Brenda Sue stepped aside and took the tall man's hand, pulling him forward. "Jonathan is a lawyer too."

"I haven't," Carolyn said, extending her arm to shake his hand. "I'm Carolyn Page. It's nice to meet you," she said, smiling politely.

Jonathan shook her hand, giving it the hard squeeze that Carolyn had come to recognize as a male lawyer letting the woman lawyer know he was in charge. When he didn't say anything else, Carolyn asked, "Where are you practicing?"

Brenda Sue answered, "His law office is in downtown Greenville. He does all of my daddy's bank work, and he's taking care of all the big cases in the county. We're so fortunate to have him in the community. He's from up East, you know."

Big cases? Carolyn thought to herself.

"It was soooo good to see you, Carolyn," Brenda Sue said over her shoulder as she steered her husband toward another table of people.

Lou Ann gave Brenda Sue's back a sour look and then turned to Carolyn. "Listen, honey, there's a barbeque tomorrow night at Kenny Prichard's house. Kenny still talks about you as the one who got away and he isn't married yet."

In high school, her relationship with Kenny had turned into more than just best friends, as they began to date. He was the quarterback on the football team and class president senior year. Besides that, he was her first love. They broke up when she went to Southwestern and he went to TCU to study ranch management, both of them intent on their own career goals.

"Anyway," Lou Ann said, "all the old crowd will be there. Why don't you come. It'll be fun."

Carolyn's first thought was that she had come home with a mission of talking to her father and thinking through what she should do about the Laura Petrillo matter and didn't have time to go to a party. Then again, it felt good to be among her old friends. There was no need to make an impression or prove herself in any way. They knew her for who she was and accepted her as such. In fact, they seemed really happy to see her. She decided she would think about it after she'd done what she came home for.

It was close to sunset when Carolyn drove by the small wooden Methodist church that her family had attended for generations. She sighed as she passed the cemetery where her mother was buried. She stopped the car and rolled down the passenger side window. The air felt fresh and she could faintly hear the choir practicing for Sunday service inside. She remembered all the years she had sung at Sunday service, funerals, and weddings before she went to college. She felt a pang of guilt that she hadn't been to church since she moved to Houston. But Sunday mornings were the best time to get some work done at the office alone, so it seemed like something she could put off and come back to later.

She turned onto the dirt road that led to the two-story white ranch house where she'd grown up. Page Ranch was painted in black high on the white sign over the front gate, although she noticed the paint could use some refreshing. The house had two stories, but the best feature of the house was a long, wide porch that ran the length of the first floor. Old pink floribunda rose bushes surrounded the porch, and purple Mexican heather grew near a weathered pair of mesquite wood Adirondack chairs that had always been on the front lawn. She looked for the rocking chair and the porch swing where she liked to lounge on warm summer evenings, reading novels and drinking sweet tea. The cicadas were already singing their evening song, and a breeze ruffled the leaves of the wild oak trees in the yard. Everything was as she remembered. She smiled to herself. *This place never changes.*

The family dog, a six-year-old border collie named Shep, heard her tires on the gravel in front of the house. He immediately began barking in order to let everyone know that company approached.

Suddenly, the front door shot open and the tranquil scene transformed. Carolyn's brother stomped out of the house, yelling, "Shut up, Shep!" He stomped over to his old blue pickup truck, yanked the door open, got inside, and slammed the door shut. Then he gunned the motor, backed up, and tore out of the driveway. Dust and gravel flew up after him. Carolyn waved at him as he passed her car, but he ignored her.

What in the world is wrong with him now? Her brother could be moody and even angry at times, but he always calmed down. She wondered what had set him off this time. She shrugged, picked up her purse, got out of her car, petted Shep, walked to the front porch, and went inside.

"Dad?" Carolyn called.

"Well, look what ray of sunshine just dropped in," she heard her father say. He was sitting in a corner of the room on what had been her mother's favorite upholstered chair. He hadn't turned on any lights in the house yet. *Typical,* Carolyn thought. The room looked like it always did. Pictures of her grandparents hung over the fireplace, and a few of the bright-colored abstract paintings her mother loved to paint hung on the other walls. They looked wild and seemed out of place in this otherwise cozy room. In contrast, her grandmother's cream-colored crocheted throw hung on the back of the floral sofa. The ceiling fan offered a slight breeze, although it was still warm in the room.

"Oh, Dad," Carolyn said, wrapping her arms around him. He was tall, muscled from hard manual work, and spare on idle conversation. Carolyn took in the familiar scent of Old English shave lotion. "I'm so glad to see you," she said. They stood like that for a minute, Carolyn savoring the feeling of calm strength that had always made her feel safe.

"I didn't know you were coming, honey. I'd've had Maria cook up some of those cheese enchiladas that you love. But there's sweet tea in the refrigerator."

"That's why I didn't warn you. I can't afford to eat all those yummy, high-calorie things anymore. I need to watch my weight. I'm twenty-eight, you know."

"I do know," he said. "I've been waiting to hear about you finding a nice young man and settling down, producing a grandson or two."

"Well, don't get your hopes up, Daddy. I work too much to have time for a husband. That will have to wait until after I make partner."

"Don't wait too long. Your mother and I had Cody when we were only twenty-two."

"That was a different world, Daddy. Thank God, it's progressed a bit." She was anxious to change the subject. "I saw Cody tearing out of here when I pulled up. What's he riled up about this time?"

Her father sighed and a pained look crossed his face. "Oh, nothing new, honey. He'll get over it. I don't want to talk about that when I can talk to my beautiful daughter."

"Why don't you talk your son into producing a grandson if you're so anxious for one?" Carolyn asked. "All the girls around here were always chasing him."

"I reckon he's more interested in making money now than getting a wife," her father mumbled.

"I thought his ambition always was to take over the ranch and be a rancher."

"It was, but that darn young lawyer in town has put other ideas into his head that go beyond ranching," her father said.

"Who?" Carolyn asked.

"Never mind, never mind," her father said. "Let's see what I can find to feed you in the kitchen."

"I stopped at Frank's. Lou Ann and a bunch of my old friends were there. I ate with them."

"Well, they probably caught you up on all the gossip around here, such as it is. I've got an idea. How about a high-stakes game of dominos before bed? I've got a couple of Shiner long necks in the fridge."

"You're on!" Carolyn laughed.

While her father took the well-worn dominos set out of the cabinet next to the fireplace, Carolyn thought about what he had said about Cody. *I wonder what he's thinking that's got Dad so upset.*

• • •

Carolyn always slept well in her old bedroom. The last color she painted it before she left for college was lilac, which she considered childish after graduation but now found comforting. White muslin curtains kept out the light or opened to a clear view of a green pasture studded with pecan trees. Only once did she wake up, when Shep started barking about two a.m. She heard the front door open and shut, and boots shuffling across the wood floor toward Cody's room. When that door closed, she slipped back into a deep sleep.

The next morning, she woke at seven as usual. Pouring herself some coffee in the kitchen, she picked up one of Maria's special warm biscuits and a slice of country ham and wandered out onto the front porch. To her surprise, Cody was sitting on the porch swing, lacing up his work boots.

"Good morning, brother. I heard you come in and you weren't walking real steady," Carolyn said in a teasing voice.

Cody grunted in acknowledgment.

"What's going on with you? Yesterday when I drove up you looked like you were in a huge hissy fit and took off in your truck without even stopping to say hey to me."

"It's Dad," Cody said. "He's a stubborn old man stuck in the past and not seeing the opportunities lying right under his feet."

"What opportunities?" Carolyn asked.

"You should know, Carolyn. You know where the real opportunity has always been in Texas." He sounded bitter.

"I don't know what you're talking about. Dad has been a pretty forward-looking rancher, always buying the latest equipment and trying new techniques as soon as the farm bureau suggests them."

"Ranching is a dying industry in Texas!" he shouted. As he stood up, he ran his hands through his thick hair. "I'm talking about oil, Carolyn. Oil is the lifeblood of Texas and the source of most of the fortunes that have been made in this state."

Carolyn sat down on the swing that Cody had just vacated. "What makes you think there is oil under the ranch?" she asked him.

"I don't know for sure," he answered. "But Jonathan thinks there might be, and he's got contacts. He says he could get an oil company to lease our mineral rights to find out if there is oil down there. But Dad won't hear of it. Says this is God's country and good ranch land and he doesn't want a bunch of outsiders digging it up and ruining it."

"Who's Jonathan?" Carolyn asked.

"Stevenson," Cody answered, seeming happier now that Carolyn was at least listening to his idea. "He's a real smart fellow. He married Brenda Sue Pinkney. Has an office on Main Street."

Oh, that's right, Carolyn thought. *Well, Brenda Sue always loved to stir the pot.*

"I ran into them yesterday at Frank's," she said. "Is he the one who put this idea into your head?"

"Don't put it like that, sis. I can come up with my own ideas," Cody said, striking a defensive posture. "Jonathan just agrees with me, that's all."

"And what does Jonathan get out of this?" she asked.

"Nothing," Cody said. "He's a friend."

"Cody, I know lawyers and the oil business. He would be a most unusual lawyer if he didn't expect to get something out of this."

Cody walked over to where Shep was sleeping on the porch. He gave him a scratch on the head. Then he turned toward the edge of the porch and spit his tobacco on the ground.

"I wish you would stop dipping Copenhagen and spitting. It's crude, Cody."

Cody frowned at her. After a pause, he said, "Well, I suppose Jonathan might get some legal fees out of it."

"Look, I can handle the family legal work if anyone approached us about wanting a lease," Carolyn said, exasperated. "I'm a lawyer who reviews them all day. We don't need to pay an outside lawyer."

"I guess I hadn't thought of that."

Nice sarcasm, Carolyn thought but did not say. Now she was annoyed. She could see why her dad was frustrated with Cody if this is what they had been arguing about. She walked back and forth across the porch, trying to keep calm.

Then she pulled the rocker across from him and sat down so that she was facing him. She talked slowly, hoping to make her point and not offend her touchy brother.

"Cody, there are hundreds of exploration and production companies constantly scouring the geology of Texas to find any sign of producible hydrocarbons. Don't you think that at least some of them have researched this area? If no one has approached us yet, there probably isn't any oil and gas that can be economically produced. We *don't* want to sign a lease with just anyone to tie up our land for a period of time unless they're ready to drill. Otherwise, if a reservoir of petrochemicals were discovered, the lease would become more valuable, they could assign the lease for a profit, and we would lose out. Besides, we should only want to deal with a reputable company I research ahead of time."

Cody's face grew red. He threw his cap on the ground and turned his back to her. When he turned around, he said, "You may be book smarter than me, little sister. Lord knows I've been hearing that all my life. But just because you work for a fancy law firm, you don't know everything. Jonathan is damn smart too and he agrees with me."

At that Cody picked up his hat, shook the dust off it, and walked off the porch and toward the barn. Shep got up and followed him. He turned around and yelled back at her, "And I'll spit wherever I want to, just like all the other boys around here. Maybe you're just too good for this place now and best stay away."

Cody's last comment made Carolyn feel sad. She and Cody had been close as children, especially before their mother's death. Sibling rivalry from time to time occurred, of course. But she had loved her brother nonetheless. It was undeniable now that there was a rift between them.

Later, Carolyn couldn't decide whether to go to the party at Kenny's house or not. She'd only intended this to be a quick trip so she could talk to her dad about whether she should try to find out what had happened to Laura Petrillo and if she was safe and well.

But she hadn't had a chance to talk to her father yet and was bothered by her conversation with Cody. A party with old friends sounded much more appealing. After putting on mascara and lipstick, pulling on an old dress pair of cowgirl boots, and tying up her hair in a ponytail, she dug around in her closet for a suitable top. She found a white eyelet off-the-shoulder blouse from her college days and decided, *Why not?* She took off the glasses she wore at work. She didn't really need them, but she thought they made her look like an older, more serious lawyer. Then she gave a last look in her mirror and smiled. *What would my colleagues in Houston think of me if they could see me now?*

The room was crowded when Carolyn walked into the Prichard's large living room. Jerry Jeff Walker was singing about how he loved Texas, and the smoke from a mesquite wood fire in the large fireplace made the air smell sweet. The Navaho rugs that Kenny's parents had collected on trips to New Mexico, as well as Western art on the walls, and a real Remington sculpture of a cowboy on his horse rearing up to avoid a snake, gave the room a slightly sophisticated Texas air. It was a comfortable room where Carolyn had spent a lot of time as a child and later, when they dated in high school.

Kenny's mother was a small, pretty woman with a warm, matronly personality who had become like a second mother to Carolyn after her mother's death. She loved Carolyn like the daughter she never had.

"Carolyn!" Mrs. Prichard greeted her with a hug. "You are a sight for sore eyes, honey. I am so glad to see you!"

"Hey, Mrs. Prichard," Carolyn said, returning the hug. "It's so good to see you too. I've missed you. Lou Ann invited me. I hope I'm not intruding."

"Carolyn, you could never be an intruder here. You know I think of you as family. How's your dad, honey?"

"He's good. I think my brother is driving him crazy, though."

"Well, Cody's always been a handful. But he'll straighten out one day."

"I hope so," Carolyn sighed.

Lou Ann interrupted their conversation, pulling Carolyn away to a group of her high school girlfriends who were excited to see her. They plied her with lots of questions about living in Houston. Margarita Pena proudly told her she already had two babies, and of course wanted to know about Carolyn's love life.

Carolyn laughed. "I don't have a love life," she said. "I'm too busy for that. Besides, I work mostly with men all day. I get enough of them there!"

Everyone laughed. "You'll change your mind one of these days," Lou Ann said. "You just haven't met the right one. Or maybe," she dropped her voice to a whisper, "you just don't realize it."

Just then, Carolyn felt a familiar firm hand on her shoulder and Kenny spun her around. He was grinning that great big grin of his. She had forgotten how good-looking he was. His dark hair was long-ish now, and made his blue eyes look even bluer. She hadn't seen him in six years. He'd been in ROTC in college and spent four years in the Marines. After his father died two years earlier, he'd come home to help his mother with the ranch. Hard ranch work had kept him tanned, muscled, and slim.

"Hey, girl," he said. "I knew the wind would eventually blow you back home." Looking her up and down, he added, "And you are look-ing prettier than ever!"

This comment made her girlfriends scream with delight.

Carolyn felt her face flush. It had been a long time since anyone had looked at her as an attractive woman instead of as a sexless professional.

"You need a beer," Kenny said, taking her arm and steering her away from her girlfriends and toward the kitchen, where there was a crowd around a keg. Lindel, who was a committed bachelor, always played bartender and poured her a mug of Shiner.

Mrs. Prichard had been baking all day, and there were assorted cakes and pies set out on the kitchen table. She had also made some potato salad and coleslaw, which filled two pottery bowls. Tommy Nicholson walked in from the back porch carrying a tray of ribs and sausage he had been cooking on the grill outside. Carolyn thought it all smelled delicious and realized she was starving. "Let's get something to eat," she said to Kenny.

Having loaded their plates with food, Kenny steered Carolyn to the front porch. They sat down on the porch swing to eat. Friends that Carolyn hadn't seen in a long time stopped by to say hello and how glad they were to see her. She thought of her last exchange with Cody. *I belong here as much as you do, brother,* she told herself.

After they finished eating, Kenny stood up and took Carolyn's hand. "Let's dance," he said. "For old times' sake."

George Strait was singing now, and a lot of people were dancing. The furniture had been pushed against the walls and the rug rolled up to make room for a dance floor. "Kinda reminds me of senior prom," Kenny said in a soft voice.

"Now that's a thought I haven't had in a long time," Carolyn said.

"I have." Kenny smiled.

Carolyn had to admit that it felt good to feel Kenny's strong arm around her waist. They had always had an easy relationship, sharing their day-to-day experiences, as well as their career dreams. When they went outside again to get some cool air, she decided to tell him about her conversation with Cody.

Kenny's smile vanished. "I admit, Carolyn, I don't like Jonathan Stevenson. He's an outsider who only sees this place as a way to make his fortune. He thinks all you have to do is stick a straw into the ground anywhere in the state and oil will flow like an endless fountain and make him rich. He's been trying to persuade a lot of young ranchers into getting their families to lease their land without any geological indications that oil or gas is under it. Of course, he would be the agent in the process and take a piece of the action. He approached me, and it was clear as day he only had air in his head and dollar signs in his eyes."

"Just great," Carolyn said with a grimace.

"Don't worry. Your father's one of the smartest men I know. He won't let Cody talk him into anything stupid. C'mon. Wipe that frown off your pretty face."

Lou Ann and Billy came out on the porch to join them. The four of them had double-dated a lot in high school. "Seems like old times," Billy said. "Hey, do you all remember that old truck of mine that we used to pile into to go to San Marcos and float the river? Remember the time Kenny and I got so drunk we floated over the dam? You girls had to pull us out on the other side?"

"I was so mad at you I almost let you drown," Lou Ann said, pretending to still be mad at her husband.

"Lou Ann had to drive that old hunk of junk home while I poured coffee into you two so your parents wouldn't know you'd been drinking," Carolyn laughed. "We did have some good times."

After half an hour of reminiscing, Lou Ann said they needed to get home for the babysitter. "I should get going too," Carolyn said. "I have work I need to do before Monday, and I've got the drive back to Houston."

Kenny gave her a big hug goodbye as she was leaving. "Don't be such a stranger," he said.

She'd enjoyed herself more than she expected, and Carolyn slept late on Sunday morning. She realized that she had been dreaming of Kenny. Now there was barely time to have lunch with her father before she needed to start the drive back to Houston. Traffic was heavy on Sunday afternoons. Cody was at the table and in a calmer mood.

"Dad tells me you went to Kenny Prichard's house last night, Carolyn," Cody said. "Was it a party?"

Carolyn detected a bitter undertone in Cody's question so decided to tread carefully. "Oh, Kenny and I and Lou Ann and Billy were just catching up," she replied.

"Uh-huh," he said.

"Son, we need to work on getting more water in the tanks in the back pasture," her dad said, changing the subject. "It's been so hot they're running lower than usual."

"Okay, I'll start on that after breakfast," Cody said, reaching for the syrup to pour more on his pancakes.

With what seemed like peace at least temporarily restored, Carolyn didn't want to tell her father about what she'd seen after the beach party or about Laura, not to mention her indecision about whether to pursue the situation, in front of her brother. She knew he would offer an opinion, but it would be full of snide innuendos.

Now her dad was walking her outside to her car, and she had just a few minutes to tell him that something had happened that was bothering her and that she didn't know what to do about it. He listened to a shorthand version of the events and then said, "I brought you up right with God, honey. Listen to your heart and He'll tell you what you should do."

Carolyn had been looking for more practical advice, but she realized he was preoccupied and that was all she was going to get. Her conversation with her brother had also unsettled her. She hoped Kenny was right and her dad was strong enough not to let Cody do anything stupid. She wasn't so sure.

8

————

arolyn arrived at the office early Monday morning. She wanted to catch Will before he got started with his day's work. Her mentor was at a point in his career where he spent most of his time on the telephone with clients or counseling young lawyers on projects.

He smiled when he saw Carolyn knock at his open door. "Come in, Carolyn. I hope you had a good weekend."

"Yes, sir, I did." Carolyn smiled. "I went home and visited with my family and some old friends. But I wonder if you have a few minutes to discuss something."

"Well, I have a lot on my desk. Why don't you come by around six? We'll have a cup of coffee and talk about it," he said, picking up the stack of pink telephone message slips his secretary had laid on his desk.

At six p.m., Carolyn was waiting outside the door of Will's large corner office.

Will stuck his head out the door and motioned for her to enter his office. He shut the door behind her and settled back into his desk chair. Motioning to her to take a seat opposite him he said, "Tell me what is on your mind, Carolyn," in a tone that indicated to her he understood she had something serious to discuss. One of the things she admired about him was that he was very perceptive.

Carolyn sat down, crossing and uncrossing her legs. While he picked out one of his pipes from his desk drawer, she scanned the framed pictures on the bookshelf behind him. There were pictures of young women and children she assumed were his daughters and grandchildren. A professional group picture on a beach showed him and his wife and the whole family.

"Well," she began, "something happened the weekend before last and I'm not sure whether I should do something about it."

Will didn't say anything. He began to fill his pipe with tobacco, which Carolyn knew was something he did when he was thinking.

"It's work-related," she continued. "I was at an informal recruiting party at a beach house in Galveston the weekend before last."

"Informal?" Will asked. "As in unsanctioned?"

"I think so. I'm not sure." Carolyn blushed.

"Go on," Will said, tolerantly. "It wouldn't be the first one." He lit his pipe.

"Some of us spent the night rather than drive home after drinking all day. It was a large house with room for a lot of people to sleep. It was all very proper. During the night, I noticed that Laura Petrillo, the UPenn summer intern who was sharing the room with me, wasn't in her bed. I went downstairs to find her. Two of the partners were there. When I finally found Laura, she was, um, lying on the floor, unconscious and bleeding. She hadn't been drinking much so I was surprised." Carolyn paused. "She wasn't completely dressed." The last sentence came out in a rush.

"I see. What did you do?" Will asked, leaning forward in his chair and slowly drawing on his pipe.

"I asked if they had called 911, and they said they didn't want the police to come. They seemed confused and helpless and drunk. I knew she needed medical attention, so I drove her to the UTMB emergency department. She was still unconscious when we got there, and they admitted her."

Will rose from his chair and turned his back as though he was looking for something on the credenza behind him. When he turned back around to face Carolyn, he looked concerned. "And how is she now?" he asked.

"That's just it," Carolyn said. "The doctor told me to leave her until the next day so they could observe her. I went to the Tremont Hotel to get a few hours of sleep. When I went back to check on her on Sunday, she was gone. No one at the hospital knew when she left or with whom and they didn't seem concerned."

"Has she contacted you?"

"No. And I haven't had a chance to bring it up with the partners who were at the beach house. But one of them reported at the recruiting committee meeting last Wednesday that she told him the previous Friday that she decided to drop out of the clerkship program and go home because she missed her boyfriend."

"It wouldn't be the first time one of our Ivy League clerks left the program early for whatever reason," Will said. "Sometimes, they can't take the heat of the Texas summer. Some are just taking a vacation and aren't serious about joining a Texas firm. And some get homesick."

Will put his pipe down and walked over to the window facing west. He lowered the shades to cut some of the late afternoon glare from the sun out of the room. He continued standing, looking thoughtful.

"But I'm her associate sponsor," Carolyn said. "We talked a lot on the way to Galveston. She didn't say anything about having a boyfriend. She seemed happy and looking forward to the summer here. I know she was enjoying herself on the ride down and at the party. And it doesn't make sense that she would have told the partner on Friday that she resigned and then go with me to the party on Saturday and not say anything."

Will walked slowly back to his desk and was silent for a minute. Then he asked, "What do you want me to tell you, Carolyn?"

"Should I tell someone? Recruiting? The police? No one seems to care that she's gone or interested in making sure she's okay."

"Do you want my honest opinion?"

"Yes," Carolyn said. She felt sure that what happened wasn't Laura's fault. "I want to do the right thing."

"I'm sure you do. But tell me, Carolyn, do you like your job?"

"Of course I do. You know that. I want to make partner and have a career at the firm more than anything!"

Will leaned back in his desk chair and was silent for a few minutes. Then he leaned forward and looked her straight in the eyes.

"Then do nothing," he said in a calm voice. "You don't know for sure what happened that night. You did the right thing to take her to get medical help. But there isn't anything else you can do that won't get you, and perhaps an innocent party, into a disastrous situation. Everyone involved, including the summer intern, was an adult and responsible for their own actions. If you stir up an investigation, no one at the firm will appreciate it, and you'll get a reputation for being a troublemaker. You could ruin your own career. That may not be the most moral answer to your question, but it's the most practical advice that I can give you. In any big institution, the key to survival is to learn the rules that govern, even if they aren't the ones you learned growing up, and then play by them."

"It just doesn't seem fair," Carolyn said in a weak voice.

"Life's not fair, Carolyn."

"Do you want to know who the partners were who were involved?" Carolyn asked.

"I would rather not," Will said, picking up the telephone receiver as if preparing to make a call. Then he stopped and gave her a kindly look. "I have learned over my time here that what goes around, comes around. God or karma or whatever has a way of taking care of these things. Focus on your career and know you did all you could do under the circumstances."

Carolyn thanked Will, and then got up and walked back to her office. No, she didn't want to jeopardize her future at the firm. But could she ever forget what happened? How could she not feel guilty about not following up about Laura? And furthermore, could she trust Paul and Trey? After sleeping on it that night, she decided she had no choice.

• • •

A few weeks later, life came to a stop when two airplanes crashed into the World Trade Center in New York City. Like most businesses, Edwards and Harrison closed for a week while the world figured out what had happened and if it were going to end. But eventually, everyone returned to work and life went on.

In the last week of September, Paul sent a message that he wanted to see Carolyn in his office. Carolyn had never worked with him. She knew that his group worked on complex oil and gas transactions, and that they used confidential code names like "Eagle Wing" or "Thunder Head," which made the deals they worked on sound secret and important. Paul had a coterie of bright young men like himself working with him—a close-knit group of good-looking, preppy young men who drove high-powered BMWs and dressed in designer suits that they ordered at Norton Ditto. They were all native Texans, and most of them had gone to private schools in the Southwest Preparatory Conference in Houston, Dallas, Fort Worth, or Oklahoma City. After doing their undergraduate work at top Texas schools or Ivy League colleges, most of them returned to the University of Texas for law school. There had never been any women in the group.

When Carolyn entered Paul's office, notepad and pen in hand and ready in case he was going to give her an assignment, she saw that a group of five men had already gathered.

The office was big enough to hold a leather couch and two guest chairs, besides a large, burled wood desk and credenza. The walls were painted hunter green, and the hardwood floor was partially covered by a beautiful Persian rug. Stuffed bird trophies hung on the wall next to Paul's framed degrees. Several pictures of a lovely blonde woman and two tow-headed children sat on the bookshelf. She assumed the woman was Paul's wife, Ashley.

Trey moved over to give her room to sit beside him on the couch. Paul acknowledged her in a friendly way before he began to speak.

"I've assembled this team to work on a new deal for our good client, JBH Oil," he said. "JBH is going to acquire most of the assets of Oakland Oil and Gas Company in Tulsa. It will more than double our client's production. As most of you know, Joe Bill Hawkins is demanding. And as usual, we're on a short timeline. Both companies are private, so that makes things simpler, but the owner of Oakland has been difficult to work with. In fact, he seems downright hostile for some reason."

"Why?" Mark asked. "Does he have a specific beef with Joe Bill, or is he just a sonofabitch?"

"Who knows," Paul said. "Our job is to get the deal closed, and we'll just have to work with it."

"Trey, you'll be the lead on the negotiations with Oakland's lawyers. Mark, you'll head the property transfer team. Dick and Carolyn will assist you. Oakland's headquarters and a lot of the properties are in Oklahoma, so you'll need to go to Tulsa. I'll handle Joe Bill."

Paul walked toward the couch and stood next to Carolyn.

"Carolyn hasn't worked with us before, so I expect you guys to show her how we do things. Carolyn, this project will require your full time. I've already cleared it with Will. We'll meet again at nine a.m. tomorrow. Now, let's get going on Project Sooner!"

Everyone got up to leave, including Carolyn. She was surprised at being brought into this deal and that Paul had already cleared it with Will. On the other hand, she thought, this could be a real opportunity to advance within the firm—or to visibly fail. But she determined that wouldn't happen. Carolyn left the office with the others, noticing that Trey was the only person who stayed behind.

• • •

Paul closed the door behind them. Trey stayed on the couch, but sprawled his arms over the back. While the others were leaving, Paul walked over to his credenza and picked up a picture of his family, which had been taken the previous summer in Aspen. His three-year-old twin boys were grinning and Ashley was beaming. He had his arm around her. He always thought of this picture as depicting the perfect family. He smiled to himself.

"What's your thinking on this?" Trey interrupted his thoughts.

"About what?" Paul asked.

"About bringing Carolyn Page into the deal."

Paul sighed and sat down at his desk. "Always keep your friends close, and your enemies closer, my friend. I'm not saying she's an enemy, but I detect from the way she looks at me that she still has questions about what happened to that summer intern. We don't need her repeating what she saw to anyone. As far as I know, she hasn't so far, although I thought Hopson seemed somewhat reserved when I talked to him about Carolyn working on this deal. We'll use this time to let her get to know us and like us—make her feel like she wants to be one of us."

"And become dependent on us?"

Paul smiled. "She's very ethical and she's very confused. I can't say I blame her, but that could lead her to make a stupid mistake. On the other hand, she's smart and ambitious. If we incorporate her into our group, we can keep an eye on her."

"Smart! But is she a good lawyer?"

"I read her associate evaluations, and everyone she's worked with says she's developing into an excellent lawyer. Besides, the firm is putting pressure on all the practice group leaders to hire more women. The league tables are starting to rank firms in order of how many women associates and partners they have. Needless to say, we're not at the top of the list. Management is obsessed with high rankings. So, we're just doing our part."

"You mean you're managing to kill two birds with one stone— keeping Carolyn silent about what she saw and gaining points with management. Always thinking strategically."

"Hmm," Paul mumbled.

"Speaking of that goddamn night, have you talked to Joe Bill and Peter about it?"

Paul frowned. "I think some things are best left unsaid."

"I guess," Trey agreed, looking at his feet. "I don't feel proud of the way things ended with that poor girl. It's going to be hard to forget about it, at least for some of us."

Paul started rifling through the papers on his desk as if he were looking for something specific. But then he got up and walked back over to the bookcase where he stood looking at the picture of his family again.

"You have a beautiful family, Paul," Trey said.

"Yeah, my greatest achievement in life so far."

9

———

A week later, Carolyn was knee-deep in conveyances, leases, and miscellaneous documents in Oakland Oil Company's offices in Tulsa, working with Mark, a second-year partner, and Dick, a sixth-year associate. The company had closeted them in a poorly lit, unventilated, dusty room with hundreds of files that were more or less disorganized. Surprisingly, almost nothing was digitized. *It was 2001, for God's sake*, Carolyn thought. There was only one bathroom in the building, which she decided was disgusting and served as the de facto men's room since no women worked in the legal department. She had to walk one hundred yards outside to the building where the administrative staff worked if she wanted to use a clean ladies' room. There wasn't a coffee pot or copier until Ken sent Carolyn to Walmart to purchase a cheap copy machine and coffee-making supplies.

Two steps forward, one step back, Carolyn thought, in regard to her important assignment.

Dick had worked on many acquisitions and was used to these due diligence trips. But he had never experienced such poor working conditions. In the morning, when they were all getting their coffee and standing around the portable card table that Carolyn had requisitioned from the facilities staff, Dick asked, "What's the deal, Mark? No one here talks to us. I've never seen such unfriendly people. I'm getting a complex."

Mark stopped and wiped the sweat from his forehead, looking at

Dick and Carolyn. "I don't know. All I know is that this is a hostile takeover of a sort and the seller is intent on making our work as difficult as possible. I'd like to know the source of the hostility, but it's as if the employees were told to not talk to us except when absolutely necessary."

"I've had to ask some of the administrative staff for supplies. They didn't seem overtly hostile," Carolyn said.

"Lucky you," Mark gave her a tolerant look.

Carolyn grimaced but didn't say anything, even though she thought his comment was patronizing.

She was not thrilled with the menial tasks Mark assigned to her. She was anxious to find a way to make a good impression. She noticed that some of the administrative staff hung out in the ladies' lounge in their building during their afternoon break. Aside from comparing their children or complaining about their husbands, they spent most of that time on office gossip.

The next day, she timed her trip to the ladies' lounge to breaktime in the main office. It was a large room with six stalls and an area outfitted with a small sofa and some chairs off to the side. She arrived early and waited in the last stall for the women to arrive and settle in. Then she listened to their conversation.

"I just hope we all have jobs when this acquisition is over," said a woman Carolyn recognized as Mr. Oakland's secretary.

"I do too," the comptroller's secretary responded. "But I'm still looking around for someplace to go, if what the boss says about the new owner is true."

"He won't bother *you*," the first woman replied. Everyone laughed.

"How's Oakland taking it now?" the comptroller's secretary asked.

"Still madder than a hornet."

Another woman stood up to fix her lipstick in front of the mirror. She said, "I still don't understand why he's selling half the company to Hawkins when he hates the man."

"No choice," Mr. Oakland's secretary replied. "Mrs. Oakland's daddy left her the company when he died. When she got married, she let him change the name for his ego's sake, but her lawyers made sure it was separate property as much as possible. She divorced Tom to marry Joe Bill Hawkins. The divorce decree lets her take half of the assets, and she's giving them to Hawkins as a wedding present."

"No wonder he's pissed!" the comptroller's secretary said.

The first woman continued. "Tom thinks Hawkins went after his wife just so he could get the properties and build up his own small company. Tom's still coming out of this with money and assets, but he's lost his empire and that infuriates him. He says the boys down at the Petroleum Club are laughing at him behind his back. He swears he'll get back at Hawkins one day. Long as I've known him, he does what he says he's gonna do."

Carolyn had been quiet while she listened to the women talk. But she had heard enough. She flushed the toilet and came out of the stall to wash her hands.

Mr. Oakland's secretary got up and walked toward the stalls in the back of the room, seeing Carolyn for the first time. "Oh, dear," she said to Carolyn in a loud voice. "We didn't realize you were in here, hon. You shouldn't take for fact our idle gossip. This is just bored women talk."

Carolyn smiled innocently. "Don't worry about me, ladies. I didn't hear a thing." She put her index finger on her lips, picked up her purse, and left the room.

She was still smiling when she reentered the property room. "Well, I know why Tom Oakland is so hostile to us," she announced.

Everyone else stopped work and looked at her with dubious expressions. "Right!" Mark said. "You found this out in twenty minutes on your way to the ladies' room."

"No," Carolyn replied. "I found it out *in* the ladies' room. It's a great place to overhear the latest."

The men gathered close to her now. Mark got up and closed the door to the hallway.

Carolyn repeated the conversation she had overheard. When she finished, she saw something new in Mark's face. She wasn't sure it was respect, but it was definitely a realization that she had something to contribute to the team. *Victory! Another step forward,* she told herself.

. . .

The Oakland deal dragged on for several months. Either as the junior associate or as a female—she wasn't sure which—Carolyn's role seemed to be to do the most tedious things that needed to be done to document the transaction, regardless of the intelligence she'd provided. She wasn't included in any of the client meetings. Only Paul, Trey, and Mark met with their client, who didn't attend the closing.

When that deal closed, just before Christmas, Paul called her into his office back in Houston and asked her to work on another, suggesting she join their practice group permanently.

"Look, Paul," Carolyn said, "I loved working on the Oakland project, and I think the work you all are doing is important and exciting. But I spent the two years before that proving myself in real estate. Will even made me first chair on some smaller transactions. I don't want to have to start over again at the bottom, especially making trips to buy coffee at Walmart. I need some assurance from you that I'll be doing meaningful work, not just first-year associate work, if I join you."

She felt truly ambivalent about continuing to work with Paul. She respected him as a professional, but she still felt uncomfortable around him after what had happened to Laura. He'd never offered a good explanation, and she didn't think he ever would. But she didn't have the courage to confront him about it.

Paul seemed taken aback by Carolyn's frankness, but he spoke to her understandingly. "I'd probably feel the same way," he said, surprising her. "Mark told me you did a terrific job up in Oklahoma, even doing some undercover work that helped us learn what we were dealing with. I know you didn't get the credit you deserved for that. So you have my word: stick with us, and I'll fast-track your career. I'll make you second chair on some large transactions, and once you master the elements of oil and gas, you'll be first-chairing your own deals. It will be career-making work. How does that sound?"

Can I trust him? Carolyn asked herself. *I know he lied about Laura resigning, and it bothers me that he's never explained to me what really happened to her. I don't know if it's smart to put my fate in his hands. Then again, energy work is more exciting than real estate. My time is billed out at a higher rate, which is good for my potential advancement. And he is promising to promote me.*

"All right," she finally said. She had decided to throw the dice and see what happened.

• • •

True to his word, over the next few months he loaded her up with prize assignments.

Everything was new and she was constantly learning. Most days, she ran downstairs to the sandwich shop in the tunnel under the building, picked up a chef's salad, and ate lunch at her desk. In the late afternoon, Paul's secretary would call and ask her what she wanted to order for dinner from one of the restaurants downtown, since the team worked until ten most nights. Dinner was delivered to their offices. She noticed that the guys usually went out for lunch. They never invited her to join them. *Eventually,* she thought, *I'll be included.*

She still had time for Cynthia, who would sometimes drop by her office at lunch to chat while they both ate. Cynthia was also working long hours and progressing with her career, showing a talent for speaking at tax conferences and client seminars once she mastered a new regulation or subject. She was not only brilliant, but also had beauty and flair, which an audience of mostly male tax lawyers responded to with appreciation.

Cynthia was curious about Carolyn's move within the firm. All the associates knew that Carolyn was the first woman to be included in Paul's growing practice group. Some associates envied her rapid rise. They knew Cynthia and Carolyn were close. And because they were, Cynthia wasted no time in telling Carolyn when a few of them approached her, asking her to tell them the real reason Carolyn had been brought into the boys' club. Some even wondered who Carolyn was sleeping with.

One day, the two friends were sitting in Carolyn's office eating a Thai food lunch delivered from a restaurant in the tunnel system that underlay virtually all of the Houston business district. After Carolyn had formally joined the energy group, the firm had moved her to the fortieth floor, where Paul, Trey, and the other members of the group were situated. It looked the same—standard associate fare—but Carolyn had become confident enough to bring a few items from home to personalize it. She still had her law degree on the wall but had added a grouping of Texas wildflower prints above the bookcase and some photos of her father with herself and Cody and a picture of herself with Mrs. Prichard and Kenny, taken at their high school graduation. There was another photo of herself and some girlfriends from college on a spring break trip to Mexico. She spent most of her time in her office and wanted it to feel more like home.

"So how's life in the fraternity?" Cynthia asked, teasingly.

"Oh, come on," Carolyn said.

Cynthia smiled. "Are you wearing the official T-shirt yet? Although I guess they'll have to get one in your size, which would be a first."

Carolyn found Cynthia's question amusing. Being around men all day didn't feel like anything unusual, although she was aware that she still had things to learn about energy law and big business in general.

Carolyn leaned back in her chair. "I was surprised when they asked me to work on the first deal. But they've been good. I mean, I don't get to meet with the clients. I don't even get included in lunches outside of the office with the boys. I admit that bothers me. But I'm low man on the totem pole. I have a lot to learn and I'm still proving myself," Carolyn hurried to add. "Eventually, they'll include me."

"Sure, honey, you tell yourself that," Cynthia said, making a mock yawn.

Carolyn put down her sandwich. "You are such a cynic!"

"I'm a realist." Cynthia shrugged.

Carolyn perceived that Cynthia was serious, and her friend usually knew what she was talking about when it came to firm politics. That worried her. Maybe she would never be fully integrated, and there was a ceiling beyond which her career could not progress. Had she been naïve about her situation?

Carolyn decided to ask Cynthia something that had been on her mind. "When Paul asked me to join the energy group on a permanent basis, he promised to give me 'career-making work.' What do you think he meant by that—specifically?"

"Oh, my little country girl," Cynthia laughed, stretching her long legs out in front of her.

"What's so funny?" Carolyn asked, a little embarrassed, although not knowing why.

She knew that all work wasn't career making. There was legal work that was just drudge work or low-fee work that any lawyer could do, but would never lead to partnership. Career-making work was legal work for clients who paid high hourly rates or big fees. But she wanted Cynthia's opinion of whether her joining Paul's group was a good step in her goal of making partner.

Cynthia took a sip of her Fiji water before she spoke. "Everybody knows that Paul Robinson is destined for greater things. But he can't do it alone. He needs other lawyers to do good legal work on the deals he brings in to make him continue to look good. Those lawyers hope to ride on his coattails on his journey to the top of the pecking order."

"Like Trey Jorgenson?" Carolyn asked.

"Trey and Mark and others—potentially you." Cynthia looked at her and went on. "Paul will probably be elected to the management committee before long. Then he'll be jostling with other superstars in other practice areas for a few years to become managing partner one day. He'll take those who made the journey with him to partnership, high sharing ratios, and prestige within the firm and in the community."

"So you really think that being in the fraternity could get me there?"

"Exactement, mon cher," Cynthia said. "If you work hard and do good work. Energy is a practice that can support more partners because their hourly rates and total billings are high. You increased your chances of making partner significantly when you switched from real estate to energy. You just need to be careful not to let the boys keep you in a supporting role—and believe me, they'll try."

Carolyn thought back to her first deal with the group in Tulsa. She had been relegated to shopping for supplies and organizing documents, even though her intelligence work had significantly added to the success of the transaction. "I understand," she said.

"Look for opportunities to take the lead on transactions. Even better, bring in some clients of your own, train associates, and make yourself indispensable, not by being a helper, but a fee generator for the section and the firm. Remember, in a big law firm, it's all about your contribution to the bottom line."

There was a knock on the door and Carolyn's assistant stuck her head in to tell them that she was going to a training seminar for an hour. "Not a problem," Carolyn told her, eager to resume the conversation with her friend.

"So, what about you?" Carolyn asked Cynthia. "You must have a well-thought-out plan at this point, right? I know you want to make partner, but is there something else you have in mind?"

Cynthia smiled and leaned forward as if to impart a confidence. "Well, now that you ask, yes. I chose employee benefits work because it's really hard, brings in high fees, and it's a necessary aspect of big corporate transactions. The boys have to include me. Fortunately, I'm good at it. Another benefit is that I'm part of the tax section, but also apart from it. I'm not competing with umpteen other tax nerd associates to stand out. My clients are the big, powerful companies among the firm's clients. Because I sometimes get to meet with the key executives one on one to discuss their compensation or benefits packages, I get to know them well. And they get to know me, and hopefully speak well of me to management."

"And that gets you a higher sharing ratio, obviously. What else?"

"Well, a side benefit is that I am privy to a lot of amusing gossip." Cynthia fanned herself with her hand and gave a sly smile.

Carolyn laughed. "So that's where it comes from."

"Some of it. I have other sources. But seriously, I'd like to be head of the tax section someday. Most of all, I'd like to be on the management committee. You see, Paul Robinson isn't the only person who has ambitions. I do too."

Carolyn was impressed. She got up from her chair, walked around her desk, and sat down opposite her friend.

"You never told me all this, Cynthia."

"You didn't ask before now. You're just focused on making partner. I am too. But people like Paul and I, who grew up in the rarified atmosphere of River Oaks, have more experience and insight into what there is beyond mere partnership. It's just a matter of where we started from. After you spend a few years here, your horizons might expand. You might decide you want more. Wouldn't it be fun to be on the management committee together?"

"Maybe we could insist on holding our retreats at spas instead of golf resorts?" Carolyn laughed.

"Well, I like golf trips actually. My handicap is lower than ninety percent of the boys'. But spa trips would be nice for a change. Can you see some of those old guys in robes getting a mani-pedi?"

"It's a frightening thought."

Cynthia looked at her watch. "It's 1:30 already. I've got to prepare my comments for the State Bar tax conference next week. But as always, I've enjoyed catching up."

"Wait a minute, Cynthia. Since you're revealing secrets today, how do you know all these things about getting ahead in the firm? You make me think that I don't know anything."

"Well, you're lucky. You have your best friend as your fairy godmother, and I intend for us to walk down the aisle as new partners one day together. One step at a time."

"Seriously," Carolyn said, "how did you become so . . . knowledgeable and strategic?"

"Promise not to tell anyone?"

When Carolyn nodded affirmatively, Cynthia leaned forward and whispered, "My mother's brother is Arthur Hollingsworth. He is my godfather and has been my personal coach since the day I started looking at law schools."

Arthur Hollingsworth is the managing partner of Brown and Adams, the other large law firm in town, Carolyn realized. All she could say was, "Wow!"

"Relationships are everything in law and business." Cynthia smiled. "For good or bad, so choose your friends carefully."

10

———

The day that she left the hospital without any luggage, Laura arrived at her parents' house in the early morning hours of the following day, exhausted and upset. She had taken a cab from the train station in Atlantic City, and the driver seemed impressed when he pulled up in front of the two-story wood Victorian with gingerbread on the eves and a tall widow's watchtower forming the third story. It was dark, so he didn't see that the whole house could use a new coat of paint. The house had been built in 1856 by one of Laura's mother's ancestors and passed down in the family. It was situated on several acres fronting Route 9 at the edge of the Great Egg Harbor Bay and surrounded by white oak and pine trees. Laura didn't have her key, so she had to ring the doorbell until she woke her parents.

"Who's there?" Salvatore Petrillo asked in a loud voice a few minutes later.

"Daddy, its me, Laura. Please open the door," she replied.

"Laura?" Her father sounded shocked to hear his daughter's voice. When he opened the door, Laura practically fell into his arms with her last bit of strength.

Donna, her mother, was right behind Salvatore in the entryway. She turned on the sconces for light. "Laura!" her mother cried. "You look awful. What happened to you?" She was looking with dismay at the bruise on Laura's face and sling on her arm.

"We need to get her to the hospital right away," her father said.

"No, Daddy, please, I'll be all right. I just want to go to bed. I'm too tired to go anywhere. I just want to go to sleep."

"What are you doing here? Did you come all the way from Texas?" her mother gasped. She touched Laura's face on the side that wasn't bruised.

"I'll tell you tomorrow, Mom. I can't talk now. I need sleep," she replied, pulling away from her father and walking up the staircase to the room she had left just a little more than a week ago.

The next day, Laura slept until five p.m. Her mother fixed a hot dinner and insisted she come downstairs and eat with her parents, despite her protestations.

When the three of them were seated at the dining room table in a room with a black iron chandelier, flowered wallpaper, and lots of antique cut glass objects on display, her mother set a hot chicken pot pie in front of each of them. "Sweetheart," her mother said, "now please tell your father and me why you came back from Houston after only one week and without any luggage?"

"I don't want to talk about it, Mom."

"Can you tell us what happened to hurt your arm and how you got that bruise on your face?"

Laura said nothing. She just stared at her food.

"Did someone attack you, baby?" her mother persisted.

When Laura still refused to talk, her father lost his temper. "Goddamn it, Laura Ann. I want to know who the son of a bitch is who hurt my girl? You tell me, you hear? I'm gonna break his neck. I don't care if I have to go to Houston to do it. And then I'm gonna turn his ass over to the police to deal with!" Salvatore was prone to having a hot temper when provoked, and now he was furious. He slammed his hand on the wooden table, making the glasses shake.

"No, Daddy! I don't want you to do that. It wouldn't help. Besides, I'm not clear on exactly what happened," Laura sobbed. "All I know is that I'm never going back to Houston again."

Laura was sad, confused, and embarrassed by her ordeal. She kept to her bedroom most of the time, opera music playing at a low volume. Her rescue Chihuahua, Duke, who pawed at the closed door and whined for her to let him in, seemed to be the only companion she wanted. When she came down for meals, she only ate small amounts and wasn't interested in conversation, especially about her experience in Texas. The only time she left the house in the first month was to let her mother take her to the doctor to treat her broken arm, which had not fared well during her trip home.

At the end of the first week, when no one from Edwards and Harrison—not even Carolyn—tried to contact her to ask why she had left her internship, she felt hurt and then ashamed. *Obviously, they were just glad I went away quietly,* she thought. As more time passed and she still heard nothing from anyone, she grew quietly angry.

Her parents continued to try to get her to tell them what had happened, but she was too embarrassed. *I'm not exactly sure what happened myself,* she thought. *I remembered bits and pieces of what happened while I was in the hospital. But other parts of that night are still a* blur, *especially after I felt dizzy and fell on the floor.* But Laura knew she would never forget the sound of those men laughing at her while they were pulling off her clothes. The thought always made her feel sick.

Laura's father tired of watching his formerly energetic and ambitious child wasting away. One night, she had agreed to watch a show on television. Salvatore was a big man and he was settled in his La-Z-Boy recliner. Laura was curled up on the couch with Duke and an afghan her grandmother had crocheted.

"Laura Ann," he said, "I accept that you don't want to tell us what made you come home from your internship, though I don't agree with it. But if that's your decision, I think it's time you get a job, any job, to get out of the house and be among people again."

"I don't want to be around people," Laura quickly responded, drawing Duke closer. She'd messed up badly on her first trip away from home and didn't want a repeat.

Nevertheless, her father persisted and, one day, he told her to come downstairs and talk. He sat in his recliner and motioned for her to sit on the couch. "Your uncle Nicky needs someone to help him work the cash register at his hardware store while his regular girl is out having her baby," he told her. "You need to get out of this house and start living again, Laura Ann. I told him that you would be glad to help him out."

"No, Dad," Laura protested. "I just don't want to be where I have to talk to people."

"That's exactly what you need, honey. You need to learn to live again. I don't know why you gave up on your law career. You wanted to be a lawyer your whole life. It's pretty obvious those people in Texas harmed you in a physical way. Is that what happened?" She could tell that her father was angry. "I'll bring the law down on them."

No, Laura thought. *I don't want him to do anything like that.* She knew she'd be too embarrassed to have to testify in court about what happened. "I'm not completely clear about what happened, and so I don't know for sure which one of them to go after. I mean, I have an idea, but . . ."

"But what?"

"It would just be too humiliating, and no one cares or would believe me probably. They are important people in Houston and I'm nobody. It would be a 'he said/she said' issue and I wouldn't win. The best thing to do is just try to forget it."

Her father hung his head in frustration. "Well, whatever happened to make you change your mind about the law after all your hard work and the money we spent on it, you need to move on. It's not what you aspired to, but it is work and work always leads to good things." Her father had founded and operated a heating oil business in the small South Jersey town of Seadrift in northern Cape May County, and believed work was the solution to every problem and the key to every opportunity.

He moved over to sit on the couch beside her. "You know I don't have anyone to take over my business when I retire. You can always learn the heating oil business," he continued. "Lots of young women are running service companies today. If you don't want to help out your uncle Nicky, then you'll start working with me on Monday." Laura was an only child and she had heard this offer before, but she was no more interested than she ever had been.

Not wanting to be around her father day and night, she reluctantly went to work at the hardware store, although she tried to avoid making small talk with the customers. The narrow building on Route 9, across the Great Egg Harbor Bay from Ocean City, was stuffed from floor to ceiling with hardware and appliances. It felt claustrophobic. Uncle Nicky smoked Marlboro cigarettes with his old cronies, who hung around the store passing time. The smoke and the banter of old men added to the oppressive atmosphere. She watched the clock every afternoon, wishing it were five already.

The customers, many of whom she knew, were surprised but glad to see her back home. Her classmates had voted her Most Likely to Succeed in high school. The thought of it made her cringe now. Most of them were too polite to ask why she had quit law school. Content with their lives, they assumed that Laura had just come to her senses about staying where she was born and raised with people who knew and loved her. The ones who did ask received a curt reply when Laura told them, "Law practice wasn't what I thought it would be." She lived day by day, not thinking of the past or the future. She settled into a routine.

"Yo, Laura, I heard you were back in town. You good?"

Laura looked up from the invoices she was sorting one day to see Joey Meyers standing across the counter holding a new power drill with a big smile on his face. Joey was a sun-bleached blonde with green eyes, a Jersey Shore lifeguard's tan, and muscular build. They had dated in high school, but when she went to Rutgers, Joey had gone to Drexel University in Philadelphia to get an electrical engineering degree. Occasionally they would do something together—go surfing or to a bar—during summer breaks.

"My goodness, Joey, it's been a long time," she said, involuntarily smiling for the first time in months. "I see by that tan that you're still getting to the beach."

"You know me, babe. Work for the money, but never miss the fun."

Laura laughed for the first time since she had come home. His easygoing, good-natured attitude had always had that effect on her.

"Some of our old friends are going to a clam bake benefitting the Cape May Beach Patrol Saturday night," he said. "Can I pick you up?"

"I don't go out much, Joey. I'm pretty busy," she responded.

"Doing what? Counting how many screws are in the screw box? Helping your mom bake a cake for after church on Sunday? Come on. It'll be like old times, just chilling, eating clams, and drinking beer."

Laura considered Joey. She didn't feel comfortable around men anymore, but this was Joey, an old friend and a good guy. *Maybe this is what I need right now,* she told herself. She loved being at the beach, and she wasn't looking forward to another Saturday night watching TV with her parents. "Okay," she said, "I'll go." Her uncle Nicky had been eavesdropping on the conversation, and Laura was embarrassed to see him give his buddies the thumbs-up sign.

• • •

Within two months, Joey and Laura had become a couple again. Laura's parents were delighted. Their daughter seemed more content, although not as lively and optimistic as she had once been. She began working in Atlantic City in the business office of one of the big casinos. It wasn't very far up the Garden State Parkway, and the casinos provided the best jobs in the area for women with an education. The work wasn't intellectually challenging, but it paid well and there was room for advancement.

Six months from the day they started dating, Joey proposed marriage and she accepted without even thinking about it. It seemed like the safe thing to do. After a big wedding at St. Michael's Catholic Church and a reception at the Flanders Hotel Ballroom in Ocean City, she became Laura Ann Meyers on June 1, 2002. Her large Italian family on her paternal side celebrated the event for days. The day after the wedding, she woke up wondering what she had done.

Joey, Laura, and Duke moved into a small furnished bungalow in Beezleys Point. Laura liked the view of the bay out their bedroom window. It was just down the road from the historic old Tuckahoe Inn, where she'd worked as a waitress during summers in college. She had fond memories of evenings sitting outside at the tables after work, drinking beer and listening to someone play guitar.

From the beginning, however, there was a problem with their marriage. Try as she might to be a good wife, Laura couldn't put that awful night at the beach house out of her mind. When Joey wanted to make love, she sometimes froze. She knew it didn't make sense. Joey was not those men. He was kind and good and loved her. She knew she was safe with him, but something she couldn't overcome made her not want to be touched. For months she tried to pretend that she was aroused, but she didn't really feel anything. In fact, she felt cold inside. She would find excuses not to go to bed at the same time he did in order to avoid his advances.

Finally, one night he confronted her. They had been sitting on the front porch on separate chairs just before Joey's usual bedtime. He got up and knelt down beside her chair, taking her hand.

"Laura, I love you and I didn't get married to just be friends. I want a good sexual relationship with my wife. I've tried to please you, but I feel like you recoil from me when I touch you. Do you know how bad that makes me feel?"

Laura saw pain in Joey's eyes, and she felt terrible.

"I'm sorry, Joey," Laura said, tears welling up in her eyes. "I do love you, but I don't know what's wrong with me. Maybe my hormones are screwed up or something. I don't want to make you feel bad. You're wonderful. Please don't let this problem I'm having make you feel bad. It's all my fault, I know." She put her other hand over his.

"Is there something that is bothering you? Did I do anything to offend you?"

"No, no, it's not you. It's me. But maybe it's temporary."

"I hope so," Joey said, releasing her hand and slowly getting up. He picked up his jacket, left the porch, and got in his car.

Watching him drive off, Laura let her tears flow. *If I tell him I was raped, he might not want me anymore*, she thought. The memory had come to her just before the wedding, clear as day—after they had pulled off her clothes, they raped her, laughing all the while. She was afraid Joey might not want her after that. She was so ashamed. She'd just try harder to be a responsive wife. That night he came home very late and very drunk.

Laura believed you could learn anything from a book. So the next day, she drove to Barnes and Noble after work and purchased the only book she could find on recovery from sexual abuse. She read that what she was feeling was not at all unusual, but putting words into action was more difficult than she thought. She kept trying, though, and their relationship improved somewhat.

Before their wedding Laura had obtained a prescription for birth control pills and took them religiously. But one evening Joey came into the kitchen carrying a bouquet of flowers. Laura thought it was a sweet gesture and kissed him on the lips.

Then Joey announced, "It's time we started a family, Laura. I'm making good money, and my dad just told me he's going to give us my grandmom's old house. It needs a little work, but you know how handy I am. It's next door to my parents and has lots of bedrooms. You can quit your job and stay home with the kids. It'll be perfect!"

Laura didn't say anything to Joey. Her first thought was, *Why didn't I see this coming?* It was what everyone did in a small town. It was what she always said she didn't want. God, she'd been stupid.

"We haven't been married that long, Joey. I didn't know you were already thinking about children," Laura finally managed.

"Of course," he replied. "I just needed to know I could provide for a family. And I'll bet that little problem of yours will go away once you see how happy you are with a baby boy—or girl."

Laura was resigned to the life she had settled for, but if she had a child, things would change. She cared deeply for Joey. It was his good nature and encouragement that had brought her out of the depressed state she was in when she came home. But he was gone a lot. In addition to his job with the Atlantic City Electric Company, he worked as a substitute lifeguard on weekends or played rugby and drank beer with his buddies. Trying to have a serious conversation with him was impossible. He mostly talked about rugby or the Eagles or the Phillies. He told jokes when she wanted him to be serious. She took refuge in reading good books and driving alone into Philadelphia to the museums or to attend opera and symphony matinees. If she had even one child, she thought, that wouldn't be possible. She'd be trapped.

After mentally struggling with the prospect of motherhood for a few months and continuing to take her birth control pills in secret, Laura gave up. After dinner one night when they were sitting at the table in their kitchen, Laura broke the news. "Joey," she said, "I think we should get a divorce."

"What? Are you kidding me?" Joey exclaimed. "We've just been planning to start a family."

"You've been planning to start a family, Joey. I'm just not ready for that, even though I understand that you are. I wouldn't be a good mother at this point in my life—I haven't even been a good wife so far."

"But nobody in my family or yours has ever been divorced. I love you and I'm happy with our life. Aren't you? Our sex life is better and could be much better yet. The only thing we're missing is children. Children cement a family."

"I love you, Joey, but I don't want to have children, at least not anytime soon. I'm too young. There are things I want to do. You should find someone better, or more normal, who wants the things you want, and who does want children now. I'm so sorry. I shouldn't have married you. I fucked up again."

Joey had never considered that Laura wouldn't want children. But after many discussions, he finally agreed that they should move on. Neither of them was a devout practicing Catholic, and it would take too long to get an annulment from the Catholic Church, so they quietly divorced. Joey had become attached to Duke and asked to keep him. Laura couldn't refuse.

After that she felt guilty, but a new thought occurred to her: *I guess I'm narrowing down the things I don't want to do with my life.* She didn't want to go to work for a big law firm, and she didn't want to be a wife and mother. She resolved to go back to what she'd always wanted to do, which was to be a lawyer. But she'd be the kind of lawyer who helps other people. That would be her penance, as it were.

Laura's parents were shocked when she told them she and Joey were getting a divorce after only one year of marriage. She went to their house the day after Joey finally agreed to the divorce, when she knew her father would be home from work. Her mother had just taken a lasagna out of the oven, and the familiar, favorite smell made what she had to tell them even harder. She gave them the news when they were sitting around the dining room table.

"Are you crazy, Laura Ann?" her dad asked. "Joey's a good man. He makes a good living and can provide for a family. He loves you, too."

"I know, Dad. Joey is a good man. This is all on me. I made a mistake marrying him and I'm sorry. I always knew I would be bored if I stayed in the area. I guess I'm selfish. I need more challenge in my life. I need people I can exchange ideas with. I came home from Houston with my tail between my legs, and I guess I thought I could adjust to a simpler life. But I know now that's not possible. Joey deserves to find someone else who will love him and want the same things out of life."

Her father was angry. He got up and took a bottle of Seagram's Seven and a bottle of 7UP out of the cupboard and fixed himself a drink. Her mother looked like she was in shock.

"Like what?" he asked in a loud voice, turning around.

"Like children," Laura said quietly.

Both her parents were aghast. "How can you say you don't want to have children?"

"I'm sorry, Mom. I just don't feel the need to have children—at least for now. I find more satisfaction in doing something mentally challenging."

Laura's mother started crying. "I never knew you could be so selfish!" she said. She left the room and went upstairs.

Laura knew she was breaking her parents' hearts. They'd never understand. They wanted her to have children and she was depriving them of that. And they couldn't have been better parents to her. *First I failed at being a lawyer,* she thought. *Now I've failed at marriage and at being a daughter. Why am I such a disaster?*

"Maybe I'll change my mind later on," Laura said, trying to minimize the damage. "I'm just saying that I'm not ready to be tied down now. I'm only twenty-six. There's lots of time to have a baby," Laura murmured.

Laura's father had already finished his first Seven and Seven and fixed himself another. Then he came back to the table and sat down opposite his daughter.

"So, what now?" her father asked, after a few awkward minutes had passed.

Laura got up from the chair where she had been sitting and stood facing him. "I've decided to finish law school. But I'll never work for a big firm like Edwards and Harrison. I want to help the public, not corporations." She still had a bitter taste in her mouth from what had happened to her in Galveston, intensified by the fact that no one from the law firm ever tried to contact her and check whether she was all right. *Big firm lawyers are as callous as their corporate clients are greedy*, she had decided.

"I applied to Rutgers Law in Camden. I can finish my third year there with in-state tuition, giving me credit for the two years at the University of Pennsylvania. I'll move to the area outside Philadelphia, get a job, and pay for it myself. You and Mom will never have to pay another dime for my education. I'm sorry for how I've hurt Joey and hurt you. But I need to get my life back on track and that's my responsibility."

Not even waiting for the divorce to be final, she moved to Cherry Hill, near Rutgers Law School. She let her hair grow out to its natural dark brown color and replaced her contacts with glasses. She stopped wearing makeup. She started wearing loose-fitting black pants and sweaters that hid her figure. She was trying to look much more serious. Whether or not she also looked much less approachable didn't matter to her.

She decided that her new life required a new identity, too, and she began using her middle name, Ann, in law school. She took a part-time job clerking with a state social services agency and took out a student loan. By June of 2005, Ann Meyers had her law degree.

When researching legal careers that were public-service oriented, she determined that if she worked for the federal government in Washington, D.C., she could be four hours from home, which was just far enough. Before graduation, she applied for an entry-level position at the Securities and Exchange Commission. Instead of representing big corporations, she was now going to make sure those companies, their executives, and advisers abided by the law. In September of 2005, Ann Meyers reported to work, intending to put everything else that had happened before, especially her disastrous internship and her misguided marriage, behind her—never to be thought of again.

11

———

Over the next few years, Carolyn focused on learning as much as she could with the goal of making partner. She dated occasionally, but there was no one special. She watched other female associates marry and have children. The juggling act proved too much for many of them, who ended up leaving the firm to stay home, or they took jobs in-house with a corporation, which was more nine-to-five. Most of the survivors either had a practice that didn't involve a lot of travel or irregular schedules, had a husband who worked at home, or employed an army of nannies. Only a few managed to stay on partnership track while raising children.

Although her father brought up the issue of grandchildren often when she went home, Carolyn simply didn't feel the need for them. *I wonder if the stress of raising Cody and me was what made our mother kill herself,* she wondered. Mrs. Prichard had told her that her mother might have had an undiagnosed mental issue that no one knew about at the time. But Carolyn was sure too that she and Cody in particular had been a handful. In any case, she wasn't even dating anyone seriously, so it was a moot point as far as she was concerned.

She travelled for work once or twice every week and worked late most nights, eating takeout if she didn't have a client dinner. Her friends worked at the firm or were fellow professionals or clients. Business development lunches and dinners were her social life for the most part. She realized that she was good at connecting with people. She was friendly and down-to-earth, and people liked that about her. But she never again agreed to be a mentor for a summer intern. She always told the recruiting office that she was too busy with client work. Soon she was acquiring clients on her own and people started calling her a rainmaker.

Cynthia had told her that, to make partner, women had to work harder, bill more hours, and be smarter than their male counterparts. Carolyn made sure that she always billed the highest number of hours of all the associates on any project she worked on. Nevertheless, it bothered her that she was still the only woman in the energy group. One day she suggested to Paul that they bring some women associates in from that summer's class of new lawyers.

"Carolyn," Paul said, "you've been a positive addition for us. But you know what people say about a group if it has too many women."

"What *do* people say?" she said, not smiling.

He shrugged. "You know. That our work isn't all that important or difficult."

This was exactly the kind of thing that made her consider changing working groups again, not for the first time. But she didn't. She had too much invested in the practice she was building. At times like this, when she needed encouragement, she would often drop in to have a talk with her old mentor, Will Hopson. He always encouraged her to stay the course she had chosen if she wanted to make partner at the firm.

One morning during the summer of 2004, Carolyn was listening to the morning news while getting ready for work. The news anchor was interviewing a woman named Lucille Post, who was part of a group planning to open a new nonprofit shelter for girls and women who had been sexually assaulted or who were the victims of domestic violence. Carolyn stopped what she was doing and listened. Suddenly she was back in Galveston, seeing a bleeding, unconscious young woman lying on the floor of the beach house. She wrote down the woman's telephone number.

Carolyn called Lucille Post that afternoon and accepted her invitation to a planning meeting at her home in Tanglewood. The women Carolyn met there were both professional women and stay-at-home mothers, all of whom had an interest in providing a safe place for victims to go and receive help in the form of medical care, temporary housing, or counseling. The existing shelters were overloaded. Some bravely shared stories of having been raped or their daughters being the victims of sexual assault. They related the devastating effect it had on their lives and their ability to form relationships with men for a long time afterward. *These seem like strong women and yet they all say the trauma never fully goes away,* Carolyn thought.

Before the end of the meeting, Carolyn had volunteered to join the initial board of directors of the organization they would name the Women's Refuge. She knew it was going to take up a lot of her time, but maybe, she thought, helping other girls was a way she could make up for what she hadn't done for Laura Petrillo.

She worked hard on the board and spent one Sunday each month manning the phones and taking calls from victims. She listened to their pleas for help and their stories. She learned how traumatic sexual assault was for the victim initially and how it could adversely influence the rest of their life. Others noted her passion for the mission of the organization, and the board elected her as chair the next year. The night after she was elected, she did a computer search for the name "Laura Petrillo." When there were no results except for Laura's student article in the *University of Pennsylvania Law Review*, she gave up.

The next year, the managing partner of the firm asked Carolyn to use her new contacts with other professional women in the city to form a professional women's group to benefit the United Way. A female client of the firm realized that there were successful women who had their own money to give to charity, and she wanted to harness that power. Carolyn was a natural to work with the client on her project, and it was an immediate success. Cynthia knew a lot of Houston-born professional women and helped recruit the initial members.

This led to Carolyn becoming known as a young mover and shaker in Houston's nonprofit world. The firm promoted her community service by featuring her and her projects in a quarterly newsletter sent to clients. The *Houston Business Journal* listed her in their annual salute to Forty under Forty. At first she was embarrassed by the praise. But she secretly enjoyed being someone of importance among Houston professional women. She was achieving the position in the community that she had dreamed about.

Once every couple of months, Kenny came into Houston and managed to persuade her to spend a few hours with him over dinner. He liked a good steak, so they usually went to Brenner's or Taste of Texas, which he thought were more comfortable than some of the glitzy steakhouses her clients preferred. Every March, they caught some of the country music performances at the Houston Livestock Show and Rodeo and wandered around the Livestock Pavilion. They would laugh about things that happened when they were kids showing their livestock or even trying to rope a calf in the calf scramble. Carolyn found herself looking forward to his visits. She went home to the ranch for holidays and always spent time with him and his mother. The peaceful Prichard home was a refuge when her brother and dad argued about leasing land for oil and gas exploration or her brother shirked his responsibilities around the ranch.

Sitting on the Prichard's porch one evening, when the air was cool and the cicadas were serenading them, Carolyn leaned back on her arms and sighed contentedly. "You know, this is where I feel most relaxed," she said.

"You could make that permanent, you know." Kenny put his arm around her.

"Oh, Kenny, you know I love spending time with you and your mom and my dad, but I could never live in the country. I'd go crazy with all this quiet." Carolyn laughed, even as she blushed. "I complain about it, I know. But I thrive on the hectic pace of the nonprofit stuff and big energy deals. It's exciting and I feel like I'm doing something meaningful. Oil and gas are coming back. Making America energy-independent benefits the entire country, and I'm playing a role in it!" She blushed again, realizing she sounded like she was giving a speech.

"I guess my worldview is closer to home, darlin'," Kenny said in a serious voice. "A productive working ranch makes me feel proud. I find satisfaction taking care of my mom and helping my neighbors when I can. The entire country is way beyond my pay grade."

"Oh, Kenny. I didn't mean that I don't think what you do is important. It is. It's just not what I want out of life."

They sat quietly after that.

Her relationship with Cody had grown strained. The stress of dealing with him clearly was wearing on her dad. She worried about his health. In 2005, she purchased a remodeled 1920s arts-and-crafts bungalow in the Woodland Heights area of Houston, with room for her dad to move in with her. Considering her schedule and how infrequently she was home, however, she didn't think it would be fair to uproot him and move him to an empty house in the city.

Once, she suggested the idea to him, to see how he would react.

He shuddered and said, "Cities suck the soul out of a human being."

They never discussed it again.

• • •

Working with Paul over the years, Carolyn's feelings about him gradually changed from distrust to reserved comfort. He supported her and she appreciated that. But she thought he was self-centered and manipulative, and she never completely let down her guard. It was easier to feel comfortable with Trey, even though he had also been at the beach house that night and hadn't given her an explanation of what happened either. He had expressed concern and backed her up on wanting to call 911, though, and he had helped her get Laura to her car that night. Since she'd joined Paul's group, Trey had been patient and generous with his time, helping her to understand the energy industry and the way deals worked. Once she asked Trey what his ambition was within the firm. He laughed and said it was "to do good work for his clients and provide a secure life for his family, obviously."

Trey's wife, Emily, was an elementary school teacher at a private school. They spent a lot of time with their daughter, Claire, and their respective parents. Carolyn admired how close their family was. Several times each year, Emily invited Carolyn over for dinner at their beautiful new home on Sunset Boulevard in West University, a distinct upgrade from the house in which Trey had been raised. Emily always invited a single male friend for Carolyn to meet. Occasionally, she went out with one of them, but she never became seriously interested. She had her priorities and marriage was not one of them.

The energy section became her work family. Paul still had parties at the house in Galveston, but Carolyn always found an excuse not to attend and Paul never pushed it. Mention of the house brought back bad memories.

Knowing them more closely now, Carolyn found herself wondering whether either Paul or Trey, no matter how drunk they'd been or how entitled Paul was, could have assaulted a summer intern. They both had beautiful, sweet wives. Carolyn hadn't known Laura all that well, really. Could she have been a willing participant in whatever happened? She remembered that Laura had said Paul was handsome and that she and Trey had hit it off at the party. Could Laura have gone downstairs to party with them, and something gone wrong?

Each time she thought about it, she remembered the pragmatic advice Will gave her: to wipe the event from her mind. She tried to lessen her guilt by telling herself that after she made partner and had the time, she would try to find Laura. She didn't know what she would do when she found her, but the intent was enough to let her forget about it for a while.

As Paul's client list steadily expanded and he added associates to the working group, the management committee named him head of the energy section. He was getting closer to achieving his dream of becoming managing partner. He continued to support Carolyn, nominating her for several important firm committees.

Eventually Carolyn talked Paul into including a couple of female associates in their practice group. She personally mentored them and tried to get them good work assignments, passing on what she had learned about succeeding as a woman in a large law firm. In the year they were up for partner, she and Cynthia talked the firm management committee into forming a women's initiative, designed to mentor the firm's female associates.

The once-small Oklahoma company for which Carolyn had done due diligence work when she first joined the group was Paul's most important client in terms of billings. Joe Bill Hawkins changed the name of "JBH Oil" to "JBH Energy" after the acquisition of the Oakland properties. The company borrowed voraciously in order to acquire several other smaller drillers and hundreds of leases in Oklahoma, Arkansas, Louisiana, and Texas. Then, with the help of Edwards and Harrison and Peter Kaufman's accounting firm, Kaufman Stone, he took the company public. A successful IPO made him a very rich man. Despite Paul and Peter cautioning him about being too highly leveraged, debt was not something that worried Joe Bill. He told them he was destined to be the richest man in Texas, and they should just enjoy the ride.

After the IPO, Joe Bill occasionally disappeared for a few days, sometimes even a week. Paul would grow frustrated about not being able to reach his client for important decisions. One afternoon, when Carolyn ran into Paul in the empty snack bar, she heard him arguing with someone on his mobile phone.

"Goddamn it, Joe Bill, you need to be available to me whenever I call. Telling me to get a message to you through Diego Soros is bullshit. Members of the Midnight Poker Club can't cover each other's backs if there's a go-between in the flow of communications!"

When she first joined the group, it had bothered Carolyn that she didn't do any work for Paul's most important client. But soon she had more good work of her own than she could do, so it didn't matter to her. Then one very long day, when Carolyn and Trey were working together with a couple of paralegals on a preclosing in a small conference room, she mentioned a recent article in *Texas Monthly* about JBH Energy.

"You've known Joe Bill Hawkins for a long time, haven't you, Trey?" Carolyn asked.

"Yes, ma'am," Trey answered brightly.

"I'm curious," Carolyn said. "Is the article an accurate portrayal? It's a little light on his history."

Carolyn watched as, predictably, Trey smiled at the opportunity to show how close he was to this important client. He leaned back in his chair. "Joe Bill grew up in the Panhandle close to the Oklahoma border. He's a big guy with natural athletic ability, and he's always been competitive. He played football and competed in rodeo when he was a kid. *Texas Monthly* got that right, but what they didn't say is that he had a good life until his father was convicted of fraud and making false statements about the quality of seed that he sold the Bureau of Land Management for their reforestation program. He had a heart attack and died in prison. Joe Bill never got over the humiliation. He likes to say he left West Texas in his rearview mirror and wasn't going back until he could hold his head up high as a rich man. I think that's the reason he's so driven to succeed."

"What's his education?" Carolyn asked, picking up a stack of legal opinions and organizing them by subject.

"He studied petroleum engineering at Texas A&M University, where Paul and I got to know him playing dominos and cards off campus. He's smart and a risk-taker. He usually came out the big winner of the night. A few guys grumbled about his constant good luck, but no one ever caught him cheating. After his father went to jail and his mother had to sell the ranch to pay the government fines, I suspect that gambling became a necessary source of income."

"Did you think he was cheating?" Carolyn asked idly.

Trey stopped what he was doing. He got up and went over to the sidebar in the room and poured himself a fresh cup of coffee. Then he picked up one of the chocolate chip cookies from a tray and started slowly eating it before he answered.

"I don't think he ever cheated when he played with us. I can't say what he did when he played with other people. Considering his win record, I've wondered if he did cheat and if I should have said something about it. He didn't play with people who couldn't afford to lose the money, for one thing. And we were such a close group of guys that it would have seemed like disloyalty or something. Maybe that shows a lack of morality or ethics on my part. That's what my father, the coach, would probably say. But that's all in the past now, so it's irrelevant." Trey shrugged and sat down again.

"How did you and Paul and Joe Bill get so close?" Carolyn got up to get a cookie for herself.

"Joe Bill lived with us at the house Paul's daddy bought in Austin while Paul and I were in law school and Joe Bill was getting his MBA at UT. Paul never charged us rent, saying his dad could afford to subsidize four bright young men destined to be leaders in Texas one day. Joe Bill learned to play poker and he got addicted to it. He taught the rest of us, and the four of us became close. We called ourselves the Midnight Cowboy Poker Club." Trey laughed. "That sounds corny now."

Carolyn's legal assistant, Melissa, said she was making a Starbucks run and asked if they wanted anything.

Carolyn and Trey both said they were good. "Who was the fourth member of the club?" Carolyn asked.

"Peter Kaufman. He went to Rice for undergraduate and was getting a master's in tax at the University of Texas. Joe Bill met him somewhere and brought him in. They couldn't be more different. Joe

Bill has a strong alpha personality, and Peter is sort of a wimpy guy. Peter's only fault is that he mistakes Joe Bill's bravado for genius, and nothing endears a person like blind adulation. Peter would do anything to get Joe Bill's approval. The funny thing is, Peter is smarter than any of us. He just lacks self-confidence. I think it has something to do with being in his father's shadow. You know he works for his father's firm, and he's said he can never do enough to impress his dad. May be why he sometimes did stupid things in order to get Joe Bill's approval."

"Like what?"

"Nothing important or serious—just pranks, usually involving girls."

Carolyn got up and retrieved a fresh set of documents from one of the boxes in the room. When she returned to the table, she said, "Go on."

"After graduation, Joe Bill worked for several small drilling and servicing companies before borrowing enough money to start his own company. He's not a geologist, but he has an instinct for where oil and gas can be found, a businessman's skill in securing financing, and a ruthless desire to make money. He's a wonder to watch and a great friend to have."

"He sure generates a lot of legal work for the firm," Carolyn commented.

"You bet. From day one, he's sent all his legal work to us. The members of the Midnight Cowboy Poker Club are as tight as brothers. Joe Bill generates the deals. The rest of us make them happen. We have each other's back. You know what they say: loyalty's everything if you want to be successful in business."

Trey's legal assistant interrupted their conversation. "The clients have arrived, Trey. Do you want me to go get them?"

"I'll do it, Susan. But thanks." After Trey left the room, Carolyn reflected on their conversation. She thought that Paul and Trey were fortunate to be part of such a productive team right from the beginning of their careers.

• • •

A couple of days later, Carolyn and Cynthia were having a late Friday lunch at Quatro in the Four Seasons Hotel. The restaurant was a power breakfast and lunch site right in the middle of a cluster of office buildings filled primarily with lawyers and oil companies on the east side of downtown near the Convention Center. The ambiance was modern Italian and featured a famous chef. The hotel bar downstairs was a good place to see music or sports celebrity guests visiting the city or big-time trial lawyers having drinks and telling war stories after work. Carolyn often met male clients there. They seemed to enjoy seeing and being seen.

Carolyn mentioned her conversation with Trey to her friend.

"Will you be working with Joe Bill too?" Cynthia asked.

"No," Carolyn said. "I was curious about the *Texas Monthly* piece. That's why I grilled Trey about him. Honestly, I was just shooting the breeze, because I don't know enough about sports to chat up what happened last weekend with the Astros or the Rockets. Trey's a nice guy. He's not a gossiper, but he seemed to love telling me what a good friend Joe Bill is to him and Paul."

"Honey, I'm sure he gave you the guys' version. Want to hear what's not in the article, although it's mostly River Oaks gossip?"

"Of course I do."

Quatro was not very busy for once, and the waiters seemed to be hovering, so Cynthia motioned their waiter over and asked him to bring them cappuccinos, along with a piece of chocolate lava cake and two spoons. Then she leaned across the table to talk. Carolyn knew that she had a tendency to be dramatic when she shared gossip, which amused her.

"Joe Bill is one of those bigger-than-life Texans—a dying breed. He always wears custom-made cowboy boots, a big silver A&M buckle on his leather belt, a huge turquoise ring, and a Stetson cowboy hat. He smokes awful Cuban cigars, so don't ever sit downwind, if you know what I mean." Cynthia crinkled her nose in distaste.

I think I smelled cigar smoke in the beach house when I went downstairs that morning, Carolyn realized. *Could Joe Bill have been the fourth man in the room? Peter Kaufman was there. That would make sense.*

Cynthia continued her story. "Not long after Joe Bill started his company, he had an affair with the wife of the owner of Oakland Oil Company. She was much older than him, and it's a small community, so people talked. They got engaged even before her divorce was final. Once he completed the acquisition of her share of the company's assets, he left her standing at the altar. Both of the Oaklands were embarrassed and furious for different reasons. I know their daughter, Katherine, from my days at Camp Waldemar. She's a little intense, but really smart. She was close to her mother and was devastated by what he did to her family. I ran into her at a tax conference a few years ago. She's a CPA. She was still angry at Joe Bill."

"That's really callous," Carolyn said.

"When oil prices hit bottom, he married Lois Ann Chambers, the heiress to a large oil field services company. They seemed happily married until shortly after their prenuptial agreement allowed him to take millions of dollars with him along with their divorce. His bride was a native Houstonian and well liked in River Oaks society. Texas old money circles rallied around his wife and excluded him for a while from polite society. My mother and her friends refer to Joe Bill as 'that crude man that the Chambers girl married.'"

Cynthia stopped her tale to take a sip of her cappuccino and to taste a piece of the cake. Then she leaned forward again.

"After a respectable amount of time, of course, the men forgave him. He was back attending matches at the Polo Club and playing poker after golf with members in the men's locker room at the River Oaks Country Club. I wouldn't trust him as far as I could throw him," Cynthia said. "But I wouldn't touch him with a ten-foot pole."

"Well, he sure doesn't sound like anyone I want to do business with, so I'll steer clear," Carolyn said.

Cynthia looked at her watch and said, "My goodness. I've got a conference call in just a few minutes." She waved to their waiter to bring the check.

"You go ahead," Carolyn said. "I'll get this after I finish what you left of the cake. This intelligence is well worth the price of lunch."

12

———

t was January 2006, and Ann was sitting in an uncomfortable chair in a gloomy basement room of a government building, attending a tedious continuing legal education seminar for federal government attorneys. The subject was one of environmental law—specifically, landfill dumping of hazardous materials. She wasn't interested in the topic, but she was facing a deadline to report the required annual number of continuing legal education hours to complete in order to maintain her law license. This was the only course that was available at a time that she could fit into her busy schedule. It was the end of the day and the speaker was using technical terms she didn't understand. Her eyes were closing and she was having a hard time staying awake.

Suddenly someone placed a paper cup of hot black coffee on the table in front of her. She looked up and saw a tall, attractive Black woman about her age, with long braids tied back behind her head and sparkling hazel eyes. She had picked up coffee from the sideboard for the both of them.

"You're a lifesaver," Ann whispered. "Thanks."

"I'm sitting next to you and I was afraid you might fall over on me when you totally nodded off." The woman smiled. She sat back down beside Ann.

When the speaker finally finished, Ann turned to the woman and introduced herself. "I'm Ann Meyers with the United States Securities and Exchange Commission."

"Aren't you in the wrong subject area?" the woman asked. "I could have suggested a much more interesting topic if I knew you were thinking of changing agencies."

"This was a continuing legal education emergency." Ann smiled. "Otherwise, I wouldn't be here."

"I'm Amanda Smith," the woman said, extending her hand. "And I'm a genuine environmental lawyer with the Environmental Protection Agency. I'm done for the day. Do you want to join me for something more stimulating off campus?"

Amanda seemed like a nice person, and Ann could use more friends since she moved to D.C. Some of her old friends from Rutgers were in town, but they were all just getting started in their careers, working hard to make an impression, and didn't have much time for socializing. Occasionally she would run into someone she knew from Penn Law representing a large corporation, but she tried to avoid having to make small talk with them. They would always ask, "What happened to you?" That was a question she didn't answer, giving some reason to cut short the conversation. One former male classmate asked her, "How in the hell did you end up working for the government with your brains?" She didn't bother to even acknowledge him when she saw him later.

Amanda seemed like a friendly female government lawyer reaching out to her. "I'd love to," Ann said. "Where should we go?"

"How about the Old Ebbitt Grill?"

Ann and Amanda ended up drinking martinis, ordering salads, and talking until after eight. They shared a lot of the same interests and insights about working in the Washington bureaucracy. Amanda was outgoing and had a wry sense of humor. She could mimic some of the older bureaucrats at the EPA who took themselves too seriously, in her opinion, which made Ann laugh. Ann recognized their counterparts in the SEC. On the other hand, when they discussed why they had chosen to go to work for the federal government, Amanda was suddenly quite serious.

"I grew up in Cleveland, Ohio, on the shores of Lake Erie," Amanda said. "As a child I listened to stories about how Lake Erie was a dead lake in the 1960s and 1970s because of the unregulated waste runoff from municipal sewer systems, factories, and fertilizer used by farmers, which drained into the shallow lake. The resulting pollution was the impetus for creation of the Environmental Protection Agency in 1970 and the passage of what became the Clean Water Act in 1972. There were continuing issues, though, due to the buildup of phosphorous and other pollutants that drained into the lake.

"I was disgusted by the lack of responsibility on the part of local government and industry. I studied biology and chemistry as an under-graduate at Ohio State and then went to Case Western Reserve for law school. I always knew I wanted to practice environmental law. Almost all private law firms defend the 'boys in the black hats.' The EPA is the only way to see that clean water laws are enforced," she said.

"So why did you choose to go to work for the government?" Amanda asked.

Ann hated this question, but she already felt comfortable with Amanda. "I interned with a couple of big law firms after my second year at the University of Pennsylvania law school," she said. "I was turned off by the people. I found them arrogant and callous. I knew that their clients were probably the same. I actually took a break from law after that experience."

She paused, sipping her martini. "But I always wanted to be a lawyer. So eventually I went back to law school and finished at Rutgers Camden. Like you, I wanted to work where I could make a difference by holding people who considered themselves above the law accountable. I liked business law and administrative law, so the SEC seemed like a logi-cal place to go. Since I came here, I feel more and more passionate about enforcing the laws that are there to protect—well, real people."

"I guess that makes us the girls in the white hats." Amanda grinned.

"Something like that," Ann laughed.

Amanda soon became Ann's closest friend. They were both ambitious to get ahead in their agencies and worked long hours. Amanda's husband, Deshaun, who was an assistant U.S. attorney for the Justice Department, travelled often with his litigation cases. When it was time to get away or have the kind of talk that only good friends can have, the two women turned to each other. When they were promoted within their agencies, they celebrated together. When one of them lost a case they were passionate about, they met for a good consolation chat. They shared their dreams and secrets.

But one secret Ann didn't share with Amanda was the experience that had changed the course of her life. She remained ashamed and embarrassed, occasionally still waking up in a cold sweat, hearing those men laughing at her. She'd changed her name and filled her time with work, and she told herself that, over time, the nightmares would cease.

• • •

Like all upwardly mobile attorneys working for the federal government, policy at the top affected their climb. During the George W. Bush administration, the press and environmental lobbyists were often at odds with the administration's more business-friendly actions. Amanda was particularly unhappy when she heard that the administrator was planning to eliminate enforcement of some of the provisions of the Clean Water Act.

The friends were meeting after work one day at a crowded bar on Pennsylvania Avenue near the White House. A baseball game was being broadcast on a television above the bar, and a group of men in suits and ties were crowded in front of it. The crowd was professional and young, and the talk seemed to be about politics, for the most part. Amanda and Ann were seated at a table in the middle of the room drinking martinis, and Amanda was blowing off steam.

"The need to protect the nation's waters is the reason I joined the agency," she said in an angry voice. "I don't mean just clean, healthy drinking water—also our rivers and streams. People end up eating the fish that swim in that water. Their kids play in that water. Our bodies are mostly water. And where do you think that water comes from?" As she raised her voice, people nearby started to look at her.

"Cool down," Ann said to her friend, putting her hand on Amanda's arm, which was visibly trembling. "People can hear you. It's not the end of the world. You know that's how it works. It always takes a while for these policies to take legal form and become enforceable. Four years later, another administration with different priorities will come into power and everything will change."

Amanda motioned for the waiter to bring her another martini. "I don't care who hears me. Clean water is something I'm passionate about!"

"I know, but it's safer for your career to tell me, not every person inside the Beltway, that you disagree with the administration." Ann made a funny face and tried to force a smile out of Amanda. Eventually, she succeeded.

"Okay, you're right. I'm not being politic."

"That's okay. I'll reign you in and you can reign me in when I'm frustrated and not politic. Deal?"

"Deal!" Amanda said.

"C'mon, let's get out of here. It's so noisy I can't hear myself think," Ann said.

"Okay."

"Hey, I have an idea of something to cheer you up," Ann said as they left the bar. "You said that Deshaun is out of town, and I don't have any work I have to do tomorrow. Let's do something really wild."

"Like what?"

"I don't know. How about we drive up to Annapolis and do the historic sites? We can even go shopping and have lunch al fresco. I read about it in a local magazine and it looked like fun. We're both from out of town, yet we never take time to see the sites. Let's be tourists for a day! What do you say?"

Amanda seemed amused at the suggestion from her workaholic friend. "Well," she said, "I guess if you can be a tourist, I can be a tourist. I'm game. I'll pick you up at nine so we'll have plenty of time to see those sites, whatever they are."

The women laughed. Ann put her arm around her friend and they walked on.

13

———

It was a heated conversation that Paul and Trey were having in Paul's office in September 2008. Paul was angrily pacing the room, and Trey sat in his guest chair wearing a defensive look; Paul's assistant knew enough to get up and close his door.

"Goddamn it, Trey," Paul said, frustrated. "I told you to stay with him at all times in New York."

"Look, I tried to be a good babysitter. But he's a cagey bastard. He didn't tell me about the meeting with those bankers until we were walking into the Ritz-Carlton bar to meet them for drinks. Then, without talking to me about it, he asks them for a loan and offers to pledge the wells in Bell County as collateral. He claimed they were producing twice as much crude oil per day, as the geologists' data indicates. What could I do? Contradict my client in front of investors? Shit! I hate it when he does these things. It puts me in a bad position." Trey slammed his fist against the arm of the chair in frustration.

"Not to mention the firm," Paul said grimly. "There's a limit to how nearsighted the management committee will be if fraud is behind the shit pile of revenues JBH's work produces for the firm. That could be the end of our careers." He stopped pacing and looked at Trey with a hopeful look. "Tell me the bankers didn't bite."

"Hook, line, and sinker," Trey said glumly.

"Well," Paul said after thinking for a few minutes, "line up plenty of associates to paper the deal right away. We can rack up a hell of a lot of billable hours. But let's hope the bankers have a valuation consultant who tells his clients to quietly walk away." He sighed.

On his way out the door, Trey turned back. "Do you think Joe Bill is getting a little out of control lately?" Trey ventured. "He seems to be driven more than before to make short-term profits."

"We just need to keep tighter control of him," Paul said. "I didn't like the way he tried to make me go through Soros to reach him, and I've told him not to do that again. Don't worry—he'll listen to me."

Trey gave him a questioning look, which irritated Paul.

After Trey left, Paul looked out his window at the building where JBH Energy had its offices. He just didn't understand Joe Bill. He knew he was making a killing with his business, and he'd had good find after good find. Why did he have to push the envelope and lie? *It's stupid and dangerous for all of us*, he thought.

• • •

A couple of weeks later, Paul and Trey were having lunch with Joe Bill at the private, exclusive Petroleum Club on the top floor of the Exxon Building in downtown Houston. The club took up the whole floor with a ballroom and numerous private dining rooms. It had large windows all around so that the diners could look down at the city that was their milieu and feel like they were on top of the world. At night, it was the best location to see the lights of the city, especially the colored neon lights that rimmed the tops of many of the major buildings. After ordering drinks, Paul casually asked, "How's that deal you discussed coming with the New York bankers? The one where you agreed to pledge the output of the wells in Bell County?"

Joe Bill frowned. "Those damn Wall Street guys hired a valuation consultant who told them that the crude production was exaggerated and the wells were only worth half of what they agreed to lend," he complained. "They were madder than hell at first. I calmed them down though by telling them about a new venture I'm starting and offering them the chance to buy interests."

Paul was not happy that he had not heard about this deal before Joe Bill was out shopping it. *This shit is getting to be a pattern,* he thought. He and Trey exchanged worried looks.

Their waiter appeared with the drinks, and conversation halted while everyone got situated.

Joe Bill looked around to make sure no one was near their table. Then he leaned forward and spoke in an uncharacteristically low voice. "I've been watching how George Mitchell has been successful in using a new technology, hydraulic fracturing, to tap oil and gas pockets that were untouchable, even unimaginable, with traditional, vertical drilling. They inject a mixture of sand, water, and chemicals into shale deposits at a high pressure to break up the rock and release the oil and gas. The Barnett Shale in North Texas is producing millions of gallons. Some other boys have started horizontal fracturing the shale in the Permian Basin in West Texas with good results."

Paul thought that Joe Bill looked very pleased with himself. "What does that have to do with you?" he asked.

"I've had my eye on a field that my geologists suspect could be just as productive for a long time. It's called the Eagle Ford Shale. A small, independent driller is putting in a well as we speak."

"Where is that exactly?" Trey asked.

A couple of oil men from Zeron Energy were walking by when they saw Joe Bill. "How's it going, big boy?" one of them asked, smiling.

Joe Bill immediately put on his self-confident smile. "Couldn't be better, boys. Good to see you." They all shook hands, and then the men proceeded to the elevator.

After he watched them leave, Joe Bill scanned the room to be sure no one else was about to interrupt them. Then he drew a map on the tablecloth with his finger. "It could be an enormous area. My guys think it starts at the Mexico border and runs northeast all the way up to the Fort Worth area." His outstretched finger knocked over a salt-shaker. A waiter immediately appeared and removed it.

Joe Bill waited until he was gone. "I've secretly been signing up leases with long terms in the counties southeast of San Antonio for the past several years. Rather than send landmen to the area, which would alert competitors, I've been working through small town local attorneys who have contacts in the community. I pay them to talk ranchers into signing leases. I figured that if I could tie up the land for long up-front terms at a low price, my investment would eventually pay off."

"You offered the venture capital group a piece of these new wells?" Paul asked. Paul and Trey exchanged concerned looks. It was the first Paul had heard of the deal, and Joe Bill hadn't run it by him for legal analysis and disclosure issues. He was afraid to ask what his client had told potential investors.

"Listen, boys, I have a feeling this deal is going to be the best one yet. I have great ideas about how the whole situation down there will make us a lot of money."

Then he laughed. "Enough business. When are we going to go out to your daddy's lease again, Paul? I've got new artillery I want to try out."

Paul did a quick search of his calendar. "How about next Saturday?" he suggested. "Ashley is taking the kids to the Alamo and the River-walk in San Antonio with her girlfriends. In the meantime, why don't you send over the details of what you are proposing on this new deal? We can talk about it next weekend. We should make sure there aren't any legal issues that need to be ironed out before you get much further down the road."

"Sure, sure, buddy. I'll do that," Joe Bill said before getting up to greet some executives from Exxon who were having lunch on the other side of the dining room.

Paul and Trey walked back to the office together after the lunch. "What do you think?" Trey asked.

"I wish he'd run his new deal by us first. On the other hand, I see a ton of work ahead for us and that's good," Paul answered.

"Still, I feel uneasy about his cavalier attitude lately to the legal issues in what he's doing," Trey said, while they were waiting for a light to change at Main Street. "I wonder what he meant by 'the whole situation.'"

"Maybe he's invented some new drilling technique he's trying out there."

"It sounded more grandiose," Trey said.

"Don't make too much of it," Paul responded. "Along with Peter, we've always been able to keep him doing things legal—or at least clean up the mess before it goes too far. And it has proved very profitable for all of us. When Joe Bill says 'new deal,' I hear 'higher billings.'"

Paul was trying to sound unworried. But inside, he was concerned that Joe Bill was moving too fast on his latest ventures and not thinking them through. Worse, he wasn't sharing what he was thinking about with his support team.

The Midnight Cowboy Poker Club hadn't met to discuss deals Joe Bill was proposing in more than a year. Prior to that, the four of them had met in Joe Bill's office regularly, at least once per month, to review all the deals JBH Energy was involved in or considering. They would dissect the deal from the legal, accounting, and financial perspectives. Only then would Joe Bill give the go-ahead and tell Paul to prepare a term sheet. After that, Joe Bill would move forward with seeking financing.

But now Trey was right: Joe Bill was cutting all his old friends out of his business decisions. He seemed to be relying more on Diego Soros, his COO. Diego tended to just agree with anything Joe Bill wanted to do without question. And Paul instinctively didn't trust him, although he couldn't say exactly why.

14

———

n December 2009, the management committee named Carolyn to the partnership class of 2010, with Paul backing her all the way. Cynthia was also part of the partnership class of 2010, along with seven men. That meant the percentage of women partners at the firm had gone up to eighteen percent, an all-time high. There was a dinner at the ultra-exclusive Buffalo Club, secluded in a corner of Memorial Park near where I-10 and Loop 610 West intersect. A one-lane road—one that people who didn't know the club was there would miss when they drove past—led to the entrance. The club building was an elegant antebellum mansion with a long pool surrounded by fountains and flowers. Situated within the park, evergreens and live oaks draped with Southern moss enveloped the property. The club's members carried the last names that were on the most prominent buildings in Houston, as well as its world-class medical center. The dinner was served by white-gloved waiters in the dining room, and the meal included quail, steak, scotch, fine wines, and cigars—all to celebrate the new partners. As was the tradition, the inductees were required to make a toast after dinner.

The male new partners toasted the partnership and said how humbled they were to join such an old and prestigious law firm. Carolyn thought their toasts were pretty similar and boring. Soft chatter began to be heard at the tables. But then Cynthia, who was never afraid to speak her mind and had the pedigree to shield her from recriminations, stood and raised her glass. In contrast to her usual dark conservative suit and pumps, tonight she wore a red Valentino dress, dangling 18K gold earrings, and fashionable gold four-inch Jimmy Choo heels. Her long hair was fastened in the back with a gold barrette in a chic chignon. The chatter ceased, and Carolyn could see that her friend was making a favorable impression on the men in the room.

"I would like to toast Edwards and Harrison for coming into the modern age and admitting not one but two hard-working women to the partnership in one year. Here's to a bright future and more opportunity for this generation of women at Edwards and Harrison!" She finished by giving a big smile to everyone.

Carolyn could detect a few grumbles and "ahems" at the retired partners' table, but for the most part, the crowd, which was well into cognac and cigars at that point, clapped enthusiastically.

Finally, it was Carolyn's turn. Unlike her friend, Carolyn had played it safe with a black Escada shift dress and pearls. She rose and looked around the room. Then she lifted her champagne flute and said, "It takes mentors to teach and guide young lawyers so that they develop the skills and judgment to be initiated as a partner of this esteemed group of lawyers. I have had the good fortune to have been mentored by the best. Thank you for your efforts and for your confidence in me." As she spoke, she looked across the room and caught Will Hopson's eye. He gave her a big smile and silently raised his champagne glass to toast her. The crowd clapped.

After the dinner, Cynthia joined Carolyn at her house for their own private celebration. It was one of the few rare cold nights in Houston, so Carolyn made a fire in the fireplace. She put on a Dolly Parton CD, and they curled up on club chairs in the living room. Carolyn had bought some bright-colored balloons to create a celebratory atmosphere, and Cynthia supplied a box of expensive Belgian chocolates. Carolyn lit some scented candles for atmosphere.

Cynthia twirled a glass of the Dom Perignon champagne that had appeared on Carolyn's desk that morning. "By the way . . . who's the big spender who sent you the Dom?"

"I don't know," Carolyn replied. "I thought of my dad or Kenny, but I don't think either of them would splurge this much. There wasn't a card, so it's a mystery."

"Maybe it's from a tall, dark, handsome stranger who has been admiring you from afar," Cynthia whispered.

"He must be real far off, because I don't recall meeting anyone of that description," Carolyn laughed.

"Speaking of mentors, I should have toasted Uncle Avery for the advice he gave me," Cynthia said. "Although toasting the managing partner of the rival law firm wouldn't be politic."

"I didn't think you were worrying about being politic tonight," Carolyn teased. "That red dress was amazing! I thought some of those guys' eyes were going to pop out of their heads. When did you buy that?"

"Years ago, pre–Edwards and Harrison, at Paris Fashion Week. This is the first time I wore it. I think I'll make it my official celebration dress."

"You can wear it on your first day on the management committee!" Carolyn suggested. "I'd love to be a fly on the wall for that."

"More?" Cynthia asked, holding the champagne bottle over Carolyn's glass.

"Mm, I've probably had enough," Carolyn said. "I was thinking about that tall, dark, handsome stranger you mentioned." She stretched out on the couch. "Do you ever think—that we gave up too much to get here?"

"You mean like husbands, kids, vacations, girl trips, not to mention lying in bed eating bonbons?" Cynthia laughed and finished off her champagne in one big swig.

"Sort of," Carolyn replied. "You can throw in integrity," she mumbled.

"What in the hell are you talking about?"

Carolyn caught herself and changed the subject. "Nothing, nothing," she said. "I mean I love the work I'm doing, and I love my clients. And I make more money than I ever dreamed I would make. But it's been such an unending grind that I don't even have time to spend it."

"Are you having second thoughts about the hot cowboy back home? Kenny, is it?" Cynthia teased.

"I'll always love Kenny in a way," Carolyn said. "But I think about my mom, who didn't consider life on the ranch worth living. I might have turned out just like her if I'd stayed in the country, and ended up going crazy too. And Kenny Prichard is a lot like my dad. Neither one of them will ever leave their land. It's part of their identity. Besides, this partnership in a major law firm is what I've always wanted."

Cynthia tossed a throw pillow at her. "And you've got it!" she said. "Liven up! This is a celebration. Not a wake."

"I'm just exhausted at the moment. I don't know what I'm saying." *I'm not saying that I never want to get married or have children though,* Carolyn thought. *It just has never been my first priority.*

"Look, we're on top of the world. We caught the golden apple," Cynthia said. "Life is just going to get better from here on out! You'll see."

On Monday, Carolyn was feeling good when she went into the office. The last year leading up to the partnership vote had been especially nerve-racking, with her feelings continually going up and down as she contemplated her chances. She decided to swing by Will's office and thank him again for his support.

Boxes were strewn about, and Will's secretary was busily packing them with the books and memorabilia that were on the furniture. Will was sitting on the couch, out of her way, smoking his pipe and looking dour.

"What's going on? Moving offices?" Carolyn asked. It was not unusual for lawyers to move to different offices or floors from time to time.

"Yes," Will answered. "Across town, actually."

"What do you mean?" Carolyn asked, surprised. "You're not leaving the firm, are you?" She sat down across from him.

"That's exactly what I'm doing," he said.

"But you built this practice, and I assumed you'd be here until you retired. Where are you going? Why?"

"I'm joining Smith and Loggins, a real estate boutique firm of good solid lawyers." Will got up to get an ashtray off of his desk and tapped his pipe ashes into it.

"But why?" Carolyn asked again.

Will asked his secretary if she would get Carolyn and him a cup of black coffee. When she left, he told Carolyn to close the door.

"Of course," she said.

"You may as well know, Carolyn. In the last two years, management has been quietly telling partners when they reach sixty that it's time to move on, even though the partnership agreement says you don't have to retire until sixty-five. I guess I should be honored that I'm only coming up three years short."

"What? They can't do that. The partnership agreement is a contract. You should protest it."

"No matter how mad this forced retirement makes a partner, nobody talks about it because no one wants other firms to know that they've been asked to leave. They don't want to look like damaged goods. The firm can replace us old guys with higher sharing ratios with younger partners who cost a lot less."

Will suddenly seemed older to Carolyn.

"Like me?" Carolyn asked, suddenly regretting her decision to celebrate with her mentor.

"Like your generation, Carolyn—not you in particular." Will gave her a fond smile.

"That seems so unfair, so cold. If one of us should be here, it's you, not me."

"Big law firms certainly aren't the gentlemanly families they were when I started in the practice of law, that's for sure. Profits per partner and where the firm ranks in the national league tables is what's most important. Nothing's personal—it's all just business now."

"Oh, Will. This firm won't seem the same without you. You've been my model of what an excellent, honorable lawyer should be. I'll miss you."

Carolyn couldn't stop thinking about Will, even if the following week was filled with congratulatory calls from clients and other lawyers and paperwork that accompanied becoming a partner. One evening, while enjoying a glass of wine and the first hot scented bath she had allowed herself in a long time, she suddenly started thinking about Laura Petrillo. *I wonder where she is now,* Carolyn thought. They'd both had the same ambition, and she'd gotten what they both wanted, but she had no idea whether Laura had managed to persevere. Carolyn reminded herself that once she made partner, she'd promised to try to find her. She wondered what she would say to her. *At the least,* she thought, *I owe her an apology.* Maybe Laura was happy and successful somewhere else.

The next week, Carolyn searched for Laura's name again online, but there was only the one entry from the law review article she'd published when she was a student at Penn. Martindale Hubbell, the official directory of all US attorneys, didn't have a Laura Petrillo listed either. *Maybe she got married and has a different name,* Carolyn thought. Or perhaps she'd given up on law and never became a lawyer.

The University of Pennsylvania was a dead end as well. After Carolyn was shuttled among several administrators, an officious-sounding woman in the legal department told her that privacy laws prevented the school from giving her any information about present or former students. Of course, Carolyn had known that, but she'd hoped to at least find some sort of clue.

She visited the attorney recruiting office at the firm and asked if she could see Laura's file. Perhaps if she could find her old address, she could follow her trail. But it had been too long since Laura's unfinished clerkship, and the file had been destroyed.

She briefly considered hiring a private detective to find Laura. The firm had one they used. But somehow that felt wrong, too intrusive.

All Carolyn remembered was that Laura had grown up in a small town in New Jersey—only one of the most populous states in the country. If Laura hadn't become a lawyer, or if she'd gotten married and changed her name, she'd somehow left no trace. *I always thought that I would find her someday,* Carolyn told herself, *but I guess that's just not going to happen.*

· · ·

After all the partnership celebrations were over, Carolyn drove home to the ranch to spend the Christmas holiday with her family. It was an unusually cold December, and she was looking forward to sitting beside the mesquite fire she expected would be burning in the fireplace. Maria's family always made tamales for Christmas Eve dinner, which they ate after returning from the service at Locust Grove Methodist Church. But Carolyn would have to go to the meat market in town on Christmas Eve morning to pick up a beef tenderloin to cook for Christmas dinner.

Shep, who had been sleeping on the front porch, started barking excitedly when she got out of her car and followed her into the house. She was surprised when she found it nearly as cold as the air outside. The fireplace was empty of wood, and a tree had been cut down and brought inside, but no one had set it up or decorated it.

"Dad? Cody?" Carolyn called. When no one answered she began looking for them in the kitchen and then in the bedrooms. Her father's bedroom was at the end of the hall, and he hadn't changed anything since her mother died. The quilt on the bed was a girlish light blue color, and the curtains were white lace. Several framed pictures of her parents in happier days were set out on the vanity where her mother used to sit, sometimes for hours, looking in the mirror and brushing her long auburn hair before she went to bed.

She found her father in his bed with the covers pulled up tight. He was asleep. Carolyn had never seen him sleeping during the day. Alarmed, she called to wake him.

"Oh, honey, you're home," her father said, after opening his eyes and beginning to sit up in bed. "I'm sorry. I should have remembered you were coming home this afternoon and lit a fire."

"That's okay," Carolyn said. "But are you sick?"

"No, no. I'm fine. I was just taking a little nap."

"It's freezing in here," Carolyn said. "Why didn't you turn up the heat? Where's Cody?"

"I don't know where Cody is. He doesn't come home much these days. He has new friends in town."

Carolyn was alarmed. This was not like her father. She wondered what Cody was up to now and grew angry. She counted on him—gullibly, she now realized—to take care of their father. He obviously wasn't doing that.

"I'm going to start a fire," Carolyn said. "Why don't you get dressed and I'll fix us something to eat."

Carolyn went to the kitchen and opened several cabinets before she found a can of Wolf Brand Chili. She took out some dubiously fresh-looking saltines and set a place for her dad and her at the table. She sat and waited for her dad, cursing her brother.

The next day on her way into town, she stopped by Kenny's house. His mother told her he was out in the pasture, so she wrapped a wool scarf around her neck, buttoned her jean jacket, and went to find him.

"Hey, Carolyn," Kenny said when she found him by the horse barn. He put down his tools and gave her a hug.

"Hey yourself," Carolyn replied. *His hug feels really good,* she thought.

Detecting the frown on her face, he stepped back and asked, "I see you've been home. How's your dad?"

"Not good. He was in bed at four in the afternoon, and there was no heat in the house when I arrived. Do you know what's going on?"

"Not directly," he replied. "But we have a pretty efficient gossip chain around here."

"Dad said Cody's been living somewhere else. What's that all about?" she asked.

Kenny took her hand and led her to his double cab F-150 and opened the passenger door. "It's freezing out here. Let me turn on the heater," he said, helping her get in. "You remember that lawyer, Jonathan Stevenson? He's been stirring up the young men since he got here about signing leases for drilling on their family's land. Some of the oil companies that've had success with hydraulic fracturing are looking at this part of the state.

"Jonathan's been giving Cody the rush for years. Hell, he's even given him a room in the swankienda Brenda Sue's daddy built for them where he can crash, drink on Jonathan's tab, and party with Brenda Sue's divorcee girlfriends."

"That's where he's been staying instead of with Dad?" Carolyn was angry.

"Seems like Cody prefers it to hanging out with his father at the ranch and hauling hay or moving cattle. When he does go home, he pesters your dad about leasing the ranch. Mom has been over there looking in on your father from time to time."

"Oh, Kenny," Carolyn said. "I had no idea it was this bad."

Kenny laid his hand on hers before continuing. She was shivering still.

"I hate to lay this on you, Carolyn. I held off while you were in the final stretch of your partnership run. I know how important that is to you. Anything my mom and I can do to help, you know we will. But Cody's been mad at me since I told him I thought Stevenson was a fraud and that he should steer clear of him."

"What's Cody done?" Carolyn asked, afraid to hear the answer.

"He's signed a lease for horizontal drilling on your ranch," Kenny said.

Carolyn was stunned. "What? How could he?"

"Here," Kenny said, reaching behind him and pulling out a thick wool Pendleton blanket. "You're still shivering. Let's put this around you.

"He talked your father into giving him power of attorney over the mineral rights. Some of the other boys around here signed leases too. Stevenson brought in this company and promised them all they would get rich. He said they would be bringing up millions of barrels of crude in no time. Jonathan and Brenda Sue have been wining and dining the bunch of them for years, preparing for this."

Carolyn felt her fists clench. "I told him we didn't need any outside lawyer getting involved in the family business. I review leases for a living. And Dad's will divides his property evenly between the two of us. What right does he have to lease our property without my approval?"

"Don't blame your dad, Carolyn. Cody has been relentless. Mom thinks he just broke your father down over time. She says your dad feels terrible about the whole mess. He hardly leaves the house anymore—just stays by himself."

Carolyn stared out the window for a minute, while Kenny pulled the blanket tighter around her. He kept his arms around her. "Maybe I'm to blame," Carolyn finally said. "I've been off in Houston. Maybe if I'd been coming home more, I could've given more support to Dad. It was selfish and stupid to ignore this leasing thing as Cody's pie-in-the-sky idea. I shouldn't have let Dad fight Cody off alone."

"Don't beat yourself up too bad. You know Cody's always had a chip on his shoulder about how his little sister was smarter and better than him in school. Now that you have a successful career in Houston, I think he's jealous. Stevenson came along and put it in his head that he could outshine you financially by leasing for oil."

"That's ridiculous," Carolyn said.

"It wouldn't be the first time sibling jealousy caused a rift in a family." Kenny smiled. "Kinda makes me glad I'm an only child."

He reached into the back seat and pulled out a thermos. He poured a cup of hot coffee. "Here, drink this."

Carolyn took the stainless steel cup from his hands.

"You know," he went on, "I've got my own reason to be angry at your brother."

"What's that?"

"Well, the site where they're planning to drill is the closest they can get to my property line legally. Cody didn't give me the courtesy of telling me that, but I can see where the frac crew is working. If they hit, they'll be draining oil and gas off of my property too."

"What are you going to do?" Carolyn asked.

"I don't know," Kenny said, sitting close beside her now and rubbing her hand to warm it. "I'll probably have to take legal action. I never wanted to disturb my land for drilling. I make more than enough money from ranching to have a good life and I love this land. I don't want big trucks and workers digging it up and creating a toxic mess."

Carolyn gave Kenny a kiss on the cheek. "You're a good man, Kenny Prichard." Then she opened the door of the truck and jumped down.

"Where are you going?" Kenny asked.

"To find Cody, and I will not be held responsible for my actions after that!"

15

———

ody didn't return Carolyn's telephone calls, and he stayed away from the ranch. He called his father on Christmas Eve and said that he had been invited to go on a hunting trip to Montana to hunt bighorn sheep over the holidays, and they didn't hear from him or see him after that. Carolyn did her best to decorate the house, prepare a Christmas dinner, and try to raise her father's spirits. She gave the clothes she had purchased at Pinto Ranch as a present for Cody to Maria to give to her husband. She was furious. When it was time to go back to Houston, she nuzzled Shep and told him, "Take care of the old man, okay?" Her father waved goodbye to her from the driveway.

Despite all her best intentions to call her father every day and make the trip home once a month, back in Houston, work took over once again. Most of her deals were time sensitive, in the financial or the energy markets, and she rarely felt able to get away. She was finding that the responsibility to bring in new clients that came with partnership presented new pressures.

When she finally made the trip home in February, she was shocked to see what was happening at the ranch. Large trucks carrying equipment or products to be used in drilling had torn up the front pasture as they made their way to a drill site near Agua Pura Creek. Workers in hard hats, steel toe boots, and safety vests were everywhere. There was a lot of noise where there had always been cattle and horses grazing in a peaceful green pasture. Some of the beautiful old live oaks had been cut down and were lying on the ground. She rolled down the car window and called, "Shep! Come here, boy." She was worried that the dog, whose eyesight and hearing were not what they once were, would get run over by one of the big trucks. She drove slowly up to the house, calling his name. When he finally came bounding out from inside of a shed, she was relieved.

Carolyn had always considered drilling and fracking a good thing. It was innovative technology that brought jobs, revenues, and energy independence back to America. She believed the industry was responsible about not harming the environment any more than necessary. She felt proud that her legal work played a small part in the shale revolution.

But those were opinions she had formed while seated at her desk on a high floor of a downtown Houston office building. This noisy, smelly disruption of her family land was not how she had envisioned the process. *This must be tearing Dad apart,* she thought.

She drove quickly up to the house and went inside, where she found her father sitting at the kitchen table with his head bowed, his hands covering his ears. There was an untouched cold bowl of soup in front of him.

"Dad?" Carolyn said softly, taking one of his hands in hers. "How are you doing?"

"Oh, I'm fine, honey. Did you see your brother's project on the way in? He's making a real mess of our family's heritage. I always felt happy when I imagined passing the care of this land on to my children. But not like this. Your granddaddy is turning in his grave right now."

Carolyn didn't know what to say, so she went to the refrigerator and looked inside for something to drink, expecting to see the pitcher of sweet tea that was always there.

"Dad, there's hardly anything in the fridge," Carolyn said in a worried voice. "Are you eating?"

"When I'm hungry," he replied. "I just don't seem to be hungry as much as I used to be. Old age, I guess. They say you eat less and sleep less as you get older. Funny, though, I seem to sleep more these days. But let's not talk about me, honey. Tell me what you've been up to."

Carolyn searched her mind for a topic, but all she could think of was oil and gas deals.

That night, she was awakened by Shep barking and the front door opening and closing. She looked at her alarm clock: It was two a.m. It had to be Cody.

He'd managed to avoid her calls and emails, but Carolyn was determined. She got up, put on a robe, and walked stealthily toward her brother's bedroom. Only one bedside lamp was turned on, but she could see him picking through his dresser drawers. A duffel bag sat on the bed. Carolyn quietly entered his room and shut the door behind her. Only then did Cody realize he wasn't alone.

"You must be a burglar," Carolyn said in a whisper. "What are you stealing now?"

Cody turned and looked at her, abashed. "I thought you were asleep," he said.

She could feel the anger rise up inside her. "You haven't answered any of my phone calls or emails."

"I've been busy. Taking care of things." Cody stood up and pushed his chest out defensively.

"What things, exactly? Certainly not our father or our ranch. I come home to find the family land being torn up, our father depressed, sick, and the livestock looking like skeletons. What the hell, Cody?"

Cody looked unnerved. But then he straightened himself up to his full six-foot-two height as if to let her know he was standing his ground. "It's the twenty-first century, sis. Fracking is the future, and I've got a gold mine right under our feet."

"This ranch belongs to the *family*, Cody—not just you!" Carolyn picked up a shirt that was on the bed and threw it at him. "And the other members of the family have a say in what is done with it. You may be driving our father to an early grave, but he's still aboveground. And I specifically told you not to enter into a lease without my reviewing it and researching the company first." Carolyn realized she sounded like she was talking down to Cody, something she usually tried not to do, but she didn't care.

"I had it reviewed by a local lawyer who knows more about leasing in this county than some Houston law firm," Cody said.

"Are you talking about Brenda Sue Bubblebrain Pinkney's Yankee husband?" Carolyn asked in a terse voice.

Carolyn was angry and pushed the duffel bag so that it fell off the bed.

Cody didn't say anything.

"Is he representing you in this transaction?"

"He's my good friend."

"But did he tell you he was your lawyer? Did you sign an engagement letter with him?"

Cody looked around before he answered.

"We made a handshake, Carolyn. Don't you know that's all you need in Texas? What a dumb question." Cody shrugged his shoulders dismissively.

"Did he send you a bill for his legal services? I'm sure he wouldn't forget to do that."

"That's one of the best parts of this. He doesn't have to. He said the company is paying him."

"Oh my God!" Carolyn exclaimed. She hung her head and then looked straight at her brother. "Stevenson's not representing your interests. He's representing the oil company's interest! I bet that lease is written one hundred percent in their favor. How could you be so stupid?"

Cody turned pale when he realized what Carolyn was saying. But then he turned red as he grew embarrassed and angry. He picked the duffel bag off the floor, threw it on the bed, and then stared at her defiantly.

"Give me a copy of that lease," Carolyn demanded. "Maybe there's still time to fix this mess."

"I'm not giving you anything," Cody snapped, taking a step toward her. "You've always thought you were smarter than me. You've always tried to make me look stupid. I won't let you make a fool out of me in front of my friends. Go back to Houston. When the money starts pouring in, I may send you some of it. If you get off your high horse, that is."

Their voices had grown loud by that point and it woke their father. He shuffled into Cody's room in his pajamas and asked, "What's going on in here?"

The siblings suddenly stopped when they saw their father. Carolyn struggled to calm down. Her dad was already weak. She didn't want to worry him further.

"It's nothing, Dad," Carolyn said, walking over and putting her arm around him, and trying to calm herself down. "We were just having a little discussion. I'm sorry we woke you. Come on, I'll walk you back to your bed and tuck you in."

Carolyn's father let her take him back to his room.

Her father got into bed. "Nothing seems right anymore, Carolyn. No one is happy. People seem to want more than they have. What happened to us?"

"Oh, Dad. It's just a temporary thing. You know how Cody flares up and does impulsive things sometimes. But we'll work it out. Everything will be all right again. Please don't worry yourself. I can't stand to see you so worried."

Carolyn tucked her father under the blue cover.

When she could see he was drifting off to sleep, she left her father's bedside. She walked directly to Cody's bedroom. She wasn't surprised to see that he had left. She had heard his truck tires on the gravel road in front of the house while she was taking care of their father.

She conducted a futile search through all the drawers and closets in Cody's room to see if she could find a copy of the mineral lease, but she didn't find anything.

He had to be keeping it somewhere else—if he even had a copy of it, she thought. And she'd forgotten to ask him the name of the company he'd signed the lease with.

The next day, Carolyn looked out the kitchen window and saw that some trucks were gathered in a spot in the front pasture and men were unloading equipment. She put on her work boots, jeans, and a warm jacket and got in her car. She drove to the work site. There was enough noise to frighten the cattle and drive them into the far pastures. She got out of her car and walked up to a tall, burly man with a mustache who looked like he was a supervisor.

"Hold it, ma'am," he said, frowning and raising his right arm as if to block her. "This here's an active work site. You can't come on this property."

"Since it's my property, I can damn well go anywhere I want to on it," Carolyn replied, growing angry. "I'm Carolyn Page, and this is my land you are proposing to drill on." She surveyed the operation.

"I was told to only deal with Cody Page, ma'am. Does he know you're out here?"

"It doesn't matter what my brother knows and doesn't know," she answered in a cool voice. "This is my property, no matter what he told you, and I have every right in the world to be here. What right do you have to be here?" she asked, taking a step toward him.

The man backed away and looked perplexed now. He started to dial a number on his phone, but Carolyn said, "I asked you a simple question. Who are you working for?"

The man put his phone back in his pocket. "I'm the project manager with DiIorio Field Services. We're the servicer for this well. We were contracted by the lease holder, Hilltop Oil Company."

"And who is your contact at Hilltop?"

Suddenly, the project manager frowned. "If you are the landowner, you should know who you leased the land to, lady. I'm not sure I should be talking to you." He looked down at her muddy boots, flannel shirt, and jeans with suspicion.

Carolyn stood there for a minute, gaining control over her temper. Then she dug into her purse and pulled out her driver's license and her Texas bar card. "Here is my identification," she said. "Carolyn Page. It's the same as the name over the gate to the front drive. I am an attorney and partner with Edwards and Harrison in Houston and represent my family on legal matters. Now, who is your contact with the company?"

"Well, most of my dealings have been with their agent in town, Mr. Stevenson. His office is . . ."

It was just as she had suspected. Cody had been hoodwinked by his friend. "Never mind," she said. "I know where to find him."

Carolyn drove back to the house and went straight to her room. She hadn't brought any business clothes with her, which made her even more frustrated. If she was going to go up against a sleazy country lawyer, then she wanted to look like a powerful big-city attorney and not a mud-spattered young ranch hand. Will Hopson had told her during her first year in practice that looking powerful and successful was half the battle in a legal fight, especially if you were a woman. She mulled over her alternatives while sitting on the bed. She could either put on the best ranch clothes she had at home or put off the confrontation until she had a chance to cool off and prepare. Actually, if she went back to the office, she could research the servicer and the lessor, neither of which she had heard of before. It might be better to be fully informed and armed before going into battle, she told herself. Besides, she needed to find that lease.

16

———

arolyn had just turned on her computer on Monday morning when her telephone rang. Her secretary wasn't in the office yet, so she picked up the receiver and said, "Carolyn Page here."

"Carolyn, it's Brian Robinson. I hope you remember me. We met in Galveston several years ago in the Emergency Department at UTMB."

Of course, Carolyn thought. Paul's brother, who had helped when she'd brought Laura Petrillo to the hospital.

"Brian," Carolyn said. "Well, this is certainly a surprise."

"It has been a long time," Brian said. "And right after that the whole world blew up on September 11. But that doesn't mean I haven't thought about you. How have you been?"

Back then I thought he was patronizing, Carolyn remembered. But he was also very handsome, and she'd been frightened and exhausted. She shouldn't judge him on the basis of having met in a bad situation, she told herself.

"I've been fine," she said. "Just terribly busy with work."

"How was your holiday?"

"I've had better ones," Carolyn sighed. "Family issues, you know."

"Believe me, I do," Brian laughed. "I heard that you made partner. Congratulations. Did you drink the champagne that night to celebrate?"

"That was you? But there wasn't a note, and I didn't know who sent it or who to thank."

"Guilty," Brian said. "But don't hold that against me. I've been keeping tabs on you from a distance, even though I've been too busy to do anything about it."

"Well, I don't know what to say," Carolyn said, meaning it.

"Say you'll have dinner with me Saturday night. I'm back in Houston for good now. I finished my residency in Galveston and then did an orthopedic surgery fellowship at Johns Hopkins and a fellowship at the Mayo Clinic. But I've joined Houston Orthopedic Group and I'll be working in the Texas Medical Center. I have this fantasy that I can actually have a real life now. And I'd like to start it off with dinner with you."

Carolyn hesitated. It would be nice to dress up and have a nice dinner and wine with a non-lawyer. And she remembered him as being very handsome.

"I'd love to," she finally said.

"Great! I'll pick you up at seven tomorrow night. Do you like Italian? How about Da Marco on lower Westheimer? It's quiet and we can talk."

Da Marco was one of Carolyn's favorite restaurants. It was located in a small old house on Lower Westheimer and served authentic Italian food in a cozy atmosphere. "I'll look forward to it," Carolyn said, as she hung up.

She was still smiling when she buzzed Melissa, her legal assistant, to come to her office. Melissa was her right hand. She had earned her master's degree from Berkeley in history and was bright enough to be a lawyer herself, but was happy doing the job she had and, as she put it, having a life. She was the same age as Carolyn and an attractive, energetic young woman. They had an easy relationship, respecting each other's work.

"Can you please go on the Secretary of State's website and see what you can find on DiIorio Field Services and Hilltop Oil Company?"

"Sure," Melissa replied. "Anything else?"

"Actually, yes," Carolyn replied. "Do a Google search and see what you can find on a Jonathan Stevenson. He's a lawyer, so check

Martindale Hubble too. And just for the fun of it, after that, search for the last eight years in the state bar's disciplinary records to see if he's ever been subject to any proceedings."

"Got it," Melissa said.

Carolyn got up from her desk and walked over to the window. She studied the downtown view for a few minutes. Then she turned around quickly and added, "Search the Railroad Commission records to see what kind of permits Hilltop Oil Company has filed for drilling in Kargon County. Try to pinpoint the locations on a map." Melissa made another note on her pad.

There was a knock on Carolyn's door. "Yes?" she asked.

"It's me, Cynthia. Are you ready to go to lunch?"

"Come on in," Carolyn replied.

"I'll go," Melissa said, starting to get up.

"Wait," Carolyn said. "One more thing. Check the records of recorded leases in the Texas General Land Office. See if Hilltop Oil Company has a lease with Cody or William Page."

"Isn't that your brother and father?" Melissa asked. "Why don't you just get it from them?"

"It's complicated," Carolyn said, frowning.

"Is this for a new deal?" Melissa asked. "Should I order new files?"

"No, this is personal," Carolyn replied.

"You look worried," Cynthia said to Carolyn. "What's going on?"

"It's my damn brother," Carolyn said. "He's signed a lease on our land with some small oil company I've never heard of."

"So maybe it'll make you rich!" Cynthia smiled, gracefully sitting down in the guest chair, placing her Chanel bag on her lap.

"I don't care about being rich," Carolyn said. "I care about my dad and my family land and the people I grew up with. I think the new lawyer in town has mesmerized the locals and is ripping them off."

"So now you're Nancy Drew, out to save the family farm and the community from itself. That's kind of ironic, don't you think?"

"Meaning what?"

"Well, helping oil and gas companies drill on other people's land is a big part of what you do every day."

"This is different," Carolyn said.

"Why? Because it's your land? Never mind. I'm just ragging you," Cynthia said, getting up and walking toward the door. "Come on. Let's go to lunch."

Carolyn had never looked at it that way before—*Or maybe,* she told herself, *I've been avoiding it. W*as Cynthia right? Was she a hypocrite? Sure, she knew that drilling had some adverse side effects, but, on the whole, everyone seemed to benefit. Then again, she'd just seen what the workers were doing to her family's land, and she was no longer sure if she truly felt that way. Kenny was a good judge of character, and he'd said he thought Jonathan Stevenson was a fraud. *What did Cody get us into?*

• • •

Saturday night's dinner with Brian Robinson turned out to be one of the best nights Carolyn had spent in Houston since she'd moved there. He was even more attractive than she remembered. He was a bit on the shy or introverted side, but had a great, wry sense of humor.

"I hope you won't be disappointed in me, Carolyn, but I don't know anything about law and I've heard enough talk about oil and gas from my dad and brothers, that I don't ever want to discuss it again," he told her when they settled in at a table in the restaurant.

Carolyn laughed. "I would love to not talk about either of those subjects for once myself," she said. "I'm a bit oversaturated."

"So, read any good books lately?" Brian asked.

"As a matter of fact, I have," she said. "Novels are what keep me sane. Have you read *Pillars of the Earth*?"

"No, but I've read the reviews and it looks good. Did you like it?"

"Loved it. It's a historic fiction novel about tenth-century England. Lots of intrigue, wars, monks, disinherited princesses, etcetera. It's long, though, over a thousand pages."

"I don't know if I have time for that one. What else have you read lately that's good?"

It turned out that Brian and Carolyn shared an interest in books, especially mysteries and historical novels, although neither had as much time to read as they would have liked. Both of them loved the classic films featured on Turner Classic Movies. Brian confessed he'd been collecting old movie posters since he was a teenager and promised to show them to her one day. Carolyn felt an electricity between them during their conversation and wondered about the potential for much more.

At the end of the night, Brian asked, "Can I call you again? I had a really good time."

"I did too," Carolyn replied. "I'd love to do this again."

Brian leaned down and kissed her lightly on the lips. She felt the warmth through her whole body.

Carolyn found herself feeling happy for the first time in a long time. Brian was adorable, intelligent, and sexy. She had no interest in dating another lawyer, but Brian was a professional of a different type. He was the kind of man she envisioned falling in love with.

When she walked into her living room, a framed photo of Kenny and her hugging and smiling at their high school graduation caught her eye from across the room where it sat on a table alongside family photos. Kenny was a wonderful man and a great friend, but she just couldn't see herself as a rancher's wife. She could imagine combining her life with a doctor's though.

Two weeks later, Brian invited Carolyn to accompany him to a gala benefitting his hospital. He said he usually avoided such events, but they'd both been busy and it would give him a chance to see her again.

She accepted right away. She had to attend charity galas and fundraising events at the invitation of clients, and she usually enjoyed them. She smiled imagining herself with urbane Brian Robinson as they mixed with bright, interesting people.

The gala was held in the ballroom at the Hyatt Regency Hotel downtown. The theme was Winter Wonderland, and the room was draped in white chiffon with crystal snowflakes dangling from the ceiling. In keeping with the theme, the host committee and many of the guests wore white, and white roses were the centerpieces atop silver linens on all of the tables. The effect was enchanting.

"Oh, isn't this just lovely," Carolyn said when she surveyed the room.

"And I have the loveliest lady at the ball on my arm," Brian said.

Carolyn blushed as a distinguished-looking older couple stopped and greeted Brian.

"Who is this very attractive young lady that managed to drag you out of the hospital for an evening of frivolity, Dr. Robinson?" the woman asked in a teasing manner.

"Dr. and Mrs. Cummings, may I introduce Carolyn Page. Carolyn, Dr. Cummings is my department head at the hospital."

"Pleased to meet you," Carolyn said, smiling.

"My dear, how did you and this young man meet?" Mrs. Cummings asked. Carolyn thought she seemed genuinely fond of Brian. She obviously knew him well.

Carolyn had to think about how to answer this. "We met through Brian's brother. He is my partner at Edwards and Harrison."

"Oh my, a brain and a beauty," Dr. Cummings said. "Well, I'm pleased to meet you, Carolyn. Brian's parents are longtime friends of ours, and we have watched him grow into a fine young man and an outstanding physician. I look forward to seeing more of you." Then they drifted off to another group.

The evening was more of the same. Doctors, philanthropists, vendors, and other supporters of the hospital stopped to speak with them.

The collegial young group of doctors and their spouses and dates at their table joked and laughed through dinner. The band played soft music for the first two hours and then shifted into 1970s and 1980s rock. Brian said he wasn't much of a dancer, but somehow they ended up dancing until the band ended at midnight.

When he took her home, Brian wrapped his arms around her and gave her a long kiss at the door.

"I had a wonderful time," Carolyn said, feeling breathless.

"I can't wait to do it again," he replied. They both had to work the next day, but Carolyn hated to say good night.

· · ·

In the following months, in addition to dinners out and catching art films at the Museum of Fine Arts, Carolyn also accompanied Brian to parties hosted by his family at their home on Inwood Drive in River Oaks. These were cocktail parties where everyone discussed the price of oil, Texas Republican politics, and their latest foreign travel. Paul was always there with his pretty wife, Ashley, circulating among the guests. Carolyn noticed with approval that Brian's father liked to pick up one of Paul's twin boys and carry him around for a while until the boy's brother claimed it was his turn with Papa. He was obviously a proud, doting grandfather.

Ashley impressed Carolyn as a sweet, kind person. She couldn't imagine why Paul had been carrying on a long-term and not-so-secret affair with Lisa, the head of the firm's marketing department, who was attractive but lacked Ashley's class. Lisa was vivacious but could be loud, and she wore skirts that were a little too short for the office, but that wasn't Carolyn's business. Like almost everyone else at the firm, Carolyn just looked the other way. Paul's affair irritated Cynthia too, but she'd told Carolyn that she kept quiet because she didn't want to hurt Ashley.

The second time Carolyn and Brian attended a party at Brian's parents' home, Paul pulled her aside.

"This is getting to be a regular thing," Paul said, nodding toward his brother.

"We enjoy each other's company." Carolyn blushed.

"You make a good-looking couple. I just wanted to tell you, as Brian's elder, that I approve of whatever this is. I don't think I've ever seen my intense little brother smile so much. You have a positive effect on him."

"We have a lot of shared interests, believe it or not," Carolyn said.

"I never asked Brian. How did you two meet anyway?" Paul asked. "I didn't think he ever left the medical center, and you look pretty healthy."

"Actually, you introduced us," Carolyn said in a soft voice.

"Me?" Paul sounded surprised.

"You had him meet me at UTMB the night I took the injured summer intern to the Emergency Department after the party at your dad's beach house," Carolyn whispered.

Paul stiffened. "Oh, yeah. That's right." He looked down at the floor. "That was unfortunate—not a night I want to remember."

Was that it? Carolyn wondered. Nothing about Laura.

"So how did you and Brian get together again?" Paul awkwardly shuffled his feet.

"I hadn't heard from him until six months ago, when he called me out of the blue and asked me out to dinner."

"You haven't discussed what happened the night you met, have you? I mean . . ." Paul looked around to make sure they were alone.

Carolyn was surprised at Paul's question. "Of course not," she said. "I try to block that whole terrible night out of my mind. And he's never brought it up. We don't talk about work. We stick to pleasant things . . . art, books, funny things that happened to us. I don't know where this is going. We're both married to our careers."

Paul seemed relieved. She wondered what he was thinking when he patted her on the arm.

"I've always wondered what did happen to Laura," Carolyn ventured.

Maybe it was the wine making her feel bold enough to say it. She waited for him to answer.

Paul swirled the ice around in his glass of scotch. "I can't tell you. Besides, I'm not sure I know myself. Can we just leave it at that?" he said dismissively.

Carolyn felt like he was being patronizing. "I'd rather know," she told him. "But if you won't tell me, maybe someday somebody will."

Before Paul turned and walked away, she thought he seemed angry, but she was practically his peer now and she didn't care.

17

During the spring of 2010, the lawyers at Edwards and Harrison were swamped with work caused by the economic downturn that started in the fall of 2008. Companies needed to refinance their loans, restructure their companies, or in the worst case, file for bankruptcy. Everyone was busy. It took Carolyn's legal assistant and the firm's property management team a month to present her with the answers to the personal questions Carolyn had asked them to research.

Melissa tried to hand Carolyn the report.

"Give me the shorthand version," Carolyn said.

"Okay. First, my search of Railroad Commission records showed that a few complaints about sloppy procedures have been filed against DiIorio Field Services in the Permian Basin, but no disciplinary action has been taken against them. Second, a search for well permits in the name of Hilltop Oil Company shows ten sites clustered around Kargon County."

"What about the leases?" Carolyn asked.

"Nothing for your family. Sometimes it takes a while for things to show up, so it might just be a recording issue."

Carolyn got up and walked over to the window, thinking.

"Third, as for Jonathan Stevenson, Martindale Hubble was a dead end. He is listed, but apparently didn't have enough peer reviews to be rated. This could be due to the low number of lawyers in the area who had worked with him and answered Martindale Hubble's peer review surveys. As for state bar disciplinary complaints, there was one complaint about misuse of trust fund money, but it was resolved without action."

"Well, all that is disappointing," Carolyn said, sitting down again.

"Are you ready for the big reveal?" Melissa asked.

Carolyn looked up.

"Hilltop Oil Company is a DBA of JBH Energy, the firm's big client."

In other words, Hilltop was JBH Energy. Paul's most important client was the company drilling on her family's land. On the one hand, at least JBH Energy wasn't some fly-by-night operation, as she'd feared. On the other hand, it made it more difficult for her to confront their agent, Jonathan Stevenson, much as she wanted to do so. She knew that rocking the boat and upsetting a good client was not a great career move. She remembered another piece of advice that her old mentor, Will, had once given her: "When in doubt, do nothing." As a result, she decided to hold off for the present.

"Anything else?" Melissa asked, placing the written report on her desk.

"No, that's all for now."

In addition to her legal work, which usually meant a seventy-hour week so that she could meet and exceed the firm's billing minimums, Carolyn was spending a lot of time working on the women's shelter. She learned that a bad economy was hardest on women without independent financial resources. Domestic violence across the city had increased dramatically.

She met Cynthia after work or at Cynthia's condo in the Huntingdon a few times for drinks, and she managed to make time for a couple of dinners, as well as go to a movie with Brian. He was also working crazy hours at the hospital. She felt happy anticipating these dates. In addition to the sexual attraction they both felt, she admired his drive and ambition. Their relationship had grown intimate and Brian sometimes spent the night at her place after a date. She lived not far from the medical center, so he could usually stay, even if he was on call. The fact that he didn't demand a lot of her time because he also had a busy career made their time together feel even more exciting.

One night, Carolyn and Cynthia met at Brennan's for drinks and dinner. The bar was a favorite place for professionals to meet and relax after work, especially on a Friday night. The New Orleans atmosphere suggested casual elegance. When it was nice outside, people sat at the tables on the enclosed patio with a French-style fountain in the middle. Cynthia wanted to hear all about the current state of Carolyn's relationship with Brian Robinson, and, likewise, Carolyn wanted to know more about his past.

"Brian and I were in the same classes all through St. John's School, but I lost track of him after graduation," Cynthia said. "He was more serious and reserved than Paul and William, who were very popular and outgoing. I knew he'd become a doctor, but I didn't realize he was back in town. He was super intelligent, our class valedictorian. And he was rather good-looking, as I recall. But I don't remember him dating anyone special. Is this something serious?"

"I kinda hope so. He might just be the man I always dreamed of. We like a lot of the same things and both have careers we're passionate about. We come from different backgrounds, but I've met his family and they all seem nice . . . very family oriented."

"The Robinsons are great people. They've been friends of my parents forever. Have you taken him home to meet your dad yet?" Cynthia asked.

"No, not yet."

"Why not?"

Carolyn thought for a moment. "It's complicated," she said. "There's just a lot going on there right now."

"With your cowboy?" Cynthia asked in a sly tone.

"I told you. Kenny and I are just good friends," Carolyn said. "My relationship with Brian is an entirely different thing."

"I can't wait to see how this turns out," Cynthia said. "Down-to-earth hunky cowboy or sophisticated hot doctor: Which will win the heart of the young maiden?" she said in a dramatic tone of voice. "I'm just hoping for one of your castoffs."

"Ha ha—you could have any guy you wanted," Carolyn said. "And you know it."

"They'll have to wait. I told you, I have ambitions."

• • •

The weekend before her father's birthday in August 2010, Carolyn went home. She stopped at the meat market in town to pick up some steaks and wine for the weekend. She planned to surprise her dad with his favorite dinner. The meat market had been a staple of the community for several generations. It was located on the town square next to the café. The Hoffman family had owned it the entire time and featured local beef and pork. They also carried local canned goods, fresh bread, and beer and wine, among other things.

"I'm sorry, Carolyn. I'm completely sold out of steak of any cut," Mr. Hoffman told her.

"Well, how about your best red wine?"

"I'm clean out of wine, except the box kind, which I know you won't drink," he said.

"You've got to be kidding me," Carolyn said. "There's more cattle than people in this county. Since when have the men around here given up beer for wine?"

"You'd be surprised how much has changed around here overnight, Carolyn," Mr. Hoffman said. "All this new business is good for my bottom line. But I can hardly keep up with the change in taste. I sell out of the more expensive items that sat on the shelf before."

Carolyn scanned the shelves of wine. "I'll try this Texas wine," she said. "Vintage 2009. So what caused this renaissance in taste all of a sudden?"

"It's all this oil money that's fixing to come to town. Right now, people are mostly spending up-front rental payments. I am afraid, though, that if all these new wells come in like people expect, Walmart might hear about it and put us small boys out of business. All of the merchants are worried."

When the phone rang, Mr. Hoffman excused himself and picked up the phone. His son, Harry, hurried in from the back of the shop to take care of Carolyn.

"Have any of the new wells produced yet, Harry?" Carolyn asked.

"Yep. One of the first wells fracked over on the Jacobs ranch is flowing oil like a river. J.R. and his wife went into San Antonio, and he bought her a big white Cadillac and himself a new Ford F-150. They have been driving around waving at folks out the windows and showing off. But instead of people resenting them, they see it as a sign that everybody's gonna be rich too when their own well comes in. It's the darndest thing, Carolyn!"

"I wouldn't have expected this."

"How's it going on your daddy's ranch, Carolyn? I seen the crews and equipment out there. Hit anything yet?"

"Not that I'm aware of. But thanks for the information, if not the steaks. I'll take that rack of ribs over there and some baking potatoes—and this wine and a six pack of Shiner beer, if you please."

Cody showed up for dinner. He was in the best mood Carolyn had seen him in in years. When she asked why he was in such good humor, he gave her a smile that indicated he was pleased with himself. "Why not be happy, little sister? It won't be long before we are all richer than Houston lawyers. I told you oil was the future."

"Have any of those wells that have destroyed our peaceful front pasture started producing yet?" Carolyn asked.

"Not yet, but the Jacobs' land is producing and it's only a matter of time before ours does too. Ain't that right, Daddy?" Cody looked at his father, who gave a fierce dig with his fork at his baked potato. "Sure, son," he mumbled.

Carolyn didn't know why, but she didn't visit Kenny and his mom this trip as she usually did. Saying that she was swamped at work and had to go back to Houston, she left first thing Sunday morning.

"I wish you didn't have to go so soon," her father told her as he walked her out to her car. "Even though Cody stays around more, it gets lonely here. Shep's good company, of course," he said as he petted the dog's head, "but the conversation is limited."

"Why don't you pay Kenny's mother a visit, Dad," Carolyn suggested, getting in behind the wheel. "She probably gets lonely too. You have always enjoyed her company."

"Hm, maybe I'll do that, honey. She makes the best pie in the county, come to think of it."

"Oh, Dad." Carolyn smiled. "That's not what I meant."

"I know what you meant, honey. But that pie is really tasty too."

• • •

In late October, Carolyn got a call from Kenny. He was coming to Houston and wanted to see her after work the next night. He said it was important.

Carolyn met him at La Griglia for dinner. It was close to the office and always one of her favorite restaurants. The walls were painted with bright murals of Italian street life, making the casual atmosphere festive. The hostess knew Carolyn and always gave her a good table where she had privacy but could observe the crowd. Kenny greeted her with a hug. It was a warm night, so they sat at a table outside on the patio. It was near a busy street, but the trickling water of a fountain softened the street noise. The waiter brought them the signature basket of bread and pizza slices and handed them menus.

Kenny didn't waste any time with small talk. "Carolyn, we have a problem that could affect both of our families."

"Tell me," Carolyn said, surprised at how worried Kenny looked. He was always cool in any situation.

"You know how over the years we see migrants crossing our land heading north and avoiding the roads."

"Sure," Carolyn said. "That's nothing new."

"Well, I'm finding dead ones."

"Do you think the cartels are going after them on this side of the border?" Carolyn asked, alarmed at the thought.

"No. There aren't any bullet or knife wounds in them. One of them was a young woman. She was cradling an infant that is now in the hospital and may not survive."

The waiter interrupted them, asking to take their drink orders. Carolyn asked for a glass of pinot grigio, and Kenny ordered a beer.

"What do you think happened to them?" Carolyn asked when the waiter went away. "That's kind of scary."

"Not sure," he said. "I've thought of several possible explanations. The temperature has been up around 100 degrees for the past two weeks, so they could have died of heat stroke or dehydration."

"That makes sense."

"But there's another possibility. The bodies were close to the creek that runs between our ranches. I was surprised to find that the vegetation along the creek has turned yellow and much of it is dead. I've never seen that before, even when it's been just as hot. It seems like something in the water is killing the vegetation. Maybe the migrants drank from the creek water and got sick."

"Do you think that the creek is polluted?"

"It's possible."

The waiter came back with their drinks and handed them menus. Carolyn said, "We need a few minutes, please."

"Take your time," he said and moved to the next table to take their order.

"I hope the creek isn't polluted," Carolyn went on to Kenny. "Besides the fact we don't want anyone dying, we might have liability for whatever it is that is toxic."

"Spoken like a lawyer," Kenny teased.

"Oh, Kenny. That's not what I meant. Have you notified anyone?" Carolyn asked.

"I called the sheriff, but he didn't seem interested. It's not that unusual to find one dead. He chalked it up to heat stroke."

"You don't think he could be right?" Carolyn asked hopefully.

"Maybe. I want to send a sample of the water in the creek to the testing lab at A&M and see what they say, just to be safe. Only there's a problem."

"In addition to dead people?" Carolyn asked, raising her eyebrows.

"I would like to take a sample of the creek water upstream. You have access to it on your property. I went over there with a mason jar to take a sample and your brother confronted me with his shotgun. He told me not to touch any part of his land or water or he'd shoot me in the knee. I told him about what I found and asked him if he'd seen anything like that on his side of the creek. He said that nothing had died on his land . . . that it must be something on mine."

"What?" Carolyn raised her voice and then realized people were looking at them. "Damn Cody! He's so hardheaded and mean lately."

"Carolyn!" a man at a nearby table said, waving to get her attention. "I knew I recognized that voice."

"Hi, George. Good to see you," she replied with a wave.

The man smiled, obviously curious about the tall, muscular man in jeans and boots that Carolyn was having dinner with, but she didn't continue the conversation and turned back to Kenny.

"Sorry for the interruption," she said. "Go ahead."

Kenny looked amused at her being recognized out in public, but then he continued. "Cody's also creating quite a spectacle of himself. Since they started pumping oil from the wells on your land, he's got himself a new, big-ass truck with 'Page Ranch' on the side. He drives around town with a flashy blonde he picked up in a Sixth Street bar in Austin riding shotgun."

"Oh my God." Carolyn cringed. "I'm glad I'm not there to see it."

"Would you call him and get him to let me onto the land? He's been madder than hell since I signed a lease with an Oklahoma oil company to pull from the same reservoir as his wells. I didn't want to drill on my land, but the alternatives were letting him drain all the oil and gas under my property or drill my own wells. As I understand the rule of capture, whoever captures the product first, gets to keep it even if the reservoir extends under land you don't own. Right?"

"Right, and that was perfectly reasonable. He shouldn't be angry at you. He started this oil grab. I'm so sorry."

"We both know your brother doesn't always listen to reason. As a landowner, he should be worried about this too if he had any sense."

"I'll call him in the morning," Carolyn said. "And if he gives me a hard time, I'll come down there and get the sample myself!"

With that, Carolyn signaled to the waiter to come back. "You must be starving, after that drive," she said to Kenny. "Let's order and have another drink."

• • •

Carolyn waited until nine next morning. Then she called Cody's cell phone. It went to voicemail almost immediately. "It's your sister. Call me," she said. "It's urgent."

Cody didn't call or text all day. At five Carolyn called his cell again. When he didn't pick up, she left the same message. That night, she called the landline at the ranch.

Her father picked up, sounding delighted to hear his daughter's voice. "How are you, Dad?" Carolyn asked.

"I'm just fine, darlin'," he said. "How's the smartest girl in the county?" He sounded more like his old self.

"I'm just fine, Daddy," she replied. "Is Cody there? I need to talk to him."

"He drove to Austin this morning with friends. He probably won't be back until Monday. Is there anything your old man can do for you?"

Carolyn paused. She didn't want to involve her father in what might be a nasty situation with her brother. Instead, she impulsively said, "I just wanted to let you know I'm going to be home for a bit this weekend. I miss you."

After hanging up, Carolyn emailed Brian. She told him that she was sorry, but that something had come up and she had to go home this weekend, cancelling plans for their dinner Saturday night.

He emailed back that he understood. Then he made a surprising suggestion. He offered to drive her to the ranch. He said he'd like to meet her father since she always talked so highly of him.

Carolyn hesitated. On the one hand, she was pleased that Brian wanted to meet her family. On the other hand, there was Kenny. She always told herself that Kenny was just her oldest friend. But she also felt like she didn't want them to meet. She emailed Brian that she would love for him to meet her father, but that this was going to be a quick visit about family business. It would be better for him to come when she had time to show him around.

18

O
n Saturday morning, Carolyn left early to make the drive to the ranch. She planned to stop at the café on the square in town to get a cup of coffee and some kolaches. Before she got there, she noticed that the new McDonald's on the highway that had been under construction for the past three months had opened. The parking lot was full of cars and trucks, many of them brand-new models. Curious, she pulled in.

It was noisy inside. Parents were trying to keep their kids in their seats until they ate their food, but the children wanted to escape to the attached playground. Two women were waving at Carolyn. It was Lou Ann with Kayla, who had also been part of her elementary and high school crowd.

"My goodness, girls," Carolyn said, "I almost didn't recognize you. You've traded in your jeans for yoga pants and cut off your ponytails? And what's with the lipstick in the middle of the day?"

Lou Ann and Kayla looked at each other and laughed. "It's the product of prosperity, girl," Lou Ann said. "We've got a well on our land that's pumping out money." Holding out her left hand, she said, "Look at this rock Billy gave me for my birthday. Do you remember the teeny-tiny diamond he gave me the last year in high school as an engagement ring?" She giggled.

Carolyn estimated the diamond was at least two karats set in 18-karat white gold with baguettes on either side. "That is impressive!" Carolyn said sincerely. "You deserve nice things, Lou Ann. I'm so happy for you."

Then she asked, "Is everyone swimming in money?" She was thinking of the cars parked outside. It was so loud with children screaming and adults laughing that Carolyn felt like she was yelling. But it was good to see everyone so happy.

"Well, no, of course not," Lou Ann said. "The ranchers with oil or gas under their land are doing well. And I guess the business owners are prospering. The bars are doing well as a result of all the oil workers in town." In a lower voice she said, "Although some of them are not the kind you want to socialize with, if you know what I mean."

"Oil field trash and that sort," Kayla whispered. "But mostly they stay out of town during the week at least. The oil companies have built what they call man camps to house their workers. Best stay away from those places. Although there's a rumor one is going up on the back part of your ranch, Carolyn."

"What?" Carolyn asked. "Definitely not!"

"Let's not talk about that," Lou Ann stopped Kayla. "Hey, Billy and I are having a few old friends over tonight. Billy is perfecting his grilling technique with bone-in rib eyes. No more hamburgers. Why don't you come?"

"I don't know if I'll have time," Carolyn said. "I'm only here for a short visit to see my dad. I'll add the rumor you heard to the list of items I want to talk to Cody about."

"Bring your dad, honey. I'm sure Cody's busy though."

"Thanks. That sounds like fun, but I'll have to see how it goes."

"Okay, honey. But we'd love to have you and your dad. Why don't you call Kenny and ask him to pick you up?" she added, winking at her.

"Why do I get the impression you're trying to be a matchmaker?" Carolyn asked.

"Why not?" Lou Ann asked, as one of her children came up to ask her for money for a game machine. "None of us are getting any younger, you know, and your biological clock is ticking, girl. I can't think of a better man for you than Kenny Prichard."

"Honestly, Lou Ann," Carolyn sighed. "I'm getting a cup of coffee. I'll see about tonight."

• • •

Carolyn stopped at Kenny's house before she went home. She wondered if anything else had happened that she needed to know. Mrs. Prichard greeted her at the door, wearing one of her flowered home-made aprons, her hands white with flour.

"Looks like I got here right on time, Mrs. Prichard. Is that the beginning of pie crust?"

Kenny's mother smiled. "Mabel Shouse brought some peaches back from visiting her son in Fredericksburg. She gave me just enough for my recipe. It won't be out of the oven for thirty minutes though. Can you stay?"

"I should get on over to the ranch and see Daddy. But thank you. I was hoping to talk to Kenny. Is he here?"

Just then Kenny walked into the room. "Thanks for coming home, Carolyn."

"Of course," Carolyn replied. "I've been worried about what you told me. I wanted to check in and see if you'd learned anything else before I ride out to the back pastures to get a water sample from the creek. Dad told me Cody's in Austin. I should also get a sample from the old well behind our house to check the groundwater."

"I'm glad you came by before you went out there. I can't see what all is going on at your ranch, but there's a lot of activity—more than I would have expected in the back pasture. Lots of trucks and men. I don't want you going out there alone," he said.

"Sure. Come over to our place in a half an hour. I'll say hello to Dad, put on some boots, and saddle up Brownie. Then we can ride cross-country."

"Right behind you," Kenny said.

Turning to leave, she whispered in Mrs. Prichard's ear, "And when we're done with business, Dad and I will be back for some of that pie."

When Kenny met Carolyn at her stable, she was surprised to see that he had his shotgun across the saddle and a pistol in his belt. "Are you riding the back pastures or going into combat, Lieutenant?" she asked.

"Don't know yet." He shrugged. "Some of those fellas I've seen on your land don't look too genteel, and I've noticed one or two are carrying firearms."

Carolyn was uneasy. "Most companies have a policy against having firearms on-site unless they're locked in their truck in full view."

"That's my understanding," Kenny said.

Carolyn had talked to her father long enough to know he had no idea what was really happening on his own ranch. He was only in his sixties, but she detected he was not the mentally sharp, focused man she once knew. She noticed the buildings needed some maintenance and the vegetation in front of the house was overgrown. Brownie looked like she needed grooming. She made a mental note to ask Kenny if she could board her horse at his place.

They decided to ride to the farthest point in the ranch, where the creek entered the Page property, to take their first sample. Shep ran alongside Carolyn's horse. When they came over a rise and down the other side, not that far from the creek, Brownie stumbled. Carolyn was an accomplished rider and she caught her balance. But she looked back to see what Brownie had tripped over.

"Oh my God!" she shrieked. Behind her, sticking out of a patch of high weeds, was the blue-jean-clad leg of a little boy. Shep saw it and started barking loudly.

Kenny rode up from behind and looked where she was staring. "Damn! Another one!" he said, getting down from his horse. He brushed the weeds aside so that he could see whether the child was alive. He wasn't, although it didn't look like he had been there for very long. The turkey buzzards had not started circling overhead. Kenny checked to see if there were any signs of gunshot or knife wounds, or of a struggle. "Nada," he said to Carolyn.

"What should we do?" Carolyn asked Kenny. She was shaking.

"Let's finish what we came out here to do. Then we'll go back to your place and I'll call the sheriff to send someone out here to get this poor boy."

"Let's not go all the way to the back of the ranch today," Carolyn said. "We're beyond where the creek enters your land. Let's take our sample now. If there is something in the water here, it makes sense it's upstream."

Kenny didn't agree, but it was obvious that Carolyn was anxious for their expedition to end before they found any other dead bodies. He took the clean mason jars they had brought along over to the creek, filling them with samples of the water. Mounting his horse, he said to Carolyn, "Let's go."

When they approached the ranch, Carolyn was disappointed to see her brother's new truck parked out front. He heard their approach and met them at the front door, legs spread, arms crossed, and a scowl on his face. "Where've you two been?" he growled.

"We need to talk," she said in an angry voice.

Her brother glared at Kenny. "I thought I told you not to set foot on my land, Prichard."

"Kenny is our neighbor and my guest. He is welcome here anytime. You have no right to talk to him like that," Carolyn retorted.

Kenny stared Cody in the eyes, standing his ground like the Marine he was.

"I'll talk to him any way I want to, sis. I'm running the ranch now, or haven't you noticed?"

"I've noticed you making a mess of the ranch. I heard a rumor in town that one of those man camps is going up at the back of the ranch. Is that true? You don't have authority to permit that, and I certainly wouldn't agree to it. This is my home and our dad's ranch as long as he is alive, not *your* ranch."

A short, well-endowed young woman with a sorry bleach job, wearing a lot of makeup and a tight pair of jeans and boots, got out of Cody's truck and slowly walked onto the porch. She wore a tightly stretched T-shirt that said, "Willy." "Ain't you goin' to introduce me to these folks?" She stared up at Cody with a bored smile. Then she looked up at Kenny and her smile changed to one of seduction. "I don't think we've met," she said. "I'm Angela."

"Hey, Angela," Kenny said.

"I told you to stay in the truck!" Cody barked at her.

"Damn, don't get your panties in a wad," the woman retorted, but she waved "bye" at Kenny and returned to the truck, sulking.

"Really?" Carolyn said to her brother, looking after Angela.

"Look, I'm making us rich while you're off in Houston playing lawyer. That makes it my ranch," he stormed at Carolyn.

"I haven't noticed any money flowing into my bank account from these wells yet," Carolyn retorted. "And I'd wager neither has Dad. Why is that?"

"You'll get your share," Cody mumbled, taking a step back from her.

"I'd like to see the books from these enterprises of yours. Give them to me. I'll take them back to Houston with me."

"Can't do that," he said, on the defensive now.

"Why not? You're such a great businessman, you must have them in shipshape and close at hand."

Cody didn't say anything. He looked at the truck and gave Angela an irritated look. She had turned on the radio, raised the volume, and the Charlie Daniels Band was wailing "The Devil Went Down to Georgia."

"We'll put that aside for just a minute," Carolyn said. "How about this: Have you found any dead migrants on the ranch lately?"

Cody didn't answer, but she could see his face turning red, even under his tan. Finally, he blurted, "Of course not!"

"You sure about that? Because Brownie and I just stumbled over a dead Mexican boy not a quarter mile from here on our property. And Kenny found two dead migrants on his property last week—not to mention dead livestock."

"What exactly is all that activity on your back pasture?" Kenny asked. "There're rumors going around about illegal activities—underage girls and whatnot."

"You're lying," Cody yelled. "If you found dead Mexicans on your land, maybe the cartels are chasing them. And what happens on my property is none of your damn business, Prichard."

Cody pushed past Carolyn and retreated to his truck with Shep on his heels, barking loudly. Cody kicked Shep out of the way and got in the driver's seat. He was talking on his cell phone by the time he turned on the motor.

• • •

Kenny's mother prepared a true country supper of fried chicken, collard greens, and mashed potatoes that evening. It was just what Carolyn needed after their unnerving confrontation with Cody, and she could tell her father was enjoying it too. It was after they had devoured the peach pie and Kenny and Carolyn were sitting on the porch swing drinking beer that the sheriff called. Kenny went inside to talk to him.

When he came back outside, the screen door slammed shut and he was swearing to himself.

"What did he say about the dead boy?" Carolyn asked.

"He said two deputies went out there and looked all over. They didn't find any bodies."

"Someone took it?" Carolyn asked. "Who would do that?"

"I don't know," Kenny said. "But I'd bet you a hundred dollars your brother does."

"I hope not, but I won't take that bet," Carolyn sighed.

19

When Ann first arrived in the District of Columbia in 2005, she rented an apartment in Alexandria, Virginia. It was cramped and undistinguished, and she had to walk a half mile to the nearest metro stop, but it was all she could afford on her new government salary. She had a student loan to pay off too. She found furniture, which she painted or repaired, at second-hand and consignment shops. It was only a slight improvement from her lodgings the previous year while she was finishing law school and counting every penny.

But there was an electricity about D.C. that made even the most mundane job feel special for small-town young people beginning their careers. In particular, Ann was excited about joining the Securities and Exchange Commission. In recent years, the agency had scored several major coups against companies and agencies that regularly tried to game the system by regarding financial regulations as impediments to be gotten around. An investigation of the insurance giant, AIG, for improper accounting of sham reinsurance transactions resulted in $800 million in disgorgement and penalties. Tyco International was investigated for utilizing unlawful accounting practices in a scheme to overstate its reported financial results by $1 billion. And in 2004, Royal Dutch Shell was cited for overstatement of hydrocarbon reserves and paid $120 million in penalties. In that year alone, the agency produced over $3 billion in penalties and disgorgement. The agency's prestige was at a high point. For a young lawyer, it seemed an exciting place to build a career.

Ann believed all her hard work had paid off. She had found the perfect job. She would be part of a team that held the high and mighty accountable for abusing and defrauding the investing public.

There were other reasons that Ann liked living in Washington. Her paternal grandfather had been born in Italy. He loved opera, and the thing Ann remembered most about him was that he always had opera music playing in his house, especially Verdi. For Ann's twelfth birthday, her grandfather had taken her on the train from Atlantic City to Philadelphia to attend a performance of a Verdi opera at the Academy of Music. Ann thought she had gone to heaven when she entered the ornate building with its many gilded balconies and stories. Even though they sat far from the stage, she thought it was the most magical night of her childhood. She took every opportunity to attend performances by opera companies that came to the D.C. area, often dragging Amanda, who preferred jazz and R&B, along with her.

Except for her friendship with Amanda, during her first two years in D.C., Ann kept to herself. Mentally, she was still stifled by what she considered her mistakes in the past. But as she scored small victories at work, she became more self-confident. When coworkers invited her to go for a drink after work on Friday night, she usually made herself go with them. She avoided men's flirtations, however, and she didn't stay out late.

She had taken up running after she married Joey. At first, she would run when she felt depressed or upset. She especially loved to run on the Ocean City boardwalk where the sea breezes off the Atlantic Ocean, and the exercise always calmed her down. After she moved to D.C., running became almost an obsession. Every Saturday morning, she ran the National Mall. She ran in the Marine Corp Marathon one year and was hooked. After that, she and Amanda, who she persuaded to take up the sport, ran at least three marathons all over the East Coast every year, eventually getting their times down so that they qualified for the Boston Marathon.

Despite good intentions, she didn't follow up on her plan to make the four-hour trip home regularly. She felt guilty. But she cringed when her mother asked her if she was seeing anyone seriously or her father bemoaned the fact that there was no one in the family to whom he could pass on his business.

One time, when she did make the trip, she ran into Joey and his new wife, a girl from Atlantic City, and their baby at Midnight Mass at the church in which she and Joey had been married. They hugged awkwardly and Ann admired the baby. She was glad that Joey seemed happy, but she still felt pained about what she had done to him. She determined to avoid such encounters in the future. Her trips home to the Jersey Shore became even more infrequent.

After four years in Alexandria, she was able to move to a small apartment in Georgetown. She had painted the walls light gray and hung modern art prints on the walls. It became her peaceful retreat in the middle of a charming city neighborhood.

She made friends with several of the single women who lived in the same neighborhood, but she avoided men. She told herself it was because she was focusing on advancing her career. But the real reasons were that she didn't trust men and she felt guilty for what she had done to Joey. Once, Amanda made a suggestion.

"I work with this really nice, smart guy at the EPA that I would love for you to meet," she said one day. "He's very attractive and he's nice-looking."

Ann didn't say anything, so Amanda persisted. "He told me he isn't seeing anyone seriously and would like to meet new people. I was thinking it might be fun if you guys double-dated with Deshaun and me one night. There's a new Ethiopian restaurant we've been wanting to try. How about it?"

"Thanks," Ann said. "I appreciate the offer, really. But I'm coming off of a bad relationship and I'm just not interested in meeting anyone right now."

"Is it something you want to talk about? You know I don't believe in dwelling on old problems. Maybe I could help?"

"You're sweet, Amanda, but I'm just not ready to talk about it. Maybe one day."

She had been at the SEC for only three years when the collapse of the Wall Street banks occurred. It was 2008. Bear Stearns, Lehman Brothers, and other entities that had promoted risky collateralized debt obligations, particularly subpar mortgage-backed securities and fee-generating derivatives, failed, crashing the entire financial market. Ann and the other agency lawyers struggled to figure out what had happened to cause the implosion and who the culprits were in the complicated derivatives market with uneven success.

Two years later, a new chairman of the commission was named and announced a more aggressive policy for the agency's division of enforcement. The director of that division had heard about Ann's reputation for toughness, diligence, and hard work, and promoted her to a senior attorney position. Ann was elated. She felt like going after the bankers and others that caused millions of average citizens to lose their life savings was a mission from God. She threw herself into her work even harder.

One Friday evening in July 2010, after another long workweek, Ann picked up the new *Forbes* magazine from the unopened mail that had piled up on her coffee table. When she saw the picture on the cover, she gasped, feeling her face flush as her heart raced. Under the heading "King of the Texas Frackers" was a photo of the man whose face had appeared in her nightmares, although she had tried for years to forget it. Seeing that face made her feel sick. She trembled so hard that she had to drop the magazine.

After a few minutes, she felt her heart rate become more even. She was able to pick up the magazine again and study the picture. He was wearing jeans, cowboy boots, a white western shirt, and a belt with a silver A&M belt buckle. On his hand was the huge turquoise ring that she had noticed when he handed her the aspirin that night at the beach house in Galveston. *It's him,* she thought.

She flipped to the story. The article said that the man's name was

Joe Bill Hawkins and that he was president of JBH Energy. The second page had a picture of four men dressed in camouflage hunting clothes. They were standing together in a field under a sprawling live oak tree. Two short Hispanic-looking men stood in the background. Hawkins was holding a shotgun, and there was a pile of dead birds on the ground in front of them. The caption read, "In Texas, business is made building relationships in the outdoors as much as the office."

Ann studied the faces. She recognized one of them as the man who had hosted the recruiting party—Paul Robinson. She thought she might have talked to the man identified as Trey Jorgensen, but she didn't think she had ever seen Peter Kaufman. They were all standing tall, with broad, self-satisfied smiles.

The article described in glowing terms the rise of the company from its humble beginnings as JBH Oil Company in Oklahoma, to a publicly traded, highly successful Houston energy company in a relatively short amount of time. The writer credited the four men with a long relationship that was the secret ingredient in the success of the company. Robinson and Hawkins were described as best friends and compatriots.

Ann closed her eyes and leaned back against the couch cushions. She felt the emotion that she had felt when she learned what the investment banks had done to crash the US economy—righteous anger. *They look so smug*, she thought. They ruined people's lives and became prosperous and carefree, with no adverse consequences for their actions. Hawkins and Robinson, she decided, had caused her to lose years of her life and her dignity—someone they could treat like a joke and throw away.

Ann had tried hard not to think about her disastrous experience in Texas. When a nightmare, after reading or hearing the name Edwards and Harrison, which had an active securities practice, caused her to remember, she still felt shame. She avoided working on any projects in which the firm was involved. At the time, she thought the incident was a moral failure on her part as much as anything.

But she was older, more experienced, and self-confident now. She examined what had happened that night from a new, more mature perspective—the perspective of a seasoned, expert investigator. She hadn't had too much to drink, she knew. Maybe the aspirin had been a date rape drug. She'd read about men taking advantage of women that way.

She got up and went to the kitchen to find the bottle of vodka she kept to serve company. She poured some Grey Goose into a martini glass, twisted some lemon into it, and lifted it as if to make a toast. *Here's to you bastards,* she thought, looking once more at the cover of the magazine. *Enjoy the good times for as long as they last. I'm finally on to you.*

The first thing Ann did after returning to the office the following Monday was to run internet searches of JBH Energy, Joe Bill Hawkins, and Paul Robinson. As the *Forbes* article stated, JBH Energy had grown to be one of the biggest players in the fracking industry. They had operations in several states, largely as the result of acquisitions of smaller companies. She made a note of the companies.

A search under its prior name, JBH Oil, unearthed a 2001 article from an Oklahoma newspaper that recounted in scathing terms the story of Joe Bill's acquisition of a large part of Oakland Oil's properties. There was a quote from the owner, Tom Oakland, that "Joe Bill Hawkins is an unethical man who doesn't give a damn about ruining the lives of innocent people to get what he wants." *You can say that again,* Ann thought.

Next, she typed in the name Paul Robinson. There were links to legal articles he had authored, mostly in the area of mergers and acquisitions, articles about large deals he had closed and a link to Harrison and Edwards' website. She read his bio. He was from Houston and spent his entire career at the firm. He graduated from Texas A&M University and the University of Texas Law School and was married to Ashley Masters Robinson. They had two children. Paul had been a championship tennis player.

Searches for the other two men revealed that Trey was also a corporate partner at the firm and Peter was a CPA with Kaufman and Stone, a midsize Houston accounting firm. She wasn't certain that she saw Trey at the beach house and knew she hadn't seen Kaufman, so she didn't go any further.

Finally, she did a search of Carolyn Page.

So she's a partner now, Ann saw. She wondered what Carolyn had done to get where she wanted to be. *She's probably never given me a second thought,* she thought bitterly.

She started to read an article about Carolyn's work with abused women when her secretary knocked on the door and entered.

"Ann, you have a ten o'clock meeting upstairs. Did you forget?"

"I guess I did, Marie. I was preoccupied." She grabbed a folder off her desk and started for the door. "Oh, would you pull all the filings for JBH Energy since it went public?" She tucked the information she had gathered away in her mind.

At the SEC, Ann had developed a style of working that involved gathering as much background information as possible about a company or transaction, analyzing it carefully and devising an action plan to pursue the target she suspected of breaking the securities laws. She was thoughtful and intentional, never rushing to take action before she had all the facts. In the same way, she thought about how to exact her revenge on the men who had abused her. But she also had a lot of work on her desk, and was mindful not to let her personal agenda get in the way of her success.

• • •

In October, Ann got an opportunity to find out more about Paul Robinson. She was on a panel on new SEC regulations at an American Bar Association Corporate Law Section conference in New York. One of the other panelists was a senior associate female lawyer from Harrison and Edwards, and Ann met her when the panelists gathered beforehand in a small meeting room at the Marriott Times Square Hotel to plan their session.

"Hi, Amy." Ann offered her hand. "My name is Ann Meyers. I'm the representative from the United States Securities and Exchange Commission on the panel."

"I'm so glad to meet you," the young woman said. "I am excited about the opportunity to be on the panel with you and hear what you have to say."

After exchanging the usual pleasantries, Ann asked, "Are you alone in New York too?"

"I am."

"Well, since we are both flying single, would you like to join me for dinner tonight? I've always wanted to go to Buddha. I hear it's very good."

"I'd love to," Amy said. "How about seven?"

"Perfect," Ann said. "I'll get the concierge to make a reservation. I assume you're staying at the convention hotel too?"

• • •

Buddha was full of customers and the atmosphere was electric. It was a dark, large, high-ceilinged room with Asian artifacts on the walls, incense in the air, and a large statue of Buddha as the centerpiece. Electronic music was loud and tables were close together, so the noise was at a high level. It was the kind of place in New York City where the diners felt like they were in the middle of the most exciting place in the world. Ann and Amy got along immediately. Amy reminded Ann of herself in a way, and she could tell that the younger woman was happy to make such an important contact at the SEC.

By eight, the women had finished their martinis at the bar. When the maître d' seated them at a table, Ann ordered a bottle of good wine.

"So," Ann said, "I've been boring you about the SEC. Tell me about your firm. What is it like working there?"

"It's great," Amy said. "Lots of friendly people and good work for great clients."

"I saw the article in *Forbes* about your client, JBH Energy. That sounds like a great client to have. Is it yours?"

"Oh, no," Amy laughed. "Paul Robinson's. He and Joe Bill Hawkins are like brothers. I hear they are glued at the hip."

"Oh, dear, that must be inconvenient for their families." Ann smiled a wicked smile.

"I don't know about Joe Bill, but Paul does. He has a wife and two children. I guess they are used to him being gone *all* the time though." Amy giggled.

"Is he with his client at night too?" Ann winked at Amy, who had finished her second glass of wine.

"I wouldn't say it's his client he was with exactly," Amy said. "If you know what I mean."

"Ah, men in power," Ann whispered. "They do enjoy the perks of the office, don't they? I see it in government all the time. Tell me, is it the proverbial secretary?"

Amy hesitated. Then she giggled again. "No, it's the marketing director. They've been an item forever. It's not much of a secret. Everybody knows about it. Except his poor wife. Or maybe she does but doesn't want to rock the boat. I guess sometimes the wife of the cheater likes having the benefits of being Mrs. Whatever and tolerates the infidelities until they become an embarrassment."

"I've heard that," Ann said. "I see what I wanted here," she said, laying her menu aside. "What did you decide to order?"

• • •

As soon as Ann returned to D.C., she called Amanda and invited her over to have a glass of wine. Amanda said Deshaun was in Denver, so she'd love to.

"How was New York?" Amanda asked after they had settled in with their wine and brie.

"Informative," Ann said.

"What are the defenders of big business up to now?"

"It's more like a couple of particular defenders of big business," Ann said. "Now I need to figure out what, if anything, I should do about it."

"You know what to do. Go after them, girl!"

"It's more complicated than that. Actually, it's personal, and that makes it tricky," Ann said. "That's why I asked you to come over. I need an objective opinion, and I trust your discretion."

Amanda made a motion like she was locking a lock in front of her lips.

"This is something that I have never told anyone. Not even you." Ann hesitated for a minute. She didn't like revisiting Galveston in her mind, but it was time to get past that.

"Sometimes it's better if you get it out, rather than reliving it in your mind, whatever it is," her friend said softly. "You can trust me not to repeat whatever is bothering you."

Ann nodded in agreement. "I told you I was coming off of a bad relationship. Actually, it was a series of bad experiences that have haunted me. After my second year in law school at the University of Pennsylvania, I took a summer internship at Edwards and Harrison in Houston."

"That's a prestigious firm," Amanda commented. "How was it?"

Ann grimaced. "At the end of the first week, my associate sponsor took me to a party at a partner's beach house in Galveston. There was a lot of drinking and it was a big house, so some people, including us, spent the night. It was all proper, but I had a headache about two in the morning and went downstairs to see if I could find some Tylenol. A man I hadn't seen at the party offered me a couple of aspirin. Almost immediately, I felt dizzy and fell on the floor. I felt someone pulling

off my pants and laughing at me. I was raped! Then I blacked out," she
said to Amanda.

"Oh my God," Amanda said. "That's horrible. Did you report it?"

"I was twenty-four years old, in a strange new city where I knew
no one except the people who had abused me, and some of them were
with the law firm where I was clerking. Who would I tell and who
would believe me? I felt embarrassed and ashamed. Like I said, I've
never told anyone. Not even my parents or my ex-husband."

Ann stopped and took a sip of her wine before continuing. "I woke
up in a hospital. I have no idea how I got there. But as soon as I could
get out of bed, with a broken arm and horrendous headache, I fled on
foot and got a flight home."

"What did you do then?"

"I gave up on having a legal career and did what everyone does at
home. I married the first guy who asked me. I told you I was divorced.
Poor Joey; I was a wreck when I married him, hoping to forget about
law and change my life. I wasn't suited or ready for marriage and children, which he wanted right away, so I asked him for a divorce. That's
the kindest thing I did for him. He's happily remarried and has at least
one child."

"What did you tell the law firm about why you were leaving early?"

"That's the worst of it. No one at Edwards and Harrison ever called
to ask why I left or to check if I was okay. That made the shame even
worse." Ann looked away.

"What bastards!" Amanda exclaimed, getting up and sitting beside
her. She wrapped her arms around Ann and held her.

After a few minutes when Ann stopped shaking, Amanda asked,
"So what made you want to tell me now?"

Ann picked up the *Forbes* magazine and opened it to the page with
the picture showing all four of the Midnight Cowboy Poker Club and
pointed at Joe Bill and Paul.

"I didn't ever want to talk about it. Until I saw this. I'll never forget
their faces, and now I know their names."

"So what now?" Amanda took the magazine from Ann and examined the faces of the men, grimacing.

"That's what I have to decide. I thought I had put it behind me, but reading this article made me furious. I still am! These self-satisfied, arrogant bastards have gone about their lives with no recriminations, while I have been suffering ever since."

"You should be furious!" Amanda said, tossing the magazine back on the coffee table like it was something distasteful.

"I've done a little due diligence on them since I read this article. Both Hawkins and Robinson are bad characters in general. Hawkins is a bully and a cheat according to another oil industry man who Hawkins cheated. I met an associate with Edwards and Harrison in New York who told me that Robinson has been carrying on an open affair for years while he is married with two small children."

"Of course," Amanda sneered.

"Do you think their business dealings bear looking into with a fine-tooth comb?" Amanda asked with a sly smile. "I think you would be justified."

"I wouldn't be surprised if one or both of them didn't run afoul of the law eventually. I just need to be patient and on the alert. But I would be using the power of the federal government to prosecute people who did me a personal insult. Is that wrong?"

"No. You're totally justified," Amanda said. "I've had to deal with my share of harassment from predatory men in my career, especially when I was just starting out—but nothing as horrible as what you went through."

Ann picked up the magazine again, which was open to the picture of the Midnight Cowboy Poker Club. "I can't help it. I want to see them get their just deserts!"

"I'll keep my ears open. Cheaters have a way of keeping on cheating."

20

One Monday morning in early November, Carolyn could tell something was out of the ordinary. Her office was on the other side of the building from Paul's, but she had to pass his office to get to the ladies' room. As she drew near, she saw that his door was closed, but she could hear people yelling inside. The loudest voice was Paul's. She had never heard him raise his voice in the office. He was usually cool and totally professional. The other voice was unfamiliar. Then someone opened the door quickly and a man came out, turned toward the elevator bank, and didn't look back. Paul slammed the door shut behind his visitor.

All morning, Paul and Trey were closeted in Paul's office. Just after noon, a sharply dressed older woman wearing stylish sunglasses and carrying a Hermes Birkin bag and a slim leather briefcase arrived. Paul's assistant ushered her into his office and closed the door.

Everyone on the floor knew something was going on but didn't know what had happened. At five p.m. Carolyn's assistant buzzed her and said that Brian wanted to speak with her. She picked up the receiver.

"How was your trip home?" Brian asked.

"I wouldn't say it was a lot of fun," Carolyn answered.

"Well, I don't think I can cheer you up," Brian said, "but I'd like to talk with you. How about if I pick you up around six and we have a drink at the Lancaster? I'll take you back to the office after we talk if you like."

The Lancaster was a small boutique hotel nestled in the heart of Houston's Theater District. The bar was a narrow, dark, quiet area frequented by guests and favored by theatergoers. Seated at a table in the corner away from the crowd at the bar, Carolyn and Brian settled in. Brian ordered a glass of Roederer chardonnay for Carolyn and a Maker's Mark Manhattan for himself.

"Carolyn, I need to ask you something delicate."

"Of course," Carolyn said. *He's acting very serious.*

"Ashley filed for divorce today. A processor served Paul with the papers this morning."

"Oh! So that's what the uproar was about," Carolyn said. "I knew it was something bad, but I didn't think of that. Every time I've seen them together, they seem like a perfect family." Carolyn pictured the cute blonde little boys she had seen running around their grandparents' house.

"I always thought so," Brian said, "although I haven't been around much until recently. I've known Ashley my whole life and think of her as a big sister." He sighed.

"What happened?" Carolyn asked.

"According to my mother, someone—who Ashley won't name—told her that Paul has been having a longtime affair with a woman who works at the firm. They told Ashley that everyone at the firm knows about it." Brian leaned forward with a questioning look.

"Oh," was all Carolyn could say, but she shifted self-consciously in her seat.

The waiter brought their drinks and she took a sip of her wine.

"Paul is denying everything to my parents. Mother has been driving me crazy with calls all day. She can't believe her golden child would do such a thing. She's afraid this could ruin his chances of becoming managing partner of the firm someday. You probably know that's always been their goal. She's up in arms, furious at Ashley, and telling Paul he should fight for full custody of the children." Brian slumped back in his chair and waved an arm in the air, as if to indicate he thought this was absurd.

"He doesn't have time to raise children," Carolyn said.

"Of course not. But I need to know how to deal with my mother," Brian said. "So tell me: Is it true that everyone at the firm thinks Paul has been having an affair? Just tell me honestly what you know. I'll never tell anyone I heard it from you. Promise."

Carolyn studied Brian. He didn't appear to be upset. His demeanor was calm, but his gaze was intense. She sometimes wondered if his training as a doctor caused him to approach difficult diagnoses with a clinical detachment. She remembered how noncommittal he'd been the night she first met him. She'd been a bit suspicious then, but now that she knew him better, she realized that was just his very rational way of looking at problems and holding off on a decision until he had all the facts. Then she thought about his parents and how this scandal would rock their perfect world.

Carolyn shifted in her seat again and chose her words carefully. "I don't know anything about who told Ashley," Carolyn said slowly. "But many people have thought for a long time that Paul and Lisa, the head of marketing, have been in a relationship."

"Is she married?" Brian asked.

"She was, but I heard that she recently got divorced. I don't know why."

"Do you believe the rumors are true?" Brian asked, looking at her with a steady gaze.

"You are putting me in a bad situation, Brian," Carolyn protested. "What Paul does is none of my business. Besides, your brother is my section head. Paul has a lot of power over my career."

"He'll never know that you told me anything," Brian said. "I swear I'll deny it if he asks me if I discussed any of this with you." He reached out and put his hand on her arm.

"At the risk of sounding cynical," Carolyn said, "a lot of morally questionable things go on in law firms that you just have to ignore. Otherwise, you wouldn't last very long."

"Do you believe it's true?" Brian asked again.

Carolyn thought back to the night at the beach house when Paul and the others had put her in a terrible situation. She'd seen Lisa and Paul coming out of his office late at night many times. Sometimes they left the office together after work, and they were usually together at firm events. They didn't really try to keep their relationship a secret. Paul assumed he was invincible.

Carolyn had been spending all her free time with Brian. She cared for him, and she hated to see him caught in the crosshairs. A picture of Ashley and her beautiful children formed in her mind. Finally, she said, "Yes, I believe it's true."

"Thank you," Brian said. "I know I'm putting you in an awkward situation. I promise I'll never do it again. But I just had to know. I don't want Ashley to be mistreated. She and the kids are the victims here, despite what Paul and my mother think."

Brian's last comment hit a nerve for Carolyn. She knew that she had grown cynical since she went to work at the firm. She'd considered the painful effect of Paul's infidelity on Ashley and his children, but hadn't thought about it too deeply, certainly not enough to do anything about it, even if she could. *Unlike his brother,* she thought now, *Brian is a truly kind, caring man. I'm lucky to have found him.*

· · ·

Paul and Ashley's divorce became a hot topic of gossip in the firm and River Oaks society. It went unusually fast, but Ashley told friends that she had been suspicious for a long time and she was adamant about cutting ties. Carolyn learned from Brian that Paul and Ashley were sharing custody of the children, but that Ashley had primary control. Through Cynthia, she found out that the management committee called Paul on the carpet for engaging in an improper affair with an employee. He received a slap on the wrist and was told that if Lisa filed a sexual harassment lawsuit, he would experience more stringent punishment. Lisa was forced to resign from her position, receiving a generous separation package in return for signing a confidentiality and non-litigation agreement.

• • •

One night at the end of November, Kenny called Carolyn just before she was getting ready for bed.

"I'm sorry for calling so late," he said, "but I knew you would want to get this information as soon as possible."

"What information?"

"I got the report back from Texas A&M about the water sample I sent them. The water contains a high level of residuals or drilling waste product. The chemicals are a bucketload of various toxic chemicals and heavy metals." Carolyn could tell that Kenny was angry.

"Drilling waste?" Carolyn exclaimed.

"It looks like some disposal company has been illegally dumping. We need to report it," Kenny said, "before more damage is done. When it has water in it, the creek feeds into the river that runs through several small towns downstream. The report says that drinking the water won't kill you instantly, but exposure over time can cause cancer, learning disabilities in children, or other health issues."

"Damn!" Carolyn said. "I've read about that happening in other places in the country, but I never dreamed it would be a problem in rural Kargon County. Can you notify the Texas Commission on Environmental Quality in the morning?" Carolyn asked.

"I'll call them first thing." She thought he sounded seriously worried.

Carolyn called him three days later to ask him how the state was reacting to the pollution of the creek running through their ranches.

"Nada," Kenny said. "I don't understand it. They're usually pretty quick to act. I thought that there would be inspectors out here right away, but it seems to be business as usual with the drillers and not a state person in sight. The only unusual thing is that a fire started in my barn last night. It could have caused a lot of damage except that I drove in late from an electric cooperative board meeting and saw it before it could really blow up. I was able to put it out with a hose."

"You sound frustrated," Carolyn said.

"I am."

Carolyn felt a chill. "You don't think it's related to your report, do you?"

"I hope not, but a lot of suspicious things seem to be happening in our quiet little piece of paradise lately." Kenny sighed.

"Do you think it would do any good to alert the sheriff about what you've found?" Carolyn asked.

"I plan on visiting the coroner's office when I'm in town tomorrow," he told her. "I want to find out what he determined was the cause of death for the migrants we found on our land. Then I'll go see Sheriff Jones."

"Let me know what you find out," Carolyn said. "I think we have a responsibility to the community to warn them of the danger. And, Kenny," she said, "please be careful."

Kenny called Carolyn again the next evening. "I visited the medical examiner at his office this afternoon and asked him what he determined was the cause of death of the dead migrants on our land."

"Was it poisoning?"

"We'll never know," Kenny said, in a disgusted tone of voice.

"Why not?"

"Dr. Sekula told me the county doesn't spend resources on doing autopsies on dead illegals. They just go ahead and bury them in the back of the county cemetery with the other itinerants and unidentified bodies. Hold on, I'm making a turn here." *He must be on his cell phone,* Carolyn thought.

She put down the documents she had been working on at her desk.

"It would be a public health issue if they died from drinking polluted water. Did you tell him that?"

"I did. I even suggested they dig up one of the bodies and run some tests. I offered to pay the costs."

"And?"

"He said he had too much work to fool around with random suspicions. He said that illegals have been dying along the way from heat stroke or dehydration or starvation for decades. I asked him if Sheriff Jones knew what had been done. He said the sheriff had given the orders, not that he would have done things differently otherwise. Hold on, Carolyn, I have to open the gate. I've started closing and locking it after the fire in my barn the other night."

When Kenny came back on the line, Carolyn said, "I thought he'd be more concerned about the safety of the community."

"I know, but let's face it, migrants have been dying on the way north for decades and nobody cares. What the locals do care about right now is the money they are making from the fracking boom, whether as mineral lessees or business owners. The sheriff is up for reelection next year. Illegal immigrants don't vote—at least they're not supposed to. Doing something that has the potential to cause those wells to shut down could make him unpopular with the voters."

"That's disgusting," Carolyn said.

"Actually, that's politics. It will take a beloved local citizen to die before anybody will look into it," Kenny said.

21

I n 2011, Joe Bill was on top of the world. His company had gone public in a successful initial public offerings three years earlier, just before the extent of the economic bust became evident. He was now a multimillionaire and a big name in the Texas oil patch. In the recent interview with *Forbes,* he referred to himself as "the King of the Texas Frackers."

Since his divorce, Paul had spent a lot of time with Joe Bill, who was currently single. He had plenty of toys, including a red Lamborghini, a small Learjet, and a condo in Vegas. Joe Bill was careful about his image with the workers in the field, however, and always drove a ten-year-old Ford pickup when visiting his drill sites or meeting with subcontractors. He told Paul that his truck was for work, and his toys were for play.

Sometimes Trey and Peter joined them at the ranch. After the details of Paul's affair with Lisa and divorce became public, however, Trey's wife, Emily, was less tolerant of his overnight trips with Paul, which put a strain on the old friendship.

On a relatively cold morning in January 2011, Paul, Trey, Joe Bill, and Peter were sprawled on cowhide upholstered couches and drinking single malt scotch in the great room at Joe Bill's sprawling new ranch in the Hill Country west of Austin and south of Lake LBJ. He'd bought the ranch from the bank that recently foreclosed on it. It came with a herd of animal trophies collected by the former owner, who was now living as a guest of the state of Texas in a minimum-security prison due to a busted Ponzi scheme. Bighorn sheep, antelope, deer, a brown bear, and other trophies filled the walls of the stone and log entry hall and great room. A floor-to-ceiling stone fireplace big enough for a man to stand in was on one side of the room. Mesquite wood burning in the fireplace gave off a sweet aroma. Windows lined the wall looking west, providing a view of the rolling countryside covered with scrub brush, live oak and mesquite trees, and breathtaking sunsets. Joe Bill's newly acquired German shepherd, Rambo, was lying by the big hearth.

"Whoever thought, when we were sharing that little house in Austin, living on beer and barbecue, and playing poker for quarters into the wee hours of the morning, that we'd end up living like this?" Trey asked.

Joe Bill took a puff on his Cuban cigar and smiled broadly at his friends. "Well, I can't say I didn't have aspirations, but I believe we have exceeded them, boys. Can you believe this place? I just wish the people I grew up with in that piss-ant town in the Panhandle could see me now."

"Didn't you say *Texas Monthly* wants to interview you?" Peter asked. "I doubt that *Forbes* piece made it to the folks north of Amarillo, but everyone in Texas reads the *Monthly*."

"You're right, dammit," Joe Bill said, slapping his knee with his right hand. "I'll make them put a picture of the ranch in the article. They will know that Joe Bill Hawkins is a successful man."

"And of course, you'll mention the indispensable legal services you received from Edwards and Harrison in building your business," Paul commented.

"Here, here, fellas!" Joe Bill raised his glass of scotch to make a toast. "Here's to the success of the Midnight Poker Club! All for one and one for all!" The men stood and raised their glasses in response while the fire, which was burning low now, crackled behind them.

"So what's it like being CEO of a publicly traded company, instead of a lone wolf?" Trey asked when he settled in on the couch again.

"Well, boys, its kinda like being a wild bull penned up before they open the chute at the rodeo. You know you want to run and don't need no man sitting on your back, so you gotta hold on until you show him who's tougher and knock him off." Joe Bill made a motion with his arm as if he was swatting away an irritating bug.

"Brilliant analogy," Peter said dryly. "Thank God you didn't share that one with the *Forbes* reporter."

Everyone except Paul laughed. He excused himself and walked out onto one of the decks. He was feeling sad, missing Ashley and his children. Despite his infatuation and long affair with Lisa, he had always loved his wife. *I never thought she would leave me over a little dalliance,* he thought. All successful men had them. It was one of the perks of success and providing a good life for his family. He didn't think Ashley was being fair.

Trey came out on the deck to join him. "What's goin' on?"

"Sometimes, I just get tired of hearing Joe Bill's bullshit, that's all," Paul said.

"It can get kinda thick."

After a few minutes, Paul leaned over the railing and said, "It's a beautiful sight out here. Everything seems so simple and uncomplicated. Makes you think sometimes that we're crazy living in the rat race we're in."

"You'd go nuts in a week, Paul. You were born for the rat race."

"Yeah, you're probably right. And our buddy in there was born to bullshit."

• • •

The next day, the men went out to inspect the ranch on four-wheelers. When they returned, tired and dusty, Joe Bill excused himself and went into his big study full of brown leather furniture and an enormous, burled wood desk to make a telephone call. At the last minute, he motioned for Paul to come along.

Paul followed him, noticing a wall of expensive leather-bound books that he assumed were purchased by a decorator and left behind by the previous owner, who probably hadn't read them either. He doubted Joe Bill would have bought them. The titles were ones he recognized from the few English literature classes he took in college.

Joe Bill offered Paul a cigar, but Paul declined.

"They're real Cuban," Joe Bill said. "Lighten up. You're getting awful serious lately. I know you're still moping over Ashley kicking you out, but you've got to look on the bright side. I always thought she was kinda snooty—cold to me. I bet she was cold to you too and didn't put out much. Now you can find a friendlier woman." He lit a cigar for himself and took a puff.

This angered Paul. "You don't know what you're talking about. Ashley's the love of my life and a wonderful wife and mother. She's kind to everyone. I'm the stupid asshole who screwed things up between us. I'd give anything to have her back."

"Okay, okay. Forget I said anything." Then he punched the speaker button on his desk telephone and typed in a number he knew by heart.

"Attorney Stevenson's office," a woman's voice said.

"This is Joe Bill Hawkins, Dolores. Is the man in?" Joe Bill leaned back, extended his legs, and rested his boots on the desk.

Suddenly a man's voice broke in. "I'll take it, Dolores. Hey, Joe Bill. How's it going?" Paul detected a bit of a Yankee accent.

"Couldn't be better," Joe Bill said. "How are things down there?"

"Excellent," the man said. "We've got seven wells producing now and the boys are working on three more. So far, production is better than predicted."

"No problems?" Joe Bill asked in a stern voice.

"Well, there's one problem. I told you that one of the ranchers, Kenny Prichard, isn't exactly a fan of mine. He's from a longtime ranching family, former high school football star, decorated Marine, and most people around here look up to him. He wouldn't sign a lease with me. But when we drilled close to his boundary on the ranch next door, he decided to play defense. He signed a lease with Oakland Oil. Oakland is starting to drill in the same reservoir. It could have an adverse effect on our production."

Joe Bill took a few puffs on his cigar and sat thinking. "Well, don't worry about it; I got the best of Oakland once and I can do it again. He's not exactly a fan of mine either." Joe Bill grimaced.

"Have you set up that other project we discussed? I think that was genius on your part. It should produce a nice little nest egg, if you know what I mean." Joe Bill winked at Paul.

"It's up and running."

"You set it up so that there's no obvious ties to me, right?"

"Don't worry. I got locals to capitalize it. It's incorporated so no one can look beneath the sheets."

"Okay, I'll check in with you in a few days," Joe Bill said, hanging up. He looked at Paul to see his reaction.

Paul had been silent. Now he asked, "Who was that?"

"Oh, that's my other lawyer," Joe Bill grinned, flicking his ashes, pushing his chair back and putting his legs up on his desk again.

Paul was annoyed. He thought he'd been doing all of Joe Bill's legal work since he first set up his business. "What do you need another lawyer for?"

"You know how to do your high-class stuff, Paul. But sometimes you just need a local to handle other things. Someone who knows how the people think and who they trust. I learned that growing up from my daddy."

Paul thought, *Didn't your daddy end up going to jail?* But he didn't say it.

"So what exactly is this local lawyer helping you with that is in his particular area of specialization?" Paul asked in a sarcastic voice.

"Let's just say I'm branching out. Isn't that what big corporations are expected to do? You know, what they say: If you're not growing you're standing still, or something like that."

"Do I want to know what this special project is that your local lawyer put together for you?" Paul asked.

Joe Bill gave a hearty laugh. "Probably not. C'mon. Let's go join the boys and play some poker."

Paul got up and followed Joe Bill to the game room, where Peter had laid out the cards and poker chips and turned on some background music. Kenny Rogers was singing about The Gambler, which Paul thought was ironic. He didn't push Joe Bill to tell him what the lawyer in Greenville was doing for him. He decided to let it go.

Paul prided himself on being a creative thinker and can-do deal lawyer. He adhered to the law but could be creative in figuring out ways to get around it. He considered it being flexible. *Lone Star Lawyer,* the state's preeminent newspaper for lawyers, gave him five stars for deal-making ability. He was careful, however, not to look beyond what was strictly within a lawyer's purview when it came to his old friend's business dealings. Later, he would ask himself if that had been wise.

22

nn was meeting in her office with Michael Mears, the head of the SEC Office of the Whistleblower in January 2011, to review recent tips. One of them immediately caught her attention. An attorney for an employee of JBH Energy had sent a letter to the director of the Division of Enforcement saying that he had a client with original, timely, and credible information about violations of the securities laws by that company.

"Tell me about this one," Ann said, leaning forward in her chair and struggling to hide her excitement.

"I've talked to the attorney briefly," Michael said. "The potential whistleblower works in the company's accounting division. They claim to know about accounting fraud, as well as other unspecified illegal activities." Michael handed Ann the letter from the whistleblower's attorney.

"I read that JBH Energy is becoming big in the oil and gas industry," Ann said. "There have been a lot of complaints from the public about these companies that employ hydraulic fracturing having a cowboy mentality and riding roughshod over laws and regulations. If this turns out to be true, this might be an opportunity to send a message to the industry, Michael. Make arrangements with the lawyer to interview this person, and let's explore whether the information warrants being a matter under investigation. I'd like to attend the interview personally," she finished, gathering up her papers and putting them in her briefcase.

"Will do," Michael said, the look on his face making it clear that he was surprised that Ann wanted to spend her time on the matter at this preliminary stage.

Ann, Michael, and two staff attorneys from the Fort Worth office flew to Houston the next week for the meeting with the whistleblower. The meeting took place in the Galleria area offices of the whistle-blower's attorney, Joshua Evans. Everyone was gathered around a small conference room table and making introductions when the door opened and a petite young brunette woman in an attractive but con-servative black dress and jacket entered the room. She wore glasses and had a serious demeanor. Joshua got up and introduced Mrs. Katherine Eason to the SEC contingent. He explained that she was a CPA and the head of the accounting department at JBH Energy.

Ann evaluated Katherine while Michael led the conversation with her and her attorney, concluding that she was a poised, well-spoken young woman. She said she had been working at JBH Energy for only two years but knew the company well.

"Katherine," Michael asked, "you say you have knowledge of accounting fraud at the company. Can you explain what you mean by that?"

"Well first, the revenues and expenses at the end of each quar-ter are manipulated so that revenues exceed expenses by a certain amount if they don't actually do so." Her words were crisp and effi-cient, Ann observed.

"Why would they do that?" Michael asked from across the table.

"The CEO receives a bonus in any quarter in which revenues exceed expenses by a certain percent. In the past two quarters, for example, expenses exceeded revenues. Consequently, expenses were deferred in order to reach the bonus threshold. The quarterly finan-cials give the impression that the company is more profitable than it actually is. As a result, the CEO receives more money than he should."

"How did you discover this?" Michael asked, typing on his laptop.

"The CFO, Diego Soros, ordered me to hold back on reporting certain expenses at the end of each quarter. When I protested that we were not following generally accepted accounting principles, he told me that is the way most oil companies handle things. I told him that had not been my experience. He said that if I didn't like the way the company did things, I could always find another job." Katherine looked around the table.

"Are you aware of any other accounting irregularities?" Ann asked.

"The CEO's personal travel and related expenses are sometimes accounted for as capital expenditures, and I suspect that at least one recent company acquisition was overvalued."

"That's quite a lot of irregularities," Ann said. "What about the board's audit committee? Haven't they noticed any of this?"

"The audit committee wouldn't know a debit from a credit," Katherine sniffed. "The board is made up of good old boys who are friends of the president. They would go along with anything he wanted to do."

"Do you think the company's outside auditor is aware of these issues?" Michael asked, his fingers poised to take down her answer.

"I honestly don't know how they couldn't be, but the firm has an excellent reputation. I haven't been able to reconcile that."

Ann nodded to Michael that she wished to speak with him privately in the hall. Michael excused himself and he and Ann left the room.

Outside in the hall, Ann stifled her pleasure. "What do you think?" she asked in a serious voice.

"It's not the first time I've seen this, and I'm sure it won't be the last."

"She seems credible to me," Ann said. "But let's find out what other matters she knows about."

Seated at the table again, Michael resumed his questioning. "Ms. Eason, you claim you might have knowledge of other illegal activity by the company. Can you explain that for us?"

Katherine looked at her lawyer, who nodded for her to go ahead.

"I suspect that there is a side deal or off-balance sheet company that may be draining the revenues of the company. When I've tried to find out more about it, I have been shut out."

Ann was intently listening to this.

"Please go on," Michael said.

"The company has been paying legal fees to a law firm in Greenville, Texas, for a long time. Since the drilling began, those fees have increased by quite a bit. Also, JBH has been making substantial payments to the company that disposes of the residual wastewater, sand, and chemicals from their wells in the Eagle Ford Shale. These amounts are much higher than market."

"Have you actually compared the rates to other contracts in Texas, or are you just speculating?"

"I grew up in an oil family, sir. My maiden name is Oakland, and I worked for my family company, Oakland Oil, part-time, from when I was a teenager until I got out of college. I know more about the oil business than the typical accountant and, frankly, I don't like seeing bad actors, like Joe Bill Hawkins, giving the oil business a bad name."

"Is there anything else?" Michael asked.

"I suspect that the company has been inflating the value of its reserves in order to make up for the drain on revenues being diverted to the local lawyer and the wastewater disposal company," Katherine said. "Although I will stipulate that I am not an expert on evaluating reserves." She looked around the table as if to calculate the response.

When the meeting broke up and Michael was discussing next steps with Katherine's lawyer, Ann approached her. "Katherine, I keep thinking I've seen or heard the name Oakland before. But I can't remember where it was."

"I don't think we've met, Ms. Meyers, and Oakland is a private company." Katherine gave Ann an innocent smile.

"Well, thank you for coming forward. You are doing a great public service. I'm sure we'll be talking again."

• • •

That night, when she came home to their house in Memorial, Katherine Oakland Eason opened a bottle of blanc de blanc, poured two glasses, gave her husband a peck on the cheek and a thumbs-up, and went out onto her patio with her wine. She could still hear her children playing in the background, but her husband made them quiet down by reading a book to them. Then she called her father on her cell phone.

"Hey, sweetheart. How'd it go today?" Tom Oakland asked.

"Great, I think. The SEC seemed very interested in my whistleblower letter. Frankly, I'm surprised how quickly they acted on it. They had a lot of questions, and I was able to give them plenty of information about different ways Hawkins is cheating the company. It was like teaching the elements of commercial fraud in a first-year accounting course." Katherine laughed and took a sip of her wine.

"Who's leading the team? Did they seem competent? Not some young bureaucrat who'll drop the ball as soon as it's punted to him, I hope."

"A senior attorney named Ann Meyers seemed to be in charge," Katherine said. "She appeared very interested, although another agent asked most of the questions. She left her card with me at the end of the meeting and praised me for coming forward. Let's hope the ball starts rolling now."

"That's my girl!" Tom Oakland said. "We'll make Hawkins pay for the torment he's put our family through."

23

─────

The letter in his inbox from the SEC on March 15, 2011, was addressed to Paul Robinson, Esq., attorney of record for JBH Energy. Paul picked it up, looked at it, and frowned. Unsolicited communications from the government were usually not good news.

When Paul read what was inside, he had to sit down. The envelope contained a letter from a senior attorney with the Securities and Exchange Commission, informing him that the Division of Enforcement of the United States Securities and Exchange Commission was looking into where there were irregularities in JBH Energy's filings with the SEC. It gave a name and number of the person to whom Paul was to respond to discuss the process going forward.

"Damn!" Paul muttered under his breath. Then he buzzed his secretary. "Marie, get Trey in here right away."

When Trey entered Paul's office five minutes later, Paul handed him the letter.

"Holy shit!" Trey said.

"I don't know what they are talking about," Paul said. "We know Joe Bill can be a wild card, but we have been very careful to make sure the company's disclosures are accurate and complete. Peter has signed off on all his financial statements."

Trey read the letter. Then he turned to Paul. "Does Peter know about this?"

"I was just about to call him."

Paul punched in Peter's office number. When his secretary answered, he told her he needed to talk to Peter immediately. She put him right through.

"Peter, I just got a letter from the SEC informing us that they are looking into JBH Energy's filings with the agency. They've classified it as a matter under investigation."

Peter didn't answer right away. After at least a minute, he asked, "Do you know what they're concerned about?"

"No, it's a short letter. There's a person for me to call. I want to huddle with our group first, before I contact him. Do you have any idea what the issue may be? Was there anything unusual in the financial statements?"

"I don't think so," Peter said. "You know my firm is pretty conservative."

"I do. And we did due diligence on everything else," Paul said.

Paul was speaking in a voice louder than usual. Since his divorce, he'd been feeling a persistent, low-grade anxiety.

Trey motioned to him to lower the volume on the speakerphone.

"Well, we'd better alert Joe Bill," Peter said. "Why don't you call this person at the SEC and get some more information. Persuade them to let us run an internal investigation first. We want to control the narrative. And we don't want a bunch of SEC people descending on Joe Bill's offices. You know how he will react."

"Unfortunately, I do," Paul said. In his mind, he could see Joe Bill's reaction, and it was not a pleasant picture.

Trey moved closer to the speakerphone and interjected, "This is probably just a disgruntled employee and a minor matter, if anything. Let's not get all bent out of shape until we know what in the hell we're dealing with."

Peter hung up.

"I guess there's the silver lining that the investigation will generate loads of billable hours," Paul said to Trey, although he said it in a less exuberant voice than usual.

Paul called a meeting at his office for the next day. Peter and Trey were already assembled and seated around Paul's desk when Joe Bill arrived. The mood in the room was gloomy. Their client didn't engage in his usual flirtatious banter with Paul's assistant, but barged directly into Paul's office without waiting to be announced. Trey had been sitting in the guest chair directly in front of Paul, but Joe Bill stood and glared down at him until he got up and made an exaggerated gesture for Joe Bill to have the seat.

Paul got right to the point. "Good news. I persuaded the SEC to stand down until we could run an internal investigation."

"Excellent!" Peter said. "That will enable us to control the process. It's important that they believe we are taking this seriously."

"This is bullshit!" Joe Bill said, glaring at Paul.

"This sort of thing happens when you're a public company," Paul said in a voice that was calm. "But you run a clean company and we'll get through this. A year from now, you'll barely remember it."

"It damn well better turn out that way," Joe Bill grumbled. He turned to glare at each of them.

"What's that supposed to mean?" Paul asked, caught off guard by Joe Bill's hostile attitude.

"I pay you boys good money and you are supposed to have my ass covered," he said. "That's all."

"If you have nothing to hide, and you don't as far as I know, you have nothing to worry about," Paul said, growing irritated.

Paul turned to Peter. "Can you go back to the sources and rerun the numbers in the financials to check for any errors?"

"Already on it," Peter replied. Peter was trying not to look at Joe Bill.

Joe Bill got up and started walking toward the door before he turned around.

"Don't expect me to roll out the red carpet for these goddamned Washington bureaucrats," Joe Bill growled.

Paul rose from his chair. "I'd be careful about showing that attitude,

Joe Bill," he warned. "Let us run with this. Why don't you take a few days off? Go out to your ranch and relax."

Joe Bill was boiling, but he knew Paul was right. "Maybe I'll do just that," he growled, as he opened the door and left the room.

Once Joe Bill was gone, the others began to plan. Paul called his assistant to come in and take notes. "We're going to need some manpower to do this quickly," Paul said. "The SEC has us on a very short timeline."

"I'll reassemble the team that put together the quarterlies," Trey said.

"No," Paul stopped him. "We should take a fresh look at everything. The original team will be defensive of their work. They might not examine things critically. I think we should get Carolyn involved. We can redirect some of the original team to help on her ongoing projects."

"Why Carolyn?" Peter quickly asked. "I thought you wanted to keep her, you know, isolated." He nodded at Paul's assistant.

"I do. But she's the smartest, most detail-oriented partner we have. And she has a team of associates that works well and efficiently together. She's the best choice in this situation, unfortunately." Paul grimaced. "We'll give her a narrow scope of looking at all the facts about the company in the filings. Your team will recheck the numbers. Pick someone else to coordinate with her."

"Okay. I'll have one of my managers contact her," he said, but not looking happy about it.

After Peter left, Paul punched in Carolyn's number. When she picked up, he asked her to come to his office as soon as possible.

Five minutes later, Carolyn joined Paul and Trey. Paul motioned for all of them to sit down on the couch and club chairs. They told her what had happened and what they wanted her to do.

"I don't know anything about JBH Energy's business," she protested. "And I'm board chair of the Women's Shelter this year. I need all my spare time for that." Carolyn stood up as if to leave.

"The fact that you have no preconceived ideas about JBH Energy makes you perfect for this assignment," Paul said. "You can put fresh eyes on the filings—tie everything back to the source without having preordained assumptions. You're also the most detail-oriented partner we have in the group."

"Is that another way of saying this is women's work?" she asked, raising an eyebrow.

"Of course not. You're not going to turn into one of those feminist-ball breakers on us, are you?" Paul asked. "We've always treated you right."

"Yes, you have," Carolyn said. "But seriously, I've thought of a bigger problem. My older brother signed a lease with JBH Energy. I didn't have anything to do with it, but they're drilling on my family's land. Doesn't that present a conflict of interest?" She was obviously trying to avoid this project.

"Maybe," Paul said. "But this whistleblower thing is unrelated to that. It's probably nothing and it'll be over in no time. Most likely it's a mistake in the numbers. If it makes you more comfortable, I'll have Joe Bill sign a waiver of any conflict on your part and you can delegate as much of the work as feasible."

"Come on, Carolyn," Trey urged. "This is really important to the firm. We don't want this inquiry to become a big deal. It might if we don't get on this and resolve the matter within the next sixty days."

"And don't worry about having to deal with Joe Bill," Paul said. "Trey and I will interface with him. You'll be coordinating with a senior member of Peter's team. Peter will have him call you."

• • •

Carolyn already had a lot of work to do for her regular clients, not to mention her work with the Women's Shelter and whatever was happening at the ranch. She wasn't at all enthusiastic about taking on a new project—especially one that was cleaning up someone else's mess.

But she told herself she was a team player, chose two associates, and directed them to go over the filings with a fine-tooth comb. James Rodriguez was a CPA and worked for a few years as an IRS agent before he went to law school. She knew Peter's team would be checking the financials, but she thought James's background as an investigator could be helpful. The other associate, Diane Andrews, had worked on a lot of operating contracts and oil field service contracts.

"Do you expect to find a smoking gun?" James asked.

"I think you spent too long as an IRS investigator," Carolyn laughed.

"You never know what lies beneath the ground until you drill for it," James said in a deep, dramatic voice on his way out the door.

Carolyn and Diane laughed.

• • •

After meeting with her team, Carolyn decided to call Kenny and check on whether the TCEQ had finally taken any action regarding the pollution of the creek. She called his mobile number, but it went to voicemail. Then she dialed the home number and Mrs. Prichard answered the phone. Her usually chipper voice sounded strange, broken.

"Hey, Mrs. Prichard, it's Carolyn. Is Kenny around?" she asked.

"Oh, Carolyn, I am so upset," she answered.

"Has something happened to Kenny?" Carolyn asked. She felt panic at the thought.

"No, not Kenny," Mrs. Prichard said.

"Dad?" Carolyn gasped.

"No, honey. It's Lou Ann Schultz. She was driving over here to pick up a pie that I made for her to take to the Methodist church bake sale. When she passed the Baptist church where the farm road intersects the main road, a big tanker truck drove right through the stop sign. Mr. Langbein was in the car behind Lou Ann's on the road and saw the whole thing. Fortunately, he was able to stop. The tanker hit Lou

Ann's car going fast. Most likely, Lou Ann was killed instantly. Thank God her kids weren't in the car with her. Kenny is at Billy and Lou Ann's house. He says Billy is a wreck. It's just too terrible, Carolyn," Mrs. Prichard sighed.

Carolyn was speechless. Lou Ann had been one of her closest friends from back home. She was the sweetest person, always cheerful and doing something for others. She remembered the last time she saw her and how happy she was, showing off the diamond ring that Billy had just given her.

"Mrs. Prichard," Carolyn finally said, "I am so very sorry. I need to process this. Please tell Kenny to call me when he has time."

It was late the next day when Kenny called Carolyn back. Carolyn was still at the office. He had been with Lou Ann's husband all night, keeping him company and doing whatever he could to help the family. Some of Lou Ann's women friends were cooking and taking turns caring for the children. He sounded weary and sad.

"Is there anything I can do?" Carolyn asked.

"No, we have it handled. The services will be Friday and Saturday. Can you come?" he asked.

"Of course I'll be there," Carolyn said. "How did this happen?"

"It shouldn't have happened. The driver of a truck carrying drilling waste residual didn't stop at the stop sign where Farm Road 1420 intersects with the main road. Lou Ann was travelling down the main road, and it appears he slammed into her going full speed. The impact was hard enough to cause drilling waste to spill out all over. People who know about this stuff are speculating that the valve wasn't closed tight when the impact occurred. The Department of Transportation and the state police have closed off the road and are all over this, labeling it a Recordable and Hazardous Spill. The damn fool driving the truck knew he had caused the crash and sped off. The sheriff is looking for him."

"How is Billy doing?"

"He's almost out of his mind with grief."

On Friday, Kenny and Mrs. Prichard picked up Carolyn and her father on their way to the visitation. Mrs. Prichard told Carolyn to take her seat in the front, and she got into the back of her SUV with Carolyn's dad. The mood in the car was somber, reflecting a gray sky before the approach of an afternoon storm.

"Has the sheriff learned anything more about the driver of the truck?" Carolyn asked as Kenny drove out of their ranch gate.

"Not much," Kenny replied, when he got back in the car after locking the gate. "No one seems to know anything about the company. From what I hear, they just show up, fill up, and go on without the usual chitchat. The workers around here say the driver who hit Lou Ann didn't speak much English. The company doesn't even have their name on their trucks. Neither the servicer of your wells nor Tom have a favorable opinion of them."

"Who's Tom?" Carolyn asked as she pulled the visor down to cut off the glare of the late afternoon sun.

"Tom Oakland. He's the owner of the company that's drilling on my land. He's been working the oil patch for most of his life. He's seen their trucks hauling residual from your wells. Folks here are anxious for the sheriff to arrest the driver at the least. He was clearly negligent." Kenny turned onto the main road behind several other cars also headed to the funeral home.

Carolyn thought for a few minutes.

"You know, I did some work at Oakland's offices years ago, when I was an associate. He's in Oklahoma, right? Our client, JBH Oil as it was called then, was acquiring some of his company's properties. It was a pretty unfriendly transaction as I recall," Carolyn said, remembering the cramped, dusty room where she had spent several months.

"Tom doesn't have anything good to say about Joe Bill Hawkins," Kenny said. "It's clearly personal and he's pretty bitter about something."

"I know a little about that," Carolyn murmured. "Joe Bill had an affair with Oakland's wife and used her to acquire a lot of Oakland's properties for free. Then Hawkins dumped the woman after the deal closed." This elicited a *tsk-tsk* from Kenny's mother, who had obviously been listening to the conversation in the front seat.

"Damn! That's really low," Kenny said. "I think Oakland and his wife are back together. I met her once when she came out to the site. I really like her husband. He seems like a hard worker and a solid guy. He strikes me as someone who does what he says he's going to do no matter how hard it is or how long it takes."

"I wouldn't blame him if he wanted revenge on Joe Bill Hawkins. But Joe Bill's riding pretty high in the saddle these days. His company has gone public, and he's a multimillionaire at least."

"Do you still do work for him?"

Carolyn grimaced. "JBH Energy is an important client of my firm, but I haven't done any work for the company since that first deal in Oklahoma and I've never met Hawkins. My section head asked me to do a little job for the company just now, but I've delegated most of the work. I'm glad it'll be over in a few days. I'm not comfortable about the conflict of interest with them drilling on our ranch, but I was pressured into it."

"Can you refuse to do it?" Kenny glanced at her.

"That's not how it works in corporate law," she sighed.

"I don't think I'd fit in in corporate law," Kenny said with an impish grin.

"No, I don't think you would." Carolyn managed a smile. "A cowboy has got to be free to do what he wants to do, right?" She gazed off into the horizon.

"Something like that." Kenny grinned, reaching over to give her arm a squeeze.

Carolyn gave a wry smile back. "Must be nice to be in control of your own life."

Kenny pulled into the funeral home parking lot. It was almost full, and they had to drive around looking for a space. The funeral home was a Victorian house with an attached brick one-story addition that had been owned and operated by the Wimberg family for four generations. The current Mr. Wimberg was prone to saying that "Sooner or later, everyone in Greenville passes through Wimberg's on their way to heaven." Carolyn had always considered this in bad taste, but most of the town respected the Wimbergs, who had historically been one of the wealthiest families, and appreciated this hopeful thought.

Practically everyone in the county had turned out to pay their respects to Lou Ann's family. She had been active in many charitable organizations, her church, and Future Farmers of America. Both Billy and Lou Ann's families had lived in the area for several generations and were well liked. Billy had played varsity baseball in high school and continued to play in a league that was countywide after that. They had a wide group of friends.

When it was their turn to pay their respects, Carolyn hugged Billy tight and tried unsuccessfully to hold back her tears. Overcome with emotion, she found herself unable to verbalize what she wanted to say, but she knew she would have other opportunities to talk to him later. She hugged each of Lou Ann's children, realizing that they were about the age she was when her own mother died. She was glad they had grandparents who could give them the emotional support they would need.

Joining her dad at the end of the visit, Carolyn was overcome with the thought that life was fragile and that he too could be gone at any time. She decided that she would make a greater effort to come home more often.

24

A month after their initial meeting, Carolyn met with James and Diane in a small conference room for a status report. The windows looked out at the side of a black building, which made it feel slightly claustrophobic. Carolyn had never liked this room. Her associates were reporting on the results of their due diligence review of JBH Energy's most recent SEC filings. Copies of the documents requested by the federal agency were piled up on the table.

"So far we haven't come up with any red flags in our review," James said. "Everything appears to be accurate."

"That's good," Carolyn said. "Only I detect a 'but' in that word 'appears.'"

James nodded. "I did note something that may warrant the accountants digging a little deeper." He picked up a file folder that had been set aside for him to show Carolyn.

Carolyn sat down on an empty chair across from him. "What's that?"

"I went back and looked at Joe Bill's contract with his board. He's entitled to a bonus in any quarter in which earnings reach a specified level. For the last three quarters the company just barely exceeded that number, and just before the end of the quarter. Here's the pertinent section," he said, handing it to her.

"Why is that suspicious?" Carolyn asked.

"When I was with the IRS, I sometimes saw that pattern. It can just be coincidence that money tends to come in at the end of the period. On the other hand, it can mean that the company is revenue shifting or manipulating earnings and expenses in order to meet a target that benefits management. I don't know that that is what's happening here, but I think I should bring this up with their outside accountants."

"Okay," Carolyn said. "Do that and let me know what they say."

James looked pleased with himself.

"Anything else?"

"Just one other thing seemed a bit unusual," he replied. "I'm sure there's an explanation."

"What is it?"

"Well, I thought we did all of JBH Energy's legal work. But they've been making big payments for professional services to another law firm. I asked Diane if she had seen its name on any of the contracts she reviewed. She said there wasn't an engagement letter or any mention of them or their role. I can't figure out what the company is paying them to do." James looked perplexed.

"That is strange," Carolyn mused. "I'll ask Paul if he knows."

Carolyn took out her notepad and made several notes to herself. She poured a glass of ice water from the pitcher on the table and took a drink.

"What about you, Diane? Did you find anything odd?"

Diane was sitting at the end of the table with ten stacks of contracts in front of her. "I've looked at most of their contracts with servicers and vendors and other contractors. There are a lot of them. And there are a few contracts missing," Diane said, sounding tired.

"Have you requested they be produced?" Carolyn asked.

"We've represented the company on most of their significant contracts, so most of them are on our hard drive, but there are a few minor ones that the staff didn't give me and that are not on our system. I have asked the company's accounting and operations departments if they have copies, but so far, I haven't seen anything," Diane said.

Turning again to James, Carolyn asked, "How much longer will it take you to go through all of this?"

"At least another four or five days to be thorough."

"Okay, well, good job. Keep on it."

When she went home that night, Carolyn changed into the pair of silk pajamas that Cynthia had given her for her last birthday, poured herself a glass of Rombauer chardonnay, and tried to read a book in bed. She felt the need to relax after the events of the past month. But her thoughts kept circling back to Lou Ann. Even though she hadn't seen her much since she moved to Houston, she'd always thought of her as one of her best friends. She was angry that a careless drilling waste truck driver had caused her death. All of a sudden she had a thought. *Damn,* she said to herself. *Why didn't I think of this before?*

As soon as she arrived at the office the next morning, she called Diane and told her to come to her office with her due diligence list of JBH Energy's contracts. "You've looked at the contracts JBH Energy has in the Eagle Ford Shale. What about the contract for residual disposal?" Carolyn asked.

"I don't have one," Diane replied. "I've requested it. I've never seen a trucking company paid such high rates. That company is raking in the money."

"Can you call the person you are working with at JBH and ask them who the contractor is for that work?" Carolyn asked.

"Sure," Diane replied. "Do you want me to do it now?"

"Yes, use my phone," Carolyn said, moving aside to make way for Diane.

Carolyn found herself pacing while she waited for the young woman to make the call.

Diane dialed the number of the person who was producing contracts for her at JBH Energy. She asked if she had located that contract yet. After a few minutes, she shook her head negatively at Carolyn.

"Ask her if she knows what the name of the company is," Carolyn whispered.

Diane did as she was told. A few minutes later she said, "Nevoz-mozhnoe Trucking? How do you spell that?"

Carolyn gave Diane a thumbs-up.

"Good work!" Carolyn said. She made a mental note to call Kenny and give him the name of the company to pass on to Sheriff Jones. *Maybe that will help him find the driver,* she hoped.

That week Carolyn's team also met in a conference room with Paul and Trey to see where they were with the SEC investigation. Carolyn asked James to tell them what he had observed in the financials. It was raining hard that day and they could hear the raindrops hitting the windows.

He repeated his suspicions about the revenues just meeting the projections each quarter so that the executives would receive their bonuses.

"Did you contact Peter's team and ask them to check it out?" Carolyn asked.

"Peter told his team leader that it was probably a coincidence and not something to be worried about. He said we should wait and see how the numbers come out at the end of the current quarter before we conclude there is a pattern."

"I guess that's reassuring," Carolyn said. "What do you think, Paul?"

Paul got up from his chair and walked over to the window as if he were studying the rain against the skyline and the Texas Medical Center in the distance.

He turned around and said decisively, "I've always trusted Peter's firm. So I guess that's what we should do."

Carolyn asked Diane to report on her fact-checking.

Diane said that she had received a few of the missing contracts she had requested and brought everyone up to date. "I'm still missing the residual disposal contract though."

"Did you find out anything about the company?" Carolyn asked.

"I found something peculiar." Diane frowned. "Nevozmozhnoe Trucking is organized in the Cayman Islands."

"What? That's odd," Carolyn said. "Did you find out who is on the board of directors or organizers?" She got up and peered over Diane's shoulder at the printout she was looking at.

"Cayman Islands law shields that type of information," Diane said. "I just have an address for its agent for service, and it's a generic servicer agent."

"I don't think I like this," Paul said. Now he was also studying the printout. "What exactly does this company do for JBH?"

Carolyn spoke up. "They have a contract, which JBH can't seem to locate, to dispose of the used drilling fluid from the wells fracked in several counties in the Eagle Ford Shale, including the wells they are drilling on my family's land."

"And why is that important?" Paul asked.

"It gets personal, Paul," Carolyn grimaced. "Last week the driver of one of their tanker trucks ran through a stop sign and crashed into a car driven by one of my best friends. She was killed and drilling waste spilled out onto the road. The DOT has labelled it a hazardous spill. The bastard took off after the collision and hasn't been located yet."

Paul looked unsettled. "Shit! This is really not good," he said.

"I'm so sorry, Carolyn," Trey said, walking over to Carolyn and putting his hand on her arm in a consoling manner. "Did she have a family?"

"She had two children and a wonderful husband. We all grew up together and were close through high school. They were the most wonderful couple. The sheriff is searching for the driver, but he says he hasn't been able to track him down. Sheriff Jones is old and not used to this much excitement, I'm afraid. A friend who owns the ranch next to mine told me he is going to talk to the district attorney about getting either the Criminal Investigations Unit of the Texas Attorney General's Office or the Texas Rangers involved in the search. The sheriff will be furious that the DA went over his head. But the whole town is impatient to make the guilty parties pay."

"Do you think Joe Bill knows this about his subcontractor?" Trey asked Paul, looking worried.

"If he does, he hasn't mentioned it to me," Paul said. "Just what we need in the middle of an SEC investigation!"

The unease Carolyn had felt when she agreed to take on this assignment was growing. Cynthia had warned her to stay far away from Joe Bill Hawkins, but events were drawing her more and more into his orbit—a place she didn't want to be.

25

arolyn went home the next weekend. Lou Ann's death had hit her hard. She was distracted and found it difficult to concentrate on work. She felt sad and wanted to see her father. He hadn't been in the best health, and she couldn't shake the thought that he could be gone any day, just like Lou Ann. She also planned to visit Billy Schultz on Saturday.

Shep started barking, which alerted Carolyn that a visitor was in the yard just after dinner Friday night. It was Kenny. He asked her to go with him to a community meeting being held at the local rural electric cooperative meeting room. "I think you'll find it worthwhile," he said.

John Hoffman, the county district attorney, was sitting in the back seat of Kenny's truck. Carolyn knew that John and Kenny were friends, and that Kenny was thinking about discussing with him his concern that Sheriff Jones was not up to the task of finding the man who killed Lou Ann or getting to the bottom of the pollution in the creek, so she wasn't completely surprised.

When they entered the hall, she thought about the many times she had been there while she was growing up. Built in the late 1950s, the cooperative building provided the largest meeting room in the county. Besides the annual members' meeting, the room hosted numerous community events. The décor was midcentury utilitarian, the pictures on the walls standing witness to the local men who had brought electricity to the rural area in the 1940s and more recently internet service. Carolyn's old crowd was sitting together in folding chairs in the front rows on one side of the room, encircling Billy Schultz. They all wore black ribbons pinned to their shirts. The fluorescent lighting in the room made everything seem stark, out of the ordinary.

"Everyone is really upset—especially how it happened," Lindel said, handing ribbons to Carolyn and Kenny and John. "What if her kids had been in the car? Several of us have had our own near misses with those big trucks. These roads weren't built for the kind of traffic on them now."

"Is that what this meeting is about?" Carolyn asked.

"That and a few other issues," Lindel said, a serious look on his usually animated face.

She looked at Kenny for explanation, but he was staring straight ahead, his eyes steely and his mouth set. She had known him practically all her life, but she had never seen him look so serious, so intent, so impressively handsome.

In the front of the room were Sheriff Jones, three men she didn't know, and Darryl Hines, the general manager of the cooperative for the past twenty years. He was the presiding officer. Everyone knew and respected him. Sitting behind the others was Jonathan Stevenson. She scanned the crowd, but noted that she didn't see Brenda Sue. She looked for her brother. She hadn't seen him at the ranch and she didn't see him here either. *I would have thought they'd be here. Everyone else in town seems to be,* she thought.

Mr. Hines turned toward the crowd and lifted his arms as a signal for everyone to be quiet. "All right now, folks, let's get this meeting started," he said.

The undercurrent of talk ceased, and the room became quiet. "You all know Sheriff Jones and lawyer Stevenson," he said. Pointing to the other men sitting around him, he continued, "These here fellows are the representatives of the three oil companies currently drilling in the county: Oakland Oil, JBH Energy, and Torrance Oil. I'll let them introduce themselves when they speak."

Mr. Hines looked at Kenny. "Mr. Prichard, I believe you requested this meeting. Would you like to say something?"

"Thank you, Mr. Hines, but I'll let you run the show," Kenny said in a strong, even voice.

"Well then, we all know what's been on folks' minds this past couple of weeks. I'll take questions from the floor and ask the gentlemen to address them. We don't want to be here all night, so please keep your questions to the point." Then he sat down.

Lindel's hand shot up and Mr. Hines recognized him. "I want to know what the oil companies are going to do to prevent their big trucks from causing another death on our county roads?"

Before anyone could answer, Billy Schultz, Lou Ann's husband, stood up, his hands tightly gripping the chair in front of him. "I lost my wife, my best friend, and the mother of my children because of the reckless negligence of one of your drivers," he said in an emotional voice. "I want to know when the son of a bitch who destroyed my life and the life of my children is going to be brought to justice. What are you doing to find this guy, and who is responsible for hiring him? I heard he didn't even speak English. Did he have a driver's license?" A rumbling of outraged voices shook the room.

Tom Oakland stood and addressed Billy. "I'm Tom Oakland," he said, "owner of Oakland Oil. I'd like to extend my sincere condolences to you and your family."

Carolyn thought he expressed himself in a sincere, almost fatherly tone, and the crowd quieted down.

"Your wife's death was a terrible tragedy that never should have happened. You should address your question directly to JBH Energy's representative, son. The waste disposal company was their contractor."

All eyes turned to the representative of JBH Energy. He wore the only suit and tie in the room, appeared to be in his late twenties, and looked pale and uncomfortable. It was clear he knew very little about Lou Ann's death. His superiors had thrown him to the angry crowd to be the sacrificial lamb.

Billy looked directly at the JBH Energy representative. "Where are you in your search for this man?" His voice was loud with anger.

The young man reluctantly stood and responded in a shaky voice. "I believe the company is looking into this matter with the utmost concern."

Carolyn whispered to Kenny, "Meaning he doesn't have a clue."

Then Billy gave a sneering look at Jonathan Stevenson. "What do you have to say, Stevenson? You've been so buddy-buddy, representing JBH Energy in getting us to sign leases; maybe you can get them off their asses. I want this man found and fried!"

A chorus of "Yes" and "That's right" rose from the crowd. Tension was high in the room.

Stevenson looked pale and didn't respond.

Kenny whispered to Carolyn, "Looks like the crowd is noticing the emperor has no clothes."

The crowd was fired up now. Everyone's eyes were glued to the men in the front of the room.

Mr. Hines stood and raised his voice above the tumult. "Now, now, let's have an orderly process here. We all feel terrible for Billy and Lou Ann's family. But we won't solve anything like this. I believe there were other matters that people wanted to discuss. Can we move on to those?"

Several people at the same time expressed dissatisfaction with noxious odors, sporadic earthquakes, and the behavior of some of the roughnecks who came into town on Saturday night and drank too much, causing fights. But when the wife of the Baptist minister stood to speak, everyone finally grew silent.

"Sheriff, some of the young boys in our youth group were sneaking around one of those camps where the workers live. I believe it was on the back part of the Page Ranch."

"What?" Carolyn heard herself gasp.

Kenny placed his hand on her knee as if to calm her.

"They shouldn't have been there, but boys will be boys. They reported to my husband that they saw some very young Mexican girls being dropped off by a white van. Their hands were tied with rope. I suspect there's immoral activities going on. Sheriff, you need to go out there and investigate soon." This caused another angry buzz in the room. Sheriff Jones looked like he was frozen.

Then Kenny raised his hand to be recognized. He stood up and spoke in a strong, steady voice. "Sheriff, I once asked if it would take the death of one of the good citizens of this county to get you to do something about the pollution in Agua Pura Creek. Lou Ann's death was not what I foresaw. But was I right? Is this finally enough for you and the state to stop turning a blind eye and do something about the problems these outsiders have brought into our community?"

All eyes turned to Kenny, who was standing tall and looking steely eyed at the sheriff. Carolyn thought, *This is what a Marine in control looks like.* She thought they knew everything about each other. But she found herself looking at him in a different way, and it was unsettling. This wasn't her childhood friend or her high school boyfriend. Had she really appreciated what he had become before now? She felt her face grow hot.

Sheriff Jones was speechless. His hands trembled.

But Kenny didn't stop there. "Six months ago, I reported to you and to the TCEQ that I found dead migrants, including a mother and a critically ill baby on my land. Later, I informed you that Carolyn Page and I found a dead Mexican boy on her land, although the body mysteriously disappeared. You dismissed the deaths as dehydration, which is a possibility.

"But I also told you that I sent samples of the water from the creek to the lab at A&M. The test came back showing that residual, or a toxic mix of water, sand, and chemicals, is in Agua Pura creek. Despite this, no one has looked into the source or extent of the pollution. Will one of us, maybe a child playing in the creek, have to get sick or slowly poisoned before anyone takes action to protect the public?"

The crowd in the room erupted. Kenny Prichard was not someone to make things up or cause a stir unnecessarily. If he believed there was pollution in the creek, people were going to believe him. Two men stood up and shouted at the sheriff. One woman wailed about drinking poisoned water.

Sheriff Jones looked terrified. He had been sheriff for over thirty years. He was not accustomed to having his decisions challenged. These were usually reasonable folks, not inclined to making an uproar about anything. But the anger and outrage in the room was impossible to ignore. He looked at Jonathan Stevenson. They'd become close since the lawyer moved to town. The Stevensons had been big supporters of the sheriff in the last election. They threw fundraisers and donated to his campaign. The sheriff hissed at Stevenson to "say something."

Jonathan stood up and raised his voice in order to be heard. "Let's calm down, folks. We're here to talk this out, but we won't get anything done if everyone is talking at once."

Slowly, the crowd quieted down.

A man in the front row stood up. "You've been a big proponent of this fracking business, Stevenson. It's true that a lot of us have benefitted from it financially and we were glad to have the money. But you didn't warn us of the dangers that go with it. What do you propose to solve these problems?"

Before the lawyer could answer, another man stood up and said, "Some of us citizens don't own any land or oil. But we're having to put up with the mess that comes with it. Don't seem fair to me." A few voices shouted agreement.

Jonathan straightened his sport coat, gritted his teeth, and looked around the room. "I did do a lot to bring the oil companies here. And you were thrilled when they paid you royalties and when stores opened up in town that had never been here before. I didn't force anyone to sign a lease. You did it because you wanted to get rich. And some of you did. Fracking is a new technology, and there are going to be unforeseen consequences in any new industry or with any new technology. It's just a matter of dealing with the problems as they become apparent. That's why we're here tonight. To work together to solve any problems." Jonathan forced a slight smile.

"You talk pretty, Mr. Stevenson, but do you have any concrete solutions?" an older woman in the middle of the room stood and asked.

Jonathan looked at the oil company representatives. "You've made your concerns known to the oil companies about their trucks using the county roads. They'll convey the message to their companies to train their drivers to be more vigilant about cars and trucks on the road and to obey all safety laws. I suggest we form a committee to meet with the Texas Department of Transportation to see if we can get the narrowest roads widened."

The same woman stood up and said, "We don't want a committee— we want action, son."

"What about the pollution in the creek?" a woman in the back yelled. "My kids play in that creek."

Another woman yelled, "Mine too!"

"Now that we know there may be a problem, I suggest everyone stay away from the creek until the sheriff can contact the TCEQ and get them to do a thorough investigation. This may be an isolated incident or there may be another explanation for the unfortunate accidents that Mr. Prichard claims occurred."

Carolyn looked around the room to assess the crowd. There was a lot of grumbling and side conversations. But the mood was less intense than it had been earlier in the evening, for the most part because people were tired and anxious to get home. She saw Cody in the very back of the room, standing in a slouched position just inside the door. When she looked back five minutes later, he was gone.

Mr. Hines stood up. "Well, folks, we have some things to do. It's nine o'clock and I know that is bedtime for many of you. Let's call it a night and reconvene in a month to see where we are." He looked at the representatives of the oil companies. "Is that okay with you, boys?"

They nodded their assent, looking relieved that the meeting was over. Mr. Hines showed them to the back door so they could make a quick exit without having to brave the crowd. Slowly people filtered out the front doors into the night.

"What do you think is going to happen now?" Carolyn asked Kenny and John when they were back in Kenny's truck.

"I think there's a whole lot more that's gonna come out," Kenny said. "I think the horses have left the barn."

"Unfortunately, I think you're right," John said. "It's clear to me that Jones isn't up to handling these issues. I'm disappointed, but it might be time for him to retire. I think I should ask for help from the state in searching for the truck driver and investigating the pollution issue. I can claim that I have a conflict of interest since I've known the sheriff all my life and that this investigation exceeds the county's resources. I don't want anyone else around here getting sick or dying."

26

I n April, Paul convened an early morning meeting of the team leaders working on the company investigation into JBH Energy's SEC filings. In addition to Carolyn, Peter, Paul, and Trey, there was Diego Soros, the COO at JBH Energy, and Rebecca Smith, the CFO. Paul had asked Joe Bill to attend, but his secretary called and said he was hunting in West Texas.

Everyone was seated at a conference table in a small room adjacent to Paul's office, where he held meetings that he wanted to be especially private. The room's dark wood panels mirrored the gloomy mood of the attendees. There was a small bar with crystal decanters and top-line liquors behind the doors of a wooden cabinet in one corner of the room. When everyone had been served breakfast tacos, coffee, and orange juice, Paul's secretary left the room, closing the door quietly behind her.

"People," Paul said, "we have a problem. We have one week to complete the company's self-investigation and so far, we have nothing to report. The only issue we have come up with is a possibility of revenue manipulation in the financials, although Peter insists there isn't any problem."

Paul looked at Peter with a desperate tone in his voice. "I'm not trying to second-guess your people, Peter, but I'm grasping at straws here. Perhaps we should bring in an independent accounting firm to look at the financials. That's the usual protocol in these situations, and it would signal to the SEC that the company is trying its best to find what it is they are looking for or to prove that there is nothing wrong."

"Now wait." Peter stood up in protest. "Are you questioning my firm? I don't like this. I think we should just tell the SEC that we've conducted a thorough investigation and that they're on the wrong track." Peter's voice, normally reserved, was shaky, angry.

"Right, Peter! We'll just tell them to please go away nicely and they'll do it. You know better than that," Trey said in a sarcastic tone. "Get real."

Carolyn noticed that Rebecca kept tapping her pen on the table.

"Don't let your pride get in the way of good sense, Peter," Paul said. "If there is a mistake in the financials, it's better that we find it and put forth a plan to remediate future errors than that the SEC staff comes in behind us and finds something egregious. We could all lose our licenses if that happened."

"Tell them Diego and Rebecca have reviewed everything and tied the numbers back to the sources. That should be good enough. You need to be firm and tell them no further investigation is warranted."

Paul sighed and said, "Look, we can make any self-serving statement you like, but they will still come in here like a hornet swarm and go through everything themselves. The only good defense with the SEC is a plausible explanation for the problem, apologies and promises not to do it again, and payment of a fine." He turned to Carolyn. "Has your team come up with anything else suspect in their due diligence review?"

"We've gone through all of the contracts with vendors and servicers, but there is still one missing. It's the one with Nevozmozhnoe Trucking for drilling waste disposal for the Eagle Ford Shale sites. According to Diane, who has negotiated many such contracts, JBH Energy has been paying them above market rates."

Carolyn got up from her chair and paced nervously. Finally, she said, "I'm anxious to get that contract for personal, as well as professional, reasons."

"What personal reasons?" Peter asked.

Paul turned to Peter. "One of their drivers ran through a stop sign and caused the death of Carolyn's friend. The driver took off, and no one seems to know much about the company. It's incorporated in the Cayman Islands, of all places."

No one said anything, but Diego started shuffling papers as if he was preparing for the meeting to be over.

"There's one more thing," Carolyn said. "Diane noticed that significant amounts of money are being paid for professional services to both the trucking company, as well as a small law firm, The Law Firm of Jonathan Stevenson in Greenville."

"I might have an idea about the law firm," Paul said. "I'll look into it, but let's discuss that later."

After the meeting, Carolyn went back to her office and dialed Kenny's cell number. He picked up almost immediately. "Kenny, I think I found out something that could be helpful in locating the trucking company. It's just a hunch though."

"I'll take whatever you've got," Kenny said. "I'm meeting with John in his office right now and we have nothing."

John's office was in the courthouse on the square in Greenville. The building dated from the nineteenth century, and the rooms were small and dark. John preferred to conduct business in the café, but he and Kenny were discussing what to do about going over Sheriff Jones's head in the investigation of the missing truck driver and needed ultimate privacy.

After exchanging greetings, Carolyn said, "We know Nevozmozhnoe Trucking was subcontracted by JBH. But our firm didn't prepare the contract. I can't say why, but I suspect Jonathan Stevenson may have done it. He acted as their agent in getting my brother and the others to sign leases. He may know more about that trucking company than he has let on."

"I don't think he would tell us, darlin'. Remember, we're not on his list of favorite people."

"Okay, let me think about this a bit more," Carolyn said.

"Well, John and I have news on our end too," Kenny said.

Carolyn heard John's voice. "Hi, Carolyn. After the public meeting, I called one of the top guys I know at the TCEQ and asked him why they hadn't responded to Kenny's letter about the pollution of the water in Agua Pura Creek. He couldn't explain why they hadn't acted sooner, but they're looking into it and doing a test next week. They're also going to test for groundwater infiltration just to be safe."

"Great. Thanks, John. I'm glad you're getting involved in this," Carolyn said.

"I'm glad Kenny brought this to my attention."

"We're just wrapping up," Kenny said. "I'll call you this afternoon, okay?"

"Sure," Carolyn said.

Kenny returned Carolyn's call later that afternoon. She expected him to tell her about his meeting and what they planned to do with the state investigators now that John was fully involved. So she was surprised when Kenny asked, "Do you have any plans this weekend?"

"Not especially," she said. "What's going on?"

"I've just been thinking. I spend a lot of time thinking about you. But whenever we're together, we're talking about pollution or dead migrants or negligent truck drivers or your goddamned brother or some other damned unpleasant subject. I need a break and I think you could use one too."

Carolyn listened closely to every word. She'd thought about him too a lot after that night at the town hall. "I can't argue with you," she sighed.

"So what if we take a weekend and just spend time together away from here and all these problems, and away from Houston and your work? Kinda like the old days, but not exactly. We might consider what it's meant to be together again—as grown-ups." Kenny said this last sentence hesitantly.

Carolyn was surprised, but she felt herself getting excited at the thought of them going off alone somewhere together. She fiddled with a pencil on her desk.

"What did you have in mind?"

"Somewhere outside Kargon County," he said. "New York City is an idea."

"Do you really want to go there?" Surprised, Carolyn laughed at the thought.

"Not really," Kenny said. "Maybe I'm just trying to get your attention. But as a fallback, how does San Antonio sound? I'd pick you up at the airport. We could stay at one of those really nice hotels on the River Walk—anyplace you like."

"So, would this be a real date?" Carolyn asked.

"That's the general idea, darlin'."

• • •

Friday afternoon, Carolyn caught the five p.m. flight from Hobby Airport. Kenny was waiting for her when she came through the gates. He walked up to her and kissed her on the lips with a kiss that said they were more than old friends. "Welcome to Alamo City, ma'am," he said, smiling as he took her overnight bag.

Kenny had booked a suite at La Mansion del Rio with a view of the River Walk. He'd also made a reservation for dinner at Boudro's, and they walked to the restaurant. She'd been to the walk along the San Antonio River as a child and a teenager, but it had been a long time ago and she had forgotten how beautiful things looked at night. Flat-bottomed boats with sparkling white lights passed each other, carrying tourists or lively dinner parties with mariachis playing Tejano music and margaritas flowing. Small white lights twinkled in the trees. The river was below street level and had several forks where charming stone bridges spanned the water. The air was filled with romance and excitement.

Carolyn looked at Kenny in the candlelight at their table during dinner and felt relaxed and happy. They talked about everything except the problems they had been dealing with in Kargon County. Kenny reminded her of some of the things they had done when they were dating in high school, and she reminded him of some of the crazy things they had done when they were kids on the ranch.

"What did you do during the four years you spent in the Marines?" she asked him at one point.

"Thought you'd never ask," he said with a big smile. He then regaled her with tales about missions and his buddies and the places he had travelled. She was amazed at the breadth of his experiences. She had only thought of him in his jeans and boots on the ranch.

"For my last two years of active duty, I was assigned to the White House," he said. "I was part of the president's personal detail. I got to see a lot of the world and meet some interesting people."

"Wow! Why didn't I know this?"

"Maybe you never asked," he replied. "Seriously, Carolyn, that's why I wanted to have this time to ourselves. We're not the kids we were when we were growing up. But we haven't had time or the opportunity to get to know each other as we are now, as grown adults who've been doing things and going places and changing into who we are today." He reached across the table and took her hand.

Carolyn smiled at him.

"I already know one thing, though," he continued. "I'm still in love with you. I always loved you, even as a kid. But now it's a grown-up love."

The rest of the weekend was a blur when Carolyn thought about it later. They had visited the Japanese Gardens and La Villita and gone to the top of the Hemisfair tower to look down at the city. Each night, they talked and made love and, when the weekend was over, Carolyn's view of herself and Kenny had changed. Of course, she thought at times of Brian and felt conflicted and guilty, but she was having a wonderful time. She decided to put off sorting out her relationship with both of them until after she got back to Houston.

27

nn was waiting for Amanda at their usual meeting place on the running trail in Rock Creek Park after work on an evening in May. Her friend had called her just after noon and told her she had news that she was sure Ann would want to hear. There were always a lot of people on the trail, but most of them had earphones in their ears and were in their own world listening to music or a book. The women could talk while they ran and not have to worry about someone listening to their conversation.

The rhododendron and azaleas were blooming, making the air fragrant. Ann loved being outside when the air was still cool, but spring was in the air. A cluster of daffodils around a large rock made her think of her parents' garden and how her mother always had whatever flowers were blooming in vases throughout the house.

She looked down at the creek, which was running unusually fast, as a result of several recent rainstorms. Then she heard footsteps behind her. Amanda had a big smile on her face when she jogged up to Ann. After a quick hug, they stretched before starting their run.

When they took off, Amanda began to talk.

"I had coffee this morning with one of our new lawyers, Juan Martinez. He came to us from the Texas Commission on Environmental Quality. He was telling me about the TCEQ. Among other things, he told me that one of his former colleagues in Austin called him and complained that he'd received a reprimand for misplacing evidence. While his friend was out on parental leave when his wife was having their first child, a letter from a rancher in Kargon County, together with a water analysis from the lab at Texas A&M University, was overlooked and not forwarded to the Texas Railroad Commission, which regulates the production and transportation of oil and gas in Texas. A county district attorney has complained to the commissioners about it. The letter stated that there's drilling residual in a creek where there's fracking going on."

"That's illegal, of course, but I wouldn't imagine it's very unusual," Ann said.

"It's not. Except that one of the companies drilling in the area is JBH Energy. They have wells close to that creek and the production residual could be coming from one or more of them."

Ann stopped suddenly, raised both arms, and exclaimed, "I am very interested in that information!"

Amanda laughed. "I thought so. But keep going. I told Juan to tell the TCEQ that we'd like to receive the results of their testing as soon as it is available. You told me the SEC is already looking at the company for the possibility of accounting fraud. That's a civil law matter. But they may have broken the law under state and federal environmental laws too. The SEC can only assess civil law penalties. But there could be a criminal case there."

"Oh my God, Amanda. That would be incredible! I took a brief look at the report their law firm just sent us for the self-investigation. They insist there is no problem in the company's financials or disclosure. But I wouldn't be surprised at anything Hawkins did," Ann said. "I told you about the quote from an oilman—I can't remember his name—whose company Hawkins raided early on in his career. Now a whistleblower has accused the company of accounting fraud, not to mention that we know he drugs and abuses young women!"

Ann ran quietly for a few minutes, thinking about this new information and how it could be used against the man who wronged her. She was smiling.

Amanda interrupted her thoughts. "The EPA has been looking for an opportunity to make an example of a bad apple in the fracking world. Hawkins could be that bad apple. What do you think about a joint agency investigation?"

Ann navigated around two little boys on the path in front of them, shooting each other with pretend ray guns.

"Hit him with both guns blazing?" Ann laughed.

"That's what I'm saying!" Amanda said.

"When is the TCEQ scheduled to do their testing?" Ann asked.

"Soon."

"Depending on the results, I think a joint EPA–SEC investigation sounds like a great idea," Ann said, feeling a wicked grin spread across her face. "I'll make the case that the whistleblower is credible and the law firm has a conflict of interest."

A vendor selling Italian ice called to them from across the street, offering his wares.

Ann pointed to him and said, "We should have a toast! Cherry or lemon?"

"I think lemon is appropriate if I'm thinking about JBH Energy." Amanda laughed.

The women ate their Italian ice before they started running again. Once they were back on the trail, Ann asked, "Is Deshaun home this weekend?"

"He's leaving early Sunday morning to fly to New Orleans. I can't wait until this one ends. He's been gone even more than usual lately. But he says it's a career-advancing case if his team can wrap this one up successfully. I sure hope so. I feel like I rarely see him anymore."

They were coming to a crowd of people on the track, gathered around something they couldn't see. Ann motioned to Amanda to swing wide of the group.

"I'm sorta worried about my marriage, to be honest," Amanda confessed when they were alone again.

"Why?" Ann said, looking at her, surprised. "I've always thought that you two are the perfect happy couple. Haven't you been together since college? Like forever?"

"Yes, and I love him. But we're both ambitious and competitive by nature. And as my career has advanced faster than his, I detect some resentment. He's picking apart things I say, disagreeing with me for the sake of disagreeing."

"Well, you can't hold your career back for the sake of his ego," Ann said with a firm tone.

"Ha! I don't have holding back in me. So, I guess the only thing I can do is support him and hope he gets credit for rounding up the sex traffickers in New Orleans. If he got a promotion within the bureau, he might be home more, and we could work this out."

"I'm so sorry, Amanda. I didn't realize you were going through this. Is there anything I can do to help?"

"Just keep being my good friend," Amanda said. "I can't tell you how much it's meant to me the past few years. I wish Deshaun had some guy he could talk to, but guys aren't like that. They keep everything inside until it all boils over."

Ann thought back to her own marriage to Joey. She remembered how miserable she'd been when they were having problems. At the time, she didn't have anyone she could talk to about her feelings who understood. She knew how lonely and hopeless she felt then.

• • •

That night when Ann was getting ready for bed, she was listening to a Bruce Springsteen CD and thinking about the next steps in her attack on JBH Energy. Amanda had brought up a good point: The SEC could only assess civil penalties, but the EPA had many more arrows in its quiver, including criminal charges.

She made a mental note to always have the Department of Justice involved in what they did. *They have a prosecutorial nose for issues I might miss where we could go after Hawkins,* she thought.

Then a funny thought occurred to her. *I met Amanda at a continuing legal education seminar on illegal disposal of hazardous waste in landfills. I thought it was a total waste of time. But perhaps Amanda spotting that exact issue now was the key to my getting justice. Wasn't that serendipitous!*

28

P aul had had no choice but to submit the result of the self-examination of JBH Energy to the SEC without having found any issues in the company's recent filings that could have caused the SEC's interest. On the day it was due, he called Trey and asked him to sign the letter, since he was out of the country at a meeting in London. This seemed to irritate Trey, since Paul was the attorney of record, but in the end he did as Paul asked and signed the letter stating that they had found no problem issues with the SEC filings.

Paul called Joe Bill to tell him that the firm had made the submission.

Joe Bill was at his ranch. "I told you my business is clean as a whistle," Joe Bill said on hearing the news. "Those damn government bureaucrats cost me time and money for nothing."

"Remember," Paul warned, "I told you to be cool. Just keep your fingers crossed that this is the end of the matter."

Deep down, Paul worried that the SEC saw something he didn't and that something was not right with JBH's reporting. Peter's defensiveness about his firm's work was concerning. Peter was an old friend who had always been reliable, however, so he decided to chalk it up to Peter's insecurities and try to forget about the matter. He would just hope that the SEC accepted their conclusion that there was no fraud at the company. He turned his attention to other deals.

Only a few weeks later, however, Paul's contact at the SEC called.

"Paul," James Craig said in a more formal voice than he had used in the past, "there's something we need to discuss."

Paul assumed it was the report he had just filed. He was confused when Craig told him they had not yet looked at it.

Craig continued: "The Environmental Protection Agency has opened an investigation of Hilltop Oil Company, a DBA of JBH Energy, that could have serious repercussions for your client."

"The EPA?" Paul asked, surprised.

"Yes, they received a report from the Texas Commission on Environmental Quality and the Texas Railroad Commission that water in a creek running through one of the sites where JBH Energy is drilling tested positive for toxic waste of the type that's commonly found in fluids extracted from fracked wells. That's a clear violation of the federal Clean Water Act, as well as other environmental statutes. The Texas agencies are looking into where the fluid originated and if it was improperly disposed of, and the EPA and SEC are in the process of organizing a joint investigation of JBH Energy."

Paul thought quickly. He didn't remember what the company's filings said about how the company was disposing of drilling waste, but he didn't remember any mention of a problem.

"Are you there, Mr. Robinson?"

"You caught me a little off guard," Paul said, absently running his hand through his hair. "This is news to me. How did this come about?"

"Some local citizens found dead migrants in the vicinity of the creek," Craig said. "A real tragedy. The vegetation along the creek was yellow and dead too, so they sent samples of the water in the creek to Texas A&M's lab and then notified the TCEQ of the results some time ago. It was unintentionally overlooked, with no action being taken until the local district attorney decided to get involved and stirred things up."

"Did you say dead migrants?" Paul asked. "Wait, do you mind if I put you on speakerphone?"

"Go ahead." Craig continued after a minute. "There was a group, a man, woman, and young boy, perhaps a family. The woman had a baby with her who survived and is currently in the custody of Texas Child

Protective Services. They probably crossed the border illegally. The lab report says the toxic chemicals in the water usually only result in death if ingested over a period of time. So it's more likely they died from other causes, but the locals are still concerned about the long-term effects of the pollution on the community."

"And how did this come to the attention of the SEC?" Paul asked, looking at his bookshelf where he kept his statutes and codes for the Texas Administrative Code, which contained the environmental statutes.

"The supervisor at the EPA who received this report is a friend of my supervisor, Ann Meyers, who's in charge of this case. They are friends, and she was aware that Ann was already looking into accounting issues with JBH Energy and mentioned it to her. This will be a joint SEC–EPA investigation, and there will be coordination with the Texas regulators. We've sent a Wells Notice spelling out the details of the suspected violations to the company."

Damn! Paul thought. He didn't know what to say. He was thinking.

"Are you there, Mr. Robinson?" the lawyer asked.

"Yes, go on," Paul said.

"We're sending you a subpoena for documents, including the contract between your client and their residual disposal subcontractor as soon as possible. I'll be getting back to you on what else we will need."

"Thanks for the heads-up. I'll get right on it," Paul said, trying to sound more confident than he felt.

Shit! he thought after he hung up, as he sunk down into his big leather desk chair.

What is going on?

• • •

The next morning, Trey, Paul, Carolyn, and Peter were seated around a burled wood table in the Edwards conference room. Carolyn had always loved this particular room, which looked out to the green vista across Allen Parkway and Buffalo Bayou. You could see the trees of the Memorial area on a clear day. The art on the walls was of Texas Hill Country landscapes, contributing to the feel of being outside rather than in a high-intensity downtown law office. Today, however, she had a lot on her mind, and she was far from being able to enjoy the view.

From the frown on Paul's face, she knew he had something serious to discuss.

She was surprised when she saw that he had brought copies of the SEC report. She hadn't expected the staff to get to it for months.

Peter was shifting in his chair, looking impatient. "Can we get started with whatever this is? I've got a lot going on right now."

"I've been waiting for our friend and client," Paul said irritably, "but I guess he's a no-show again."

The room was silent.

Paul cleared his throat. "I had a call from the SEC yesterday. My contact told me the EPA notified the SEC that they're investigating pollution of the water in a creek that runs through land where JBH Energy is drilling. Combined with the whistleblower complaint, the two agencies are putting a joint investigation of our client on the front burner."

Carolyn stared straight ahead. *I knew there was a potential conflict of interest in my working on this case, but I didn't realize how big the conflict was.* She and Kenny had started the pollution ball rolling, and she could no longer rationalize the implications of her actions being adverse to a firm client. What if she'd violated the code of disciplinary procedure and was subject to discipline by the state bar?

"Carolyn!" Paul said her name for the second time and she almost jumped.

"Where are you?" Paul asked. "I asked if you had received that contract for the residual disposal yet. The SEC is issuing a subpoena for it."

"Um, no," Carolyn said. "I think it may have been prepared by a local lawyer. Our research shows that JBH has been paying a lot of money to The Law Firm of Jonathan Stevenson, a local firm—more than I would expect for them to just do a few land transactions. I think they may have prepared the contract and that's why it's not in our system."

Paul turned to Trey. "Trey, I want you to handle this yourself. Call these local yokels and tell them we need a copy of the contract yesterday. And get the contact information for the people who signed the contract."

Suddenly, Carolyn heard herself say, "I'll do it. I've met Jonathan Stevenson." *And then I'll recuse myself from this mess,* she thought grimly.

"Damn," Paul grumbled. "This could have criminal implications. Somebody needs to find Joe Bill and hope he has a good explanation for all of this. Peter, are you in contact with our friend?"

"I'll try to talk to him," Peter said in a sober voice, grabbing his briefcase and getting up to leave.

Carolyn thought she heard him mumble, "This has gone too far."

29

———

The Law Firm of Jonathan Stevenson was located in a one-story brick 1950s building that seemed out of place on the square in the middle of downtown Greenville. Virtually all of the other commercial buildings had been constructed of stone or wood in the nineteenth or early twentieth century and were several stories high. Carolyn had always thought it was ugly and looked out of place.

There was a sign on the office door that read, "Closed for Lunch." But when she tried the door, it was unlocked. Carolyn went inside and looked for Jonathan's office. Loud male voices coming from behind one of the doors to her right caught her attention. She decided to wait until they were finished with their business, but the door was thin and the voices were loud. If she stood near it, she could hear everything the men said.

She recognized Sheriff Jones's voice. He was shouting, obviously angry. "Look, Stevenson, you said you had everything under control— that this was a slam dunk for us. It's looking like we could be the ones who get dunked."

"Now, Jimmy," Jonathan Stevenson said, "this will all come to nothing. Cayman Island law shields the ownership of corporations and bank accounts. There isn't any contract they can tie to us. Remember, this is a handshake deal among good friends. Just keep stalling. Everyone assumes the driver is long gone across the border by now, and that's probably where he is."

When the sheriff didn't agree or disagree, he went on. "It's a tragic accident. Brenda Sue and I feel terrible about Lou Ann's death. But any of us could get run over by a car any day. It's just that it's especially bad when it's someone we all know and love."

Bang! Carolyn heard someone give a hard blow to a solid surface. "Don't play like you give a damn about Lou Ann, Stevenson! She was a fine woman, and I'm feeling a world of guilt for my part in this. No amount of money is worth the life of a good wife and mother. I'm ashamed I let a greedy, slick-talking lawyer cloud my good judgment. You said the return on my interest in the trucking company would more than make up for the money I used to buy in. How can I replace the money I took from the jail fund before anyone notices? Now that we've shut down operations, it'll take every penny of my savings and then some to pay it back. Hell, I could go to jail! Do you know what happens to law enforcement officers in jail?"

Carolyn looked around to make sure she was still alone and then took a few steps closer to the door. She couldn't believe what she was hearing. She had no doubt Stevenson was crooked. But she'd known the sheriff for all of her life, and he was highly regarded in town. She attributed his failure to act when Kenny showed him proof of a problem in the creek and failure to find the driver of the truck that killed Lou Ann to incompetence. He was old and perhaps burned out. She never thought he could be mixed up in something illegal. *So Stevenson and the sheriff are behind Nevozmozhnoe Trucking,* she thought. Why would they start a business they knew nothing about? And why would they incorporate in the Cayman Islands? Judging by the lawyer's earlier comment, they were trying to hide something.

Carolyn heard the front door open and close, and she quickly edged away from the office door. When she looked, she saw a courier dropping off a FedEx envelope on the first desk. The young man nodded at her and left.

But she had found out what she had come to get—the reason they couldn't get the contract between JBH Energy and the trucking company was because there wasn't one. A handshake deal, Jonathan had said. So who did the other hand belong to? Someone at JBH, of course. But who? And who owned the other interest in Nevozmozhnoe Trucking?

She heard the sheriff's chair being roughly pushed back on the floor in Stevenson's office and knew their meeting was over. Quickly, she walked back to the front, left the building, and ran around the side to keep out of sight. She waited until she was sure the sheriff had left. Dolores, Stevenson's assistant, came back from lunch and entered the building. Struggling to subdue her anger, Carolyn reentered the building as if it were the first time.

Before she could say anything to Dolores, Jonathan was standing right in front of her. He was carrying his briefcase and obviously going somewhere in a hurry. When he saw Carolyn, he frowned briefly. Then he gave her a tepid smile.

"Carolyn," he said, "I'm on my way out. Can we visit later today?"

"This will only take a minute, I promise," Carolyn said, giving him a sweet smile. "I need to get back to Houston."

"Well, if it's only a minute," he said, ushering her into his office. He closed the door. Carolyn scanned the office. There were bookcases with Vernon's Texas Civil Statutes and various codes, and a few Western novels on the shelves. Framed pictures of Brenda Sue, her family, and the two of them in various locations in Texas and Mexico were interspersed among the books. A Persian rug was on the floor under the desk, and some Longhorn memorabilia hung on the walls along with his law degree from UT Law. There was nothing relating to his life before law school, which she thought was curious.

"Now, what can I help you with? I'm sorry that we haven't had time to get to know one another. I am very fond of your brother, and Brenda Sue always speaks highly of you."

Carolyn smiled politely. "You know that my firm, Edwards and Harrison, represents JBH Energy," she began. "We are doing a little due diligence work and we need a copy of the contract between them and their residual disposal company. JBH's people told me you did all the work on that matter."

She watched the color drain from the lawyer's face before he answered. "No, I don't know who told you that," he said. "I've just done a little of the usual local land work for that company. I know when I'm out of my league."

"Oh, so you don't know anything about that contract?"

"I'm sorry I couldn't be more help, but I really need to get to my next appointment. I'll walk you out to your car." Jonathan opened the office door, indicating Carolyn should leave.

But Carolyn wasn't finished. "Since I'm here, there's another personal matter I need to discuss. Cody told me that you represented JBH Energy in getting the lease to drill on our land. Dad wants to see it since it affects the entire family." Carolyn sat down on a chair, indicating she wasn't ready to leave.

"I'm sure you can get it from Cody," Jonathan said sharply.

"Cody is so disorganized. He can't seem to find it. He told me I should get it from you. I know you're in a hurry, but I promise to leave you alone if you just instruct Dolores to make a copy for me. I'll be glad to wait here." Carolyn smiled and gave a friendly wave to the woman now seated at a desk outside Jonathan's office, who was listening intently while pretending to be working.

"Honestly, Carolyn, all my dealings have been with your brother. I don't feel right about giving it to someone else." Jonathan was shuffling his feet now, looking nervous.

"But my father is the landowner and mineral rights owner. My brother and I are equal heirs. Cody claims Dad gave him a limited power of attorney over the mineral rights. Something I haven't seen, incidentally, and frankly I'm not sure it exists. Dad's beginning to rethink the whole matter after what happened to Lou Ann. A lot of people are uneasy these days, as you know." Carolyn frowned.

"That was a tragic accident," Jonathan said, looking at Dolores.

"Besides, Dad complained to me that he hasn't seen any royalty money in his bank account, even though the wells have been producing for quite a while now. I think if he sees the contract it will put his mind at ease." *Such a snake,* Carolyn thought. *I can hardly stand to be in the same room with him.* Her expression was stern now.

Jonathan's smile was long gone. He was glaring at her now. He walked over to the outside door, opened it, and faced her.

"I'm very late now for another appointment. I'll send it to you in the next few days. Goodbye," he said in a curt tone. When Carolyn didn't move toward the door, he walked outside, got in his car, and drove off.

As Carolyn was leaving, she noticed a copy of the *Forbes* magazine with Joe Bill on the cover lying on the coffee table in the entry.

She turned to Dolores, who had been hanging on every word. "Dolores, does Mr. Stevenson know Joe Bill Hawkins?" she asked.

"Yes, of course," Dolores said uneasily.

"Mr. Stevenson does a lot of work for Mr. Hawkins? That's pretty impressive for a lawyer in a town as small as ours."

"Well, Mr. Hawkins depends on Mr. Stevenson's advice about how things are done around here. That's not unusual, is it?" Dolores looked uncomfortable.

"No, not at all. Good to see you, Dolores. Please tell Mr. Stevenson that I'll be expecting that mineral lease at his earliest convenience." She smiled and walked out the door.

Carolyn thought about stopping by the Prichards' ranch before she left town. She had been thinking a lot about Kenny since their weekend in San Antonio. But she had a long-planned date with Brian Robinson that night. They were having dinner with Dr. and Mrs. Cummings and another doctor and his wife from his department. It wasn't something she could cancel.

After she pulled onto I-10, Carolyn punched in Kenny's number. When he answered, she told him most of what had happened in

Jonathan Stevenson's office, leaving out her suspicion that someone at JBH was involved in whatever scheme Jonathan and the sheriff had cooked up. He didn't seem surprised that Sheriff Jones was involved.

"I've seen a lot of examples of greed changing good people since the oil boom came to town," he said. "People who were perfectly happy with their lives and totally honest will do things they would never dream of doing when money is involved—especially when it's a bundle of money. And then there's the jealousy factor. A few people like the sheriff, who aren't landowners, see others getting rich and start thinking of ways they can cash in too."

Kenny paused. "I hope you'll come by the house before you head back to Houston?"

"I'd like to, but I have a deal closing tomorrow and need to get back to the office," she lied. Then she looked at her reflection in the rearview mirror and confirmed that she was blushing. "I've been thinking," Carolyn changed the subject. "It can't be just the two of them behind this. They would need more capital than either of them have to buy a trucking business. Where did the money come from?"

"I don't know, but you be careful about talking on the phone and driving back to Houston, darlin'," Kenny said.

Damn! Carolyn thought. *I hate lying to Kenny. And to Brian.*

There wasn't a lot of traffic, and the drive gave Carolyn time to think. She hadn't seen Brian since before the weekend she'd spent in San Antonio with Kenny. Brian had been busier than usual at work and she didn't mind, since things were more complicated now. Before San Antonio, she had been certain that he was the man she wanted to marry one day. He was sensitive, kind, and professional—the type she had always dreamed of marrying. They liked and wanted many of the same things. Their professional lifestyles were compatible, and she enjoyed being with him. She had told herself that Kenny was her good friend, that was all. But the Kenny she now knew was a wonderful man too, and the physical chemistry during their getaway in San Antonio had been incredible. He was strong and good, and fun, and being with him felt natural. But he would never leave his ranch and the life she'd always known she didn't want. She knew they both loved her. Now she was confused. Now she didn't know what she wanted.

30

---

aul was surprised to see Carolyn sitting on one of his guest chairs when he opened the door to his office the next morning with a frown on her face. "Is something wrong?" he asked her. It wasn't like her to just stop by for a friendly chat with him.

"Actually, something is wrong," she said. "Do you have time to talk? It's about the JBH disclosure issue."

He buzzed his secretary to bring each of them black coffee and then asked her to hold his calls. He pulled the other guest chair to face Carolyn. "Tell me," he said. "Although I came in with a headache and I don't think what you have to say is going to make it go away."

"I hardly know where to start," Carolyn sighed.

"Start at the beginning." Paul waved his arm in a broad circle.

"I told you my brother entered into a lease with JBH Energy to do fracking on my family's land. He talked my father into giving him power of attorney over the mineral rights. I only found out about it later. I can't seem to get a copy of the lease from either him or the local lawyer involved, Jonathan Stevenson. My brother thought the lawyer was representing him, but he was actually being paid by JBH to get leases signed. He signed up a lot of the younger ranchers in the area."

That's what Joe Bill told me about when we were at his ranch, Paul remembered. *It seemed harmless.*

"About six months ago," Carolyn continued, "Kenny Prichard, whose family owns the ranch next to ours, called me and told me that he had found dead migrants on his land. There was a man and a woman. She was holding a baby that survived. The bodies were near Agua Pura Creek, which divides our two ranches. The vegetation along the creek had died, which just doesn't happen naturally. We wondered if there was something in the creek that was dangerous. Kenny and I rode across my family's ranch to get a sample of creek water, and I literally stumbled across another dead body. A little boy."

"You were part of the local citizens who alerted the state?" Paul asked, astonished.

"I certainly knew about it," Carolyn said, frowning.

Paul was confused. Then he pulled himself together and asked, "What do you think killed them? Couldn't it have been heat stroke?"

"That's possible. But being cautious, Kenny sent the water sample to a lab for testing. The results showed toxic chemicals. As you know, production waste is required to be profiled and disposed of in a certified landfill. It's highly likely someone has been dumping the production waste in the creek and perhaps the river. He sent the report to both the sheriff and to the TCEQ, which sends reports on production waste to the Railroad Commission, but nothing happened."

Paul walked over to the window. He didn't say anything for a while. Then he came back to his chair and sat down again.

"There's more," Carolyn said. "As I told you, a little time later, the driver of a truck belonging to a company called Nevozmozhnoe Trucking ran a stop sign at a high speed and crashed into my good friend, Lou Ann Schultz's car. She died instantly. The driver and the truck vanished, and the sheriff claims he hasn't been able to find him. The crash caused the truck to leak hazardous waste and crude on the road, and the road was closed down for days while the highway department and TCEQ did the cleanup. That's probably where the EPA investigation originated."

"What else do we know about this company?" Paul asked.

"Not much," she said. "JBH subcontracts with Nevozmozhnoe

Trucking to dispose of the residuals from the wells on my family's land and other wells in the Eagle Ford Shale. That's the same contract the SEC told you they want us to produce."

Paul got up sharply and motioned for Carolyn to stop. He had to think. *Have I been blind to what Joe Bill has been up to? Is this the whole situation that he alluded to when we had lunch at the Petroleum Club? Goddamn, I should have paid more attention.*

Paul reached into the bottom drawer of his desk and pulled out a bottle of Oban scotch. He poured himself and Carolyn a shot and handed her glass to her. After taking a drink, he looked at her and said, "Okay, let me have the rest of it."

"Yesterday, I told you I thought Jonathan Stevenson might have drafted the contract because the financials show JBH has been paying him a lot of money every month since the drilling started. I drove to his office to confront him. When I arrived, the staff was out to lunch. I could hear Stevenson and our local sheriff, Sheriff Jones, arguing in his office through the closed door. I learned several unsettling facts. First, there is no contract between JBH Energy and Nevozmozhnoe. Jonathan described it as a handshake deal.

"Second, Jonathan and the sheriff are partners in the deal. The sheriff is worried because of the pollution in Agua Pura Creek and Lou Ann's death that people will trace the trucking company back to them. He diverted public funds in his custody to buy an interest in the company and won't be able to pay it back now that the company is shut down."

"In other words, there was a conspiracy to commit a crime involving Joe Bill's lawyer and the sheriff," Paul groaned.

"Third, it is obvious that someone at JBH is working with them. I don't know who.

"And fourth, I don't know where the other capital came from to set up this fly-by-night company."

"Is that all?" Paul asked with sarcasm in his voice.

Carolyn took a deep breath. "More or less. And now that we know all this, the question is, what should we do?"

"What are you thinking?" Paul asked, afraid of the answer.

"I think that I, at a minimum, should withdraw from representation of JBH Energy as a result of my conflict of interest."

"Don't do anything rash just yet," Paul said. "I understand how serious this is, and I'm shocked and disappointed that our client may be involved in illegal activity. But give me a little time to think about all this. I promise I'll get back to you." He stood and held out his hand to Carolyn to try to show they were in this together. At the same time, he was thinking, *Damn her, she's too smart for her own good—and certainly mine.* He couldn't let her blow up this representation. There had to be a better way of handling this and not losing the client.

• • •

Paul and Trey were at Paul's new furnished apartment in the Four Seasons Hotel downtown, a place Paul hated but found convenient. The apartment came furnished, so it was stylish and comfortable, but there was nothing personal about it. Despite his infatuation with Lisa, he had always loved Ashley. He missed his home, and Ashley and the children. But Ashley was deaf to his apologies and pleadings for her to forgive him. Mrs. Robinson had told him that she'd even seen Ashley with another man at the country club at dinner in the Grill and that she seemed happy. He thought Ashley was being unfair, but there was nothing he could do about it. As for Lisa, she had moved to Miami. She'd opened a boutique on the beach with the money she got from the firm's settlement with her and wouldn't return his calls or emails.

"I can't believe Joe Bill has done this stupid thing," Paul said to Trey. "I should have questioned him, damn it! I honestly don't know if I didn't think it was important or if I didn't want to know more because it might be incriminating." Paul slammed his fist into the couch pillow.

"We were supposed to be a team, watching each other's backs. But he's been hiding things from us lately," Trey said. "And it's because he knew we would tell him not to do it."

There was a loud noise outside and Trey walked over to the balcony to see what was going on. "Hey," he said, "looks like a rally for the Rockets in front of Toyota Center. Come check this out."

"You know," Paul said, joining him on the balcony, "Joe Bill once told me that cheating was what his daddy did compulsively. He made up aliases, applied for agriculture insurance, and made false claims. He made a lot of money doing that and was living high until he got caught cheating the government under the Federal Grass Program."

"Yeah, well, it sounds like the apple didn't fall far from the tree."

The friends watched and listened to the crowd for a few minutes.

"I wonder if his luck at the poker tables finally ran out. He's spending like crazy. Cars, the ranch, trips. It's possible that he's spending and losing more than he's bringing in," Paul suggested.

"I feel like I don't know him anymore," Trey said, shrugging.

"At least we can claim we didn't do anything wrong, and we certainly didn't know about this fly-by-night residual disposal company," Paul said, trying to sound upbeat. "We signed the letter to the SEC saying our internal investigation of JBH's filings were clean."

"You mean I signed that damn letter, because you were out of town. Remember, buddy?" Trey frowned. "You didn't suspect he was doing anything illegal then, did you?"

"Of course not," Paul protested. "I'm surprised you would even think such a thing."

Trey was silent.

"What about Peter?" Paul asked to change the subject.

"Do you think he knew about this?"

Paul thought about the question as he went back inside the apartment to get some aspirin for his hangover. He took two and offered the bottle to Trey, who declined, and said definitively, "I don't think Peter has the balls to do anything illegal."

"Probably right."

"Although, as I think about it, this whole mess started with the SEC looking into whether there was false reporting in the SEC filings. I trusted Peter when he said there wasn't anything wrong. But the SEC obviously didn't agree. They're broadening their investigation."

"So what should we do?" asked Trey. "Should we confront Joe Bill? Maybe he has an explanation. Maybe it's someone else at the company and he doesn't know about it. He's not exactly a hands-on executive lately. I thought Diego and Rebecca seemed uneasy at our last meeting. Maybe they're doing something on the sly."

"Maybe. And now Carolyn wants to withdraw from representation, which is sure to raise questions at the firm," Paul said in a glum voice.

"But we don't know for sure that Joe Bill is implicated," Trey countered.

"And it will be a real hit to our sharing ratios and reputations, maybe our careers, if we lose JBH's billings. We've built much of our practices around representing his business."

"The TCEQ and EPA will find out where the frac water came from. And I bet it came from that Cayman Island company that was working on JBH Energy's wells," Trey said. "It could be a leak or improper disposal. Either way, there will be liability. Combined with the woman's death, could we be talking criminal liability?"

"Christ, I hope not," Paul said irritably.

"Let's just think this through," Trey said, sitting down on the couch.

"Okay, do we confront Joe Bill and, if he confesses, nobly withdraw from representation, finding someone else to represent him? Or do we wait and see how all this plays out, insisting we didn't know what was going on?" Paul mused.

"That might work if we *didn't* know what was going on," Trey responded. "After your conversation with Carolyn, we have a pretty good idea."

"Not if Carolyn doesn't say she told us," Paul said.

"I'm not sure she would do that," Trey said, sounding doubtful.

"She's been a team player before," Paul said. He thought of the incident with the summer intern, and how Carolyn had been loyal then. "And she's not only ambitious for her career at this point. My little brother is pretty serious about their relationship. I think he wants to marry her. I doubt she'd want to get her prospective brother-in-law disbarred or worse." He felt more positive as he began to formulate a plan for handling the situation.

"You'd better hope not. Otherwise our asses might be in hot water."

We didn't do anything wrong, Paul told himself. They wouldn't have even known about the migrant woman's death or the sleezy trucking company if Carolyn hadn't told them. They were lawyers, not priests after all.

31

———

The TCEQ and Texas Railroad Commission looked at the three companies that had wells producing in the area and their waste disposal procedures. After taking samples of the drilling waste from each of the frac wells in proximity to Agua Pura Creek, the agencies concluded that the pollution came from wells owned by JBH Energy and located on the Page Ranch.

The TCEQ issued a notice of violation and notice of enforcement with an order to cease and desist disposal operations. JBH Energy was ordered to present a written plan describing procedures to prevent future spills. Nevozmozhnoe Trucking, its trucks and employees, disappeared overnight. No individuals claimed ownership of the company. Legal notices sent to the agent of record went unanswered. The TCEQ referred the enforcement action against the trucking company to the Texas attorney general.

The Texas Railroad Commission notified JBH Energy that it was seeking to sanction the company for allegedly violating the Texas Clean Water Act. Since Nevozmozhnoe Trucking was a Cayman Islands company, the FBI was brought in to identify the responsible parties. Eventually, a task force consisting of the FBI, EPA, SEC, and Texas Attorney General's office took over the investigation.

The meeting taking place in a conference room near Ann Meyers's office at the SEC was small and private, but it included some influential people. They were crowded in together and it was warm. Senator Mario

Salinas of Texas was a strong proponent of the oil and gas industry. But Texas citizens living in the areas most affected by the worst excesses of the fracking revolution called his office more and more frequently with complaints about odors, earthquakes, traffic congestion, and scenic pollution. He felt the pressure to send a visible message to the fracking industry that they needed to be more sensitive to the environment and citizens' safety and comfort. Also present was Amanda, representing the EPA, and Arthur Arnold, a senior assistant US attorney with the Justice Department, a representative of the FBI, as well as some SEC staff. Ann's assistant had tacked a map on the wall, showing Kargon County and the location of the accident and spill.

"I agree with you, Ann. JBH Energy would be a good target for us to make our point," Senator Salinas said. "Most of the energy companies try to be responsible members of the community. But there's always a bad apple in the barrel that has the potential to sour things for the whole batch. JBH Energy isn't a big donor to political campaigns like the major integrated oil companies, so I don't expect too much blowback from members of Congress if we investigate them. Hiring a sloppy subcontractor leading to the pollution of a water source is a prime example of a rogue oil company not taking federal and state laws and the health and welfare of the people of Texas seriously. The case is sympathetic and more worthy of public attention since it involves one of their contractors negligently causing the death of a popular local woman."

Ann thought the senator sounded like he was practicing for a press interview with the Texas media rather than having a conversation with the group. But she was glad he was supportive.

The representative of the SEC Office of the Whistleblower spoke up. "We still have an open whistleblower complaint about their financial filings. Their outside law firm, Edwards and Harrison, did a self-investigation and opined that there was no problem. The whistleblower who brought this to our attention, however, is still employed and insists the company is engaged in accounting fraud." He looked around at the other participants to get their approval.

"And perhaps the law firm that gave that opinion should be looked at," Ann said. *This is going well*, she thought.

Everyone nodded in agreement.

Amanda jumped in. "We have been emphasizing the importance of all the states enforcing their Clean Water Act laws and regulations. The Texas agencies do a good job as a rule. But it looks like we have some particularly bad actors violating federal environmental laws as well. This could be a high-profile case, so I will continue to be involved."

"In light of all these issues," Ann said, "perhaps we should take a look back at the company's past offering documents to investors. In my experience, once a company starts cheating in one area, they usually are cheating in another."

Everyone nodded in agreement again.

Arthur had been drinking coffee and listening quietly. Now, he said out loud what he had been thinking. "I find it strange that the sheriff in this county isn't going full guns with a criminal investigation of the trucking company's role and responsibility in the death of that young mother. I've done a quick internet search. The local paper had an article about how the people in the area are up in arms that the driver of the truck that killed the local woman hasn't been found. It said that the sheriff in charge of the investigation has been the sheriff for thirty years. Seems like he would be pulling out all the stops in bringing this guy to justice."

Amanda turned to him. "I understand some local citizens actually discovered the pollution a while ago and alerted the sheriff, but he ignored it. I can give you the name of the local rancher who first discovered the pollution. Kenny Prichard seems to be heading up the local response. There's also a district attorney, John Hoffman, who has been stirring things up at the state level."

"Send me those names," Arthur said. "Maybe I'll ask a US attorney from the Southern District of Texas field office in Houston to pay a friendly visit to the sheriff, the DA, and Mr. Prichard." He was making notes on a legal pad.

"Have they identified the principals of the trucking company yet?" Senator Salinas asked.

"No," Amanda said. "But the FBI is working on tracking them down."

The meeting ended with everyone having their assignments. Ann closed the door to her office, sat back in her chair, and closed her eyes. Everything was going in the right direction, she thought. The men who had ruined her career in corporate law and caused her so much pain were back in her life and bringing a string of bad acts with them. Luckily, it was just when she was in a position to make them pay for it.

What was that old saying? she thought. *Revenge is a dish best served cold?* That was it.

· · ·

Saturday night, Ann had tickets for her and Amanda to see one of Ann's favorite operas, Puccini's *Madam Butterfly*, at the Kennedy Center. At the last minute, Amanda called and said she thought she was coming down with a cold and didn't think she should go. Ann talked her into coming, citing the high price of the tickets and raving about what a beautiful opera it was. "You'll feel better having a nice evening out," Ann assured her. They arrived just in time to be seated before the opening curtain.

As the lights were lowered, Amanda asked Ann, "What's this show about?"

"It's a love story that takes place in Japan," Ann whispered.

During the first act, when the young Japanese virgin falls in love with the American sailor and immediately marries him in a marriage arranged by a crooked matchmaker, Amanda seemed to enjoy the music. But when it becomes apparent that the American didn't intend to stay with her after enjoying their wedding night, Ann could feel her friend stiffening in her seat. As his full treachery became apparent, Amanda broke out in tears.

"What's wrong?" Ann whispered, alarmed.

"I can't stay," Amanda choked, and stood up and walked quickly out of the theater. Ann followed her, catching up with her friend in the lobby.

Ann threw her arms around Amanda, who was sobbing now. "Tell me what's wrong," she said.

"Deshaun is having an affair with the junior AAG on his team. All these nights he's been spending in New Orleans, he's been sleeping with her."

"Oh, honey, I'm so sorry," Ann said, fiddling in her purse for a tissue to give Amanda. "You've been thinking about this and I take you to see the saddest story of a lover's deceit in the whole world. I could kick myself."

"No, let me," Amanda said, getting herself under control. "It's ironic actually," she said. Then they both tried to laugh.

"How did you find out?" Ann asked.

"He talks about her a lot, but they do work together . . . I didn't think much of it until I left my laptop at the office and decided to use his last night. The whole sordid story is in the email chain. God! I've been such a fool!"

"Did you confront him?"

"Yes, and he admitted it. Said he was tired of me making him feel not as smart or successful as me. She makes him feel like a man. Not even a unique story."

"Well, he's not worth it if he can't appreciate being married to a beautiful, super accomplished woman like you."

"Thanks, babe. I don't know what I'd do without you."

"Hey," Ann said. "Let's take a cab and go someplace fun and lively for a drink. Screw Madam Butterfly. She didn't end well anyway."

32

———

wo days later, Paul was sitting in the empty bleachers at the tennis courts at the club. It was four p.m. and he should have been at the office, but he felt like he needed the fresh air and there was no one around. The club grounds were groomed immaculately as usual, and he had always felt like a winner on these courts. He called Joe Bill on his private cell phone.

"What's going on, buddy?" Joe Bill asked when he finally answered the phone.

"You tell me," Paul said. "A government lawyer has informed me that the SEC and EPA are instituting a joint investigation of JBH."

"Really?" Joe Bill responded.

"The SEC insists there are irregularities in your SEC filings. But that's minor compared to allegations of violations of environmental laws. They say one of your contractors has been dumping toxic drilling residual illegally, polluting surface water."

"That sounds like government harassment over technical issues," Joe Bill said in a dismissive tone. "You boys can take care of that, I'm sure."

"That's not the worst of it," Paul said. "One of your contractors ran through a stop sign and plowed into a car driven by a local woman who was killed. Some of the residual the truck was hauling and some crude spilled onto the road at the site. The Texas Department of Transportation and the state police are all over it and looking for the responsible parties. The driver took off, and nobody seems to know anything about the trucking company he worked for. The whole town is up in arms, wanting to hang whoever's responsible," Paul said in a louder voice. "Does that get your attention, buddy?"

Two young women on the next court started at the sound, turned, and looked at him disapprovingly before returning to play. He reddened when he realized he knew them. Paul told himself to get a grip.

Joe Bill was silent. "I don't know anything about that," he said, his bellicose tone subdued.

"Well, if my firm is going to continue to represent you, and I mean *if,* we need to discuss all of this pronto. Be at my apartment at eight tonight. No excuses. I'm asking Trey to be there too. You've been keeping things from us that could get us all in serious trouble. It's time you tell us the truth." Paul hung up the phone before Joe Bill could make any excuses. Then he sat there for a while, hoping he might see his children or Ashley.

Joe Bill arrived at Paul's apartment a half hour late and seemed unconcerned. He casually lit a cigar and tried making a few jokes. Trey sat on the couch stone-faced.

"Cut the bullshit and sit down and listen, Joe Bill," Paul said in a firm voice.

"Don't beat around the bush, Paul. If you've got something to say, say it," Joe Bill growled.

"Okay. The federal investigation puts all of us in the headlights. Now I'm going to ask you some questions—the same questions the Feds are probably going to ask you. And we want the truth—no more bullshit."

Joe Bill sat down on a club chair, stretching his legs out in front of him, as if to show he wasn't concerned.

"The first issue is the pollution of surface, and perhaps groundwater, with residual from one or more of your wells. Did you contract with a company called Nevozmozhnoe Trucking to dispose of the waste?"

"We purchased a small freight hauling company in the Valley. I don't know the name. We sold the majority interest in it to some locals who wanted to share in the fracking prosperity," Joe Bill said. "I did it as a favor. The locals operated the company. I'm not responsible for whatever they did."

"I don't recall any disclosure about that transaction in the management's discussion and analysis or the financials you filed with the SEC," Paul said. "Why not?" he said, raising his voice.

"We sold the majority interest," Joe Bill said. "It's an off-balance sheet transaction."

Which doesn't mean the purchase wouldn't be recorded on the company's financials or mentioned in the MD&A, Paul thought. He was surprised Peter had signed off on this, if he knew about it. Paul shook his head.

"Do your local partners have the knowledge, certifications, and insurance required to operate a hazardous waste disposal company?" Trey asked.

"I assume so. My local lawyer was responsible for overseeing it."

"Where in the hell did you find this B-class lawyer?" Paul asked, getting up and confronting Joe Bill.

"You're letting your silver spoon, elitist attitude show, Paul. We didn't all grow up in River Oaks," Joe Bill growled. "In fact, Jonathan, his wife, and her family are leading citizens and high society in their town. I met him recently at the poker tables in Vegas. He shares our love of cards."

"Was that who you were talking to when I sat in on your telephone conversation at your ranch some time back?" Paul felt himself beginning to shake with anger.

"As a matter of fact, it was," Joe Bill said, trying to remain cool.

"So you knew about it?"

"Right, you knew about it, buddy," Joe Bill said.

"The hell I knew about it," Paul exploded. "I only heard one side of the conversation, and there wasn't any mention of what exactly your other lawyer was doing for you."

"Oh, yeah, you said you didn't want to know."

Paul turned red. He looked at Trey for help, but Trey had a horrified look on his face. When Paul didn't say anything, Joe Bill continued.

"It was mostly his idea. He had the local sheriff and one of his landowner friends chip in. Together, they own fifty-one percent of the company. The landowner runs the operations. It seemed like a sweet deal. After taking their share of the profits, the rest of the money went into my bank account in the Cayman Islands. I don't like admitting it, but I haven't had much luck at the poker tables lately. That gave me a cash reserve."

"Son of a bitch," Paul said. He remembered Joe Bill saying that his local lawyer had been soliciting leases for him for several years. He'd clearly been lying about it being a recent relationship. And he was embezzling from a public company! What else had he lied about?

Paul was beyond anger. Now he felt sick.

Trey said, "So you're telling us that you were siphoning company money through your lawyer friend to your own account offshore to pay personal gambling debts? Does that not seem wrong somehow? Seriously? Does the word 'embezzlement' sound about right? Or how about prison?" His voice rose.

Joe Bill shrugged, but he looked scared.

"Everyone knows the Caymans are a haven for illegal business dealings. That's like waving a big, red flag at the Feds, for God's sake: Look at me; I'm embezzling from a public company!" Trey was waving his arms now. Paul knew he was really worked up, and that was unlike his normally laid-back friend.

"Like I said, I left it up to Stevenson to do the legal work," Joe Bill blustered. "Besides, there wouldn't be a company without me. I deserve a few perks when I need them."

"I'd say you get more than enough perks," Trey erupted, exasperated. "The ranch, the cars, the private planes. Did you run this idea by Peter? Did he determine that this company satisfied the requirements to be off the balance sheet of the company and not disclosed in the financials?"

"Sure, I ran it by Peter. I assume that if there was anything that should have been reported, Peter would have done so. I rely on him one hundred percent for those things."

"That's convenient, but you have an MBA, for God's sake. You know better. Did the board of JBH approve this side deal?" Trey was standing so their faces were close together now.

"Yeah, the boys approved it, at least most of it. Unlike my lawyers, they think I'm doing a great job and that everyone is benefitting from the way I run things."

Trey ran his hands through his hair. He took off his jacket and threw it on the floor. Then he walked over to the bar. Finding a bottle of Glenfiddich, he poured some in a glass and chugged it. He didn't offer Joe Bill a drink.

Paul felt like he was able to talk without blowing up now. "That local woman who was killed. Remember me telling you that this morning?"

"Yeah, you mentioned that." Joe Bill walked over to the bar and poured his own glass of scotch. "That's unfortunate. The boys down there should have been more careful in who they hired. Don't worry, though. The sheriff is in charge of the investigation and he's not too anxious to dig into the matter, seeing as how he's one of the owners of the company." Joe Bill gave a conspiratorial smile.

Paul and Trey looked at each other in dismay.

"That's your concern—that no one gets caught for killing an innocent woman?" Trey was aghast.

"I didn't kill her, Trey. But I sure don't want to get mixed up in this mess those boys created. It's not my fault."

Paul hung his head and studied his feet for a few minutes. Then he continued.

"Okay, let's talk about the thing that started the Feds' investigation—the financials. My contact at the SEC told me they still suspect irregularities. Do you know what in the hell they are talking about?"

"I don't need to know about accounting. That's what I pay Peter for. Look, I've had enough of this shit. I'm the big-picture guy. I have people to deal with the details."

"Is that how you think of us now, old friend? The little people cleaning up after your illegal activities?" Trey asked, his face red and his fists clenched. Paul got up and stood between his two friends, worried that Trey might take a swing.

Joe Bill's eyes were steely and his stance defiant. "That's what I get for thinking my friends have my back—nothing but suspicion and accusations." Turning to the door, he said, "I'm out of here."

Paul blocked him. "One more thing, Joe Bill. If we're going to continue to represent you, you have to promise us you won't have anything more to do with this local lawyer or this sleazy company. Can you do that?"

Joe Bill was angry, but his facial expression betrayed underlying panic. "Sure," he said.

"In that case," Paul said, "we need to contain the damage. I need to know everyone who knows about this off-balance sheet truck company, including who hired the driver and oversaw the work. Where did they dispose of the residual? Who else was involved besides the lawyer and the sheriff? You mentioned a landowner friend of the lawyer."

Joe Bill sneered. "Well, he won't be hard to find. His sister works for you. I think her name is Carolyn. Ask her about her big brother. He's the incompetent fuckhead who hired a damn illegal without a driver's license to drive the truck."

After Joe Bill stomped out of the apartment, Paul and Trey stood dumbfounded.

Trey looked at Paul. "Do you trust him to keep his word?"

"Let's just say I would like to," Paul said.

Trey sat down on one of the barstools.

"Do you think Carolyn knows about this?"

"No," Paul said, sitting down on another stool. "If she did, she wouldn't have told me about overhearing the conversation between the sheriff and Stevenson. But to an outsider, like a federal investigator, it could look like she did know and, by extension, that we knew what was going on and didn't report it. We all could be drawn into this shitstorm as co-conspirators."

"I really don't like this," Trey said. "I don't recognize Joe Bill anymore. His arrogance and callousness make me sick. Carolyn is right. We should walk away as fast as we can."

Paul started pacing the room. He stopped at the floor-to-ceiling window and stared out for a while at the city landscape. The Toyota Center was in view. He remembered the carefree days not long ago when they were hosting parties in the firm's private suite. *We were on top of the world,* he thought. *It feels like a million years ago.*

Paul turned to face Trey. "We can't risk the firm finding out about this mess, and they will if we resign as Joe Bill's lawyers," Paul said. "They are good at covering up careless screwups, even really serious ones that partners sometimes do, but this has the potential to be the kind of front-page news story that can't be quashed. Which means our conversation with Joe Bill here tonight is privileged. We should stick to our plan. We'll keep representing him, but deny knowing anything about his dealings with that fly-by-night trucking company."

"Too late. Carolyn knows and could be questioned," Trey said, purposely breaking a plastic stir stick that was on the bar.

"I'll deal with Carolyn," Paul said. "I can use her brother's involvement to incentivize her to keep quiet. I have a feeling that Joe Bill will be throwing everyone else involved to the dogs to save his hide. I'll convince Carolyn we'll keep her brother out of it."

Trey jumped, hearing a knock on the door.

"Are you ready for me to clean up?" a woman's voice asked.

"No, leave it until the morning," Paul replied.

"Something else is bothering me," Trey said. "I'm surprised that Peter went along with not disclosing the off-balance sheet company and Joe Bill's interest in it. I would have expected him to run something like that by us for our legal opinion to cover his own ass."

"Agreed. And the SEC still thinks there are irregularities in the financials. Peter insists they're fine," Paul said. "I'm having second thoughts. Being flexible and creative with the law is one thing. That's why we get paid the big bucks. But I never thought he would outright falsify the numbers."

"Me neither," Trey agreed. "Maybe we need to talk with Peter."

"Agreed," Paul said. But privately he thought, *The more we learn, the deeper the hole we're in.*

33

---

aul called Peter and told him they needed to talk privately. He suggested that they cook steaks at sundown on the deck at his dad's beach house in Galveston. Peter tried hard to make excuses, but Paul insisted. He said that Trey would pick Peter up at work and drive him down.

Paul arrived before the others. He picked up steaks and boiled shrimp, setting them out on the kitchen counter. With the shades rolled up, with the view of the beach and Gulf, took in the last of the sun.

Paul had continued to entertain at the house, but it suddenly occurred to him that he couldn't remember the last time Peter had been there. He hoped the relaxed atmosphere would make an uncomfortable conversation easier.

As soon as he arrived, Peter walked directly out onto the deck and selected a chair facing the water. Trey kept up a steady, light conversation with Peter while Paul cooked the steaks on the gas grill. It was a nice night, and Paul decided they should eat at a table on the deck. When the steaks were ready, Paul opened a bottle of good pinot noir and poured a glass for each of them. Peter frowned, and Paul said, "Oh, I'm sorry. I always forget that you don't drink anymore. I'll get you some Perrier and lime."

While Paul was getting the Perrier and putting on a Willie Nelson CD, Trey turned to Peter and said, "You know, I don't think you've ever told me why you quit drinking."

"I have a clearer head without it," Peter said.

After dinner, Trey cleared his throat, giving Paul an anxious look.

"Peter," Paul said, "there's something Trey and I wanted to talk to you about."

"I figured as much," Peter said, looking defensive.

"I told you the SEC and EPA are going to open an official investigation into JBH Energy. They still think that the financials are misleading. In order to defend JBH, I need to ask you if you have any idea why. Otherwise, we can't devise a defense."

"Did you ask Joe Bill what he thinks?" Peter asked in a wry tone.

"As a matter of fact, we did. He said he had no idea. He said he relies on you to make sure the financials are done correctly."

"Of course," Peter said dryly and took a sip of his Perrier.

"In addition, they suspect there's an off-balance sheet entity that should have been disclosed. It matters because the entity may be involved in a potential criminal indictment. The driver of a truck carrying drilling waste ran a stop sign and plowed into a car driven by a local woman who died at the scene. Joe Bill said you knew about the trucking company and determined it didn't need to be disclosed," Paul said. He looked closely at Peter to gauge his response. "He said he relies on you completely for your expertise in these areas."

Peter's look seemed resigned at first. Then his face turned red and his fists clenched. "That bastard!" he shouted, almost knocking over the table. "He's trying to set me up as the fall guy for his illegal activities. I never should have gone along with any of it!" The glass of Perrier, already wobbling on the table, fell onto the wooden deck, where it shattered.

Paul was startled. He had never seen Peter angry. He looked at Trey, but Trey was fixated on Peter, his eyes wide.

Paul got up and tried to put his hand on Peter's arm in a supportive gesture.

Peter pulled it away.

"Look, we aren't here to judge you. We are just trying to figure out what kind of mess we're in. Tell us what's going on so we can help."

While Trey picked the broken glass up off the deck, Peter sat down again. The tide was coming in and they all sat listening to the noisy waves as they crashed against the sand.

Finally, Peter spoke. "A while back, I caught him, the CFO, and the COO manipulating revenues and expenses so that he would get his quarterly bonus. I told him that if he falsified the financials, he would have to get a new auditor. He brought up something criminal that I did a long time ago and threatened to expose me to the police if I didn't sign off. I didn't stick to my guns. I was a coward.

"It got worse when he set up that off-balance sheet waste disposal company. I suspect he's funneling money he pays that company through a local lawyer to a bank account in the Cayman Islands. Again, when I objected and threatened to resign, he said he would expose what I had done. I can't go to jail."

Peter looked away from Paul and Trey. Paul could see Peter's shame and regret, but he was still angry with him. Paul's brain was racing, trying to figure a way out of this mess.

"Look," Paul finally said, "is Joe Bill the only witness? To whatever it is you did? When the Feds figure out all of Joe Bill's sins, his credibility will be zilch."

"Paul, I don't think Peter should add lying to law enforcement to his problems," Trey said in a terse voice.

Paul ignored him. "As far as the financials go, you can tell the SEC that you only made decisions based on what information JBH's staff gave you about the revenues and expenses and the off-balance sheet company. That's true. Look, you're a good person from a good family, a brilliant professional with an unblemished record. We all are, for that matter, so we can't let Joe Bill's sins ruin the rest of our lives and careers. None of us deserve that. What Joe Bill did is not our fault." Paul realized he sounded in control, but inside he was learning what deep-seated fear felt like for the first time in his life. His stomach felt as turbulent as the waves beyond the dunes.

• • •

Trey and Paul met for breakfast the next day at the Avalon Grill in River Oaks, which had served great comfort food to locals for decades. It had been a favorite place for both of them since they were children. They sat in a vinyl booth in the back corner. The waiter poured the first of many cups of black coffee for them and left them with the menus, which they knew by heart. The smell of bacon and fried potatoes filled the room.

Paul hadn't been able to sleep much after their emotional conversation with Joe Bill. Paul could tell that Trey hadn't slept either. He was wearing the same clothes he wore the night before when he drove Peter back to town from Galveston. Peter had a lot more to get off his shoulders, and Trey was emotionally drained.

"Can you believe this mess?" Trey exclaimed. "Peter is a wreck."

"Peter was foolish, but Joe Bill is the real villain here," Paul said. "He was on top of the world and didn't need to do this shit. It reminds me of something my daddy says: Pigs get fat. Hogs get slaughtered."

"Was that meant to be comforting?" Trey asked.

Paul didn't answer. "I've been thinking about it all night. Much as I'd like to punch Joe Bill in the face and never see him again, I think we should do everything we can to stick to our original plan."

The waiter came back and they put in their orders for eggs, bacon, potatoes, and biscuits.

"Remind me of what that is in light of our knowing our best friends have engaged in multiple felonies and violations of federal and state regulations," Trey asked sarcastically.

"We don't know anything. We certainly don't know Peter's approval of manipulated financials. We don't know about the off-balance sheet company. Peter can deny knowing anything. He was going on the information that he got from Joe Bill, Diego, and Rebecca. The fact that Carolyn's brother is one of the ringleaders of the disposal company fiasco will make her want to deny knowing anything." Paul realized he was tapping his fingers on the table and stopped.

"I'm not so sure about that," Trey said. "I think she's really upset and angry about her friend's death. I think she wants justice, and I can't say I blame her."

"We only brought her into the work for JBH recently. I'll tell her to go back to working for her own clients. It won't be apparent to the SEC that she knows anything. I assume I'll be subpoenaed, since I've always been JBH's lead lawyer. But I can honestly say Joe Bill used a different law firm for his off-balance sheet entity and that we didn't know about it."

"When are you going to talk to Carolyn?" Trey asked.

"Right after breakfast," Paul said. "I want to get this over with before any more shoes drop."

The waiter brought their orders and poured more coffee. The friends were silent while they ate, but Paul couldn't help wondering what Trey was really thinking.

• • •

Carolyn was alone in her office when Paul knocked on her door that morning at eleven. He closed the door behind him and sat down across from her.

"I've been thinking about our conversation several days ago," he began. "Obviously, there's some serious stuff going on with our client that we didn't know about. My contact at the SEC told me that the SEC and EPA have opened a joint investigation of JBH. You were correct in thinking there could be criminal, as well as regulatory penalties involved. I'm sorry I ever brought you into this." Carolyn thought he looked sincerely concerned, which somewhat relieved her anxiety.

"What do you think we should do? Shouldn't we run this by the firm's general counsel? Have you thought about whether the firm should resign from representing JBH?" Carolyn asked, speaking quickly.

"That wouldn't be a good idea. JBH is too important a client. Do you have any idea how much we bill them every year and how many associates we have working on their deals? I've decided our best course is to keep privilege with the client and not reveal what you found out. It certainly wouldn't be good for the firm if it turns out we know about Nevozmozhnoe Trucking. Besides, you have a conflict of interest in all this. You could get in trouble with the firm or the bar if they learned you had been doing things like notifying the TCEQ of suspected pollution that could prejudice our representation of the client."

"What the hell?" Carolyn exclaimed, jumping up from her chair. "I asked you specifically about my potential conflict, and you told me it wouldn't be a problem—that you'd get Joe Bill to sign a waiver."

"I never could sit him down to get the waiver." Paul was all wide-eyed innocence. "He certainly wouldn't sign it now if he learned what you found out eavesdropping on a private conversation between his local counsel and the sheriff. I'm afraid you've created a real mess, Carolyn, by poking around with this pollution issue." Paul was shaking his head as if he was perplexed.

Carolyn felt her blood rise to her face. She walked over to where Paul was sitting to confront him.

"How can you turn this against me?" she protested. "First of all, it's my family's property that your client is defiling, so I have every right to be involved. Second, you knew I was going to see Stevenson about the contract. It's your client who is at the bottom of a scheme that resulted in Lou Ann's death. Are you proposing we let him get away with this? Really?" She was getting in his face.

"No," Paul said in a sickeningly calm voice. "I'm just saying that it is probably best for all of us if we claim ignorance of anything having to do with this waste disposal company. Let's let the Feds find out what they inevitably will and stay out of it as much as we can. Joe Bill and anyone else in the company who was involved in this will be punished. I'm just proposing that we do what we can to not go down with him."

Carolyn was fuming. She wanted justice. "I don't think I can go along with that, Paul," she said. "Too many people have been damaged, including some of my best friends. And besides, I'm not the only person who knows what I found out about the sheriff and Stevenson." *Kenny knows*, she thought. *And by now, he's probably filled John Hoffman in on it. This isn't going away.*

Paul stood up in order to be able to look down on Carolyn, and the obvious attempt to intimidate made her blood boil further.

"You're a realist and a practical person, Carolyn," Paul said. "You know that sometimes when bad things happen it's best to just not say anything for the greater good of everyone. You've always been a team player. Be one now!"

Was this a veiled reference to her failure to expose the cover-up of what had happened to Laura Petrillo at the beach house all those years ago? The possibility hit Carolyn like a slap in the face. She turned away and tried to compose herself before she replied.

"I might have thought that way once, Paul, when I was young and ambitious," she said. "But I don't need to sell out my principles to get ahead anymore."

Paul held her gaze and asked, "Would you bend your principles if it meant keeping your brother out of jail?"

"My brother? What does Cody have to do with this?"

"Joe Bill says your brother was one of the people that put up the money for Nevozmozhnoe Trucking and was the man on the ground running the operation. He oversaw the disposal operations and hired the unqualified driver of the truck that killed your friend."

That's why I never saw any revenue from the wells, Carolyn thought. *That's why he didn't want Kenny and me to sample the water from upstream. Oh, Cody, how could you?* And to what lengths would Paul go to protect his career? She'd made mistakes, but she was done covering up for anyone. From now on, she was going to do what she knew was right, no matter the cost.

"I don't care what my brother did or didn't do, Paul," Carolyn said in a cool voice. "Cody's an adult and he is responsible for his actions. He'll have to live with the consequences. I'm not sacrificing my integrity again for him or for you or for a law firm."

She stood tall with a firm look in her eyes until Paul left her office. His last angry words were, "Think about what I said, Carolyn."

34

arolyn was furious. She grabbed up her purse and left the building, walking as far as Market Square Park before she sank down onto a bench. She had no idea where she could go or who she could talk to, she realized. She didn't want to go to the ranch, which had always been her safe place when life became difficult—until Cody had ruined it by allowing the fracking. She didn't want to see her brother. She thought she might strangle him herself. And she didn't want to see her father, knowing what it would do to him if Cody had done what Paul said.

She couldn't call Kenny. She worried she might tell him about Cody, and he'd surely turn him in to the police. Not Sheriff Jones, but the real law enforcement. Kenny didn't like Cody anyway, and he'd be furious if he knew he was partly responsible for Lou Ann's death. He might go after Cody himself, and then she could lose both of them.

She thought of Brian, but he was Paul's brother—there was nothing she could tell him that wouldn't hurt him. He would be upset and conflicted about what his brother had done. She cared for him too much to drag him into the mess.

Carolyn sat for a few minutes. Then she thought of Cynthia.

Eight months ago, Cynthia had invited Carolyn to lunch at Tony's, considered by many to be the best restaurant in town. The restaurant was chic, modern, and served high-end Italian food in a gracious atmosphere. It was the place for Houston society to see and be seen. After ordering champagne, Cynthia said, "This is a celebration lunch."

"Where's your red dress?" Carolyn smiled. "And what are we celebrating?" Carolyn had been very curious ever since Cynthia's assistant called her with the invite earlier that morning.

"I believe you should celebrate good fortune. A spectacular opportunity has come my way. The managing partner visited me in my office late yesterday afternoon, and he asked me out of the blue whether I would be willing to spend six months in Australia."

"Australia? Why Australia? Do we have clients there?"

"We will, if I go. The CFO of a large, growing Australian corporation with operations all over the world heard me speak a couple of months ago at an executive summit in New York. I've had this idea that if non-U.S. companies structured their compensation and retirement plans more like we do, they could draw from a larger talent pool. He went home and convinced his board that they should bring me over to work with them. Can you believe it?"

"I'm stunned. What did you tell him?"

"Well, I hemmed and hawed a bit so he would think he was doing me a favor and make the terms favorable to me, including a month on the back end to tour New Zealand, which I've always wanted to see. And then I said yes. I leave in a week."

"You are really excited about this, Cyn. I'm glad for you, though I'll miss you."

"I'm not just doing this for the sightseeing opportunities," Cynthia said in a more serious voice. "If I'm successful, it will give me leverage when the head of the tax section retires a year after I return. I've told you before, that's the next step in my ten-year plan for my career."

"Well, nobody will ever say you lack ambition, my friend." Carolyn laughed.

The friends had kept up a regular correspondence by email and occasional telephone conversations while Cynthia was on the other side of the world. Carolyn had hoped to visit her in Australia, but with all that was going on at work and at home, she never had the chance. Now Cynthia was back in Houston and had said she was taking some time off to recoup.

Carolyn pulled her phone out of her purse and punched in Cynthia's cell phone number.

"Carolyn!" Cynthia said when she picked up. "I've missed you."

"I've missed you too. How was your trip home?"

After listening to an upbeat report, Carolyn asked, "I need to talk to my wisest friend. Can I come by?"

"Come on over," Cynthia said. "I'm at my parents' house and I can't wait to see you."

Cynthia's parents lived in a large saltbox-style house in the Tall Timbers section of River Oaks. Buffalo Bayou buffered the section from the rest of the city and a forest of pine trees made the houses seem secluded. A fifty-foot-long swimming pool led up to the house.

When Carolyn arrived, Cynthia greeted her at the door in a beautiful pink and yellow silk caftan. She was not wearing makeup, but she looked fresh and relaxed. She gave her friend a big hug.

"Come on in and tell me what's so urgent that you left work in the middle of the day. Let's go out to the sunroom and talk. Frankly, you look like hell."

Carolyn replied, "I feel like hell."

The sunroom overlooked an expansive, landscaped lawn leading down to Buffalo Bayou. Carolyn had never been in this room and marveled at how peaceful the view was right here in the middle of the fourth-largest city in the country. Water trickled from a fountain just beyond the window.

Cynthia called to her parents' housekeeper and asked her to bring them some tea. Then she curled up in a wide pink and green floral upholstered chair. *She looks so calm—so different, so not intense,* Carolyn thought. Cynthia motioned for Carolyn to sit on a matching couch on the other side of the wicker coffee table. "So, tell me what's bothering you?" Cynthia asked.

"I'm having a crisis of conscience," Carolyn said.

"Uh-oh, that's dangerous in your line of work," Cynthia said.

"I'm serious. It's a complicated mess, but I have learned that at least one person at JBH Energy, probably including Joe Bill, as well as people I know at home, are involved in illegal activities that caused the death of one of my longtime friends."

Cynthia's eyes widened and her cheerful mood turned sober. "Are you sure? Who told you that?"

"Today Paul told me my brother oversaw the drilling residual disposal from the fracking operations on our land and hired the totally unqualified truck driver that killed my friend. Deep down I think I always suspected Cody might be involved," Carolyn said. "I just didn't want to admit it to myself. Paul's using it to pressure me to not tell anyone what I know about JBH Energy's involvement."

"Joe Bill did something illegal? Why am I not surprised?" Cynthia remarked sarcastically, putting her hand over her mouth. "As for Paul, I've known that he was an arrogant, narcissistic bastard since we were children," Cynthia scoffed. "Look what he did to poor Ashley."

The housekeeper had come back into the room and placed a silver tray with a tea service on the table between the women. She poured each of them a cup and offered them sugar, which they both declined.

Carolyn was quiet for a minute. Then she asked, "Are you the person who told Ashley about Paul's affair with Lisa?"

"I am," Cynthia admitted. "She asked me point blank if I thought Paul was cheating on her, and I couldn't keep quiet any longer."

"You never told me you felt that way about Paul!" Carolyn said, dismayed at this admission.

"You were working for him, and he seemed to be treating you unusually well. That was surprising, but I didn't want to interfere so long as that was the case. Besides, to be honest, I didn't want to hurt my own career." Cynthia gave Carolyn a sheepish look.

Carolyn hesitated. Then she said, "I have a feeling that the reason he was so good to me all this time was because I knew something damning, maybe even criminal that he was involved in. I've never told you this before, but I really need help sorting out what to do."

"What is it?"

Carolyn stood up and walked over to the entrance to make sure the housekeeper was not listening. "Do you remember the summer between when we were second- and third-year associates and Paul called you asking you if you knew where I was and how he could get hold of me one Sunday? You thought it was strange and asked me why he was looking for me the next day."

"I remember that, but I don't think you gave me an answer."

"No, I would have, in fact I wanted to tell you, but your assistant interrupted, and you had to go back to your office."

"Okay." Cynthia sat forward, eager to hear.

"That weekend, Paul's secretary invited me and my summer intern to a party at his parents' beach house in Galveston. We went and ended up, with a number of others, finding rooms to spend the night because we'd been drinking and it had gotten late. Nothing improper, or at least I didn't think so."

"What happened?"

"In the middle of the night, I woke up and when I looked at the other bed in the room, Laura, my summer intern, wasn't there. So I went downstairs looking for her, to make sure she was all right. Paul, Trey, Peter Kaufman, and another man I'd never seen before were in the living room, clearly drunk and confused. I kept asking them if they'd seen Laura, but no one answered me. I found her in the dining room lying on the floor, bleeding and unconscious, with a bruise on her face and a broken arm. Her pants were thrown in a pile nearby."

"Oh my God, Carolyn!" Cynthia got up and gave her friend a

comforting hug. Then she sat down on the couch again. "Then what happened?"

Carolyn returned to the other couch. She drank some tea. She was suddenly very thirsty.

"I asked Paul if they had called 911, but he refused to do it because he said he didn't want the police to come."

"What a selfish bastard!" Cynthia said between clenched teeth.

"I knew they had done something terrible to her and that she needed medical care, so I took her in my car to the emergency department at UTMB."

"Was she still unconscious?"

"Yes, and the doctor who examined her told me they would keep her overnight for observation and that I should come back the next day to get her."

"What did you do?"

"Paul had called Brian, who was a resident, and had him meet me. That's actually where we met for the first time. He wanted to take me back to the beach house or his apartment, but I didn't trust him after my experience with Paul and the others earlier in the night. So I went to a hotel. When I went back the next day, Laura was gone and no one could tell me when she left or how. I drove around looking for her and then went home. There were four calls from Paul on my answering machine wanting to talk to me to 'get our stories straight,' but I pulled the cord and went to bed. That's probably about the time he called you, looking for me."

"Do you know what happened to Laura—why she disappeared or what they did to her?"

"No. I never found out. I told Will Hopson most of what happened and asked his advice about what I should do. Bottom line, he told me that if I valued my career and didn't want to be blackballed at the firm, I should just forget about it—that I had done all I could do."

"What did you do after that?"

"Nothing, I'm ashamed to say. I didn't do a damn thing. And a couple of weeks later, Paul called me in and offered me a plum assignment. Then he invited me to join his group and promised to give me partner-track work. That's the real reason I was invited to join the fraternity."

"Wow!" Cynthia said.

"Once I got up my nerve to ask Paul what happened that night in the beach house, but he said he couldn't tell me. I never demanded to know what they did to Laura that night or if he knew where she'd gone. And he never offered to tell me. I guess you could say I made my bargain with the devil and sold my soul for my ambition to be a partner." Carolyn's eyes teared up and shame made her turn away from her friend.

Cynthia got up to get a tissue for Carolyn and then sat down and hugged her again. "I'm so sorry you've been carrying this secret for so long," she said. "I wish you'd confided in me, although I'm not sure what I would have told you to do. We were all consumed with ambition then."

"Yes, we were, all of us."

"Here," Cynthia said, pouring another cup of hot tea for Carolyn. "Drink this and let's think things through."

After taking a few sips, Carolyn felt calmer. She said, "Now I have to decide whether to get justice for Lou Ann and Billy Schultz and maybe send my brother to jail, breaking my father's heart. Or I can remain silent, let a lot of guilty people get away with murder, and keep my career intact. What would you do?" Carolyn looked beseechingly at Cynthia.

Cynthia poured herself some fresh tea while she considered Carolyn's question, but she didn't drink it. "You can maintain your life here," Cynthia said slowly. "But if you participate in Paul's cover-up, will you ever be able to face your dad and friends at home again, knowing what you do?"

The Connors' housekeeper entered the room with a tray carrying berries and whipped cream, laid it on the table, cleared the used cups, and asked if they needed anything else.

"Josefina, could you please bring my friend some aspirin?" Cynthia asked.

When Josefina left the room, Cynthia returned to the couch. She leaned back and said, "You're not the only one who's been trying to decide what to do."

"What do you mean? You said your project in Australia turned out to be a huge success."

"It was. But I did a lot of deep thinking about life while I was there, too. I think a slower lifestyle, fresh air, and distance gave me perspective. The Australians aren't as driven as we are to succeed. They take time to appreciate things. And they're extremely family oriented. My colleagues were always inviting me home with them. It was something I hadn't experienced before."

"But you've travelled all over the world," Carolyn protested.

"Yes, but always on the fast track with ambitious people like me who weren't sitting still for more than a day at a time. This was different. And at the end of my stay, I went to New Zealand and visited with friends of my Australian friends, or wandered by myself in the most peaceful, beautiful country I've ever seen. I think it changed me."

"In what way?"

"My parents are getting older, and I rarely saw them when I was working at the firm. My dad always wanted me to come to work for his business, but I resisted because I needed to prove myself on my own. I've done that. Now I'm seriously thinking about taking a position with his company as general counsel. If it works out, I may be running an oil field equipment business one day." Cynthia laughed at the prospect. "Can you see me in a hard hat out at the plant?"

"Well, not in your Jimmy Choos." Carolyn smiled.

"Maybe I'll go wild and even look for a boyfriend."

"Employee benefit plans to oil field equipment manufacturing—it's a natural progression," Carolyn said, laughing at the thought.

"I've learned from this experience that life is precious. I had a good law career. But I want to spend the rest of my life with the people I love," Cynthia said.

35

Katherine Oakland Eason, the whistleblower, helped put together the list of people who should be interviewed and the documents that should be requested in the investigation of JBH Energy. The team that Ann and Amanda assembled to investigate the company's regulatory crimes were some of their most experienced people from the D.C., Houston, Dallas, and other Texas offices. Ann's group focused on the accounting issue and the off-balance sheet entity, while Amanda's environmental team investigated violations of the Clean Water Act and other environmental laws.

John Hoffman, the Kargon County district attorney, had contacted the Criminal Enforcement Division of the Texas Attorney General's Office, as Kenny had requested. Together with the FBI, they initiated a search for the truck driver and an investigation of Nevozmozhnoe Trucking. Sheriff Jones was terrified when the Texas Attorney General's Office notified him that they were taking over the investigation at the request of the district attorney.

Ann sat in her office late one night reviewing the list of people to be interviewed in the SEC investigation. Joe Bill was at the top of the list, but they would save his interview until after they had talked to the people who worked for him, including the COO, CFO, internal auditor, and comptroller. Paul Robinson and Peter Kaufman, JBH's lead attorney and outside accountant, were also key persons. Trey Jorgenson was added, because he signed the letter to the SEC.

There is one person missing from this list, she decided. She typed in the name Carolyn Page, Esq.

"Who's Carolyn Page?" Arthur asked at the next team meeting.

"Trust me," Ann told him. "I have it on good information that she works closely with some of the people at Edwards and Harrison on the list. She may know something, or she may not, but I think it's worth pursuing. Actually, I'd like to lead that interview myself." Pointing to the most junior staffer on the team, she said, "I'd like you to accompany me, Sylvia."

"Yes, ma'am," Sylvia said eagerly. She started writing something on her notepad.

"Have we heard from the assistant U.S. attorney in Texas about his visit with the local sheriff and the rancher?" Amanda asked, joining the meeting by teleconference as she was out of town.

"Indeed I have," Arthur said, moving the conference phone nearer to him. "He used immigration issues in South Texas as an excuse to go by and talk with Sheriff Jones. He said that for someone who had been safely reelected to his position for thirty years, he seemed awfully uncomfortable talking to a federal officer."

"Anything else?"

"He asked the lawyers with the Texas Attorney General's Office about Sheriff Jones," Arthur said. "They say the sheriff has never been controversial or suspected of public corruption, but he's also not considered a crack lawman. Apparently, he's just a good ole boy in a quiet county trying to hold on until he can retire at sixty-five." Arthur shrugged.

"Did our man ask him if he knew anything about the disposal company?" Amanda asked.

"The sheriff said they had left town. His search for the driver came to a dead end. He claimed the driver was probably long gone across the border and it was a closed case."

"Okay," Amanda said to Ann's assistant, "put Sheriff Jones down on the list of people to be subpoenaed."

The CFO and COO of JBH Energy were the first people the SEC interviewed separately. Both denied knowing anything about accounting errors or the off-balance sheet company, except acknowledging they were aware that the company was paying Nevozmozhnoe Trucking to dispose of drilling waste, but they both claimed they were unable to find the contract.

When the SEC staff tried to schedule an interview with Peter Kaufman, they were surprised to receive a letter from his lawyer. The lawyer said his client was prepared to respond but wanted some assurances in return. Ann decided to turn the matter over to the Justice Department and told Arthur to have a couple of his attorneys handle negotiations with him, while her people focused on his role in the alleged accounting fraud.

Ann considered whether she should personally participate in Paul Robinson's interview. She wanted to watch him squirm on the hot seat. But if he recognized her and admitted to knowing her, he could claim she was pursuing him for revenge. Then again, he'd have to admit how he knew her, and she didn't think he wanted to do that. But it was still a risk.

In the end, she assigned her most intimidating agents to conduct the interview and told them to be tough on Paul. She also asked Arthur to have one of his assistant U.S. attorneys attend, to add to the intimidation factor. She would attend, but stay back.

The parties gathered in a small room that Ann had requested, with no windows in a government building the SEC used for storage, far from downtown. The head SEC agent, a tall, Black former college all-star football player named James Boyer, introduced the government personnel, including Ann Meyers, senior attorney with the SEC. Ann sat quietly in the back of the room watching Paul's expressions and forcing herself to keep from showing any emotion. She didn't see any sign he recognized her. But his face seemed like she had seen it close up before. Could it have been in the hospital?

"Mr. Robinson," James started, after standing where he could look down on Paul, "I understand you and your firm have been the legal team for JBH Energy from its beginning. Is that correct?"

"Yes," Paul said, smiling pleasantly.

"And in that capacity, I would think you would be privy to all of the transactions in which the company has been involved over the years. Is that also correct?"

"Well, all the transactions the company has asked us to be involved in. As you know, sometimes companies consider deals on the spur of the moment and don't always think to involve their lawyers. Or sometimes they think a matter is too inconsequential or has unique characteristics that don't require a lawyer or for which they engage a different firm with that specific expertise." Paul looked thoughtful, like he was explaining something to a class of law students.

It was difficult for Ann to not squirm because he seemed so self-confident, verging on smug.

"But your firm is the company's securities counsel in compiling its required filings with the SEC. Isn't that your specific expertise?"

"Yes, although much of the reports consist of financial data that we are not competent to prepare. For that, the company has always relied on Kaufman Stone."

"And in your letter to the SEC about the company's self-investigation, you said you found no inaccuracies in the financials prepared by Kaufman Stone. Correct?" Ann observed that James asked that question in a louder voice, while giving Paul a searching look. Ann stifled a small smile.

"We are not accountants, Mr. Boyer. We don't opine on their work. And I should point out that the report was signed by my colleague, Trey Jorgenson."

Throwing his colleagues to the lions, Ann thought. *What a dirtbag!*

"Did you think to bring in a third-party accounting firm to review Kaufman Stone's work? And if not, why not? Isn't that standard practice in these inquiries? Doesn't Edwards and Harrison hold itself out as an expert in securities law?" James almost boomed down at Paul, moving closer to him.

Under increasingly intense questioning, Paul began to perspire. Several times he glanced at the clock on the wall, the only decoration in the room, obviously uncomfortable. When the agents finished asking him questions, Ann detected a sigh of relief. She made a point of looking Paul in the eyes but not shaking his outstretched hand as she left the room.

• • •

The following day, Ann met with Amanda after work at the Old Ebbitt Grill. They were at a small table near the back where it was less noisy.

"Paul Robinson denies knowing anything more about the accounting issue than stated in the response letter that his colleague Trey Jorgenson signed. He said that he had requested JBH's outside accountant, Peter Kaufman, and JBH staff to check the numbers in the financials. He relied on their expertise and excellent reputation," Ann said sarcastically.

Amanda waved to a waiter and ordered two glasses of house chardonnay and an order of shrimp cocktail. "What about the off-balance sheet company and the environmental issues?" Amanda asked.

"He said he didn't know anything about the off-balance sheet disposal company except that his lawyers had repeatedly requested the contract between JBH and the company. Nevertheless, the company never produced one. He stressed that his firm had not written the contract and knew nothing about it. He claimed to have only a professional relationship with Joe Bill Hawkins and Peter Kaufman. When confronted with the *Forbes* and *Texas Monthly* articles describing a closer relationship, he said that the journalists had exaggerated in order to produce more interesting stories."

"How did it feel seeing him again?" Amanda asked, clearing a space for the waiter to put the wineglasses and shrimp cocktail on the table.

"I have to admit that I enjoyed watching him squirm, especially when he was claiming he only had a professional relationship with Hawkins," Ann said. "I wish I could have yelled *liar* at him, but it wasn't the place or time. I'm satisfied for now that we scared the shit out of him, at least." Ann took a sip of her wine.

"Did someone record the interview?"

"I made sure of it."

"So, all in all, how do you feel about the way the investigation is going at this point?" Amanda asked.

"I feel good," Ann said. "I've faced one of the devils and feel like we've shaken his obnoxious, overwhelming confidence, at least. He was actually perspiring under James Boyer's barrage of questions."

"No shit." Amanda laughed. "I imagine James can be downright terrifying."

"I see a crack in the brotherhood developing. Paul was quite willing to try to push the blame for wrongdoing onto Jorgenson and Kaufman. And I believe Katherine Eason's allegations that the company is cooking the books. I think we'll be able to prove it in the end." Ann reached for a shrimp and bit into it hard to make her point.

"I think you really want to find out what exactly those creeps did to you at that beach house. Am I right?"

"You're right. I do want to know, so that maybe I can put the questions behind me. I don't know any more than I did at this point, but I think I'm gaining the leverage I need to pry loose the truth—and make them pay."

36

___

Paul cut Carolyn out of all further matters relating to JBH Energy after their altercation about Cody. She was angry with him, but she tried, more or less successfully, to avoid him.

She had hoped to distance herself from JBH Energy completely, so she was disappointed when she received a written request from Ann Meyers, senior attorney with the SEC, to meet in connection with the matters currently being investigated concerning JBH Energy. At least the meeting was described as informal and was to occur in her office, rather than federal offices. She told herself it would be okay.

Carolyn had a more important issue on her mind. She had agreed to have dinner with Brian the previous night. He had made a reservation at one of her favorite places. Originally the hunting lodge of wealthy philanthropist Ima Hogg, it was a log structure on the shore of Buffalo Bayou across a pedestrian suspension bridge from her palatial River Oaks home and formal gardens. The log beams and stone fireplaces created an atmosphere that was both rustic and romantic. Brian had asked her to sit in the gazebo on the grounds with him after dinner. It was surrounded by tall old azalea bushes, which made it seem private and special.

Suddenly, he was on one knee before her. He had a little blue Tiffany box in his hands.

"Carolyn, I've never been happier than I have been since I met you. I hope you feel the same. I love you. Please be my wife."

Carolyn hadn't been expecting this, although she couldn't say she hadn't hoped for it before her weekend with Kenny in San Antonio. But now there were two problems, she realized: Paul and Kenny. Her relationship with Brian's brother had seriously deteriorated. Her relationship with Kenny was totally different now. After San Antonio, she could no longer tell herself he was just a friend.

She hadn't seen Kenny since he'd put her on the plane to Houston and kissed her goodbye in the most tender way. But she knew that he was patiently waiting for her, giving her room, as he always had. He told her that he had been waiting all his life and a little longer wouldn't hurt.

"Oh, Brian," was all she could say.

Brian looked confused, then disappointed. "Was I wrong thinking we had grown closer and you felt the same way I do?" he asked.

Carolyn felt the tears come to her eyes. He looked so vulnerable and disappointed. She felt terrible.

"I thought this would make you happy," Brian said, perplexed.

"I can't explain it to you, Brian. I'm not sure myself what I'm thinking. But I can't give you an answer right now. There are some things about me you don't know. Some circumstances have changed since we started seeing each other. I need to sort them out first. I'm so sorry."

"Are you saying no?" he asked as he stood up.

Carolyn softly touched his cheek with her hand. "I'm saying I can't say yes right away. I need a little time. Can you give me that?"

Brian put the ring box back in his sport coat pocket. Then he kissed her on the lips and said, "Please don't make me wait too long."

Carolyn just didn't know how marriage to Brian could work out— she was furious at Brian's brother, disgusted with his callousness—to Laura, to Ashley, to Lou Ann, and to herself. And she didn't know how to talk to Brian about it. This was what she was struggling with when the letter from the senior attorney with the SEC arrived.

• • •

The following week, Ann Meyers arrived at Carolyn's office with a young attorney she introduced as Sylvia Morales. Carolyn suggested they sit on the couch and club chair so they could be more comfortable. Ann struck Carolyn as a no-nonsense attorney. There was something about her voice in particular that made Carolyn think she had met her before, but she couldn't remember where. Maybe she had heard her speak at some conference.

Before they began, Ann started looking through her purse. "Oh, dear," she said, "I left my cell phone in the car. I'm expecting a call from the commissioner—Sylvia, would you mind getting it from the car? Don't rush. Grab yourself a coffee on the way back. We won't start the actual interview about JBH until you return. We'll spend some time getting to know one another. Knock on the door before you come back in."

"Okay," the young woman answered, a quizzical look on her face. Then she was gone.

Carolyn thought it odd that Ann Meyers wanted to spend some time getting to know her. Government lawyers were not usually so personal. She studied Ann's features, trying to figure out what it was that seemed familiar about her. She imagined her without the glasses. Was it the hair? Had she always been a brunette? What would she look like as a blonde? Yes, that was it!

Ann had been waiting—letting Carolyn figure it out for herself. When she realized that she had, she said, "You remember.

"You took me to a party at a beach house in Galveston many years ago. You were my sponsor and promised to take care of me. But it didn't work out that way, did it?"

"But you said your name is Ann Meyers," Carolyn said, looking confused.

"Ann is my middle name. I started using it when I had recovered sufficiently, to start my life over. Meyers was my married name. It's the kind of mistake you make after your world goes to hell."

"I tried to find you," Carolyn said. "No wonder I couldn't find any sign of you."

"When did you try?" Ann asked, her tone frightening Carolyn a bit. "I woke up in a hospital with bruises and a broken arm. Where were you then?"

"You weren't in your bed," Carolyn said, starting to relive the night she'd wanted to forget herself. "I went downstairs to find you. You were on the floor. No one—no one would tell me how you got that way. I drove you to the hospital." Carolyn's arms dropped to her side. She felt paralyzed.

"And you left me there," Ann said coolly.

"The doctor who examined you said they'd keep you for observation for twenty-four hours. He said I should go get some sleep and come back the next day. So I went to a nearby hotel and slept. When I went back, you were gone. I was so upset, so worried! Where did you go?"

"I didn't know how I ended up in the hospital," Ann said, looking away from Carolyn. It was as if she were speaking to herself. "As soon as I woke up, I just wanted to get away and I walked until I found a cab that took me to an airport. I ran home like a wounded dog."

"How could I have known?" Carolyn asked.

"You could have tried harder to contact me. Penn had my home address, but you never called. Imagine if you were a twenty-four-year-old young woman, far from home, abused by the very people who invited you to come there, and then discarded with no further thought."

"I'm so, so sorry," Carolyn said. "I never stopped thinking about you. I always wanted to apologize. I should have reported it that night to the police, I know. But I didn't."

"I've often wondered why you didn't," Ann said, leaning back in her chair with a cynical look on her face.

"I guess I was stupid," Carolyn said. "And selfish. I let my ambition for success at the firm get the better of my morality." Her eyes filled with tears.

Ann got up and reached for a tissue out of the box Carolyn kept on her desk. "Here," she said, handing it to Carolyn. Then she walked around to the other side of Carolyn's desk as if to study her from afar.

"Do you really not understand what happened to me that night?" she asked.

"No," Carolyn said. "No one would ever tell me."

"I'll tell you," she said, walking around the desk. "When I went downstairs, a man I now know to be Joe Bill Hawkins gave me a couple of aspirin that were probably date rape drugs. Then he and another man, I think Paul Robinson, pulled my pants off and raped me. *That's* what happened to me that night." She was full of anger, but she wiped a tear that had fallen on her cheek.

"I am so, so sorry," Carolyn said again, putting her face in her hands. "Please forgive me. I didn't know. I didn't know." She was sickened to know what Paul had done.

"And now," Ann continued, choking back the urge to cry and saying in a strong voice, "I'm in the position I'm in and Joe Bill Hawkins and Paul Robinson are where they are. I read once that what goes around comes around. Maybe it's karma."

I think that's what Will told me once, Carolyn thought.

"I didn't look for them to get even," Ann said. "I never told anyone what happened and for many years I tried to forget about it. I even blamed myself. That's what women do. But now, I'm pretty sure that Joe Bill Hawkins and perhaps Paul Robinson have broken the law. I can't say I'll be sorry if they get punished for it this time!"

Ann stopped talking and studied Carolyn's face for a minute. Then she said, "Are you ready to help me now? Or would you prefer to not get involved again?"

I deserved that, Carolyn thought.

"I'll tell you what I know, although I didn't learn much working on the SEC inquiry response."

There was a knock at the door, and Ann went to open it. Sylvia came in and Ann told her they were ready for her to take notes. The young woman's entrance lessened the hostile energy that had built up in the room. When everyone was seated again, Ann nodded to Carolyn to speak.

"I have never met Joe Bill Hawkins and I never did any work for JBH Energy except once when I was a young associate," she began. "But recently, Paul Robinson, who is the head of my practice group, asked me to fact-check their latest quarterly filings because of the letter from the SEC saying you were investigating whether their recent filings had issues. I'm not an accountant, although my associate, who is a CPA, thought there were indications of possible revenue shifting. I told him to have Kaufman Stone check for that and they insisted there wasn't any problem. The only thing we discovered was what wasn't there: a lack of disclosure of the relationship with their residual disposal contractor. We kept asking, but the company never sent us the contract, although the records showed that JBH was paying the company significant amounts of money."

Ann gave Carolyn a searching look, as if to ask for more.

Carolyn continued, determined now. "That's all we found out in our due diligence review of the filings. But I owe you, Ann, so I'm also going to tell you what I discovered in my personal capacity as a landowner in Kargon County." She took a breath. "My family owns a ranch where JBH Energy, under the DBA of Hilltop Oil, is drilling in the Eagle Ford Shale. My brother, Cody, entered into the mineral lease without telling our father or me. Our neighbor, Kenny Prichard, found dead migrants on his land and suspected that the creek between our properties was polluted. The Texas A&M lab confirmed that the creek was polluted with drilling residual. Kenny reported it to the sheriff and the state, but nobody did anything about it until a driver for a JBH subcontractor ran his truck through a stop sign and slammed into a car driven by a good friend of mine, Lou Ann Schultz. She was killed. The driver took off and hasn't been found. The entire community is enraged. We all want the persons responsible to be brought to justice."

"I'm sorry about your friend," Ann said dispassionately. "But go on."

"The SEC kept asking to see the contract between JBH and Nevozmozhnoe Trucking. Our firm didn't prepare it. I suspected that Jonathan Stevenson, a lawyer in Greenville, had drafted it." She filled Ann in on the rest of what she'd learned. "Kenny and I always thought Stevenson was crooked," she said at the end.

"Is that all?" Ann asked.

"The shorthand version, yes," Carolyn said. She realized she was not revealing her brother's involvement, but she couldn't bring herself to implicate him. She figured it would come out anyway eventually. *Stevenson has probably set him up to take the fall if anything went wrong.*

"You know our investigation is a multi-agency investigation," Ann said. "I'm sure my colleagues in the EPA and Justice Department will want to talk to you more about this."

"I will cooperate fully and tell them anything I know," Carolyn said.

"I have one last question. With whom have you shared this information?" Ann asked.

Carolyn closed her eyes. She saw Brian proposing to her in the garden of the old Rainbow Lodge. She realized that what she was about to say would ruin any chance of a happy future with him. But that seemed less important than being honest with the woman she had wronged. She thought of Paul and realized that she no longer wanted to work with him. *This is probably the end of my career at the firm,* she thought. *But no more secrets. No more lies.*

"Paul Robinson," she said. "And I told my neighbor, Kenny Prichard."

Ann stood up. "Thank you, Carolyn. I know this was difficult. But I appreciate your honesty. And I'm sure you can appreciate why I have to insist that you not reveal my identity to Misters Robinson, Kaufman, or Hawkins?"

"Of course," Carolyn said. "Yes. And again—I'm sorry."

"I'm sorry too," Ann said in a softer tone. "I think we were both victims in different ways. But we're older and wiser now, and this show's not over yet."

After the meeting, Carolyn felt both relieved and sad. There had been some sort of closure on the issue of Laura Petrillo—Ann. She had survived her ordeal and had a successful legal career after all. It was clear that she hadn't forgiven Carolyn, but Carolyn wasn't sure she deserved it. She was also relieved that she had told the truth about what she knew of the illegal activities of Joe Bill, Stevenson, and the sheriff.

She felt sad for Cody, although he had brought his troubles on himself. As for Paul, he had the choice to continue to hide the truth or come clean. He'd always believed that he deserved to be invincible, and he bet on his luck continuing. But his luck appeared to be running out lately.

37

A week later, Carolyn decided she couldn't put off making a decision about Kenny or Brian any longer. It was torturing her and not fair to either of them. She called and invited Kenny to Houston. Hearing his voice on the phone, she found herself excited. They set a bistro table in her backyard on a cool evening. Carolyn had picked up beef stew from the Raven Grill, which she was keeping warm in the oven.

"Where do things stand with the investigations of the waste disposal company?" Carolyn asked, pouring water into their glasses.

"John Hoffman and I are working with the Texas Attorney General's investigative division to try to find those responsible for Lou Ann's death. The FBI is also involved because there turned out to be federal issues. Hell, Carolyn, there are more people looking into this than the Kennedy assassination!"

"Have they found the truck driver?" Carolyn asked hopefully.

"The guy who was driving the truck is long gone. No one even knew his name. He was just some guy who crossed the Rio Grande without being invited. Everyone thinks he ran back across as soon as he knew he was in trouble. But John called me earlier today and told me that Border Patrol found their trucks and equipment on a trailer trying to cross the border in Laredo." Kenny sat down.

Carolyn poured wine into her glass and handed Kenny a beer, but didn't say anything for a few minutes.

"Paul told me that Joe Bill Hawkins claims Cody was handling the operations of the trucking company on the ground, including hiring the truck driver. Is that true?" She hadn't discussed this with anyone yet.

"I didn't know how to tell you that, Carolyn, but it's true. When the FBI and all the attorneys showed up to question Jones, the old guy choked. He couldn't wait to spill his guts about the whole residual disposal operation in hopes of cutting a deal. He blamed Stevenson for practically everything, but he fingered Cody too."

"I was afraid of that," Carolyn said.

"The governor has stripped Jones of his office, and the grand jury has indicted him for public corruption. His attorney has filed for a change of venue, but there may be more charges in connection with his ownership of SJP Industries. He could spend a few years of his retirement in jail."

"That's sad after all his years of public service. What did he say about the trucking company?"

"He said that Stevenson organized the entity under Cayman Island law, claiming that it gave the owners personal liability protection, which John tells me it does not."

"Of course not." Carolyn shrugged.

"JBH purchased a small trucking company in the Rio Grande Valley and transferred seventeen percent interests to the three locals in return for cash, retaining a forty-nine percent interest. Their plan was to take over disposal at all the Eagle Ford Shale operations by staying lean and keeping their rates low. That included hiring unskilled labor and dumping the residuals into creeks, rivers, and low areas instead of certified storage. He promised the investors huge returns on their investment. Stevenson's so arrogant and dumb, I suspect he even believed it himself." Kenny took a swig of his beer.

"Where did Cody and Sheriff Jones get the money to buy their interests?" Carolyn asked. "I haven't talked to Cody in close to a year.

He avoids me, and I can't say I've tried very hard to reach him. I mean, I don't even recognize him as my older brother anymore. He's turned into someone else, someone crude and greedy and mean."

"Well, I understand Cody paid for his share by assigning the royalties from your wells to JBH Energy. The sheriff helped himself to funds his office held for prisoners' food and other fees paid by the good citizens of the county who had run afoul of the law. Stevenson secretly borrowed his share from one of his father-in-law's bank accounts and his client trust fund. It seems he'd run up a mountain of debt at the poker tables in Vegas. He did all the bank's legal work and had access to the accounts. Stevenson and the sheriff thought they could replenish the stolen funds with profits from the company before it was missed." He was looking closely at her to see how this information affected her.

"Cody stole from Dad," Carolyn said sadly. "And you know, neither of us ever wanted the money. I never would have believed Cody would turn out this way."

"Cody was stupid and greedy. But if it makes you feel any better, I think Stevenson was the real snake in the garden."

A bell signaled that the stew was ready. Carolyn jumped up to get it. She first brought out some homemade biscuits, which she had started baking after her interview with Ann Meyers. She'd felt the urge to produce something tangible all of a sudden. Maria had taught her to make great, fluffy biscuits. Carolyn remembered that when they were children, Maria would call all the kids in from their play for fresh hot biscuits and homemade preserves every afternoon.

After ladling the stew into their bowls and tossing a green salad, Carolyn sat down again, savoring how nice it felt to be sharing a meal with Kenny on her patio. A three-quarter moon illuminated the blooming hibiscus and geraniums in the garden. She felt more at peace than she had felt in a long time, despite the subject matter of their discussion. She acknowledged that Kenny always had that effect on her.

"And what's going to happen to our friend Jonathan Stevenson?" Carolyn asked, as she filled her wineglass again.

"The attorney general has cited him with all kinds of legal malfeasance. The state bar has scheduled a disciplinary hearing, and I've been told he'll probably lose his law license. The FBI is going after him big-time. Stevenson, Hawkins, and some of his employees are looking at a conspiracy to commit money laundering charge because of the Cayman accounts, not to mention their parts in your client's embezzlement of his company's funds. Stevenson is also charged with bank fraud for his embezzlement of Mr. Pinkney's bank funds.

"Mmmmm," Kenny murmured, taking a first bite of a biscuit. "You know how I love these."

"How are Brenda Sue and her parents reacting to Jonathan's scandal?" Carolyn coyly asked.

"You'll love this part, darlin'. His devoted wife, Brenda Sue, has filed for divorce and gone on an extended vacation out of the country so that she doesn't have to face her neighbors for a while. Stevenson will most likely be going to prison for a long time."

"What a loss to Greenwood society!" Carolyn feigned dismay.

Kenny laughed and reached across the table for her hand. "Did I ever tell you that you are really pretty when you're vengeful?"

Carolyn didn't pull her hand away. She held on to his for a few minutes without saying anything. *This feels so right,* she thought. "I thought you might like to stay the night?" she asked him. "It's been such a perfect evening."

"I thought you'd never ask," Kenny said. "Actually, I've been afraid that you were involved with another man in Houston. You need to rush home quite a bit. Is there another man in your life?" He shifted in his chair.

Carolyn was glad he had broached the subject before she had to do so. "Actually, I started seeing someone right after I made partner. He's a doctor, grew up here, and we have a lot of the same intellectual interests. He asked me to marry him recently."

"I see," Kenny said, frowning and releasing her hand.

"But I've decided to break it off. He's a good man, but I realize now that I don't love him enough to marry him, and I don't think the life I wanted for a long time is still the life I want now."

"What do you want now?" Kenny asked, taking her hand again.

"I'm trying to figure that out," Carolyn said with a smile. "Want to help me with that? Let's leave the cleanup until morning," she said, leading him toward her bedroom and turning out the lights along the way.

• • •

Kenny stayed at Carolyn's house for two extra days, during which she called in sick to work. They stayed at Carolyn's house, talking about old times and Kenny telling her about plans he had for the future. He said that he was considering running for Kargon County commissioner. The average age of the current commissioners was seventy, and he and some of his friends felt like new blood was needed. Sheriff Jones's involvement in the trucking disaster shook people up and made them realize that longevity in office was not necessarily a good thing.

He also told her that he had been tracking the child that he found in the arms of his dead mother on his land. He'd learned that the child had been shuttled from one foster home to another and that knowledge was eating at him. He said he had always wanted children and was considering filing the paperwork to become a foster parent. "After all," Kenny said, "his mother died on my ranch while shelter-ing him in her arms. He sorta belongs there. What do you think about that idea, Carolyn?"

Carolyn was surprised, but she could see that this was something Kenny really wanted and that he was hoping for her approval. "I think you'd make the best father in the world, Kenny. I think that child would be really fortunate if you took care of him, so I say 'do it.'"

. . .

After Kenny went home, Carolyn called Brian. They exchanged the usual greetings until he suddenly said, "Carolyn, I've been as patient as I can be, but I'm miserable. I need to know. Have you made a decision?"

Carolyn felt herself tear up as she replied, "After all that's happened recently, I just don't see how we could have a happy future together, Brian. I'm sorry. I had to admit to the Feds that Paul knew much of what Joe Bill had done. Your family would never forgive me if they knew and eventually Paul will figure it out. And I don't want to come between you and your family."

"I was afraid of that," Brian said. "I could tell something was on your mind when you hesitated."

"Almost as soon after we had dinner that first night, I thought you were the man I had always seen myself spending my life with, Brian. You're handsome, brilliant, funny, and we like so many of the same things."

"I love you, Carolyn. I would devote my life to making you happy, you know."

"I know you'd try, Brian, but we can't just ignore where we come from and who our family is. In the course of the JBH Energy revelations, Paul tried to threaten me by telling me that my own brother has been involved in some pretty unscrupulous activities—worse than anything Paul has done, actually. Cody will probably go to jail. But that puts more of a burden on me to start taking care of my dad. Life is pulling me back home, I think. And I can't say that's all bad. This JBH Energy disaster makes me long for some good old country values."

"So that's your final decision?"

"I'm afraid so.

"I am really sorry it didn't work out for us, Brian." When he didn't say anything, she said what had just come into her mind, "Do you remember Cynthia Connor, Brian? She told me you went to St. John's together. She's my best friend in Houston, and she's single, beautiful, and brilliant. You have a lot in common. You should call her."

"Take care, Carolyn," Brian said. "I'll never forget you."

38

The entire firm knew that several federal agencies were investigating one of their biggest clients. An email had gone to all users telling them to preserve any files, documents, and emails relating to JBH Energy. The legal press, as well as the *Chronicle* and *Houston Business Journal*, were following the developments as the FBI and Justice Department zeroed in on Joe Bill Hawkins. The King of the Texas Frackers had accumulated a lot of enemies in his ruthless climb to the top. Fearing his retribution, most had kept their enmity to themselves. Now they gossiped openly as they enjoyed watching his rapid and very public fall from grace.

In Cynthia's absence, Carolyn relied on her assistant's participation in the administrative staff gossip chain to know what was going on at the firm. She told her that the management committee had called a special meeting to question Paul Robinson about his possible involvement in any of Joe Bill's alleged legal infractions right after the SEC notified him that they wanted to interview him. At first, Paul had denied knowing anything about what Joe Bill had been doing. But after Carolyn's conversation with Ann, the U.S. attorneys charged him with lying to federal agents. Then the management committee took steps to remove him from the partnership. The firm also reluctantly severed its representation of JBH Energy, which was the source of eight percent of the firm's gross revenues annually, in order to distance itself.

Cynthia told her she heard from her mother that Paul had packed up his jeans, boots, and T-shirts and moved to the family ranch in the Hill Country near Bandera. Soon after, Ashley filed for sole custody of their children.

After her initial anger, Carolyn felt sorry for Paul. He'd lost his wife and children, his friends, and the thing that mattered most to him, his successful position in the legal community and the accompanying prestige in Houston society. He had embarrassed his parents and disappointed his brothers. He didn't have to get brought down as a result of Joe Bill's crimes; he hadn't participated in them. But he had purposefully ignored obvious signs because of his ambition to rise in the firm. His real crime was participating in the cover-up.

It was obvious to Carolyn that Ann Meyers had used all of her relationships and power to make sure Paul was going to pay for his recent infractions of law and his past crime against her. His civil money penalty settlement amount with the SEC was substantial, and he was barred from representing clients in securities matters in the future.

Carolyn was awed by the power that the unsophisticated young intern from a small town in New Jersey had accumulated in only a little over ten years and how far she had come from a disastrous first encounter with a big, powerful law firm. She didn't fully appreciate that she had also come a long way from the ranch and become a powerful woman in her own right.

• • •

It was later in April when Trey knocked on Carolyn's office door and asked if she had a few minutes to talk.

"I wanted to tell you in person that I am leaving the firm," Trey said, standing just inside the door. "Trans National has offered me a position as general counsel. I've decided to take them up on it."

"That's surprising news," Carolyn said. She wasn't sure how she felt about Trey at this point, and waited to see what he'd say next. She didn't invite him to sit down.

"It wasn't a hard decision, really. Not after all that's happened." Carolyn knew that he'd come clean about what he knew about Joe Bill, and that as part of that, he'd had to admit what he knew about Paul. She imagined that he must have hated having to turn on one of his best friends. I'm sick of a client who lied, lawyers deliberately looking the other way, and everyone keeping secrets.

"Emily is thrilled," Carolyn heard him saying now. "By the way, she's expecting another child. We just found out."

"I understand," Carolyn said, warmly for the first time. "And I think you're doing the right thing."

Trey gave a bitter laugh. "So much for the Midnight Poker Club. Perhaps it was always fiction. I was just too dumb to realize it."

"It's unfortunate Paul didn't get it."

"He was desperate to maintain his career," Trey said. "After his divorce, that's all he had left. I think he was blinded by his ambition and arrogance."

"I would agree with that," Carolyn said.

"Of course, the Robinsons have hired the best lawyers to represent him. But his dream of being managing partner is dead. In fact, his legal career could be over entirely."

"Would you like a cup of coffee?" Carolyn asked, warming to him.

"I'd love one," he said. "I was a little afraid to come see you after all that happened."

Carolyn asked her assistant to bring them some coffee and moved files from two chairs, indicating that he should sit down.

"What's happening with your friend Joe Bill?"

"I think we both know by now he wasn't really my friend, at least not in the past few years. The SEC came down hard on him for accounting fraud for manipulating the financials and not disclosing the off-balance sheet company. They've also gone back and examined some of JBH

Energy's earlier transactions and found that he overvalued some of his acquisitions. The SEC will probably prohibit Joe Bill from ever serving as an officer of a public company and levy a huge civil money penalty. The U.S. attorneys are asking the grand jury to indict him, along with Diego and Rebecca, for conspiracy to commit embezzlement, wire fraud, and money laundering in connection with the payments to Nevozmozhnoe Trucking. He'll probably get a long jail sentence."

"It couldn't happen to a more deserving man," Carolyn sneered.

"Well, he sure won't be going back to the Panhandle and showing everyone that he's a big man, which was his goal. I'm sure people who knew him there are saying, 'Like father like son.' His greed and hubris ruined a lot of people's lives, including Paul's and Peter's."

Not to mention Lou Ann Schultz and Laura Petrillo, Carolyn thought.

"I know you're disappointed, Trey," Carolyn said, taking the cup of coffee from her assistant and handing one to Trey. "But it sounds like you'll be all right. Do you know what's happening with Peter?"

"I talked to him. He has a good lawyer and agreed to tell what he knows about whatever Joe Bill, Diego, and Rebecca did in return for partial immunity. He thinks it's a done deal. But it needs sign-off from the commissioners at the SEC."

"Peter fudged the numbers in the JBH financials, didn't he?" Carolyn asked, arching her eyebrows.

"Yeah, but it turns out that accounting fraud hasn't been his biggest worry. Joe Bill bullied him into manipulating the financials and signing off on not disclosing the waste disposal company."

Trey took a drink of his coffee. "You remember that awful night at Paul's beach house about ten years ago?"

"Yes," Carolyn said, surprised that Trey would mention it now. "We never—well, we never talked about it," she said, looking at him carefully.

Trey took a deep breath. "Paul and I really didn't know what had happened to Laura when we came in from the beach and found her on the floor. We were as shocked as you were. Peter only told me recently on a very long drive from Galveston to Houston that Joe Bill bullied him into attacking the girl while Paul and I were outside."

"She was raped!" Carolyn said.

"I know," Trey said. "And Peter told me he didn't want to do it, but they were drunk and Joe Bill called him a weak little sissy. Peter would do anything for Joe Bill's approval. I always wondered why he quit drinking. That's why. What he did has been eating at his conscience ever since, and he's been afraid of going to jail if Joe Bill told about it." Trey was looking away from her.

This was a surprising bit of information. "Are you sure Peter was the one who raped her? Not Joe Bill or Paul?" Carolyn asked.

Trey nodded. "Peter said that Joe Bill intended to rape her after him and had got down on his knees to do it, but that they heard Paul and Trey about to come in the door, so he pulled up his pants and went into the living room before they came in."

Carolyn felt sick at the picture in her mind, but somehow she knew he was telling the truth.

"I know Brian helped you once you got to UTMB," Trey said. "Monday morning when he got to the hospital and checked on her, he learned she had checked out. Paul called Brian to ask how she was, and Brian told Paul she'd disappeared. We never knew what happened to her. I'm ashamed I went along with it, but that's what Paul wanted to do. He was my best friend. As usual, I didn't resist." He had a pained look on his face.

"I always knew Paul made up that story about her wanting to go home to a boyfriend," Carolyn said.

"Paul was used to everything always turning out in his favor. I assumed it was Joe Bill who'd attacked her. I never suspected Peter, but it's a secret that Joe Bill has been holding over Peter's head ever since. That's how he got him to fudge the books. Now Peter's afraid, so he's talking first. There's a ten-year statute of limitations on rape in Texas, but it can be extended under certain circumstances."

"Oh my God," Carolyn suddenly gasped. "Ann thinks it was Paul, not Peter!"

"Who's Ann?" Trey asked.

Carolyn had finished her coffee and got up to put the cup in the trash can. "I guess I can tell you now. You've probably met her but didn't recognize her. The senior attorney with the SEC heading up the investigation? That's Laura Petrillo, but now she goes by Ann Meyers."

"Damn!" Trey exclaimed. He got up and took a few steps around. "I knew there was something about her that seemed familiar, and the way she looked at me made me uncomfortable. But it's been so long, and I only talked to her for a few minutes after drinking all day. How did you find out?"

"She confronted me during the investigation. She looks a lot different. Older, of course, but her hair is dark brown and she wears glasses and no makeup. She's taller in high heels. I didn't recognize her either at first."

"What did she say?"

"She was angry that I hadn't contacted her after that night to find out if she was okay. I can't blame her. I've felt guilty ever since. She told me the whole story about Joe Bill drugging her and being attacked. But she thinks it was him or Paul that raped her. And I never knew any different."

"Shit! Are you going to tell her now?"

"I don't know," Carolyn said. Inwardly, she asked herself, *Would it make a difference at this point?*

39

———

I t was late on a hot summer afternoon, and Ann and Amanda were meeting with the assistant U.S. attorneys in a conference room at the Justice Department. The air conditioner, ancient as it was, was noisy and didn't work very well. Everyone was on their umpteenth cup of coffee, and the attorneys brought the two women up to date on their trial preparations for their case against Joe Bill Hawkins. Ann told Arthur that she intended to be in Houston to watch his trial.

Arthur said, "Hawkins is a total scumbag. He's been trying to shift blame for everything he's done onto someone else."

"Not surprising," Amanda said. "Tell me more."

"He's claiming that he had nothing to do with Nevozmozhnoe Trucking. He says his company only entered into the deal as a minority owner because Stevenson convinced his COO that it would reduce costs. He claims he didn't know about Stevenson sending JBH Energy's share of the profits to the Caymans and that Stevenson was siphoning that money off for himself. He claims to be the victim."

Arthur stood so everyone at the table could see the first of the whiteboards he had prepared showing the parties to the conspiracy, as he put it. He pointed to a circle with the names of Stevenson, Diego, and Rebecca inside it.

"His employees and Stevenson claim the idea of the off-balance sheet company and Cayman Island account was all his idea. They say it was Joe Bill's slush fund for his gambling debts and they were only in it for a small amount."

"They're all scumbags," Amanda said.

"Hawkins is also offering us information on what he calls an unrelated, undiscovered crime and wanting to cut a deal based on the information," Arthur added.

"Which is?" Ann asked.

"He claims that he was a witness to the outside accountant, Peter Kaufman, raping an unconscious young woman. It happened in Galveston just over ten years ago."

Ann didn't move. *Kaufman?* she thought. *Could I have been wrong all this time?*

"Did you tell him that rape is a state law charge?" Amanda asked. "And that the statute of limitations may have run out?" Amanda glanced at Ann, indicating that Ann should be quiet and she would carry this.

Ann ignored her friend. "Do you think he is telling the truth about Peter Kaufman raping the girl?" Ann asked in a tentative voice. *I'm in control,* she told herself.

"Probably." Arthur shrugged. "Kaufman tried to use confessing to an old crime he committed as leverage to cutting a deal. We told him we weren't interested in a state law issue. But I'll pass the information along to the Texas AG's team that is prosecuting some of the conspirators."

Amanda was sitting next to Ann at the table and now she reached under the table and put her hand on top of Ann's. Ann looked at her thankfully.

"He's also blaming the death of Lou Ann Schultz completely on Cody Page, the rancher who hired the truck driver. The locals are fired up and a grand jury is considering indicting Page under state law for aiding and abetting in manslaughter, violating environmental laws, conspiracy to commit sex trafficking, and a pile of other charges."

I wonder if Carolyn knew about her brother's role in this mess when I talked to her? Ann thought.

"So that's about it for all of the snakes in the pit," Arthur said in closing. "Any questions?"

When no one answered, he picked up his papers and said, "Let's put these scumbags away."

On the way back from their meeting at the Justice Department, Ann said to Amanda, "Can we stop at the Hay Adams Bar for a drink? It's quiet around this time."

"Sure," Amanda said, giving her friend a hug. "It's been an unsettling day."

"It sure was. I'm still processing it."

The women walked into the stately lobby of the historic Hay Adams Hotel where they were greeted by smiling staff. They settled into a table in the corner of the bar. In the middle of the afternoon there were only a few old, retired congressmen hanging around, passing time by drinking and telling war stories.

After they'd settled in and ordered drinks, Ann reflected. "I'd decided it was either Hawkins or Paul Robinson or both. I don't remember seeing Kaufman that night. Of course, I was drugged and then unconscious."

"What do you want to do now?" Amanda asked. "You might still be able to press charges. But then again, you might not. Either way," she said, squeezing her friend's arm, "you're the winner."

"I don't know," Ann said in a quiet voice. She was studying her hands. "I guess . . ."

Amanda let Ann consider for a minute while she fiddled with her watch.

Ann finally said, "Honestly, I don't want to relive that experience. Kaufman's going to have to pay a huge fine. He's lost his license to practice accounting, but he won't have any jail time. His lawyer said he was desperate to confess. Maybe he thought that would get him absolution or something. In any case, I'm ready to finally put that part of my life behind me." Ann sighed.

"Can you forgive him?"

"No. But I suppose he's suffered enough."

Ann laid her head on top of her hands for a minute. The waiter brought their wine, giving her a strange look.

"Here's to our successes," Amanda said, raising her glass. "Joe Bill Hawkins will undoubtedly go to federal prison for embezzlement, wire fraud, securities fraud, and related charges. He's been indicted on state charges for environmental crimes, and the EPA has fined the company and him personally. He's also being sued by his shareholders.

"Paul Robinson has been fined by the SEC for lying to federal prosecutors and fired by his law firm. The Texas state bar is considering disbarment. Last but not least, we've sent a message to the industry that polluting the waters of this country will be prosecuted."

"I'll drink to all that," Ann said, raising her glass in return.

"And Peter Kauffman has lost his public accounting license and the SEC has fined him. That's probably more justice than a lot of rape victims get. Feel better?"

"I do," Ann said. "And then there's Carolyn Page. After confronting her, I have a better understanding of what happened. She did take care of me before I disappeared. And she was helpful in uncovering the Nevozmozhnoe Trucking crimes, so there's that."

"That was a big part of really putting Hawkins away and nailing Robinson for the cover-up."

"I still don't know if she knew about her brother's involvement and didn't tell me, but I'd prefer to think she didn't."

"She still has to live with herself," Amanda offered, and Ann nodded in agreement.

"A terrible event in your life will soon be history. You can think of the justice or revenge you achieved, and not the crime. Better yet, you can just wipe the whole sordid affair from your mind and move on. Who knows what financial crimes are left to be uncovered by the powerful Ann Meyers, SEC super agent?" Amanda dramatically intoned.

Ann had to laugh. She raised her glass to toast. "Here's to my best friend and fellow sleuth!" Then she got serious. "There's still the trial, though. Worse crooks have gotten off in the end, you know. I won't rest completely until the verdict is in. Now—what about you? What have you decided to do about Deshaun's affair?" She looked at her friend with concern.

"I told him to move out," Amanda said. "It's destroying both of us to keep living with his resentment and lies. I plan on moving on myself. I love what I do at the agency and I'm not going to hold back just because my success damages someone else's ego. Deshaun and I had a good run for a long time, but people grow and change. It's sad, but I'll survive."

"Well, let's have a toast to two thirty-something women in white hats starting their life over. Watch out, world!" Ann laughed. They clinked glasses again.

40

———

arolyn called Cynthia to discuss the ongoing investigation of JBH Energy one day at lunch.

Cynthia was at her new office at her father's company overlooking the busy traffic of ships in the Houston Ship Channel. "I told you Joe Bill Hawkins was trouble," Cynthia reminded her.

"I know, but what could I do when my section head pleaded with me to do a seemingly isolated, small task?" Carolyn replied.

"Actually, it's good you did. He would have continued to do bad things if your cowboy hadn't discovered pollution in your creek water and persisted in alerting the authorities. Your Nancy Drew investigation of the crooked local attorney was the nail in the coffin." Cynthia's voice grew coy. "I'd like to meet your cowboy. He must be pretty smart, and I've seen his picture in your office. He's quite handsome in a rugged he-man sort of way."

"Kenny's pretty wonderful, but he's not your type." Carolyn laughed, looking at his picture on her bookcase.

"How do you know that?" Cynthia asked. "I have time for a social life now that I'm not slaving my life away at Edwards and Harrison. I'm thinking boyfriend, but I might even entertain the idea of marriage." Carolyn imagined Cynthia putting on her seductive look.

"I can't see you riding the back pastures to help round up cattle or making preserves out of the fruits in your garden or doing the two-step in jeans and cowgirl boots at the Gruene dance hall, Cynthia."

"That all sounds dreadful!" she replied. "You're right. I'll leave the cowboys to you and find me a nice city boy who will take me to Tony's for dinner and the Opera Ball and who knows how to select fine wine." They both laughed.

"I broke up with Brian Robinson."

"Hmm," Cynthia said. "Why exactly?"

"He's a wonderful man, you know that. But I don't see how it could have worked out with all that happened between his brother and me. Besides, I realize that I've always loved Kenny, and now not just as a friend. But I had to spread my wings. I've had a career that I loved and accomplished my goals, but I've had enough. I want to go home now."

• • •

Instead of the cotton pajamas she usually wore to bed, Carolyn put on the silk ones, poured a glass of sparkling Rose wine, and curled up on her couch that evening. Then she dialed Kenny's cell.

"I'm coming home," she said when he answered.

"When?" he asked.

"I'm coming home permanently." Saying it out loud, she realized she was excited about leaving Houston. She was even more excited about seeing him. "I have a few things I need to wrap up here and clients and friends to call, but I can leave in a couple of weeks. I'm turning in my letter of resignation to the managing partner tomorrow." She waited expectantly to hear his answer.

When there was silence on the other end of the line, Carolyn worried. Then Kenny said, "That's the best news I've heard in my entire life. Come home, girl. I've been waiting for you for a long time."

On the Saturday after Carolyn moved back to the ranch, Kenny's mother held a welcome home party at her house. Carolyn's father was there. Carolyn noticed that he and Shep seemed to be at home in the house. When she commented to him about it, he shyly told Carolyn that he and Mrs. Prichard had been courting. Carolyn gave him a big smile and a hug.

Just then, Mrs. Prichard came out of the kitchen carrying a toddler, a little boy, with black hair and brown eyes.

"What a cute baby," Carolyn said.

Kenny came out of the hallway and gently took the boy from his mother. "Johnny, meet Carolyn," he said with an impish grin. "CPS gave him the generic name 'Juan,' but we call him 'John,' after my father."

He seems full of love and joy when he looks at that child, Carolyn thought.

"You'll make a wonderful foster father," Carolyn said, putting her hand on his arm. "John is a lucky boy."

Billy Schultz, Kayla, and Carolyn's old group of friends arrived for a dinner of buttermilk fried chicken, mashed potatoes, green beans, and apple pie. They filled Carolyn in on what had been happening the past few weeks. Sheriff Jones and Jonathan Stevenson were in a pissing contest to spread the blame to anyone except themselves. Both were seeking change of venue to another county for their trials.

"Good luck with that one," Lindel sneered.

Everyone was careful not to mention Cody's name. Carolyn had not wanted to ask her father, and she hadn't seen or heard from her brother in more than a year.

"You're my friends and family," Carolyn said, looking around. "Tell me what's happening with Cody. I'm sure it's not good news."

Kenny finally broke the silence. "The county grand jury has indicted him for auxiliary to manslaughter in Lou Ann's death. John Hoffman says the Feds and the state are investigating charges of human trafficking in connection with the man camp he allowed to be built on your property."

"How do you feel about all this, Dad?" Carolyn asked, putting her arms around her father and searching his face.

"I knew years ago I lost Cody," her father said. "But we've still got each other." He smiled, but Carolyn could see his pain in his eyes.

It feels so comfortable here, Carolyn thought. *But am I walking away from the identity I've worked so hard to achieve? Who am I now, and what am I going to do with myself?*

She listened to friends discuss their everyday issues and business, complaining about disputes with the oil companies and their workers. Suddenly, she realized that there was a role she could play in her own community that would be meaningful, maybe even satisfying. Jonathan Stevenson's practice in town was finished, and he would go to jail when he was convicted. The county would need an honest business lawyer to represent people in dealings with the oil companies and commercial establishments that had come to town. She'd saved enough money to not have to bring in income for a while. She could do it! Eventually, there would be the revenues from the wells on their land. She didn't have to give up the law completely; she could remake her life however she wanted to, right there.

After everyone had gone home, Kenny and Carolyn sat on the front porch swing as they did hundreds of evenings before. They were drinking beer as a George Strait album played in the background. The air was fresh and clean, not like the air in Houston, she thought.

Kenny put his arm around Carolyn's shoulders. "Have you decided what you want to do with your life now? I asked you that question our senior year in high school when we were sitting right here. Do you remember what you said?"

"Something about leaving the ranch in my rearview mirror, having a career in a big city, and doing meaningful things with important people." Carolyn smiled.

"Yep," Kenny replied, laughing.

"I did that, you know."

"I know," Kenny said. "I'm not laughing at you. I'm proud of you. So what's left?"

"Set new goals, I guess," Carolyn said.

"Do you have any in mind?"

"Actually, yes. I want to use my law license to do something good for real people—not corporations. And there are no more important people than the ones right here in this county. I'm thinking of opening a civil law practice in town. But not in that ugly building Stevenson was in. What do you think?"

Kenny laughed and gave her a hug. Being in his strong arms felt wonderful.

"I think you can't sit still for a minute, can you?"

She pushed him away. "You're making fun of me."

"No, I think that's a great idea. I'll be your first client," he said, drawing her close. "But I was really fishing to see if any of your new goals included making a place in your life for an unimportant rancher who has been trying for a while now to tell you he wants to be more than a friend."

Carolyn instinctively snuggled up against him. "That's the one thing I do know for sure." She smiled.

Kenny leaned down and they kissed for a long time. "Mmm, do it again, please," she said.

"Gladly. I'd love to do this forever."

After a few minutes, he said, "You know, if we make this permanent, we can build any type of place you want on my land, your land, or move into your dad's house, I don't care."

"Why, Kenny Prichard, are you proposing marriage to me?" Carolyn smiled.

Kenny pulled her close and wrapped his strong arms around her again. He gave her another long, slow kiss that made her feel like her body was melting and this was the only moment that mattered. "What do you think?" he whispered, nuzzling her neck.

"I think after the wedding we should officially adopt Johnny and create some siblings for him as soon as we can," she whispered in his ear.

"That's the Carolyn I know!" Kenny exclaimed. "When you chart a course, you go full speed ahead. But I never say no in a horse race, darlin'!"

41

Ann boarded a flight to National Airport on a Friday night. She'd been in Houston for the last days of the Joe Bill Hawkins trial in federal court. The first day she had run into Katherine Eason in the lobby. Katherine introduced her to her father, Tom Oakland. He was obviously in a good mood, which stood out in the somber air of the looming, brutalist-style courthouse. She thought it was curious that he thanked her profusely for her good work in putting away Joe Bill Hawkins.

She sat alone in one of the back rows of the courtroom. *He looks a lot less smug than he did the first time I saw him now that he knows he's going to prison for a long time,* she thought.

During the afternoon of the last day, Carolyn had quietly entered the courtroom, looked around, and seeing Ann in the back, sat down beside her. Ann was surprised when Carolyn handed her an envelope with her name on it and the words "personal and confidential." Then Carolyn quietly got up and left.

That night, in her hotel room, Ann opened the envelope and read the letter inside:

> *Dear Ann, I told myself after our meeting that I would tell you anything I learned that shed light on what happened to you in Galveston. I was telling you the truth when I said I didn't know. But since then, the other man who was present that night*

told me what actually happened. Not long ago, Peter Kaufman confessed to him that he had been the person who raped you. Peter said that Joe Bill bullied him into doing it when he was drunk and that he regretted it for the rest of his life. Joe Bill and Peter were alone in the house when it happened. Everyone else had gone out on the beach. Joe Bill intended to rape you as well, but Paul and Trey returned before he could do it. Paul didn't rape you, although he certainly didn't do anything to help after they found you. I don't expect a response. I just wanted you to finally know the truth.

My deepest apologies,
Carolyn

Ann carefully folded the letter and put it back in the envelope. Later, she put it away in her carry-on bag.

She took the last flight back to D.C. that evening. The flight was not full, since most people with business in Washington were going in the other direction on Friday night. She was able to get a window seat in coach on an aisle with no one in the center seat. She never liked to talk to other passengers, so she smiled politely at the man who sat down in the aisle seat. Then she opened the letter from Carolyn to read again. She had already learned the truth, but she felt pleased that Carolyn had made the effort to try to close the book for her.

As they crossed over the Mississippi River, the flight attendant asked Ann if she would like a beverage. *I should celebrate,* she thought. Hawkins was being punished. The others had gotten their just deserts as well. She was determined to put that experience behind her once and for all.

When the flight attendant brought her a glass of champagne and the man on the aisle a Maker's Mark, he pulled down the table for the seat in the middle and suggested she also put her glass there. Thanking him, she noticed that he was very attractive. He looked to be in his early forties, with light brown hair and hazel eyes. He was reading pleadings for a court filing. *A lawyer,* she thought. Of course. Everyone in D.C. was a lawyer. She put in her earphones and settled in to listen to one of her favorite operas.

Suddenly the plane hit a patch of turbulence and the two glasses wobbled on the shared table. Ann reached to steady her glass at the same time he did. When their hands bumped into each other, they both laughed awkwardly. She noticed that he wasn't wearing a wedding ring.

"I couldn't help notice that you're having champagne," he said. "What are you celebrating?"

"I am celebrating," Ann said. "But it's a personal celebration—the end of a long journey to justice."

"I won't pry, although that's not like me. It's my business to pry," he said, adjusting his glasses for emphasis. His expression made Ann laugh.

"For instance, I was wondering why you were one of the few unfortunate souls going into D.C. on a Friday night. Do you live there?" He took a sip of his bourbon.

"I do." Normally, Ann would have cut the conversation off at that point. Maybe it was the champagne, or maybe his warm smile, that made her ask, "Do you?"

"Yes. I'm with the FBI," he said. "But I'm really a nice guy. Jack Archer," he said, holding out his hand to shake hers.

Ann smiled, took off her glasses, shut off the music in her ears, put out her hand, and said, "I'm glad to meet you, Jack. I'm Laura Ann Petrillo. I go by Ann."

THE END

ACKNOWLEDGMENTS

I am grateful to my friends who gave their time to read drafts of this manuscript and give me their comments and criticism as I developed the characters and plot of *Crude Ambition*. Carolyn Truesdell, Esq., my patient and encouraging friend and former law partner, read draft after draft and helped steer the course of Carolyn and Laura Ann's struggles. As one of the first female partners in a major Houston law firm, as well as chair of the board of both the Houston Area Women's Center and Harris Health System, Harris County's healthcare safety net, she has a knowledgeable perspective on the struggles of both women. My dear friends Harriet Hart and Sonny Wallace are always faithful supportive readers. Rebecca McDonald, a groundbreaking Houston energy business executive and avid reader, gave me insightful comments from her experience that improved the plot. Ashley Allison, an environmental geologist and project manager with an international engineering firm, advised on the parts of the book relating to the environmental spill issues, and Hillary Holmes, Esq., a senior securities partner in an international law firm, advised on the SEC issues. Mathew Archer, Esq., a former Aggie who grew up on a ranch in the Panhandle, gave me helpful insights into what life would have been like for Paul, Trey, and Joe Bill at Texas A&M. F. Andino Reynal, Esq., former assistant U.S. attorney, kindly answered my questions on matters relating to the enforcement of Joe Bill's crimes. My former law partner, Kathy Lake, Esq., shared insights on ranching in South Texas amid the fracking boom. Andrew Allison, MD, helped

316 Patricia Hunt Holmes

with the UTMB triage. Susan Sorenson, PhD, CPA, gave me ideas on accounting fraud.

My substantive editor, Anne Sanow, was tremendously helpful by making suggestions that gave depth to the characters and their relationships to one another. Ava Coibion's critical copy-editing comments gave polish to the text. My publisher, Greenleaf Book Group, has been a great shepherd in the world of writing and publishing.

I am especially grateful for the encouragement I have always received from my ninety-seven-year-old mother and perpetual cheerleader, Julia Hunt.

I have to acknowledge Inprint, Houston's premier literary organization, where I participated in numerous creative writing workshops and learned the difference between legal writing and creative writing. I recommend their workshops to anyone who wants to explore an interest in writing. Finally, I am grateful to the many readers who embraced my first fiction novel, *Searching for Pilar,* giving me the encouragement I needed to write a second novel.

ABOUT THE AUTHOR

Patricia Hunt Holmes spent 30 years as a public finance attorney with a large international law firm, specializing in nonprofit healthcare finance and rural electric cooperative finance. Consistently listed in Best Lawyers in America, Texas Super Lawyers, and Top Lawyers in Houston, she was a frequent speaker at national public finance and healthcare conferences. Patricia has also served on the faculty of the University of Missouri-Columbia, University of Tennessee, and University of Texas Health Science Center at Houston. She has written and published in the fields of intellectual history and law.

In addition to her legal career, Patricia has been a member and board member of several social service organizations throughout Houston, including the United Way of the Texas Gulf Coast Women's Initiative, Dress for Success Houston, the University of Houston Women's Studies Program, University of Houston Law Review Board of Directors, is a trustee of the Houston Grand Opera, and Houston Justice for Our Neighbors.

Searching for Pilar, published on April 10, 2018, was her first fiction novel. The story centers around Houstonians of all stations helping a young stranger from Mexico rescue his sister from the horrific world of sex trafficking in Houston's glitzy Galleria-area men's clubs and barrio cantinas. Her purpose in writing this book was to make others aware of the extent of these horrifying crimes in Houston and to inspire empathy in her readers for these overlooked girls.

Since the publication of *Searching for Pilar* in April of 2018, Pat has been a frequent speaker at forums, including two universities, the Junior League, YMCA, United Way Women's Initiative, and numerous book clubs in Houston, Dallas and New Jersey. In 2019, the Portuguese Confraria do Vinho do Porto honored her for her work in fostering awareness about international sex trafficking. *Searching for Pilar* has been #1 on Amazon in Urban Fiction and #2 in Suspense. Both BookBub and Amazon have featured the book.

Crude Ambition is a story that takes place at the other end of Houston's society. It is the story of two idealistic and ambitious young women who aspire to be successful lawyers but have to overcome physical and emotional challenges in their climb to the top of their profession. It is also a story about four ambitious male friends who are determined to succeed in the powerful professional arenas of big law and oil. Will their brotherhood help or hinder them? What will they do to succeed?

Patricia grew up in Egg Harbor City, New Jersey but has lived in Houston for over 40 years. She has two daughters, Hillary and Ashley, who have successful careers as an attorney and a geologist, and three adorable grandsons. She is an avid golfer and traveler.

Patricia holds a BA in English and history, an MA in history, and a PhD in Russian and South Asian history with honors, all from the University of Missouri-Columbia. She received her J.D. from the University of Houston Law Center and was an editor on the *Houston Law Review*.

www.ingramcontent.com/pod-product-compliance
Lightning Source LLC
Chambersburg PA
CBHW050523110726
47899CB00005B/1567